THE
BERKELEY SQUARE AFFAIR

The Malcolm & Suzanne Rannoch Mysteries
by Teresa Grant:

Vienna Waltz

Imperial Scandal

His Spanish Bride

The Paris Affair

The Paris Plot

Published by Kensington Publishing Corporation

THE
BERKELEY SQUARE AFFAIR

TERESA GRANT

KENSINGTON BOOKS
www.kensingtonbooks.com

KENSINGTON BOOKS are published by

Kensington Publishing Corp.
119 West 40th Street
New York, NY 10018

All Kensington titles, imprints, and distributed lines are available at special quantity discounts for bulk purchases for sales promotion, premiums, fund-raising, educational, or institutional use.

Special book excerpts or customized printings can also be created to fit specific needs. For details, write or phone the office of the Kensington Special Sales Manager: Kensington Publishing Corp., 119 West 40th Street, New York, NY 10018. Attn. Special Sales Department. Phone: 1-800-221-2647.

Kensington and the K logo Reg. U.S. Pat. & TM Off.

ISBN-13: 978-0-7582-8395-5
ISBN-10: 0-7582-8395-4
First Kensington Trade Paperback Printing: April 2014

eISBN-13: 978-0-7582-8396-2
eISBN-10: 0-7582-8396-2
First Kensington Electronic Edition: April 2014

10 9 8 7 6 5 4 3 2 1

Printed in the United States of America

For Audrey LaFehr, a wonderful editor
and equally wonderful friend,
with thanks for your support of Malcolm and Suzanne
and of me, and for making me a better writer

ACKNOWLEDGMENTS

My heartfelt thanks to my longtime editor, Audrey LaFehr, who began work on this book, and to my new editor, Martin Biro, who helped me shape and polish the manuscript. I am very fortunate to have the insights and support of two such wonderful editors. And as always, the input and advice of my agent, Nancy Yost, was invaluable.

Thanks as well to Paula Reedy for shepherding the book through copyedits and galleys with exquisite care and good humor. To Barbara Wild for the careful copy editing. To Pauline Sholtys for the eagle-eyed proofreading. To Kristine Mills and Jon Paul for a fabulous cover that evokes Suzanne and Berkeley Square. To Alexandra Nicolajsen for the superlative social media support. And to Karen Auerbach, Adeola Saul and everyone at Kensington Books, and Sarah Younger, Adrienne Rosado, Natanya Wheeler, and everyone at the Nancy Yost Literary Agency for their support throughout the publication process.

Thank you to all the wonderful booksellers who help readers find Malcolm and Suzanne, and in particular to Book Passage in Corte Madera for their always warm welcome to me and to my daughter, Mélanie. Thank you to the readers who share Suzanne's and Malcolm's adventures with me on my Web site and Facebook and Twitter. Thank you to Gregory Paris and jim saliba for creating my Web site and updating it so quickly and with such style. To Raphael Coffey for once again juggling cats and baby to take the best author photos a writer could have. To Robert Sicular for inspiration onstage (including a memorable *Hamlet*) and inspiring conversations about books and plays, including a discussion of Hamlet's attitude toward his father. To Jayne Davis for the always erudite grammar advice. To Bonnie Glaser for always asking about my writing; and to Bonnie, Raphael, Lesley Grant, Elaine Hamlin, and Veronica Wolff for nurturing Mélanie so Mummy could get a few more words down. And to the staff at Peet's Coffee & Tea at The Village in Corte Madera for keeping me supplied with superb lattes and cups of Earl Grey and making Mélanie smile as I wrote this book.

Thank you to Lauren Willig for sharing the delights and dilemmas of writing about Napoleonic spies. I'm so excited that we now share juggling writing and motherhood as well. To Penelope Williamson for support and understanding and hours analyzing plays, including a brilliant *Hamlet* at the Oregon Shakespeare Festival in 2010. To Veronica Wolff for wonderful writing dates during which my word count seemed to magically increase. To Catherine Duthie for sharing her thoughts on Malcolm and Suzanne's world and introducing them to new readers. To Deborah Crombie for supporting Malcolm and Suzanne from the beginning. To Tasha Alexander and Andrew Grant for their wit and wisdom and support, whether in person or via e-mail. To Deanna Raybourn, who never fails to offer encouragement and asks wonderful interview questions. And to my other writer friends near and far for brainstorming, strategizing, and commiserating—Jami Alden, Bella Andre, Isobel Carr, Catherine Coulter, Barbara Freethy, Carol Grace, C. S. Harris, Candice Hern, Anne Mallory, and Monica McCarty.

Finally, thank you to my daughter, Mélanie, for inspiring me and always seeming to understand when Mummy needed just a few more minutes to craft a sentence.

Dramatis Personae

*indicates real historical figures

The Rannoch Household

Malcolm Rannoch, Member of Parliament and
    former Intelligence Agent
Suzanne Rannoch, his wife
Colin Rannoch, their son
Jessica Rannoch, their daughter
Blanca Mendoza, Suzanne's companion
Miles Addison, Malcolm's valet
Valentin, their footman
Laura Dudley, Colin's and Jessica's governess

Malcolm's Relations

Lady Frances Dacre-Hammond, Malcolm's aunt
Chloe Dacre-Hammond, her daughter
Aline Blackwell, Lady Frances's daughter
Dr. Geoffrey Blackwell, Aline's husband
Claudia Blackwell, their daughter
The Duke of Strathdon, Malcolm's grandfather

The Davenport Family

Colonel Harry Davenport
Lady Cordelia Davenport, his wife
Livia Davenport, their daughter
Drusilla Davenport, their daughter
Archibald Davenport, Harry's uncle

At the Tavistock Theatre

Simon Tanner, playwright and part owner of the theatre
David Mallinson, Viscount Worsley, his lover

Manon Caret, actress
Crispin, Lord Harleton, her lover
Roxane, her daughter
Clarisse, Manon's younger daughter
Berthe, Manon's dresser

Jennifer Mansfield, actress
Sir Horace Smytheton, her lover and the theatre's patron
Brandon Ford, actor

The Dewhurst Family

Earl Dewhurst, British diplomat
Rupert, Viscount Caruthers, his son
Gabrielle, Viscountess Caruthers, Rupert's wife
Stephen, their son
Bertrand Laclos, Rupert's lover

Others in London

Lord Carfax, British spymaster, David Mallinson's father
Amelia, Lady Carfax, his wife

Raoul O'Roarke, French spymaster

* Lord Bessborough
* Lady Caroline Lamb, his daughter
* William Lamb, Caroline's husband
* Emily, Countess Cowper, William's sister

General Hugo Cyrus

Colonel Frederick Radley, Suzanne's former lover

Paul St. Gilles, painter
Juliette Dubretton, writer, his wife
Pierre Dubretton, their son
Marguerite Dubretton, their daughter
Rose Dubretton, their daughter

Doubt thou the stars are fire,
Doubt that the sun doth move,
Doubt truth to be a liar,
But never doubt I love.

—Shakespeare, *Hamlet,* Act II, scene ii

PROLOGUE

London
November 1817

The lamplight shone against the cobblestones, washing over the grime, adding a glow of warmth. Creating an illusion of beauty on a street that in the merciless light of day would show the scars and stains of countless carriage wheels, horse hooves, shoes, pattens, and boots. Much as stage lights could transform bare boards and canvas flats into a garden in Illyria or a castle in Denmark.

Simon Tanner turned up the collar of his greatcoat as a gust of wind, sharp with the bite of late November, cut down the street, followed by a hail of raindrops. His hand went to his chest. In his greatcoat pocket, he could feel the solidity of the package he carried, carefully wrapped in oilskin. Were it not for that tangible reminder, it would be difficult to believe it was real.

He'd hardly had a settled life. He'd grown up in Paris during the fervor of the French Revolution and the madness of the Reign of Terror. Here in England, his plays had more than once been closed by the Government Censor. He'd flirted with arrest for Radical activities. He and his lover risked arrest or worse by the very nature of their relationship. But he had never thought to touch something of this calibre.

He held little sacred. But the package he carried brought out something in him as close to reverence as was possible for one who prided himself on his acerbic approach to life.

The scattered raindrops had turned into a steady downpour, slapping the cobblestones in front of him, dripping off the brim of his beaver hat and the wool of his greatcoat. He quickened his footsteps. For a number of reasons, he would feel better when he had reached Malcolm and Suzanne's house in Berkeley Square. When he wasn't alone with this discovery and the attendant questions it raised.

He started at a sound, then smiled ruefully as the creak was followed by the slosh of a chamberpot being dumped on the cobblestones—mercifully a dozen feet behind him. He was acting like a character in one of his plays. He might be on his way to see Malcolm Rannoch, retired (or not so retired) Intelligence Agent, but this was hardly an affair of espionage. In fact, the package Simon valued so highly would probably not be considered so important by others.

He turned down Bolton Street. He was on the outskirts of Mayfair now. Even in the rain-washed lamplight the cobblestones were cleaner, the pavements wider and neatly swept free of leaves and debris. The clean, bright glow of wax tapers glinted behind the curtains instead of the murky yellow light of tallow candles. Someone in the next street over called good night to a departing dinner guest. Carriage wheels rattled. Simon turned down the mews to cut over to Hill Street and then Berkeley Square. Another creak made him pause, then smile at his own fancifulness. David would laugh at him when he returned home and shared his illusions of adventure.

He walked through the shadows of the mews, past whickering horses and the smells of dung and saddle soap and oiled leather. The rain-soaked cobblestones were slick beneath his shoes. A dog barked. A carriage clattered down Hill Street at the end of the mews. It was probably just the need to share his discovery that made him so eager to reach Malcolm and Suzanne. If—

The shadows broke in front of him. Three men blocked the way, wavering blurs through the curtain of rain.

"Hand it over," a rough voice said. "Quiet like, and this can be easy."

Lessons from stage combat and boyhood fencing danced through Simon's head. He pulled his purse from his greatcoat pocket and threw it on the cobblestones. He doubted that would end things, but it was worth a try.

One man started forwards. The man who had spoken gave a sharp shake of his head. "That isn't what we want and you know it."

Acting could be a great source of defense. Simon fell back on the role of the amiable fool. "Dear me," he said, "I can't imagine what else I have that you could want."

The man groaned. "Going to make this hard, are you?"

Simon rushed them. He had no particular illusions that it would work. But he thought he had a shot.

Until he felt the knife cut through his greatcoat.

CHAPTER 1

Malcolm Rannoch glanced up from his book and tilted his head back against the carved walnut of the Queen Anne chair. "There was a time when I thought we'd never have a quiet night at home."

Suzanne Rannoch regarded her husband over the downy head of their almost-one-year-old daughter, Jessica, who was flopped in her arms, industriously nursing. "There was a time when I thought we'd never have a quiet night."

His gray eyes glinted in the candlelight. "Sweetheart, are you complaining of boredom?"

"You mean do I miss outwitting foreign agents, getting summoned by the Duke of Wellington and Lord Castlereagh at all hours, sitting up into the morning decoding documents, dodging sniper fire, and taking the occasional knife to my ribs?"

Malcolm picked up the whisky glass on the table beside him. "Something like that."

Suzanne glanced round the library. Warm oak paneling, shimmering damask upholstery, gilded book spines. Velvet curtains covering leaded-glass windows that looked out on the leafy expanse of Berkeley Square. She had never thought to live in such luxury. Or such security. "Do you miss it?" she asked.

"Sometimes." Malcolm took a sip of whisky. One of the things she loved about him was his uncompromising honesty. "But there are compensations. Like not worrying about my family."

The family she had once never thought to have. Jessica tucked warmly in her arms. Their four-year-old son, Colin, asleep upstairs in the nursery. Berowne, the cat they had found in Paris as a scrawny kitten, now sleek and well fed, curled up on Malcolm's lap. All the reasons she had to preserve her improbable life here in Britain.

Jessica stirred and stretched, her arms reaching over her head, her legs kicking the fluted arm of the sofa on which Suzanne sat. Suzanne smoothed her daughter's sparse hair. Jessica still had the high, hairless forehead of an Elizabethan lady, but she had enough hair now that Suzanne could ruffle it with her finger. The candlelight glinted off a bright gold that might one day darken to Malcolm's leafy umber, mixed with strands of Suzanne's own walnut brown. A year ago, when Jessica was born, they had lived in Paris. Malcolm had been a diplomat, not a Member of Parliament. A diplomat and an Intelligence Agent. A spy, though he didn't like to use the word. From Spain, where he and Suzanne had met in the midst of the Peninsular War, to the Congress of Vienna, to Brussels before Waterloo and Paris after, they had shared adventures and intrigue and often been one step ahead of danger. Sometimes not even that. They both had scars inside and out to prove it. Those exploits seemed a world away from this house in Mayfair and their life among London's beau monde, where Malcolm was an M.P. and she was—a political hostess? She still wasn't sure how to define herself.

"Unfair," she said, putting a touch of raillery in her voice. She tried never to let him see her qualms about the way their life had changed, because she knew it worried him and she owed him so much already. "You've played the trump card. How can I say anything weighs in the scales beside the children's safety?"

"But I owned to missing the excitement as well." Malcolm rubbed Berowne's silver gray ears. "Though I don't miss being at Carfax's beck and call."

Suzanne pictured Lord Carfax's sharp-boned face and the

piercing gaze he could shoot over the frame of his spectacles. "Lord Carfax is a spymaster. He never—"

"—really lets his agents go. Quite. With another man one might call it kindness that he hasn't demanded my services yet. With Carfax it makes me wonder what he's up to." Malcolm stroked the cat's head while his gaze moved from the glass-fronted bookcase that held his first editions to the lamplight spilling onto the library table, softening and illuminating the chestnut-veined Carrara marble. "I never thought this house would seem so like a home. You've worked wonders."

The house, a small jewel set on this exclusive square, had been Malcolm's father's until his death last summer. It was filled with memories of Malcolm's childhood that Suzanne still did not fully understand. Malcolm, she knew, had had mixed feelings about living here. He'd been inclined to sell the house at first. When they walked through it, still filled with Alistair Rannoch's furniture and art treasures, she'd seen the memories cluster behind Malcolm's eyes, more painful than sweet. But he'd looked out at the railed square garden overhung by leafy plane trees, a rare bit of greenery in the city. Perfect for the children, he'd said. How could they not raise Colin and Jessica here given the chance? So Suzanne had set about ordering new paper and paint, choosing new upholstery and wall hangings, sketching new moldings, and conferring with the builders about which walls they could knock down.

"It was good to have a project," she said. In truth, it had saved her sanity as she adjusted to life among the British beau monde— Malcolm's world, where she would always be an outsider—and struggled to come to terms with everything she had given up.

The smile he flashed her was filled with understanding. "It will get easier. Living here in London. Finding a scope for your talents."

She nodded. Malcolm understood so much and could read her so well. But there were things he couldn't understand. Such as just how much she was missing from her old life or the reasons that even in the heart of Mayfair she would never truly feel safe. For her husband, the man she had married out of necessity and come to love so much it frightened her, didn't know she had been a Bonapartist agent when they met. That she had married him to spy for the French. That she had gone on doing so for the first three years of their marriage. That even now, more than two years after she had made the choice to leave off spying, she felt the tug of divided loyalties. That she lived with the constant fear of discovery, like the nagging pain of a headache that never went away or the gnawing ache of a half-healed wound.

For every day of their marriage she lied to her husband. And the best she could hope for was that she could preserve the lie for the rest of their lives.

"I don't have any regrets," she said. Like so much of what she said to her husband, it was a half-truth. She didn't regret for a moment her marriage, her children, the life they were building here in Britain. But when she thought back over the past five years, regrets clustered thick and fast.

Berowne rolled onto his back on Malcolm's lap. Malcolm rubbed the cat's stomach. "I'd say we were tempting fate, save that I don't believe in fate. But our life has a way of not staying settled for long."

"It's different now."

"To a degree. Much as I like to claim I'm my own master, once an agent always an agent."

That ought to have been funny. Save that it tore at her throat. She stroked Jessica's tiny hand. Jessica's fingers curled round her own, the way they had when she was a squirming newborn. Suzanne tried to savor moments such as this. To commit to memory the boneless weight of the child in her arms, the tug of the small mouth at her breast, the soft translucence of Jessica's skin, and the web of veins showing at the temple. The glint in Malcolm's eyes, the angle of his head, the way his long fingers moved over the cat's fur. The rumble of Berowne's purr and the sight of his head lolling off Malcolm's knee. To store the memories up against whatever the future might hold. No matter what Suzanne missed from her old life, no matter the fears she lived with, five years ago she could never have thought she'd find such contentment simply sitting in lamplit quiet, with the patter of the rain on the windows, her baby at her breast, and the steady warmth of her husband's smile. That counted for a lot. Perhaps she should—

A thud on the window glass cut through the candle-warmed air. Malcolm dropped his book. Suzanne nearly dropped Jessica. Malcolm sprang to his feet, disrupting Berowne, and put himself between Suzanne and Jessica and the window. Suzanne tightened her arms round Jessica. Old defensive instincts sprang to life, like hairs responding to a shock of electricity. The Berkeley Square house, still so new, had perhaps never felt so much like home than now, when it was threatened.

Berowne hissed and arched his back. The window scraped against the sash. Malcolm snatched up a silver candlestick. Jessica released Suzanne's breast and let out a squawk.

"It's all right." A slurred, strained voice came from the window. "It's me."

Malcolm exchanged a look with Suzanne. "Simon?"

They both ran to the window. Malcolm pushed the sash up the rest of the way and extended a hand to haul Simon Tanner, muddy and dripping rainwater, over the sill.

Simon had lost his hat and his greatcoat was soaked and caked with mud. His straight dark hair was plastered to his forehead. And—

"You're bleeding," Suzanne said.

"Scratches." Simon pushed his wet hair out of his eyes and grinned at her with his habitual nonchalance. "Sorry for the dramatic entrance. I may not have your skills at espionage, but it seemed safer not to use the front door. Not that I think they were actually trying to kill me, but they didn't seem too concerned about collateral damage."

Malcolm crossed to the drinks trolley, splashed whisky into a glass, and put it in Simon's hand. Suzanne kissed Jessica and put her in her bassinet, then pressed Simon into one of the Queen Anne chairs. He protested, spluttering whisky. "I'll ruin the upholstery."

"The upholstery's more easily repaired than you. Darling, can you get my medical supply box?"

Malcolm ran out of the room. She could hear his footsteps on the marble tiles of the hall and the polished wood of the stairs. She helped Simon out of the sodden greatcoat and the damp coat beneath. Above his silver brocade waistcoat, blood seeped through the linen of his shirt.

"Scratches," he said again.

"Only in the sense that Berowne and a lion are both cats. Hold still. David will never forgive me if I bungle this."

By the time Malcolm came back with her medical supply box, she had Simon's cravat and waistcoat off. Malcolm helped her cut away the bloodstained shirt. The main cut was long but, if not precisely a scratch, not overly deep. It wouldn't require stitches. She cleaned and dressed it and the cut on his face while Malcolm replenished Simon's glass of whisky. Berowne, deciding there was no imminent danger, ran over to bat at a roll of lint. Jessica sat up in her bassinet and observed with wide eyes.

"I'm sorry," Simon said. His hands were steadier now. "I didn't mean to put you in the middle of this."

"I'm glad you came to us." Malcolm didn't add, *What the hell are you in the midst of?* though the unasked question lingered in parchment- and whisky-scented air. Simon was one of London's foremost playwrights, but it seemed more likely his involvement in Radical politics had led to tonight's adventure.

"I was on my way to you before I was attacked, as it happens." Simon winced as Suzanne secured a dressing over his chest. His gaze slid between them. "No, I'm not involved in a plot to bring down the government. I do recognize that you're a Member of Parliament now, Malcolm. I may not be the most considerate of friends, but I wouldn't knowingly put you in such an awkward situation."

Malcolm smiled, though the strain remained round his eyes. He perched on the arm of the other Queen Anne chair. "What then?"

Simon settled back in his own chair as Suzanne drew the folds of a blanket about his shoulders. "I wanted to get your opinion on a manuscript."

"One of your own?" Malcolm asked. Simon frequently got into hot water with the Government Censor.

"No, I'm not nearly so cautious. Not that I don't value the opinions of both of you." Simon flashed a smile between them and took a sip of whisky. His face had a bit more color, Suzanne was relieved to see. "A play I was sent. We're planning a production at the Tavistock. Read-throughs start tomorrow. Though we know it will mean no end of controversy."

"Another Radical playwright?" Malcolm asked. Jessica had begun to fuss, fretful squawks that were the prelude to cries while her hands beat a tattoo on the wicker of the bassinet. He got to his feet.

"No, the playwright's reputation is as solid as pounds sterling." Simon stroked Berowne, who had jumped up on the arm of the chair. "Though he dramatized his share of revolts and assassinations. You could say you and I and David and Oliver owe our friendship to him."

Suzanne sat back on her heels. Malcolm lifted Jessica against his shoulder and stared at Simon. David, Simon, Malcolm, and their friend Oliver Lydgate had met in an Oxford production of *Henry IV, Part II*. For a moment the air trembled with disbelief. "Simon, are you saying someone sent you a lost Shakespeare play?" Suzanne could hear the wonder in her own voice.

"Not exactly. It's a play we know well. But I've never seen this version before. It is—or purports to be—a different version of *Hamlet*."

A chill ran through Suzanne, touching a part of her that went back to childhood. To days when she had sprawled on her stomach watching her father stage rehearsals or dozed in a dressing room while her actress mother swept on and off the stage. Suzanne lived and breathed politics now, but she had grown up in the theatre. A new version of *Hamlet* was like touching Excalibur. "How different?" she asked.

"There are several scenes of Laertes in Paris. And a new scene of Claudius and Polonius plotting. Including a line that could imply Claudius is actually Hamlet's father."

Malcolm's fingers tightened against Jessica's head. "Good God."

"Yes, it does add even more layers to Hamlet's motivation."

"Could the manuscript be authentic?" Malcolm asked.

"Difficult to tell." Simon shifted against the chairback, then winced as he jostled his wound. "The language feels right. A bit rough round the edges, but that could be accounted for by it being an early version. Some of the familiar scenes have slightly different language as well."

"There are two different versions of *Hamlet* that we know of," Malcolm said. "And there are mentions of an earlier play that was a source for *Hamlet,* by Kyd, perhaps even by Shakespeare himself. A lot of Shakespeare scholars, including my grandfather, think Shakespeare was working on *Hamlet* for years. So theoretically one can imagine an earlier draft existing." He drew a breath. Suzanne could hear the shock and wonder that underlay his words. "Does it look authentic?"

"It certainly looks old." Simon stroked Berowne, who had jumped into his lap and was kneading his knees. "It's handwritten, and at least one other person has made notes and corrections on the manuscript. But I couldn't tell if either is Shakespeare's hand."

"I don't think anyone could. The only examples of his handwriting we have are a few signatures." Malcolm moved across the room, shifting Jessica against his shoulder. His voice was temperate, but Suzanne could read the excitement in the taut lines of his body.

"You know Shakespeare. Both of you." Simon's gaze flickered to Suzanne. "And you know forgeries."

"We should get my grandfather's opinion. Fortunately he's staying with my aunt Marjorie in Surrey, so I can reach him more quickly than if he were in Scotland." Malcolm rubbed his hand against Jessica's back. His grandfather, the Duke of Strathdon, was a noted Shakespearean scholar.

"Yes, I was thinking of that. Obviously it's a ticklish situation. It could be the making of the Tavistock if it's authentic. We could make fools of ourselves if it turns out to be a forgery. But it never occurred to me it was dangerous."

"Simon?" Suzanne said, watching his face. "What happened on your way here?"

"Three men jumped me. I fought back—I don't take kindly to having my possessions appropriated. But when I took the knife to the chest even I was willing to concede it was prudent to let them have what they were after."

"Do you have any idea who they were?" Malcolm asked, jiggling Jessica in his arms.

Simon shook his head. "There were three of them. English, I think, but we didn't stop to exchange pleasantries."

Suzanne closed her medical supply box. "Where did you get the manuscript?"

"From Manon."

Suzanne's fingers froze on the bronze latch. She forced them to unclench. Manon Caret had been the leading actress at the Comédie-Française. She had escaped Paris two years ago just ahead of agents of Fouché, the minister of police. For in addition to being a brilliant actress, she was a Bonapartist agent. And Suzanne had helped her escape. Which of course Suzanne couldn't say to anyone. Even her husband. Especially her husband. "How on earth did Manon—"

"Harleton gave it to her. Apparently he found it tucked away among his father's things after Lord Harleton's death."

Suzanne set the medical supply box on the sofa table, controlling the trembling of her fingers. Crispin, Lord Harleton, was a cheerful young man, a couple of years ahead of Malcolm at Oxford. He had been Manon's lover for the past year or so. His father had been one of the sporting set. Suzanne had met him once or twice before his death six months ago, a bluff man with a hearty laugh, an appreciative eye for a low-cut bodice, and hands that were inclined to wander.

Malcolm dropped down on a footstool, propping Jessica in his lap. "I'm surprised old Lord Harleton had a manuscript of such value. Though not surprised he left it tucked away."

"Crispin said ten to one his father didn't realize what he had," Simon said. "I must say Crispin quite impressed me. I always used to wonder what Manon saw in him."

Jessica wriggled in Malcolm's lap and arched her back. Malcolm set her on the carpet, and she began to scoot across the floor, heedless of the undercurrents. "Did Crispin and Manon give you any indication that anyone might be after the manuscript?" Malcolm asked.

Simon shook his head. "No. They were merely curious if it could be genuine."

"Simon." Malcolm reached down to steady Jessica as she pulled herself up on the edge of an ormolu table. "Tell me that you didn't give up the only copy of the manuscript?"

A slow smile spread across Simon's face. "I copied the whole script out the night Manon and Crispin gave it me. I was thinking of fire or damage more than theft. And then I had copies printed up for the actors." He stroked Berowne under the chin. "I'm not sure why I brought the first copy I made with me tonight. I had some vague thought that we might want to read from it to spare the original. But I'm very glad I did. Because the thieves couldn't tell my copy from the original manuscript."

Malcolm echoed Simon's smile. "You still have the original?"

"Wrapped in oilskin in my greatcoat pocket. They glanced at my copy enough to determine it was a script—which apparently is what they'd been told to look for—and then saw no need to search me further. Bring my coat over and we can have a look at it. I'm eager to see what you think of the authenticity. And more."

"More?" Suzanne scooped up Jessica, who had crawled over to grab her mother's sarcenet-covered knees.

Simon's fingers went taut against Berowne's soft gray fur. "Even when I was bleeding on the cobblestones, I felt I should put on a show of reluctance to give up the manuscript. One of the men dealt me a blow to the jaw and snatched it from my hands. Another said, 'All this fuss just for some old paper.' And another replied, 'It's not the paper. It's the secrets hidden in it.' "

CHAPTER 2

Malcolm set Jessica in her cradle, gently settling her head on the tiny feather bed. "An adventure without international intrigue."

"That we know of." Suzanne closed the door to the night nursery, where Colin was sound asleep, his arm curled round his stuffed bear. Manon's involvement danced on the edge of her consciousness. As Crispin's mistress, Manon shouldn't have anything to do with a manuscript found among his late father's things. But her involvement, combined with the talk of dangerous secrets, brought Suzanne's defensive instincts springing to life. Or perhaps she was starting to jump at shadows, like the Tory politicians who saw Radical plots behind every tree.

"Old Lord Harleton wasn't particularly political," Malcolm said, stroking his fingers against Jessica's cheek. "Difficult to imagine international secrets being hidden in papers he possessed, whether or not the manuscript is genuine. Amorous secrets on the other hand—"

Suzanne crossed the room and tucked a soft blanket round Jessica's legs. English houses were drafty and the fire in the grate (why had the porcelain stoves so prevalent on the Continent never caught on here?) could not drive out the chill. "Yes, he managed to get his hand down my bodice the one time we actually spoke. At the regent's reception at Carlton House."

Malcolm's brows snapped together. "You didn't tell me."

"You might have turned husbandly and felt obliged to do something. I may be new to London society, but I do realize that making a scene at a party hosted by the prince regent isn't the way to further your political career."

"I'm not worried about furthering my political career."

"I know, you're delightfully blind to it, which is wonderfully idealistic but not perhaps wise for furthering your agenda." Suzanne adjusted the blanket as Jessica stretched in her sleep. "Which is why your wife has to do it for you."

He grinned and pushed a ringlet behind her ear. "It's not as though I'd have challenged Harleton to a duel or planted him a facer—much as I'd have liked to."

"No, you'd have said something cutting. But it still could have caused a scene. Trust me, I dealt with it perfectly well on my own. But crude as Harleton's approach was, I gather he had a fair amount of success in the boudoir?"

Malcolm moved across the room and shrugged out of his coat. "So rumor has it. He moved in the same set as my parents." His hands stilled for a moment on his waistcoat buttons.

Suzanne watched him. She had known before they left Paris that Britain held ghosts for him. But even after almost nine months here, she was only beginning to understand the nature of those ghosts. His childhood had been lonely, his parents distant, he and his brother and sister largely packed off to the country house in Scotland. His parents' marriage, he had warned her when he proposed, had been a disaster. His mother's death was a wound that plainly still festered but which Suzanne couldn't touch. His father's death over the summer had only raised more questions about their relationship. *He didn't love me,* Malcolm had told her in a stark voice. *I didn't love him. There isn't much to mourn.*

She knew she could only watch and let the picture unfold, listen to what Malcolm was willing to reveal. She had to constantly remind herself not to push for more. And to tell herself it shouldn't matter that when they shared so much there were still secrets he kept from her. After all, she had more than her share of secrets that she kept from him.

Malcolm stripped off his waistcoat and tossed it over a chair. "I'd hazard a guess the secret concealed in the manuscript is the name of a lover."

"A love affair doesn't necessarily spell ruin in these circles." Love affairs, Suzanne had learned, were not flaunted as openly in London as in Paris or Vienna (where some of her friends could move about openly as couples with their lovers), but though the veneer of respectability was slightly stronger, amorous intrigues seemed just as common. It had been an open secret, Malcolm's cousin Aline had told her, that the late Duke of Devonshire lived in a menage-à-trois with his wife and his mistress Lady Elizabeth Foster. On the other hand, Suzanne's friend Cordelia's childhood friend Lady Caroline Lamb had caused no end of scandal with her affair with Lord Byron, because she flaunted it so flagrantly. It wasn't what one did, said Cordy, who had her own past, it was how openly one did it. "Of course talk always has more power to ruin the woman involved," Suzanne said, thinking of Caro and Cordy.

"Precisely."

Suzanne looked at her husband and could tell they were both thinking back to a matter they'd investigated at the time of their wedding. "You think Harleton devised the manuscript as a way of concealing the names of his lovers?"

"It's hard for me to imagine Harleton having the wit to devise a manuscript that could even remotely plausibly be by Shakespeare. But he could have hidden the information in an existing manuscript."

"And a former mistress is behind the attack on Simon?"

"It's the likeliest explanation."

The door creaked as Berowne pushed his way into the room. Suzanne bent down to pet the cat. "Whoever was behind the attack went to considerable lengths. Which argues wealth. And desperation. Someone with a great deal to lose. At the very least a less than complacent husband."

"Or secrets that go beyond a love affair. A child perhaps."

Malcolm didn't pause before he said it, though she could hear his questions about his own parentage, never fully voiced between them, echoing in the air. And then there was the son his late half-sister, Tatiana Kirsanova, had gone to such lengths to conceal, who now lived in London.

"It can be a powerful motive." Suzanne scooped up Berowne and held him against her. "Whoever was behind the attack isn't likely to give up. And they may realize we have the manuscript."

"I hope they do." A smile curved Malcolm's mouth. "We'll be prepared if they come calling. But we should plant guards at the theatre as well. David wouldn't forgive me if anything happened to Simon. For that matter, I wouldn't forgive myself."

"Nor would I." She pictured the precious stack of paper, now locked in the desk in Malcolm's study. "If Harleton used an existing manuscript to encode the information, the manuscript itself could be genuine. Even our glance in the library just now confirmed it's old."

He met her gaze and she could feel the air tighten between them, this time with excitement. Shakespeare was one of the first things they'd shared. Strangers in what was to all intents and purposes an arranged marriage, with so many lies between them, they'd been able to cap each other's quotes. On their wedding night, when words like "love" had seemed as distant as Illyria, they'd been able to quote *Romeo and Juliet* to each other. Shakespeare quotes had been their own private code, a way to express emotions they still couldn't and might never be able to properly put into words, a shared language that marked out territory uniquely their own.

"It could be," he agreed. He pushed his fingers through his hair. "And God help me, of course I'm sorry for what happened to Simon, but—"

She shifted Berowne against her shoulder. "You're excited."

"It is a welcome distraction."

From his father's death. From the stresses and unresolved issues of their return to Britain. From her own fears of discovery, as long as Manon's connection didn't drag them onto dangerous ground. The bond between them had always been strongest when they were able to work together on a mystery. Where some couples might bond over glasses of champagne or a moonlit stroll in a garden, they could over missing papers, complex codes, or mysterious deaths. "And a chance to work together."

A smile lit his eyes. "Quite." He crossed the room and slid his fingers behind her neck. She tilted her head back, but as he bent his lips to hers a knock fell on the door.

"I'm sorry, sir." The voice of Valentin, the first footman, came through the door panels. He was not quite three-and-twenty, but after the battle of Waterloo and the subsequent events he had gone through with Malcolm and Suzanne in Paris, he was unflappable. "But Lord Carfax is below. He's asking for you to come down at once. He says it's urgent."

Valentin had shown Lord Carfax into the library and had poked up the fire and lit a brace of candles and two lamps. Malcolm came into the room to find his mentor, spymaster, and best friend's father by the drinks trolley pouring himself a glass of brandy. Carfax set down the decanter and replaced the stopper. "Sit down, Malcolm," he said without looking round.

Malcolm advanced warily across the Aubusson carpet. Through the years, those words from Carfax had taken on an ominous ring. In Malcolm's boyhood, the earl had been a commanding but distant presence who appeared on speech days and other special occasions at Harrow and occasionally poked his head in the schoolroom or nursery when Malcolm visited Carfax Court. Carfax burdened his son, David, Malcolm's best friend, with expectations but was generally kind to Malcolm if rather dismissive. Then in the wake of Malcolm's mother's death, Carfax had found Malcolm a diplomatic post. With an intelligence component. Malcolm wasn't sure what would have become of him if Carfax hadn't come to his rescue in the midst of that personal crisis. He knew full well he owed the earl an incalculable amount. Malcolm respected Carfax, knew he would be forever in his debt, perhaps even cared for him, if one could apply such simple words to such a complex man. And at the same time Malcolm knew he couldn't trust him.

Malcolm dropped into one of the Queen Anne chairs. He remembered sitting in a similar chair at the age of fifteen when Carfax called him and David in for a rare grilling about where they had disappeared to the previous evening (he'd seemed, if anything, disappointed to learn they had slipped out of the house to go to a lecture by William Godwin). Malcolm wouldn't be a bit surprised if Carfax remembered that incident as well and had set the scene accordingly. He wasn't above making use of the past.

Carfax took an appreciative sip of brandy. "Your father kept a good cellar, I'll give him that." He ran his gaze over Malcolm, no doubt taking in his rumpled coat and lack of a cravat. "Sorry to have called so late. My apologies to Suzanne."

"Suzette's used to it. What's happened?"

Carfax regarded Malcolm over the rim of his spectacles. "I understand Tanner came to see you this evening."

"That was quick even for you." Malcolm stared at Carfax. The light from the brace of candles on the library table bounced off the lenses of his spectacles. *Good God.* Malcolm's stomach lurched. "Did—"

"My dear Malcolm. I admit to finding Tanner's views dangerous, but do you really imagine I'd have my son's friend attacked on a London street?"

Malcolm's fingers sank into the carved walnut arms of the chair. "Yes, if you thought it necessary to achieve your ends."

Carfax gave a smile that was a tacit acknowledgment of a point scored. "Possibly. But I don't dislike Tanner, you know. Nor do I actively wish to pick a quarrel with my son."

Like the rest of David's family, Carfax maintained the fiction that David and Simon were friends who shared lodgings. Simon was even invited to Carfax Court on occasion. Malcolm suspected that Carfax had known the truth of David's relationship with Simon Tanner from quite early on. He wasn't even sure Carfax had moral objections or that he wished the relationship to end. But Malcolm had no doubt Carfax expected David, as his heir, to marry and produce a son. Malcolm had seen in Paris what tragedy those tensions could lead to. Still, as Carfax said, there was no reason Malcolm knew of for the earl to have taken such drastic action now.

"Do you know who did have Simon attacked?" Malcolm asked.

"No, as it happens." Carfax advanced across the room at a measured pace and sank into the other Queen Anne chair. "Nor who is after the *Hamlet* manuscript."

Malcolm was suddenly and keenly aware of the frame of the chair pressing through the cassimere of his coat. "You know about the manuscript."

Carfax removed his spectacles and folded them. "My dear boy, that's why I called on you."

"To ask me about a manuscript that may be by Shakespeare?"

"To order you to examine it. And bring me what you learn."

Malcolm stared at his former spymaster. "What the hell is in the manuscript?"

Carfax set the spectacles on a table beside the chair. "Surely the fact that it may be by Shakespeare makes it valuable enough."

"Not to explain your interest. Need I remind you that I don't work for you anymore, sir?"

"My dear Malcolm. I won't insult your intelligence by pretending to believe you could have thought walking away from the intelligence game was as simple as resigning from the diplomatic corps."

"I'm not obligated to follow your orders anymore. I have a right to demand an explanation."

Carfax gave a short laugh. "You'd have demanded it anyway."

"Probably."

"Undeniably." Carfax picked up his spectacles and turned them over in his hands. Malcolm sometimes wondered if the earl actually needed them or if he had appropriated them as an effective prop. "How much did Tanner tell you about where the manuscript came from?"

Malcolm hesitated. He always did so before revealing information to Carfax, but there didn't seem any harm in this. "He said Crispin Harleton found it among his father's things after Lord Harleton's death."

"And Crispin gave it to the lovely Manon Caret, who is sharing his bed." Carfax lined the spectacles up on the chair arm. "Old Lord Harleton was at Oxford with your father, wasn't he?"

"I wouldn't be surprised. They seemed of an age. My father was hardly given to reminiscing about his undergraduate days with me." Malcolm swallowed. Five months after Alistair Rannoch's death, the mention of him still brought the bitter bite of an emotion Malcolm could scarcely name. Save that it at once chilled and scalded.

"They were in the same year, I believe. A year behind me. Along with Glenister and Hugo Cyrus and Thanet. Harleton always struck me as a gullible sort. A follower more than a leader. But then I imagine that's how he fell into their clutches. You'd think it would be the independent rebels, but so often it's the fools."

"The fools who—"

Carfax picked up the spectacles, unfolded them, and set them on his nose. "Harleton was a French spy."

After almost a decade in the intelligence game, hearing that someone one had considered trustworthy was an enemy agent was not as surprising as it would once have been. Even so, Malcolm blinked, trying to reconcile his image of a portly, red-faced man sitting over a bottle of port with a Bonapartist agent. "For how long?"

"Since before Bonaparte came to power. I suspect part of Harleton's idiocy was a pose, part was simply who he was. Sometimes having a less complicated brain can be an asset in an agent. Present company excepted."

Malcolm leaned forwards in his chair. "You knew the whole time?"

"No, I regret to confess it was 1802 before I discovered it. When I went to Paris during the Peace of Amiens. Don't let my idiocy get about."

"You funneled misinformation through Harleton?"

"He was useful." Carfax turned his brandy glass in his hand. "Not clever enough to realize he was being used."

"And after the war?"

"No point in causing a scandal and embarrassing the family."

"His sister is married to your cousin."

"Quite. I saw no need to do anything." Carfax settled back in his chair. "Until a month or so before Harleton's death."

"What did Harleton do?"

"It wasn't what he did so much as the political situation in general. Even you can't be blind to the risk that the machine breakers and dissenters in the north will join up with former Bonapartists."

"That assumes you see any call for reform as a step towards treason."

Carfax shook his head with a smile that was almost affectionate. "You have a keen understanding, Malcolm, but thank God men like you aren't running the country. Suffice it to say, it seemed like a good time to make an example of a man like Harleton. I was preparing to move against him when he died."

"Where does the manuscript fit in? Are you saying the manuscript is a fake? Harleton created it?" Malcolm kept his gaze from straying to the door to the study where the manuscript currently resided. He had no intention of surrendering it to Carfax. "Because from my preliminary examination, it certainly appears old."

"It may be genuine for all I know. I doubt Harleton would have had the wit to create it on his own. But Harleton used it as a codebook. I had agents look for it after he died, but they couldn't find it. I don't know where he had it hidden away." Carfax set his glass down on the table. His gaze hardened. "I need those codes broken, Malcolm."

"The war's over."

"The intelligence game doesn't stop." Carfax tented his fingers together. "It's interesting that the manuscript surfaced at the Tavistock. You know about Manon Caret."

"I know what's been rumored about her." Manon Caret, former leading lady at the Comédie-Française, had fled Paris—rumor had it only a hair's breadth ahead of Fouché's agents—while Malcolm was attached to the British delegation two years ago. "I have yet to see proof."

"With a woman that clever, there wouldn't be any." Carfax leaned back in his chair and folded his hands together. "Interesting that she became the mistress of the son of a former spy."

"You're suggesting that a former Bonapartist agent got her

hands on a codebook of another Bonapartist agent and had her lover bring it to Simon Tanner? Knowing Simon is close to me and also to your son? Whatever else she may be, I think we can agree Manon Caret is no fool."

"A point. I still find her involvement suspicious. I'm sure you'll discover the truth of whatever role Mademoiselle Caret played, Malcolm. And who else may have been involved in this along with her."

"Don't you think I'm too close to Simon to be looking into all this?"

"No." Carfax let his shoulders sink into the chairback. "I have every faith in your ability to be fair-minded, Malcolm."

"Convenient." Malcolm crossed his legs. "So you think this manuscript was hidden away until Crispin just happened upon it after his father's death?"

"Not quite. I suspect the manuscript relates to why Harleton was murdered."

He should have seen it coming. But Carfax could still catch him unawares. "I thought Harleton's death was an accident."

"Really, Malcolm. A former spy accidentally shoots himself while cleaning his gun? If you'd believe that for a minute civilian life has made you soft."

"I don't suppose I would have done if I'd known Harleton was a French agent. Whom did you task with the investigation?"

"I didn't. I suspected someone from Harleton's past got rid of him, and I saw no need to waste our energies on a Bonapartist feud. The manuscript surfacing changes things."

"So you want—"

"—you to decode whatever's in the manuscript and learn who killed Harleton. I know you now have Parliament to distract you, but really for a man of your talents it shouldn't be too difficult."

Suzanne stared at her husband across the candle-warmed rose-and-blue medallions of their bedroom carpet. "Do you believe Carfax?"

Malcolm shrugged out of his coat and tossed it over the tapestry chair. "I don't believe he made the whole story up. That's a long way from saying I believe all of it. I've learned never to take Carfax at face value. I'm not sure he's been entirely forthcoming about what he thinks is in the manuscript."

Suzanne scanned her husband's face. She could feel the intensity rippling through him. "But you're going to do as he asked?"

Malcolm's gaze shifted over the shadows cast by the dressing table and chest of drawers and escritoire. A chill coursed through her. "I'm going to decode whatever may be in the manuscript. And to learn what happened to Harleton. What I do with the information once I decode it and how much I tell Carfax remains to be seen."

There was no other answer she'd have expected Malcolm to make. And she could do nothing to dissuade him. But she felt as she had after she'd fallen into the Carrión River in January.

He moved across the room and dropped down on the bed beside her. "That is, *we're* going to decode the manuscript and learn what happened to Harleton." He gave a faint smile. "I hope. I shouldn't speak for you."

She leaned in and kissed his cheek. Her mouth felt like ash. "Of course, dearest. You can't think I'd let you have all the fun. Do we begin by talking to Crispin?"

"And Manon Caret. Carfax confirmed she's a former French spy."

"It's been a fairly open secret," Suzanne said in an equable voice. "At least in intelligence circles."

"Quite." Malcolm laced his fingers through her own and stared down at their clasped hands. "I've come to quite like Manon since she's been at the Tavistock. Whatever her activities during the war, one can't but admire what she's built here. I find myself loath to disrupt her life."

Suzanne swallowed. Hard. "Investigations have a way of disrupting lives, darling. And it may prove to have nothing to do with Manon's past activities. It seems shockingly risky for her to have given the manuscript to Simon only to try to steal it back."

"Perhaps she didn't realize what it was when she gave it to Simon."

That, Suzanne had to admit, was a possibility.

"Carfax never thought about bringing her in?" Suzanne asked, keenly aware of the pressure of Malcolm's fingers on her own.

"We never had proof, only rumors. And she quickly acquired powerful friends in England. Besides, she was spying in France on the French, not directly against us."

Unlike Suzanne herself. "Yes, of course."

"I admit I'm still adjusting to the idea of old Lord Harleton as a French spy," Malcolm said.

So was she. "If only I'd known when he got his hand down my bodice."

"Quite. But I still want to find out what the devil happened to him. It seems we're investigating a murder again."

She twisted her head round to look at him. "You're enjoying this."

He shot her a crooked smile. "Call it the lure of the challenge. A compulsion to leave no stone unturned." He kissed her hair. "Or perhaps another project we can share."

She leaned into him, craving the warmth of his arm round her and his breath brushing her skin.

She only hoped he couldn't feel the chill coursing through her.

CHAPTER 3

" 'Soft you now! The fair Ophelia.' "

The voice echoed against the wooden walls as Malcolm and Suzanne stepped into the wings of the Tavistock. Greasy light from oil rehearsal lamps gleamed against the white cravats and shirt cuffs and muslin gowns and tippets of the group seated round a table in the center of the bare stage.

" 'Nymph, in thy orisons—' " A dark-haired man threw his script down on the table. "Damn, I keep getting the old version confused with this one."

"This is the old version if it's genuine." Manon Caret leaned forwards, stretching her back. "I must say I rather like this Ophelia. She gets to stand up for herself more."

"And Hamlet does actually seem to love her in this version." The dark-haired man, who was Brandon Ford, the Tavistock's leading actor, pushed his chair back from the table.

"He loves her in the other version," Manon said. "He says so when he jumps in her grave."

"Christ, Manon, how long have you been playing Shakespeare?" Brandon grabbed a flask that, knowing him, might contain either water or something stronger and tossed down a swig. "The man doesn't always have his characters say what they think."

"No, but it's there between the lines as well. At least half the bit-terness in the 'get thee to a nunnery' scene is because he realizes the woman he loves has been set to spy on him. And then there's the letter he wrote her—"

"Where he says 'doubt that the sun doth move'? Shakespeare knew perfectly well the earth moved round the sun, not the other way round. And in this version the letter's even more nonsensical. 'Doubt that my blood is fire—' "

"It's the letter of a young, ardent man—"

"Oh, he's ardent all right. Probably wrote it when he was trying to get her into bed."

"You're being too cynical, my boy." A gravelly voice sounded from the front of the house. "I'm quite sure Hamlet loves Ophelia deeply. I've always thought the whole point of the 'get thee to a nunnery' speech is that he's trying to get her out of the way."

"Just so." Brandon set down the flask and wiped his hand across his mouth.

"Not because he's tired of her, because he wants to protect her. He's about to go off and do this dangerous thing, steep himself in blood and all that, and he wants to make sure she's safe from all the dark doings. Quite noble, really—"

"Horace, dear," said a handsome auburn-haired woman seated at the head of the table beside Simon, "you're here to observe."

"But he makes a good point." Crispin's voice came from the front of the house as well. "If—"

Simon's eye had fallen on Malcolm and Suzanne. "Edifying as this conversation is, perhaps we can continue it later. We have visi-tors I need to talk to. I think this is a good time for a break. Half an hour?"

"Thought you'd never ask." Brandon sprang to his feet. "Tav-ern, anyone?"

As the actors dispersed, Malcolm stepped forwards and glimpsed Crispin sitting in the front row of the audience. He had a fair-haired girl of about seven in his lap. An older girl was sprawled on the floor beside him with a book. A stout man with a ruddy complexion, thin-ning sandy hair, and sharp blue eyes, the possessor of the gravelly voice, sat across the aisle from Crispin and the girls.

"You know Lord Harleton," Simon said to Malcolm and Suzanne. "And Sir Horace Smytheton."

"Come to see the magic unfold, have you?" Sir Horace asked. "Once in a lifetime chance to be a part of something like this. Do you know, Simon, it occurs to me that when Hamlet calls her 'nymph' he really means—"

"Horace, dear." The auburn-haired woman slipped off the edge of the stage with the grace of a young girl. "I am quite parched. Do take me out for a lemonade."

"What? Oh, of course, Jenny." Sir Horace pushed himself to his feet.

Simon moved towards Malcolm and Suzanne. "Flattered as I am, I doubt the two of you came merely to have a glimpse of our rehearsal."

"We might have done," Malcolm said. "But no, as it happens."

Crispin got to his feet. He was a tall man with a crop of disordered golden-brown hair. In his light blue coat, buckskin breeches, and boots, he looked like a young blood out for a morning ride, but there was nothing of the pampered aristocrat in the way he swung the younger girl in the air. "We can go get ices—"

"Actually," Malcolm said, "I was hoping for a word with you as well, Harleton. And with Mademoiselle Caret."

The little girl in Harleton's arms gave a squeak of protest at the loss of the promised ices.

"Come on, Clarisse," the older girl said, getting to her feet. "We can—"

"Berthe," Manon called. "Could you take the girls out for ices?"

A few moments later, a dark-haired woman in a stylish print dress emerged from the dressing room, arms filled with pelisses, bonnets, and gloves. Crispin set Clarisse on the ground and ruffled her hair, touched Roxane's hair as well, and gave each girl a sixpence once they were bundled into their outerwear.

Manon cocked a brow at him as Berthe took the girls off. "You spoil them."

"I like spoiling them."

Malcolm felt a flash of kinship at the tenderness in Crispin's eyes as he watched the girls leave. For Malcolm as well fatherhood had brought a shock of unlooked-for delight. No matter who the biological parent. Crispin went up in Malcolm's estimation. He remembered Crispin as a good-natured boy, an excellent rider, with a good arm for cricket, not much of a student—though perhaps due more to lack of application than aptitude—with an easygoing temperament.

"Sir Horace is the Tavistock's main patron, isn't he?" Malcolm said as Manon conducted them to her dressing room.

"And always takes a keen interest in our productions. But he has a particular affinity for *Hamlet*." Simon's grin was sharp with irony.

"I think that makes the eighteenth time he interrupted this morning," Manon said, opening the dressing room door. "Not that I'm counting. Fortunately, Jennifer manages him superbly. Don't get any ideas, Crispin. I wouldn't be as patient as she is."

"I wouldn't dream of it," Crispin said.

Inside the dressing room Manon swept a bejeweled velvet robe, a doll, and two stuffed animals from a frayed tapestry settee and set a kettle to brewing over a spirit lamp. "Two years in England and I've become a tea drinker."

"No one would guess how practical you are for a leading lady," Crispin said with a grin.

She grinned back with familiar ease. "Shush, don't let it get about. I have a reputation to maintain."

"Exciting to see the play staged." Crispin dropped down on the settee with the ease of one used to making himself at home there. "Forgot what a dashed good story *Hamlet* is. And I confess there are things I like better in this version."

"Ophelia's a bit stronger, perhaps," Manon agreed. "I like the insights into Laertes. And the Claudius-Hamlet relationship is interesting."

"I say," Crispin said, as though he'd just realized his two worlds were colliding, "you have met the Rannochs, haven't you, darling? Been properly introduced, you know what I mean."

"No one could fault your manners, *mon cher*." Manon smiled at her lover. Even in a simple blue-spotted muslin round gown, her dark gold hair pulled back into a loose knot, she dominated the scene as though playing Cleopatra. "As is glaringly obvious, though you're far too polite to say it, Mr. and Mrs. Rannoch and I hardly move in the same circles. But we have met, at Simon's party after the opening of *School for Wives*. And once or twice in Hyde Park with the girls."

"And my wife and I have admired your performances many times onstage." Malcolm inclined his head.

"You're very kind, Mr. Rannoch." Manon lifted a silver tea tray bearing a set of delftware from a chest of drawers, her gaze surprisingly direct. "Mrs. Rannoch. How is your little boy? And your charming baby?"

"Jessica took three steps on her own a week ago, then dropped down on the carpet and decided crawling was safer."

"They do grow up quickly. But you didn't come here to discuss children. Or the theatre, I suspect."

"Is it to do with what happened last night?" Crispin shook his head. "Can't make head nor tail of it. Why the manuscript should seem so important. That is, I may not be bookish, but I can understand a new version of *Hamlet* creating a stir, of course. That's why we went to Simon. But to attack someone over it—"

"Do you have any idea how it came to be among your father's things?" Malcolm asked.

"I can hazard a guess." Crispin's unwontedly tense face relaxed into a more characteristic grin. "Bit of a family scandal. Back in the sixteenth century, the current Lord Harleton was an adviser to Elizabeth. And his wife—Eleanor Harleton—cut quite a swath at court. Philip Sidney wrote poems to her in a rare moment when he wasn't mooning over Penelope Deveraux. Eleanor caught Essex's eye at one point as well, and despite or because of it, Harleton was caught up in the Essex rebellion. Ended up attainted and executed. But it's always been a family legend that the love of her life was an actor at the Globe. Francis Woolright, his name was. In fact, after her husband was executed she ran off and married Woolright. Lived with him in the city, took her daughter with her, had more children by him. Family disowned her, but I always liked to think they were happy." His gaze slid sideways to Manon.

Manon gave a dry smile. "You're an incurable romantic,

Crispin. The poor woman gave up her life of luxury and had to live with an actor of all things."

"So she must have loved him," Crispin said, undaunted. "Anyway, part of the story is that Woolright played Laertes in the first production of *Hamlet*. So I can imagine him giving Eleanor an early copy of the script, when they were still lovers, before her husband was killed. She could have left it behind when she ran off with him. Odd it was hidden for so long, but you know the way things get tucked away in old houses. Not hidden so much as lost or simply forgot. Still doesn't explain why people would make such a fuss about it now. Unless it's a mad scholar. Or a rival theatre company?"

"Crispin." Malcolm studied his school friend, debating possible approaches and how much to reveal. "Your father never mentioned the manuscript?"

"God, no. To own the truth, I'd give even odds on whether the pater could even have listed a half-dozen titles of the Bard's plays." Crispin leaned back on the settee. Was there something just a bit too studied about his casual good humor? Malcolm couldn't be certain. "Does the fact that someone's after it make it more likely it's genuine?"

"Perhaps. But there could be other reasons."

"What—"

"Milk, Mr. Rannoch?" Manon held out a translucent blue-flowered cup.

"Thank you." Malcolm accepted the cup and took a sip.

Crispin regarded him from beneath drawn brows. "You're saying there's something else about the manuscript?"

"Perhaps."

"What the devil—" Crispin stared at him. "Oh, Christ, Malcolm, is the manuscript somehow caught up in the espionage business?"

"I didn't say—"

"No. But you're in the middle of it. I may not have been brilliant at maths, but I can add two and two."

Malcolm gave a faint smile. "Did you discover anything else unusual after your father died?"

Crispin frowned as he accepted a cup of tea from Manon. "What sort of thing?"

Malcolm took a sip of tea and balanced the fragile cup in his hand, while he balanced the tricky question of how much to reveal.

Crispin stared into the milky depths of his tea. "Does this have something to do with my father's death?"

Malcolm's fingers tightened round the delicate handle of the cup. "What—"

"Crispin—" Manon put a hand on her lover's arm.

"It's what he does, Nonny. Investigate things." Crispin pushed aside a script and set his cup and saucer on the hamper before the settee. "You're going to say I'm crazy, Malcolm."

"Try me."

Crispin ran a hand over his hair. "I think Father's death may not have been an accident. That is—" Crispin swallowed, looked at Manon, then at Simon and Suzanne, then back at Malcolm. "I think he may have been murdered."

Malcolm met Crispin's gaze and wondered if it was really as guileless as it appeared. "What makes you think that?"

Manon drew a sharp breath. Apparently Crispin hadn't shared this with her. Crispin cast a quick glance at her, reached for his cup, then set it down untouched. "Father'd never been in the habit of cleaning his own guns. He always had Hughes—his valet—do it. Hughes said Father hadn't mentioned anything about the pistols needing cleaning. I'll own at first I wondered if he might have taken his own life. Couldn't for the life of me imagine why he'd have done so, but then I can't claim to have known him well."

"That can't have been easy," Simon said. Manon was watching Crispin steadily.

"No." Crispin turned his cup in its saucer. "Couldn't help but wonder if there was something I should have done. But then Tom, one of the junior footmen, came up to me. Said he'd seen a man he didn't recognize outside the study window just before they found Father. I started to make inquiries, but none of the other staff reported seeing anyone. Then when I asked Tom again, he said he'd been mistaken, it had only been Wilkins the curate. But Wilkins says he didn't come to the house until an hour after they found Father. And then Tom disappeared."

"Disappeared?" Suzanne asked.

"Ran off presumably. I couldn't but wonder if he'd been paid off." Crispin ran a hand over his hair. "At least I hope to God it was that. And not—" He shook his head.

"You didn't say anything to me," Manon said.

Crispin turned to her, an odd sort of appeal in his gaze. "I half-thought I was imagining things. More than half. Not used to this sort of intrigue. And then it got worse. That is—" He drew a breath, snatched up his tea, tossed down a swallow. "After Father's death I went through his things—tidying up papers about the estate, trying to do my duty, you know the sort of thing. I found some letters. I couldn't make sense of them at first, but I think—" Crispin drew the breath of a man teetering on the edge of words that could not be snatched back once spoken. "Malcolm, could my father have been a French spy?"

Malcolm looked into Crispin's wide blue gaze. He was two years Crispin's junior, but at the moment Crispin seemed as young as Colin, brave enough to ask a question, young enough to fear the answer. Carfax's warnings reverberated in Malcolm's head. As did his own qualms about Carfax. "What makes you think that?" he said, his voice schooled to neutrality. He didn't need to glance at Suzanne to know that her own expression gave nothing away.

He saw the reality settle like a blow in Crispin's gaze. Crispin had been hoping Malcolm would laugh the whole thing off. "I found a letter. It looked as though Father had been working on it when he died. It seemed to be to his—I suppose 'spymaster' is the word. Asking for protection from Carfax. I couldn't believe he would put it down in ink."

"He may have been drafting it before he put it into code and then didn't have a chance to destroy the original draft," Malcolm said.

Crispin gave a quick nod, then turned to Manon, who was staring at him, eyes wide with shock. "I'd have told you, Nonny, but I couldn't quite bring myself to put it into words. That's also why I didn't mention my suspicions about his death. It was all twisted together."

"I understand." Manon reached for his hand. "You were hoping it wasn't true."

Crispin nodded, twining his fingers round hers. He turned back to Malcolm. "So—you knew?"

Malcolm hesitated, then plunged forwards. "Carfax told me. Last night."

Crispin's gaze darted over his face. "Did he tell you the whole?"

"He told me your father had been working for the French for over two decades. There's more?"

Crispin swallowed, and suddenly Malcolm felt their roles had reversed. It was Crispin who was looking at him with the gaze of the adult seeking the best way to break an uncomfortable truth to a child. "I found another letter with the one to his spymaster. The second letter was from your father."

CHAPTER 4

For a moment Malcolm went completely numb. A not unusual re-action when it came to his father. Malcolm had few illusions about Alistair Rannoch. He would have said there were no revelations about the man he had grown up calling Father that could shock him. But once again, even in death, Alistair had managed to drive the breath from Malcolm's lungs.

"Are you saying this letter indicated my father was a spy along with yours?"

Once again Malcolm saw sympathy in Crispin's gaze as he chose his words. "Your father talked about secrets it was imperative to keep. He said they could both ruin each other."

Suzanne's hand closed round Malcolm's own. He squeezed her fingers even as he sifted through fragments of information. Alistair's face danced before his eyes. Ironic. Imperious. Cool blue eyes that could cut through to bone and a lift of a brow that could dampen all pretensions. He had never revealed much of himself. Why should one more revelation be such a shock?

"You didn't know," Crispin said. "I'm sorry. Perhaps—"

"No." Somehow his voice came out even past the tightness in his throat and the metallic taste in his mouth. "I needed to know.

And it's hardly as though I was swimming in illusions where my father was concerned."

"Nor was I precisely." Crispin gulped down a sip of tea. "With my own father, that is. He was just the pater. Patted me on the head. Gave me a pound note on occasion. Showed up at Harrow for speech day and the occasional cricket game. Belonged to White's but seemed apolitical."

"My father was a diehard Tory who deplored my dangerous Radicalism." Malcolm shook his head. He was aware of the warmth of Suzanne's gaze on him, but he didn't dare meet her eyes. He was afraid it would undo him.

"You think your father's politics were a pose?" Simon asked.

"Perhaps. I can't claim to have known Alistair in any sense." Malcolm could hear his father's voice, mocking an article Malcolm had written as at once dangerous and woefully idealistic. "But the thought of him as a committed Bonapartist—"

"There are other reasons than ideology to become a spy," Manon said in a quiet voice.

Malcolm swung his gaze to her. He wondered how much, if anything, Crispin knew about Manon's own espionage activities. He had an image of Crispin ruffling her daughter's hair. Somehow he couldn't bring himself to mar that unexpected vision of family bliss.

"A good point, Mademoiselle Caret."

"You never guessed?" Simon asked. Malcolm could feel his friend's intent gaze.

"No. But then in many ways Alistair and I were practically strangers."

Crispin pushed himself to his feet and took a turn round the dressing room. "Our fathers were selling information to the French all these years? It's difficult to comprehend."

"Chéri." Manon reached for his hand.

"I'm all right." Crispin spun round and pushed his fingers into his hair. "That is, I'm not going to collapse. Never much of a Crown and country sort. Though to commit that sort of betrayal— My cousin died in the Peninsula."

"My brother fought there," Malcolm said. And his father had always seemed to prefer Edgar.

"You risked your life there as well," Simon pointed out.

"Which wouldn't necessarily have been a disincentive to Alistair."

"Come now, Malcolm," Crispin said.

"Truly. I know many boys claim their fathers detest them, but in my case it wouldn't be much of an exaggeration. Save that I'm not sure Alistair's feelings about his children were strongly enough engaged for detestation."

"There was a mention in the letter of something concerning Dunboyne," Crispin said. "Does that mean anything to you?"

Malcolm shook his head. "My grandfather has estates in Ireland. And the French were active there, especially at the time of the United Irish Uprising. Alistair despised the United Irishmen. Claimed to despise them."

"Harleton was using the manuscript?" Manon asked.

Malcolm nodded, relieved at the straightforward question. "We think it was a codebook."

"And whoever murdered my father was after it?" Crispin said.

"I think it's more likely your father was murdered to conceal a secret he knew that the codebook could also reveal."

Simon stared at Malcolm with a shock he hadn't shown over the revelations about Harleton and Alistair. "Harleton was using an original manuscript that may have been by Shakespeare as a *codebook?*"

"It's quite clever actually," Suzanne said. "The manuscript is unique. He'd have had to make a copy for whomever he was communicating with, and then no one else would have been able to break the code."

"So that's why the people were after it last night when they attacked Simon?" Crispin asked.

"Most likely," Malcolm said. "It's also possible Harleton or someone else encoded information in the manuscript itself. Suzette and I couldn't find anything last night, but we only had time for a cursory examination. I want to have my cousin Aline look at it. She's the best code breaker I know."

Crispin gave a quick nod. "I don't know that I mourned him as much as a son should. As much as I'd hope my son would mourn me. And then I found the letters and wondered if I'd ever known him at all. But—He was my father. I want to know who killed him. You'll tell me what you learn? I promise I won't turn Hamlet and go mad with thoughts of revenge."

"I'll tell you as much as I'm able. My word on it."

"You're working for Carfax?"

"I'm reporting to him. I'm working for myself."

Crispin's gaze flickered over Malcolm's face. "Do you think he knows about your father?"

"I don't know." Malcolm turned over every moment of his conversation with Carfax in light of this new information. "But I'm going to find out."

"I assume you want to see my father's papers," Crispin said.

"As soon as possible."

Crispin gave another brisk nod. "They're at the Richmond villa. It's late to go there tonight, but I can take you first thing in the morning."

"Thank you." Malcolm scanned the other man's face. "I know this isn't easy."

"From firsthand experience?" Crispin gave a twisted smile. "If I have to think of myself as a traitor's son, I can't imagine better company."

Suzanne looked at her husband across the Tavistock's Green Room, to which they'd repaired when the others returned to the stage for the read-through. One could become so caught up in one's own secrets one quite lost track of other people's. The fear that Malcolm would discover she had been a Bonapartist spy was part of the fabric of her life. She had grown used to it, yet it overhung everything she did. It had never occurred to her that his father, of all people, could have been a spy for the French as well.

The lamplight in the windowless room warmed Malcolm's ashen skin. His features were set like granite. As though he feared the least crack would unleash the torrent of feeling beneath. "Darling—" She touched his shoulder. He was shaking.

"It could be worse. I could have faced this from someone I truly cared about."

She was nearly sick right there on the worn carpet.

"You think you know the parameters of a person's weaknesses," he said in a low, rough voice. "You learn to live with them. And the boundaries are somehow comforting, I suppose. A bulwark against further hurt. Bad as it is, it could be worse."

She tightened her grip on his arm. She might be a hypocrite, but he needed comfort. Giving it to him mattered more than her own falseness.

"I didn't know him." Malcolm stared at a framed playbill for *School for Scandal*. "I didn't much like him. I had no illusions that he liked me. Why should learning he was a French spy make things worse?"

"He was still your father."

"Possibly my father." Malcolm gave a short laugh. "I can't even say what I'm feeling. Angry that he was cleverer than I am? That he could outwit me at a game I flattered myself I had a passing skill for?"

"Loyalty matters to you."

"Alistair was disloyal to my mother. His ideals were the opposite of mine. He was an enigma in many ways. This only renders him more so. But—Damn it." Malcolm pulled away from her and smashed his hand against the chipped white molding.

She wanted to sweep him into her arms and comfort him as she would Colin or Jessica, but there was no comfort for this. Damnable to watch someone one loved in pain. "With him gone, there are so many questions we'll never be able to answer," she said.

"Alistair was a poor relation who went to school and university on the charity of the cousin who was his godfather." Malcolm began to prowl about the room. "He came into a small fortune when another cousin died in Jamaica when he—Alistair—had just come down from Oxford. A few clever investments and he was a wealthy man. At least that's the story I grew up with."

"You think instead he used money he was paid by the French?"

"It's easier for me to believe that than that he was a committed Republican or Bonapartist. Alistair never was a committed anything. Or perhaps it's just that I can't bear the thought that his political beliefs in any way approached my own."

"You aren't a Bonapartist." Amazing her voice could be so steady as she said it.

He gave a twisted smile. "To hear my father tell it I'm a fire-breathing Jacobin who would turn England into a replica of France under the Terror. Except I don't think it ever occurred to Alistair that I was capable of achieving so much."

"On the contrary, darling. Watching from the outside, I'd say Alistair had a very healthy respect for what you were capable of."

"If you made out anything other than contempt in his attitude towards me, you're more discerning than I. It's hardly anything new. It should be rather amusing."

She swallowed. Beneath the gnawing pain of her own fears, she ached for her husband. "Dearest, you're entitled—"

"He didn't love me. I didn't love him." Malcolm's voice was as flat as a sheet of glass. And perhaps as easily smashed. "A revelation about him, however shocking, shouldn't matter."

"That doesn't mean it doesn't."

He stopped pacing and shot a sideways look at her. "I'm not going to collapse. Or otherwise cause complications. I'd be a fool to claim I'm at my best, but I'll manage to be a decent investigative partner."

"Of course. You're much too good at what you do to be anything else. But it can't help but feel like a betrayal." Stewed tea rose up in her throat as she said it.

His mouth twisted. "If there's one thing we should be used to in this business it's betrayal. What else is espionage but a series of betrayals? As one does an unconscionable amount of betraying oneself, one can hardly object."

She met his gaze, keeping her own steady. "But one doesn't expect it from those close to one."

"All the more reason for this not to matter. I wasn't close to Alistair at all."

Suzanne recalled Alistair Rannoch, his mocking gaze seeming to cut through her gown and the corset beneath. She wondered, with a stab of panic, how much else he might have known about her. "I didn't like him, either, darling. But I own I'm shocked. If nothing else he was a brilliant actor."

"Yes. To own the truth, I wouldn't have thought he had the ability. But then he had a superb instinct for self-preservation. And if he'd taken French money to build his fortune, they'd have owned him, however wealthy and powerful he became. Until the war was over."

"But the truth would have ruined him. Even a whisper of it." She hesitated a moment. "Somehow Harleton's past caught up with him."

" 'Murder most foul.' You're saying it's a bit coincidental that my father, to whom Harleton had written, died in a carriage accident less than a month after Harleton's death? So it is. We have to at least consider the possibility that Alistair was murdered."

He said it matter-of-factly. But she could feel the tension crackling against her skin. "Darling. When they asked you to look into this no one could have thought—"

He shot a look at her again. "You think I don't have enough perspective to investigate? Quite possibly. But I have you to keep me in line if I can't tell a hawk from a handsaw. And I have inside knowledge which may be of use. That has to count for something. Besides . . ."

"What?"

"Whatever I thought of Alistair, whatever he thought of me—or despite the fact that most of the time he didn't think of me at all—I confess I have the damnedest desire to learn the truth. Ironic, is it not?"

"Understandable."

"Can I count on you?"

"Always." One more lie in the legion she had told her husband.

He strode to her side and pressed a kiss to her forehead. "I need to see Carfax."

She nodded and touched his face. "I'll stay here and watch the rehearsal."

He squeezed her arm. "What would I do without you?"

The tea rose up in her throat again. "You'd manage."

The man she'd betrayed from the moment they met smiled

down at her as though she was his lifeline to sanity in a world gone mad. "I very much doubt it."

"Malcolm." Carfax set down his copy of the *Morning Post* with a rustle as Malcolm stepped into the reading room. "How did you get in here? Usually I can count on White's to be a haven from anyone who bears even the most remote taint of Whiggishness."

"Harry Palmerston brought me in." Malcolm hesitated a moment inside the doorway. The room was empty save for Carfax. It smelled of newsprint and port and expensive shaving soap as it always did. As it had on the rare occasions Malcolm had come here with Alistair. He drew a breath, crossed the room, and dropped into a leather-covered chair beside Carfax. "I needed to see you."

Carfax smoothed the crumpled newspaper. "If you were willing to stomach White's it must be serious. Have you found something in the manuscript?"

"No. But I have more information to go on." Malcolm scanned his spymaster's face. The sharp bones, the hard spectacle lenses, the opaque gaze beneath. Carfax was not an easy father, but as Malcolm had once pointed out to David, at least he cared about his children. "Why didn't you tell me my father was working with Harleton?"

Carfax released his breath in a long sigh, part surprise, part what might have been triumph. "You found proof?"

"So you did know?" Malcolm's hand tightened round the arm of the chair, so hard the acanthus leaves carved on it were imprinted on his palm.

"Interesting." Carfax regarded him for a moment. "I'd have sworn you didn't have any illusions where Alistair was concerned."

"Damn it, sir—"

Carfax folded the newspaper into neat quarters. "I've suspected Alistair for years. Unlike with Harleton, I didn't have any proof. If I had, I don't think I'd have let your father continue to operate. He had a considerably keener understanding than Harleton. In truth, one of the reasons I kept giving Harleton rope was the hope that Alistair would hang himself."

Malcolm swallowed and tasted the ashes of bitterness. He

thought he'd had no illusions about Alistair Rannoch. He thought he'd come to terms with this latest revelation. So why did he feel as though he was going to lose his breakfast over the oak furniture and Axminster carpet? "Since when have you waited for proof before bringing someone in?"

"Use your head, Malcolm." Carfax slapped the newspaper down on the polished top of the table between their chairs. "Alistair wasn't an émigré or a courtesan or a minor diplomat. If I'd taken action against the Duke of Strathdon's son-in-law who was also a prominent Member of Parliament—"

"It's not as though my grandfather was overfond of him." Malcolm could rarely remember a conversation between Alistair and the duke, but he could see the contempt that had filled his grandfather's gaze when it rested on Alistair.

Carfax gave a short laugh. "There's nothing like an outside threat to create family unity. Trust me, Strathdon would never have stood by while I took action against Alistair."

"It wouldn't have had to be public action."

"People would have asked questions if Alistair had disappeared. He was friends with half the Tory aristocracy. Your aunt Frances alone would have made a fuss I couldn't have controlled, and she didn't even much like him."

And Lady Frances Dacre-Hammond numbered two royal dukes and possibly the prince regent among her bedmates. Carfax had a point. Malcolm drew a breath. "It didn't occur to you to tell me?"

"I tell you what you need to know, Malcolm. Occasionally, I confess, what you force me to reveal. But what good would it have done for me to tell you this? When Alistair was alive, I couldn't be sure what you'd have done with the truth."

Malcolm's fingers clamped on the chair arm. "What does that mean?"

Carfax adjusted one of the earpieces on his spectacles. "He was your father."

"You think I'd have protected him?"

"I'm not sure. But I think you'd have had a hard time turning him over to face justice. You have a hard enough time doing that with some agents who aren't related to you."

Past incidents shot through Malcolm's mind, but he wasn't going to let himself be distracted. "And after Alistair died?"

"What good—"

"When you told me about Harleton?"

"I thought about it," Carfax conceded. "But to be honest I wasn't sure you'd believe me without proof. And I wanted to see what you could come up with on your own, without my muddying the waters by planting the suspicion."

"By God, sir—"

"You're in shock, Malcolm. When you can think coolly, you'll understand why I acted as I did." Carfax regarded him for a moment. "I'm not insensible of what you're going through, you know. Impressions to the contrary, I am not without feeling."

"Sir—" Malcolm swallowed. "I never suggested you were."

Carfax's gaze drilled into Malcolm's own. "What have you learned?"

Malcolm drew a breath. Why did answering feel like a betrayal? "Crispin Harleton found a letter from my father to his. Talking about secrets that could ruin them both."

Carfax's mouth curled in a smile of satisfaction. "It's ironic. You're the Jacobin with the dangerous ideas that would turn society on its ear if you ever had the chance to put them into effect. I don't think Alistair had a Radical bone in his body."

"No. I'd have sworn his politics were much like yours."

Carfax settled back in the chair. He was wiry and surprisingly slight, but somehow he turned the leather and oak of the chair into a throne. "I worried about you when you were up at Oxford, you know. The dangerous nonsense you'd spout off about in coffeehouses and write down in pamphlets. That you and Tanner embroiled my son in. But then I realized that for all your dangerous views, you'd never betray king and country."

"So sure?" For an instant, Malcolm knew a savage desire to prove Carfax wrong.

"You take your loyalties seriously, my boy."

"I never thought to find you echoing Suzette, but that's almost exactly what she said."

"Your wife is a perceptive woman."

"A few minutes ago, you suggested I'd have tried to protect Alistair if I'd learned the truth while he was still alive."

"Oh, I think you would have done. You wouldn't have stood by and let him hang for a traitor. But you wouldn't have been able to forgive him. Just as you find yourself unable to forgive him now. I hope your wounded feelings won't impede your investigation."

"I'll manage."

"Yes, I rather think you will. The one thing that may be stronger than your loyalty is your tenacity."

Malcolm forced his fingers to unclench on the chair arm. He needed every ounce of self-command he possessed. "Was my father murdered?"

Carfax smoothed his fingers over the newspaper, brows drawn in what appeared to be honest appraisal. "I wondered, of course, especially as it followed close on Harleton's death. I'd made some inquiries, but the carriage was smashed too badly to determine if it had been tampered with before the accident. I couldn't determine who'd have gone after Alistair and Harleton at that time. Now—"

"You think they were killed by someone who wants this manuscript?"

"If so, the person was singularly unsuccessful."

"Or by someone who wanted revenge on both of them for a past wrong? Or wanted to shut them both up because of some past secret? I haven't seen this letter from my father to Harleton yet, but Crispin said there was a mention in it of something to do with Dunboyne. Does that mean anything to you?"

Carfax's fingers froze on the newspaper. The look in his eyes was part surprise, part wariness, and part the scent of the chase.

"What happened at Dunboyne?" Malcolm asked.

Carfax set the newspaper on the table and cast a glance round the empty morning room. His gaze lingered on the door for a moment. "One of the drawbacks of involving you in investigations, Malcolm, is the need to reveal things to you."

"I could investigate on my own and see what I come up with."

"You would anyway. But I have a vested interest in you not blundering about as though this were a game of blindman's bluff."

Carfax leaned forwards across the table in an unusually confiding posture. "Nearly twenty years ago, in July of '98, Lord Dewhurst went from a late meeting with the prime minister to a dinner with a group of friends. He had his dispatch box with him. Containing documents relating to a secret mission he and I had just discussed with the P.M."

"In France?" Malcolm asked, shutting his mind to the instinctive recoil at the mention of Dewhurst.

"In Ireland." Carfax's mouth tightened. "It was at the height of the United Irish Uprising. We'd scattered the rebels, but they were still strong. I had just received intelligence about the location where a group of the ringleaders were hiding out in Dunboyne. At our meeting Pitt had signed off on a mission to send a special force in to take them captive."

Memory clicked into place in Malcolm's head. "Was that—"

"Yes, when the force arrived, they found the rebels were prepared for them. We lost ten of our best men." Carfax drew a breath that grated with frustration, but his gaze was uncompromising. "I believe the intelligence came from someone getting into Dewhurst's dispatch box at that dinner party. Based on who was at that dinner party, that narrows it down to five men."

"My father or Harleton?"

"No. Ironically, they were there, but they both left early. Before Dewhurst arrived. It has to be one of the five others."

"But you think whoever it was, this person was working with my father and Harleton?"

"I've always wondered. This seems to confirm it." Carfax hesitated again. His gaze shifted beyond Malcolm to the wall behind.

"You know I'll need their names, sir."

Carfax dragged his gaze back to Malcolm. "If asked I'll deny I ever said any of this."

"Isn't that true of all our conversations?"

Carfax gave a wintry smile. "Lord Bessborough."

Malcolm blinked. "The Duke of Devonshire's brother-in-law?"

"Quite. You see why this is a ticklish business. Sir Horace Smytheton."

"The patron of the Tavistock?"

"Interesting, isn't it? Not sure what to make of the connection. Archibald Davenport."

"Good God." Malcolm sat forwards in his chair.

"Yes, I know you're close to his nephew. I leave it to you how much you tell Harry Davenport, but for God's sake use some discretion. I know Davenport was in intelligence, but we don't need an outraged former agent defending the family honor."

"I don't think Harry Davenport acknowledges the existence of family honor."

"You might well have said the same before your father was dragged into this."

Malcolm shifted in his chair. "Who are the last two?"

"Hugo Cyrus."

Malcolm sorted through his knowledge of past events. "Didn't Cyrus's brother die in the Dunboyne business?"

"He did, but he joined the mission at the last minute. Cyrus wouldn't have known his brother was involved when he betrayed the mission. If he betrayed the mission. Though if that's the case he now has to live with the guilt of it. Which I admit even I would find hard to bear."

Malcolm, thinking of his brother and sisters, including the one he had lost, could not suppress a shudder.

"And the last person?"

"Dewhurst himself."

Malcolm stared at his spymaster. "Good God."

"Oh, that's right. He was involved in the business in France two years ago, wasn't he?"

"You know damned well he was."

"I did my best to stay out of that mess. It seemed to come down to a sad tangle of personal relationships and meddling by the French authorities."

"That was certainly the story we thought it best to put about. There was a fair amount of meddling and bungling on our own side as well."

Carfax smoothed a corner of the newspaper. "Precisely why I

thought it best to stay out of it. Besides, it all dealt with events in the Peninsula and France."

"Which are precisely the sort of events you expertly influence. Don't sell yourself short, sir. Suffice it to say, the events two years ago didn't leave Dewhurst and me on amicable terms. I think it's safe to say he blames me for his estrangement from his son."

"But those same events should have left you with considerable leverage over Dewhurst."

"I thought you said you stayed out of things."

"That didn't stop me from noting the pertinent developments. You have a hold on Dewhurst, Malcolm. Don't be squeamish about using it. God knows Dewhurst doesn't deserve such consideration." Carfax shook his head. "The man was a fool. By going after Bertrand Laclos, he only roused his son's anger. If he'd simply left his son alone, Caruthers and Laclos would have grown apart and Caruthers would have done what was expected of him as his father's heir."

As you're hoping your own son will do? Malcolm bit the words back just in time. Carfax never directly referred to David and Simon's relationship. Malcolm sensed that not referring to it was crucial to keeping Carfax from interfering. Lord Dewhurst's interference in his son Rupert's relationship with Bertrand Laclos two years ago had crystalized many of Malcolm's fears for David and Simon.

The events two years ago had also left Malcolm with a strong desire to draw Lord Dewhurst's cork, but such an action would scarcely produce the desired results. "You strategized missions with Dewhurst."

"Yes, I know. I watched him carefully, but he never betrayed himself. Dewhurst was in and out of France all the time in the nineties and the early part of this century. Excellent cover if he had been an agent."

"He's—"

"One of our most prominent diplomats. Quite." Carfax pushed his spectacles up on his nose. "If Harleton and your father knew who was behind the Dunboyne leak and the codebook could reveal

that man's identity, it's likely that man is also behind their deaths."
He laid his hand, palm down, on the newspaper, pressing out the
wrinkles. "Whether Dewhurst leaked the information himself or
left his dispatch box where someone else could get at it, I should
never have trusted him with the information. The Dunboyne leak is
one of my worst failures, Malcolm. I've wanted to find out who was
behind it for almost two decades. This codebook could be the
break we need to unearth the agent, but it's an investigation that
will require the utmost discretion. All of these men have powerful
friends. Even with proof, it won't be easy to bring the agent to justice."

"And accusing the wrong person could be a catastrophe."

"Quite. Even the questions have to be asked delicately."

"A lot of feathers could be ruffled."

"Precisely." Carfax tightened a spectacle piece behind his ear.
"Which is why you're perfectly placed to conduct the investigation.
Whatever your politics, your pedigree is impeccable. And I know I
can rely upon your discretion. Especially with your father involved."

"And I provide you with deniability."

Carfax settled back in his chair. "But of course."

CHAPTER 5

"Oh, dear God." Manon put her face in her hands. The read-through was over. Simon was beginning to block the opening scene with Horatio and the other guards and the ghost. Manon and Suzanne had escaped back to Manon's dressing room.

Suzanne clunked her cup of fresh tea back in its saucer. Her stomach was roiling. "You didn't know about Lord Harleton being a French agent?"

"Can you imagine I'd have involved you if I did? That I'd have involved myself?" Manon dragged her hands away from her face and stared at Suzanne. "You do believe me, don't you?"

"Yes."

"I don't know that you're wise to do so, but it happens to be the truth." Manon pushed herself to her feet and moved to a cabinet with chipped gilt paint. "You didn't know? About Malcolm's father?"

"Dear God no." Suzanne shook her head, seeing again Alistair Rannoch's mocking face and the way his gaze had at once undressed and dismissed her. "I still can't believe it. Malcolm doesn't—His family life has been unfortunate." An understatement if there ever was one. "One more betrayal—"

Manon turned to her, her hand on the cabinet latch. "I'm so sorry."

"It's not your fault."

"You've been nothing but kind to me, and I've put you at risk."

Suzanne smoothed her hands over her sarcenet skirt to still their trembling. "We're all at risk."

"You have a husband."

"You have a lover."

Manon gave a short laugh. "I'm fond of Crispin. Fonder than I intended to grow. But I have no illusions." She opened the cabinet and took out a brandy bottle. "It's better not to have illusions. Not that I don't have moments of envy when I see you with your Malcolm." Manon studied her for a moment. "He might forgive you if he learned the truth, you know."

"No." Suzanne forced herself to stare into the possible future. She could feel Malcolm's lips against her hair in the Green Room a half hour before. "He has too much integrity himself. He could never do what I've done."

Manon crossed the room and splashed brandy into Suzanne's teacup and then her own. "You sound as though you admire him."

"I do. It doesn't mean I regret what I've done."

Manon dropped down beside her. "Drink some of your tea. You could do with the jolt."

Suzanne gave a bleak smile and took a sip of brandy-laced tea.

"You can't persuade him to give up the investigation?" Manon asked, reaching for her own cup.

Suzanne shook her head.

"For a woman with a besotted husband, you're slow to use your wiles."

Suzanne ran her finger over a chip in the gilded rim of the cup. "Malcolm and I don't have that sort of relationship. We never did. It's part of what I love about him. Part of what he loves about me, I think."

"And you claim not to be romantic." Manon tossed down a generous swig of tea and brandy.

"It's the opposite of romantic. Romance is rose-colored glasses. Malcolm and I see each other clearly." Suzanne took a sip of tea and brandy. "Except for the part where he has no idea I was spying on him."

Manon flopped back in her chair and stared up at a cobweb on the ceiling. "I can't believe Crispin's father was a Bonapartist agent."

"Did you ever meet?"

"Once. He came to my dressing room after a performance. Said he wanted to get a look at his son's bit of muslin. Tried to put his hand down my dress. The usual tiresome sort of thing." Manon wrinkled her nose. "Crispin came in and grabbed his father by the back of his coat and threw him out. An overreaction, but I rather appreciated it."

Suzanne studied her friend. "I think you may have more in Crispin than you're crediting, Manon. He obviously loves your girls."

Manon's carefully plucked brows drew together. "It's dangerous, that. I don't want them to become too attached to him. They're too young to understand that he won't always be here."

"Are you so sure he won't be?"

"Oh, for God's sake, Suzanne." Manon sat up straight, sloshing her tea. "Has love addled your brain? Forget being a former French agent. I'm an actress. Even if I had any desire to marry, he'd hardly consider it."

Suzanne saw the tenderness in Crispin's gaze when it had rested on Manon. "He's in love with you."

"A lot of men have been in love with me. It passes."

"He doesn't know you were an agent?"

"Good God no. That would certainly cross a line for him." Manon gave a crooked smile. "He may not be a Crown and country sort as he says, but he's an English gentleman. Charming but decidedly set in his ways beneath the easygoing demeanor."

"So is Malcolm. Well, a British gentleman. However forward-thinking he is, he'll never get past certain things."

"Then we'll have to make sure he never learns the truth. While evading Lord Carfax." Manon twitched her muslin tippet smooth, as though armoring herself for the fight ahead. "Simon doesn't know about you, does he?"

"No," Suzanne said.

"But?"

Suzanne stared down into her tea. "I'm not sure. I've always found it harder to dissemble with Simon than with the rest of Malcolm's friends. Perhaps because he's an observer and an outsider as well."

"I'm never sure how much he sees, either," Manon agreed. "I'm only comforted by the fact that if he knew the truth he wouldn't do anything about it."

Suzanne smoothed her hands over her lap. There was a brown smudge on the amber sarcenet she hadn't seen before. Probably applesauce. These days Jessica's food ended up everywhere. "I know Malcolm. He won't rest until he learns the truth."

"The truth about Harleton and his father won't necessarily lead him to you."

Suzanne rubbed at the smudge out of instinct. "It could lead him to any number of former Bonapartist agents. I can't stand by while my husband destroys someone who was once an ally."

"So you'll oppose him?" Manon asked as though they were discussing stage combat tactics.

"If necessary. What else have I done all these years?"

"But it's different now. You left that behind."

"One can't ever leave it behind truly. You know that. I should understand it." Suzanne locked her hands together, conscious of the pressure of her wedding ring. "I knew my life would be a balancing act. I have to face the fact that it may not be a balance I can maintain."

Manon stretched out her hand. "Suzanne—"

Suzanne closed her fingers round her friend's own. "Of course I'm terrified. How could I not be?"

Suzanne looked up at the sight of the figure crossing Berkeley Square. Jessica dozed in her lap, having fallen into a milk coma, so Suzanne was careful not to move. Malcolm opened the gate of the square garden and stepped inside. Something in his posture told her the added weight his interview with Carfax had placed on him. Her heart lurched for a host of reasons both personal and practical.

"Daddy!" Colin scrambled to his feet from the flagstones where he was lining up his lead soldiers round a castle built of blocks.

Malcolm forced a smile to his face, though it didn't drive the shadows from his eyes. "Excellent job with the fortifications, old chap." Malcolm knelt down beside Colin for a few minutes, conferring over the arrangement of the soldiers. After a few adjustments, Malcolm got to his feet and moved to the bench where Suzanne sat with Jessica.

He dropped down beside her as though his bones ached. "Carfax confirmed it. Apparently he's suspected Alistair for years. He was hoping I'd stumble on proof."

"Oh, darling." She touched his arm, aching with sympathy, while at the same time she felt as though the square's gnarled plane trees were closing their branches round her.

"I don't know why—" His fingers curled inwards. "I should be used to the ground being cut from beneath my feet and my perception of reality being turned upside down. It's happened often enough."

Suzanne looked down at Jessica, her head tucked into the crook of Suzanne's elbow, one hand curled round Suzanne's breast. "It's different with your father."

"Possibly." He touched his fingers to Jessica's head. "There's more. Carfax has a theory about who killed Alistair and Lord Harleton and is after the *Hamlet* manuscript."

He quickly outlined Carfax's revelations about the Dunboyne leak and the five suspects.

Suzanne swallowed, a host of possible scenarios racing through her mind. "The General Cyrus we knew in the Peninsula?"

Malcolm nodded. "Shock waves would reverberate through the British army if he proved to be a traitor. His brother died in the Dunboyne affair. But Carfax says the mole wouldn't have known Thomas Cyrus was part of the mission at the time he betrayed it." His gaze fastened on Jessica, her face relaxed in sleep, one leg tucked under her, the other sliding off the edge of Suzanne's lap. "I find it hard to believe he could live with the guilt."

Her fingers curled over Jessica's sparse hair. "You don't know how easily he did. If he is the one. Who else?"

Malcolm reached down to pet Berowne, curled up in a basket by her feet. "Sir Horace Smytheton, who was so eager to share his thoughts on *Hamlet* at the rehearsal this afternoon. His role at the Tavistock doesn't obviously make him more likely to be guilty. But at the very least it's an odd coincidence. Lord Bessborough."

"Caroline Lamb's father?" Suzanne forced her hands not to tighten instinctively round Jessica. Lady Caroline Lamb was the childhood friend of Suzanne's friend Cordelia Davenport. Caro Lamb was also the wife of Malcolm's friend William Lamb.

Malcolm nodded, mouth grim. "Bessborough's in less of a powerful official position than the others. But he's the late Duke of Devonshire's brother-in-law. The current duke's uncle. Part of the inner circle of the Devonshire House set, which makes him minor Whig royalty. And for all the Whigs have been tweaked on sympathy for Bonaparte, to imagine one a traitor—"

The word "traitor" sliced through her. She needed to make herself hear it a hundred times a day to get past this. She drew a breath, focusing on the boneless weight of Jessica in her arms and the even rise and fall of the baby's breathing. "Who else?"

"Archibald Davenport."

Jessica let out a squawk as Suzanne's hands tightened. "I'm sorry, *querida*." Suzanne shifted the baby against her. "Harry's uncle?"

"Who raised him after his parents died, though he appears to have done so at a distance."

Suzanne had only met Archibald Davenport once, at the theatre with Harry and Cordelia. A tall man with a jovial manner, shrewd eyes, and breath laced with port. "Isn't he a crony of the prince regent?"

"One of his inner circle. Yet another who would cause shock waves to reverberate should he prove to have been betraying his country for years." Malcolm's gaze fastened on Colin as their son galloped a knight on horseback up to the castle. "I don't know whether to be in awe that Carfax has trusted me with this investigation or furious that he's blithely throwing me to the wolves. How do you feel about having to go live in exile?"

How odd to hear one's husband blithely summing up one's worst fears for the future. "Even Carfax couldn't force you into exile."

"It might not be so bad. We'd be free of my family."

"You'd miss your family." She knew now, having seen him with them, how much his siblings and aunt and cousins meant to him.

"Some of them."

The truth of course was that Suzanne wouldn't mind exile so much if she was with him and the children. But if her past drove her into exile, they almost certainly wouldn't be together.

Jessica lifted her head without opening her eyes and flopped back down in a different position. She'd left a milky smudge on the moss green velvet of Suzanne's spencer. "Harry and Cordelia could help us with Archibald Davenport and Lord Bessborough."

"I know. Carfax acknowledged as much. He said it was up to me how much I told them. Well, how much I told Harry." Malcolm's gaze returned to Colin, who was now staging a tournament with two knights on horseback. Or a fight. She hoped it was a tournament. "Harry and his uncle are far from close. But as I learned with the revelations about Alistair, that doesn't make it easier." One of Colin's knights fell to the pavement. Colin lifted the second from his horse and had him go help the fallen rider. "Carfax said he thought I'd have tried to protect Alistair if I'd known while he was alive."

"You're loyal. To people as well as countries." A conflict that would tear him in two if he learned the truth about her, she feared. He might not expose her, but he'd never trust her again. "Do you think Harry would protect his uncle?"

"I don't know. Harry can be ruthless. But Cordelia's made him no stranger to betrayal. And forgiveness. If their marriage can survive what it's been through, God knows what's possible."

Suzanne swallowed. Harry and Cordelia's miraculous marriage both terrified her with the possibilities of what could go wrong and gave her an odd sort of hope. "Yes."

Malcolm scratched Berowne's ears. "I know if I were him I'd want to know the truth. I owe him that as my friend."

Jessica's head was slipping to the side, heavy with sleep. Suzanne curled her arm up, carefully, so she anchored Jessica without waking her. "Cordy can help with Lord Bessborough. She was in and out of Caro Lamb's house growing up. Unless you don't want to involve her in something so delicate?"

Malcolm reached down and touched Jessica's tiny black-booted foot. "No, I think the more we can keep the investigation as unofficial as possible with this group, the better. And after what we've been through with Harry and Cordelia we know we can trust them." He gave a twisted smile. "I may not have known my father, but I know them."

Suzanne twitched a fold of blanket closer round Jessica. Such simple words. But in theory, Malcolm knew her far better than he did Harry and Cordy. Perhaps it was simply that some betrayals were unimaginable. "Who is the fifth suspect?"

"Lord Dewhurst himself."

For a moment, two years were gone, and Suzanne saw Dewhurst in the private parlor of an inn in the French countryside, nose streaming blood while his son stared at him with unmitigated hatred. "That's . . . unexpected."

"Lovely understatement, sweetheart. Carfax told me to use the events two years ago as leverage to get Dewhurst to talk."

"How much does Carfax know about two years ago?"

"Enough. More than I realized. He usually does."

"Dear God, if Dewhurst proved to be a French spy—"

"The irony is exquisite. But speaking of fathers and sons, it won't be easy on Rupert."

Suzanne stroked Jessica's hand as Jessica reached for the ribbons on her mother's bonnet. "I talked to Gabrielle at the Granvilles' last week. Rupert still isn't speaking to his father. She said Rupert cut Dewhurst dead at the opera."

"But hating one's father doesn't make it easier to accept his crimes."

She cast a quick glance at him. Malcolm gave a reluctant smile. "Yes, I confess I'm not entirely immune to caring about Alistair. And Rupert takes honor and loyalty more seriously than I do."

"You take honor and loyalty exceptionally seriously, dearest," Suzanne said, as Jessica's fist closed round her fingers. "In many ways you and Rupert are much alike. That was clear two years ago."

Malcolm caught her free hand in his own and squeezed her fingers. "Rupert will manage. He has the support of the person he loves. That counts for a lot."

Suzanne returned the pressure of her husband's hand and concentrated on the weight of her daughter in her arms.

"Mummy! Daddy!" Colin's voice carried across the square. "I captured the castle."

Malcolm waved to their son. "Are we dining out tonight?"

Suzanne swallowed the bitterness that welled up in her throat and waved to Colin as well. "No, but we promised to look in at Holland House."

"Let's go early and make sure we're back by eleven. I'll talk to Addison and Valentin about setting up shifts to keep watch in the study."

Suzanne scanned her husband's face. "You think they'll attempt to steal the manuscript again tonight?"

Malcolm grinned and touched his fingers to Jessica's head. "I hope they will."

Sitting in the dark, careful not to make any telltale movements, all senses keyed for the scrape of a picked lock or the creak of floorboards, one had plenty of leisure to think. To reflect on the man who had bought this house and whose works of art still filled it, for all Suzanne's wonders at redecoration. Who had given one a name and whose very absent disdain had shaped one in more ways than one cared to admit.

Malcolm eased his legs straight. It wouldn't do to let his muscles cramp. He'd always known he and Alistair Rannoch were opponents. He'd just thought that the divide was between a diehard Tory and Radical reformer. Not a British agent and a French one.

Alistair's mocking face danced just beyond the reaches of his memory. As though leaving a mystery Malcolm couldn't solve was one more way of pointing out his putative son's inadequacy. Malcolm pushed aside the image of Alistair. Instead, the image that filled his mind was Colin, flopped in his bed upstairs with his stuffed bear when Malcolm had looked into the nursery before he came downstairs to keep watch. Had Alistair ever paused to look at Malcolm sleeping, even in babyhood? Had he felt any tug of tenderness, any concern for the young life he was helping to shape, at the start at least? Or even then had he simply ignored his eldest child? Or found him a source of anger?

A cry cut the air. From the passage. Malcolm pushed himself to his feet, crossed the darkened room by instinct, pushed open the door. The acrid smell of smoke greeted him.

"Fire in the kitchen." Addison, Malcolm's valet, poked his head out the baize door at the end of the passage. "Mary Beth caught it. We have it under control."

Suzanne came hurrying down the stairs in her dressing gown. "The children are fine," she said in response to a look from Malcolm. "I'll go to the kitchen. You should go back into the study. This must have been meant as a diversion."

Though every instinct said to check that the fire was under control, Malcolm knew she was right. Whoever was after the manuscript knew they would be on their guard. The attempted theft would follow quickly on the fire. Malcolm slipped back into the study, but instead of returning to the chair, he flattened himself against the wall. He counted out a minute, then another. The smell of smoke seeped into the room. Was it just his imagination or was the smoke stronger? Good God, what was he doing here? He should end this farce—

The window scraped in its frame. Malcolm forced himself to stay stock still as the window slid up. In the thick darkness, he could hear the thud of the intruder dropping to the floor. He gauged where the intruder would have moved to, then launched himself across the room and caught the intruder in a flying tackle. A fist smashed him in the eye. He grabbed one of the intruder's wrists. With his other hand, the intruder managed to land a blow to Malcolm's jaw. Malcolm maintained his grip on the intruder's wrist and struck a blow that, judging by the satisfying crack, slammed the man's head into the floorboards.

Suzanne appeared in the doorway holding a brace of candles. "Oh, good, you've got him."

"Throw me a rope, will you?" Malcolm grabbed the intruder's other wrist.

The intruder appeared to have had the wind knocked out of him. In the candlelight, Malcolm could make out a pockmarked face and short-cropped dark hair. He looked to be in his midtwenties. "Who hired you?" Malcolm demanded.

The intruder drew a ragged breath. "No one—"

"Spare me the denials." Malcolm caught the rope Suzanne tossed him and lashed the man's wrists together in front of him. "You'll never make me believe you simply decided to break into our house on your own account. We can take you to Bow Street or you can give us an explanation. Who hired you?"

Still lying on his back, the intruder looked from side to side, as though seeking escape. "Gentleman. Older. Don't know his name. Don't expect you to believe me—"

"I believe you. He wouldn't have been fool enough to tell you his name. Who set fire to the house?"

"Didn't—"

"Your denials try my patience. You and your companion set fire to my house. With my children in it."

"My mate Bert. Was only supposed to be a diversion. Just long enough to fetch what the gentleman wanted."

"What did he tell you to take?"

The intruder glanced at Suzanne, who had advanced into the room holding the brace of candles. "Blimey, they said your wife was a beauty—"

"What did your employer tell you to steal?" Suzanne said.

"He didn't—"

"Spare us." Malcolm tugged the knot on the rope tighter.

"Papers. Some sort of old play."

"How were you supposed to get this manuscript to him?" Malcolm asked.

"He—"

"He wouldn't have given you an address. You must have planned to meet him?"

"Tonight. Monmouth Street. Off Covent Garden."

It was in Seven Dials, one of the worst parts of London. "Good. We'll go there with you."

"Who's 'we'?"

"My husband and I," Suzanne said.

The intruder stared at her, then looked at Malcolm. "You're going to let your wife go to Seven Dials?"

"My wife tends to make decisions for herself. You'll lead us to your employer."

"He'll kill me."

"We won't let him. We need your evidence. On the other hand, if we take you to Bow Street, burglary and attempted arson are hanging offenses."

"How do I know you won't take me to Bow Street when we're done in any case?"

"You have my word."

He gave a low laugh. "If I relied on any bloke's word—"

"Nevertheless. You may rely upon mine."

The intruder stared at Malcolm a moment, then snorted. "Looks as though I don't have much choice."

Addison and Blanca, Suzanne's maid, appeared in the doorway.

"The fire's out," Addison said. He had black smudges on his face and shirt. "No damage beyond a couple of scorched floorboards."

"That's a relief." Malcolm got to his feet, one eye on the intruder. "We're off to Seven Dials to discuss the night's events with this man's employer."

Blanca cast a glance at the man lying on the study floor. "His employer has to realize he might have been intercepted."

"Quite," Malcolm said. "This shows how desperate he is."

"He'll be armed when you meet him."

"Probably." Malcolm looked at Addison. "I'd appreciate it if you'd come with us."

"Of course."

"Addison should stay here," Blanca said. "In case they try anything else at the house. Take me instead."

Malcolm hesitated.

"She has a point," Suzanne said.

"You're going to take *two* women?" the intruder said from the floor.

"I've learned to rely on my wife's good sense," Malcolm said. He smiled at Blanca. "And on that of her friends."

CHAPTER 6

Shadows cloaked the street. Seven Dials was a crooked maze of winding streets, close-set buildings, and cracked cobblestones on the brightest of days. Tonight, clouds rippled over the half-moon, leaving a faint glow. The dark washed over the grime but did not take away the stench of too many people packed into too-tight quarters. Suzanne hadn't had much excuse to explore this part of London, though it was close to Covent Garden. But whether in Paris, Brussels, or Vienna, slums were remarkably similar.

Malcolm was marching the intruder along, holding his bound wrists, while Suzanne walked behind with her pistol pointed in the man's back. Blanca, armed with a knife, kept watch on the man's other side. At approaching four in the morning, Seven Dials had quieted down, though the thick yellow light of tallow candles spilled from a few windows, at least some of which were undoubtedly brothels. And they'd glimpsed more than one tired-looking woman leaning in a doorway and heard the thuds and grunts of crude lovemaking from a shadowy alley. Memories clawed at Suzanne's skin. She kept her gaze fixed on the dark outline of the intruder's back and concentrated on keeping her footing on the uneven cobblestones.

The appointed corner was up ahead. Malcolm pulled out a

knife and cut the bonds on the intruder's hands. "We'll be watching," he told the intruder. "And we're armed."

"As will he be. I can't win."

"We offer the best chance of staying alive," Malcolm said.

The man rubbed his wrists. "So you say."

They flattened themselves in doorways on either side of the street, Malcolm in one, Suzanne and Blanca in the other. The intruder advanced into the swirling shadows and gave the low whistle he had told them was his agreed-upon signal with his employer.

Suzanne stayed still, face pressed against the rotting wood of the doorframe. An agonizing minute or so later a shadowy form approached at the end of the street. Greatcoat, hat. Middling height.

"Come on," Suzanne muttered. "A little closer."

The man moved down the street. A gust of wind tossed the clouds over the moon.

The intruder reached into his coat and pulled out a sheaf of papers Malcolm had given him. The greatcoated man took a quick step forwards and snatched the papers. The wind ruffled the clouds. The light fell on Malcolm flattened in the doorway across the street. The greatcoated man froze, then spun round and ran. Malcolm lurched from the doorway in pursuit. The greatcoated man spun towards him and fired off a pistol. Malcolm fell to the ground.

Suzanne screamed and ran to her fallen husband. Even as panic drove the breath from her lungs, a part of her brain registered that she'd heard the bullet strike the cobblestones.

"Malcolm?" She knelt beside him and seized his hand. "Darling? God of my idolatry?"

He opened his eyes. Even in the darkness, she caught his grin. "Worth waking up for."

"Are you all right?" She felt his shoulder.

"Only my pride bruised. The shot whistled past me." He pushed himself up. "Is he gone?"

"Unfortunately."

"This one isn't." Blanca was holding a knife on the intruder.

Malcolm got to his feet and approached the man.

"I didn't warn him," the intruder said.

"No. You did as told." Malcolm surveyed him. "If your former employer approaches you again, you'll come to us."

The man stared at him as though he were speaking a foreign tongue. "You're letting me go?"

"I see nothing to be gained from turning you over to Bow Street," Malcolm said. "And I did give you my word."

The intruder gave a short laugh. "Men like you don't give their word to men like me."

"Many men go back on their word to others in all walks of life. I don't."

The intruder studied Malcolm. "How do you know you can trust me?"

"I don't trust you for a bit. But I don't see what else you can do to us." Malcolm inclined his head to Blanca, indicating she could lower the knife. "And there's just a chance you'll lead your former employer to us."

The intruder stepped gingerly aside as Blanca lowered her knife with obvious reluctance. "Because you let me go?"

"Because whatever he pays you I promise to double it."

The man gave a slow smile. "Do I have your word on that?"

"Would you take it?"

"I don't know about that. But at the very least it's a risk I'd run."

"Anything that would tell you who the man in the greatcoat was?" Suzanne asked Malcolm as they made their way back towards Berkeley Square.

"Middle-aged, a flash of graying hair. He could be any of our five suspects. Or another man entirely."

"He risked a lot," Blanca said. "Exposing himself. Coming to Seven Dials at all."

"Yes." Malcolm tucked Suzanne's arm more closely into his own. "Whatever's in the manuscript, he's willing to risk a great deal to recover it." He glanced at the sky, which was already beginning to hold a predawn glow. "Only a few hours until I have to meet Crispin. Hardly worth going to bed at all."

Tuesday dawned fine and Crispin offered to drive Malcolm down to Richmond in his curricle. He gave his horses, a superb pair of matched grays, their office when they left the London traffic behind, going at a clip that set up clouds of dust from the road and stirred the cool air. Malcolm could understand the desire for speed and bracing air. Anything to provide distance from recent revelations. Even if it was an illusory distance.

"Never spent much time at the Richmond villa," Crispin said abruptly. "I think Father kept it mostly for rendezvous with his mistresses. And I suppose perhaps to meet with his . . . contact? Spymaster? What the devil word does one use?"

"All of those."

Crispin's York tan–gloved hands tightened on the reins. "I confess I used to think what you did sounded exciting. Used to be a bit jealous that I was here choosing horses and going to the opera and sampling the latest port while you were helping save England from Bonaparte and the French. I don't think I had the least idea of what the reality of being a spy was. How—"

"Ugly it is?"

Crispin shot a look at him. "I didn't mean—It's different for you. You were working for your country."

A dozen compromises in that country's name shot through Malcolm's head. "So I was."

Crispin cast another look at him and once again Malcolm had the feeling the other man saw more than one would expect of him. "But it still must—"

"It still comes down to lies and betrayal."

Crispin steered the curricle round a mud puddle in the road. "You're glad to be away from it?"

"I can't really get away from it. And a part of me is glad." He could still feel the adrenaline rush of the moment he'd tackled the intruder in the study last night. "The truth is I miss the game, dirty as it is."

Crispin nodded. "I can see that. You always were clever. Need to do something with those brains of yours. I don't suppose Parliament quite fills the void."

"Parliament is its own sort of game. And its own set of compromises. But I still miss—"

"The adventure?"

Malcolm could hear his wife saying, *You're enjoying this.* "For my sins—yes."

"But you tried to give it up?"

"I have a strange desire to be my own master. And I have children now. I want them to be safe." Malcolm hesitated, then added something he didn't verbalize often. It touched too much on the personal. "And I'd like to be someone they can be proud of."

Crispin nodded. "I never thought much about the sort of man I was or what people thought of me. Simply did the expected. With Roxane and Clarisse . . . they aren't mine of course, but they make me"—he flushed—"want to be a better person."

"Nothing to be ashamed of in that. And there's more than one way to become a father."

Crispin fixed his gaze on the sleek backs of the horses. "Always liked children. But I've never had a chance to get to know any so well. Don't want to intrude, of course. I sometimes think Manon thinks I overstep my bounds."

"She's probably concerned about what would happen if you weren't part of the girls' life anymore."

Crispin's eyes widened. "But I wouldn't—"

"Love affairs have a tendency not to be permanent."

Crispin's mouth tightened. "I know. That is—" His eyes darkened, with the look of a man who doesn't want to stare into the future. A few moments later, he turned the horses in at the drive to the villa.

Lord Harleton's Richmond house was a sharp contrast to the classic Palladian style of most of the villas that dotted the Thames. Instead of symmetrical white stone, the house at the end of the avenue of pleached limes was of mellow brick in the E style common in the Elizabethan era, with banks of mullioned windows, a dormer roof, and newer wings added on either side. "It was the main family estate in the sixteenth century," Crispin said, pulling up the curricle in the gravel circle before the house. "The seventh earl—the one who got the estates restored—married an heiress with a larger property in Buckinghamshire and that became our main county seat. Father considered tearing this one down and building something more modern but never did. I'm rather glad."

A groom emerged to take the reins. Crispin ran up the steps and rang the bell. "Morning, John," he said to the footman who admitted them. "We'll be in the study."

"Father used the villa a lot," Crispin told Malcolm, leading the way down the hall to the study. "Rarely closed it up."

The study was oak paneled and filled with gilt and claret-colored leather. The typical domain of an English gentleman, though less businesslike than some. A handsome oil portrait of a man in sixteenth-century dress hung over the mantel. Even from across the room the rich colors and play of light caught the eye. "Good God," Malcolm said, "it's a Rubens."

"Is it?" Crispin looked up from lighting a lamp. "Always thought it was pretty."

"One of your ancestors?"

"No. I remember asking once. Father had the painting hung when I was a boy. He acquired it somewhere."

"And I'd swear that's Cellini." Malcolm stared at the bronze of the lamp, glowing as it flared to life. "I didn't realize your father was a collector."

"Nor did I. Would have sworn he couldn't tell a Rubens from a Rowlandson." Crispin pulled a key from his pocket and hesitated. "I left the papers locked in here." He opened a drawer in the desk and lifted out a sheaf of documents, then stepped back, almost as though afraid to touch them. Malcolm moved to the desk and studied the papers in the light of the Cellini lamp. His father's handwriting stared up at him.

Sick certainty settled like a lead weight in the pit of his stomach, and he knew that until this moment he had held out hope.

> *My dear Harleton,*
> *Don't make idle threats. You must have the wit to*
> *realize that if you could ruin me, I could just as easily*
> *ruin you. We share the same secrets and the same*
> *sins. I agree that the Dunboyne business could prove*
> *useful, but I won't commit more to paper.*

"It's your father's hand?" Crispin asked.

"Yes." Malcolm touched his fingers to the paper, not sure what he was searching for. He felt chilled to the bone and numb to all emotion. Which was much the way Alistair had made him feel in life.

"I'm sorry." Crispin hesitated. "I wasn't particularly close to my father, but—"

"You were almost certainly closer to him than I was to Alistair, but—" Malcolm met the other man's gaze and saw a reflection of his own confusion. "Yes. It still means something." He studied Crispin. The other man's face showed a newfound maturity coupled with the vulnerability of a schoolboy. "Crispin. I've known a number of spies. Duplicity and deceit go hand in hand with the work. Often one doesn't like oneself very much. I don't know that spies make the best fathers. But it doesn't mean they love their children any less."

Crispin nodded slowly. "Then that applies to your father as well."

"Perhaps. Save that I long since came to terms with the fact that Alistair didn't love me."

"You can't know—I mean at times everyone thinks their parents—"

"Quite. Save that in my case Alistair admitted it flat out."

Crispin stared at him. "He didn't actually—"

"To be fair, I was the one who brought it up. Still not quite sure where I got the temerity. I think I said that Carfax at least loved David, but I'd never say Alistair loved me. Alistair simply replied, 'What on earth would make you think I did?' "

Crispin shook his head. "That's—"

"It's all right. It relieved me of the guilt of trying to love him myself." Malcolm riffled through the papers. "These were all you found?"

Crispin nodded. "You think there's more?"

"Spies never destroy as much as they should." Malcolm glanced round the study. "People tend to make use of familiar objects. With someone with love of travel, I'd unscrew the top of the globe and look inside. With a bibliophile, I'd look for a hollowed-out book." His gaze swept the pristine glass-fronted bookcase.

"Neither describes Father," Crispin said. "Truth to tell, I don't think he spent much time in his study. He left accounts and the like to his estate agents. And when he was here—" Crispin's gaze settled on a gilded mahogany cabinet beneath the windows that held an array of decanters. "I'd try the drinks cabinet."

"Excellent suggestion."

"Seriously?"

"It sounds like just the sort of thing your father would have thought of." Malcolm moved to the cabinet and knelt in front of it. He ran his fingers over the gilded moldings, but he could feel no hidden spring. He felt down the classical pilasters on either side, then eyed the marble top. The layer of mahogany beneath was thicker than it needed to be. "Help me lift the drinks tray," he said to Crispin.

They lifted the mirrored tray of decanters and set it on the desk. Crispin gave an appreciative sniff as they set down the tray. "I'll say this for the pater, he had good taste in liquor."

Malcolm bent down with his ear against the green-veined marble that topped the cabinet and tapped. A spot in the right corner rang hollow. He ran his fingers along the molding beneath and one of the marble tiles slid back to reveal a shallow compartment.

"Good God." Crispin stared over Malcolm's shoulder at the sheaf of yellowed papers in the compartment. "This spy business really does work."

"It's not usually this neat." Malcolm lifted out the papers and carried them to the light of the lamp on the desk.

"It looks like Greek to me." Crispin gave a faint smile. "And I do know that's a *Julius Caesar* reference."

Malcolm returned the smile. "It's a book code that's then been transliterated into ancient Greek for good measure." He flipped through the papers. "At least some of these look like my father's hand."

"You think you can use the manuscript to decode them?" Crispin asked.

"We'll have to see."

CHAPTER 7

Even in early afternoon the shadows cast by the plaster and oak of the ceiling of the coffeehouse were forgiving and the thick leaded glass of the windows filtered the light in a comforting way. Ladies might be rare here, but enough actresses, milliners, and ladies of the evening were present that Suzanne attracted no more than a few casual glances. Only a half hour before she had been walking along the Serpentine in Hyde Park with Colin and Jessica and their governess, Laura Dudley. But then she should be used to combining the roles of mother and agent by now.

She waited for the glances to turn away before she scanned the crowd. Something alerted her to his presence before she actually spotted him through the haze of smoke and coffee steam. There, at a table in the corner.

She made her way across the room, careful not to walk too fast. He looked up from his newspaper, though she suspected he'd been aware of her from the moment she stepped through the door.

The strain of the past years showed in his face. He had always been thin, but he looked leaner and gaunter. As though the need to keep going had whittled away anything extraneous. The iron resilience was still there and his eyes burned as bright as ever, but the scars of defeat showed in his face. Still, his mouth lifted in a familiar smile as she approached. Despite everything, she felt an absurd wash of comfort.

"You look well." He got to his feet and pulled out a chair for her.

"Rank flattery." She sank into the chair and stripped off her gloves.

"Hardly." He returned to his own chair, picked up the bottle of red wine on the table, and poured her a glass.

She reached for the glass and took a grateful sip. The tension coiled within her was so ever present she almost forgot it was there. "I didn't think you'd be able to come so soon."

"Britain is friendlier to me these days," Raoul O'Roarke said. "My sins in the United Irish Uprising seem forgot in the wake of my supposed support of the *guerrilleros* in Spain. Ironic, is it not?"

Raoul's cover during the Peninsular War had been that he worked with the *guerrilleros* who had been allied with the British in driving the French out of Spain. He had in fact been a spymaster, running a network and passing intelligence along to the French.

"An irony that works to your advantage," Suzanne said.

"These days one takes blessings where one finds them. Not that having been allied with the *guerrilleros* is a universally welcomed calling card in Britain, either."

After the war the restored Spanish king, Ferdinand, had re-pealed the constitution and re-established the Inquisition, to the despair of the Spanish liberals who had wanted the French out of Spain but had also wanted to remake their country along more pro-gressive lines. The outcome might vindicate people like Raoul and her who had thought the best route to reform lay with the French, but she knew it sickened him to see it as much as it sickened her.

"Malcolm made a speech about it in the Commons," she said. "Our—that is, Britain's—lack of support for those who fought be-side the British in Spain."

"Yes, I know." Raoul reached for his wineglass. "I read it. I thought I detected your hand. Or rather pen."

She swallowed hard at the memory of poring over the speech with her husband late one night in his study, debating, scribbling, tossing out turns of phrase. "I may have helped with the editing, but the ideas were his. I think what's happening in Spain makes

Malcolm happier than ever that he left the diplomatic corps. He says he wonders sometimes what we were fighting for. That is, what he was fighting for. What the British were fighting for. You know what I mean."

"Quite." Raoul gave a faint smile as he took a sip of wine.

"What I'm trying to say is that Malcolm is happier in Parliament."

"And are you happy as a political wife?"

She turned her glass on the tabletop. The wine glowed a dull red in the murky light. "I won't deny I miss the excitement. But I think I'm rather a good political hostess."

"Rumor has it even Tories seek out invitations to your parties."

"I have novelty on my side for the moment."

"The English ton isn't an easy world to navigate. Speaking as one who's lived my life on the fringes of it."

She had known that, but she had still been overwhelmed by the feeling of stepping into an alien landscape when she and Malcolm had moved to Britain in the spring. Not a wild landscape but a garden laid out with meticulous care and governed by unwritten rules and indecipherable codes. "People are eager to see the Berkeley Square house. Redoing it has been a challenge. A welcome challenge, though I never saw myself as the decorating type."

"It should be child's play for one who helped stage a medieval tournament."

She smiled, remembering the Carrousel in Vienna. Dear God. In some ways the Congress of Vienna seemed a much simpler time. She'd still been actively spying. But somehow in the midst of that activity she'd given less thought to consequences. "You have no idea how exhausting choosing wallpaper can be. It's the first time we've had a proper home of our own. But I sometimes wonder if we were wise to move into the house. If Malcolm will ever see it as ours rather than his parents' house."

"It's a beautiful house."

She nodded. "I think that's what decided Malcolm. He was planning to sell it, but we walked through and Colin was running up the staircase, and Malcolm said we'd be fools to walk away from it. But I worry it has a lot of ghosts for him. Though from what I gather he and Edgar and Gisèle were packed off to Scotland much of the time and then away at school."

Raoul leaned back in his chair, wineglass tilting between his fingers. "The past months can't have been easy."

She nodded, surprised at what a relief it was to talk about it. Perhaps that was why she was prevaricating about the real reason she had asked to see him. She was indulging herself, basking in a few moments of understanding. There were so few people with whom she could really be herself. "Losing his father was hard on Malcolm for all they were never close. Perhaps particularly because they weren't close. There's so much unsettled business between them that now will never be resolved." Including the question of who had actually fathered Malcolm. "He doesn't talk to me much about it."

"I suspect he talks about it more to you than to anyone."

Suzanne studied Raoul across the table. He had been friends with Malcolm's mother and grandfather and had known Malcolm since boyhood. In some ways, she thought, Raoul knew her husband better than she did herself. "He doesn't share easily. But then I've always known that. I thought—" She bit back what she'd been about to say and snatched up her wineglass. It wasn't for Raoul to know that she'd thought she and Malcolm had grown closer only to realize, here in the world in which he had grown up, the layers still between them.

Raoul regarded her with a shrewd gaze. "One holds the hurts of childhood close. It's different from the things he's been through with you. I suspect he's afraid to burden you with those childhood hurts."

"What else does he think I'm here for?" She slumped back against the hard slats of her chair. "Damn you. I suspect you're right. As usual."

"My apologies."

She wadded up her handkerchief and threw it at him.

Raoul caught it one-handed. "How are the children?"

Their gazes locked across the table. How quickly one could step onto quicksand. "Adjusting to England better than their parents, I think. Jessica crawls all over the new house and pulls herself up and babbles as though she's telling us something very important—which I suspect she is, we just can't decipher it yet. She says 'mama' all the time, and I think she might actually have been referring to me yesterday. Colin is learning to read and loves the Berkeley Square garden. That convinces me we were right to take the house. And most of the time he's quite fond of his little sister."

"I'm glad." Raoul smoothed out the handkerchief and handed it back to her. "It's good for Colin to have a sibling. I suspect it's good for Malcolm as well."

She was silent for a moment. Of all the decisions she'd taken, having a second child with Malcolm was the one that tied her irrevocably to him. "Malcolm was happy when I said I wanted another child." She could see his face across the breakfast dishes in their lodgings in Paris, a mix of surprise and wonder. Her fingers clenched on the handkerchief. Her initials were embroidered in the corner. *S.S.V.* Suzanne de Saint-Vallier. The alias she'd been using when she met and married Malcolm that had now become a permanent part of her fictitious past. "I can't imagine my life without Jessica now. But I can't help but wonder if it was selfish. One more person to be hurt if anything goes wrong."

"All the more reason to be sure nothing goes wrong." He watched her for the length of a measure of music. "Why did you want to see me, *querida?*"

Suzanne took a sip of wine, curling her fingers round the stem of the glass. "Did you know Lord Harleton was a French spy?"

Surprise shot through Raoul's gaze. "Talk about old ghosts."

She set the glass on the table, sloshing the wine. "So you did know?"

"Oh yes. I recruited him."

The world spun, as it often did with Raoul. "You—"

"It was in the midnineties, after the Terror." During the Reign of Terror Raoul had been imprisoned in Les Carmes. He'd been days away from the guillotine when Robespierre fell. It was something of a miracle Raoul had survived this long, all things considered. Raoul reached for his glass. "It seemed important to protect the gains of the Revolution."

"So that was when you first offered your services to French intelligence?" Suzanne had never been sure of the chronology for all she knew of Raoul.

He nodded. "And what more natural than to have me spend time at the Salon des Etrangers and other haunts of British expatriates. I might be anathema to the British Crown, but I still had connections. There were a lot of heedless young aristos like Harleton sampling the joys of Parisian life. He had expensive tastes."

"Gambling debts?'

"And a woman. A very expensive courtesan named Lilliane Moncoeur to whom he'd written indiscreet letters."

"You extricated him from his difficulties in exchange for his services."

"Always dangerous to have a hold on an asset that can breed resentment. On the other hand, burning idealism can have its own drawbacks. One needn't fear disillusion when there've been no illusions to begin with."

"But Harleton continued to work for the French for over a decade. Did he still need the money?"

Raoul took a sip of wine. "Not particularly after he came into the title and estates."

"Do you think it was fear of his secret being exposed that kept him working for the French?" she asked.

Raoul twirled his glass between his fingers. "Actually, I think Harleton enjoyed the thrill of the chase. Which is also not the best quality in an agent. Though to a degree it can give one an edge."

"He didn't mind betraying his country?" Funny how the word "betraying" stuck in her throat these days.

"I don't think Harleton had much loyalty—to his country, to any cause. Perhaps a bit to his friends. He liked the challenge of the game. It amused him to appear to have less of an understanding than he did. I wouldn't say he was brilliant, but he was less of a bumbler than he let on."

"He went on reporting to you?" she asked, piecing this together with what Malcolm had learned from Carfax.

"Off and on through Waterloo. After the United Irish Uprising, I was in Paris more than ever."

In fact, Raoul had escaped Ireland by the skin of his teeth,

Suzanne knew, narrowly avoiding the fate of Lord Edward Fitzgerald and others who had died in the wake of the failed rebellion. "Did you realize—"

"That Carfax was on to him? Yes, after a few years. I funneled information through him that I wanted to get back to Carfax."

"And then?"

"Unlike most of my assets, Harleton didn't need protecting after Waterloo, so he ceased to be a concern to me. I didn't hear from him for almost two years. And then a few weeks before he died, he contacted me saying Carfax was going to bring him in."

"What did you tell him?"

"That I was hardly in a position to protect him."

"You must have wondered when he died so soon after."

"Of course. To own the truth, I wondered if he'd killed himself, though I'd have thought Harleton's sense of self-preservation was too strong for that."

"His son found a letter Harleton was drafting to you that he hadn't yet put into code."

Raoul grimaced. "I'm sorry for the son. Apparently Harleton at least had the wit not to use my name?"

He could face exposure so coolly. But then the ever-present threat of exposure was something they had both learned to live with. "Crispin Harleton would have said if his father had used your name. But could Harleton have letters from you?"

"He was supposed to have destroyed any communications from me. But even if he didn't, I doubt Malcolm could recognize my handwriting on a coded letter written in capitals."

Suzanne swallowed, aware of the ground she was stepping onto with her next question. "What about Alistair Rannoch?"

Raoul's brows lifted. "What about him?"

She kept her gaze steady on Raoul's face, the hooded eyes, the sharp nose, the ironic mouth. Trying to read the man who was so often unreadable, even to the agent he had trained. "Crispin Harleton found a letter from Alistair Rannoch to his father in his things. It implies Alistair was a French agent as well."

Raoul released his breath, his enigmatic gray gaze gone wide with shock. "Dear God in heaven."

"He didn't work for you?"

Raoul reached for his glass as though he was unaware of what he was doing with his hands. "You don't think I'd have warned you before you went off to England as his daughter-in-law?"

"Not necessarily."

Raoul gave a faint smile. "When I taught you to question everything, I wasn't extending that to my own motives."

"You'd question mine."

He tossed down a swallow of wine. "You have a tendency to see me as more of a chess player than I am, *querida*."

"Which is just the sort of thing a master chess player would say."

"It can be an advantage to see when someone is being sincere. Think what you will of me, *querida,* I didn't know Alistair was an agent." He stared into his glass, as though viewing the past through a different filter. "I don't say this often, but I'm shocked."

"Couldn't he have done it out of self-interest, like Harleton?"

"Perhaps." Raoul turned the glass on the tabletop. "Alistair's main loyalty was also to himself. He was cleverer than Harleton. And more ruthless."

"You knew him well?"

"I knew the family."

"But you believe it?"

Raoul's brows drew together. "Alistair Rannoch was a penniless young man who went to Harrow and Oxford on his godfather's charity and came into a legacy from a distant cousin in Jamaica just after he left university. Supposedly. I begin to think I was very credulous to have believed the story. He was keenly aware of being a charity boy. Cleverer and poorer than his friends. If he saw becoming a French spy as a way to make his fortune and give him the place he sought in the world—Yes, I can believe it." He was silent for a moment. "I'm sorry for Malcolm."

She nodded, not trusting herself to speak. Her fingers curled into her palms. She saw Alistair Rannoch's face again, heard him delivering a cutting remark to Malcolm, felt the instinctive recoil Malcolm wouldn't own to. "I just can't bear to think—"

"What?"

"That a man like Alistair Rannoch was in any way like me."

Raoul gave a short laugh.

"It's not funny."

His gaze skimmed over her face. "You know the game, *querida*. You know how it corrodes the soul."

She swallowed. The wine had gone sour in her mouth. "I suppose I liked to believe one could play the game and have some core of integrity left." She glanced across the room at two young men, students by the look of it, debating over a stack of books and papers, then forced her gaze back to his face. "Go on, say it. I'm a deluded fool."

"On the contrary. I think holding on to even a shred of your ideals after what we've been through is a remarkable achievement. You're to be commended."

"Don't be ironic."

"I've never been more sincere in my life. If anything, I'm envious." Raoul leaned forwards. His gaze turned compelling and unusually open in that disconcerting way it could. "You're no Alistair Rannoch, *querida*. You couldn't be if you tried."

She forced a sip of wine past the bitterness in her throat. "I betrayed my husband. He betrayed his son."

"You married a fellow spy who was already part of the game. Alistair failed Malcolm from the moment he was born."

Beneath Raoul's cool voice was unexpected bitterness. "You knew Alistair well."

"I knew him once."

Suzanne searched his face, but he revealed no further clues. No one could put up better barriers than Raoul when he put his mind to it.

Raoul picked up the bottle and refilled both their glasses. "Why did this come up now?"

She told him about the Shakespeare manuscript. "But you must have known about it if Harleton was using it as a codebook?"

"He gave me a copy of one scene we based the code on. I can't tell you how much I wanted to see the rest of the manuscript." Raoul twisted the stem of his glass between his fingers. "It seemed rather like sacrilege to use a manuscript that could be by Shakespeare as a codebook."

"But clever. No one but the two of you had a copy."

"Yes, that's what Harleton said. It was a fair point, though he didn't seem to have the least appreciation of what he had in the manuscript." Raoul took a sip of wine. "The Irish were rebelling when Shakespeare wrote *Hamlet*. I've always thought that had something to do with Hamlet's bitter take on fighting over a little patch of ground."

"Is that when your ancestor fled to Spain?" Suzanne asked, sorting through the stories Raoul had told her.

"Eventually, when the rebellion was quashed, as rebellions in Ireland are wont to be." Raoul's mouth tightened. "Though first the rebels dealt quite a blow to the British under Essex."

"Harleton's ancestor was a supporter of Essex, though I don't know if he fought in Ireland."

"A pity the investigation couldn't be confined to the manuscript and history." Raoul sat back in his chair and regarded her. "As it is, it's not an easy investigation for Malcolm. Or for you."

She tightened her fingers round the stem of her glass. "I said I'd help him. But I can't of course."

Raoul took a sip of wine. "You don't work for me anymore."

She jerked the glass to her lips and tossed down a swallow. "I can't lead Malcolm to one of our own. I can't see someone who was an ally arrested on treason charges. I may be capable of a lot but not of that kind of betrayal." She swallowed, the Bordeaux raw in her throat. "I know I've betrayed Malcolm. Horribly. My loyalty to my comrades may not be stronger, but it's older."

"Commendable."

"I don't know about that."

"*Querida*—" He scanned her face and for a moment his gaze was like the brush of fingertips. "You could walk away. Pretend you didn't know any of us or any of this."

She reached for her wine, then folded her hands in her lap. "And Malcolm's investigation?"

"Play dumb and try to stay out of it."

"He wouldn't believe me."

Raoul's mouth curled in a smile of acknowledgment. "You have a point there. Still, you're a good enough actress I think you could manage to stay out of it. Not implicate anyone but not risk yourself actively trying to protect them."

She shook her head. Her nails curled into her palms. "I can't. I told you in Brussels after Waterloo I was walking away, but by the time we got to Paris a few weeks later I knew that was impossible. I could stop actively working for you, but I couldn't turn my back on my former comrades." She forced her hands to unclench and took a sip of wine, searching for words. "I have a hard enough time remembering who I am these days. Sometimes it seems that all that's left of me is the shell I built for my masquerade as Malcolm's wife. If I stopped protecting my friends, I'd lose track of myself completely. I don't think I'd like the person who was left. I don't think I'd want her to be the mother of my children. I want to be someone Colin and Jessica can be proud of. Though if they ever learn the truth, they'll probably hate me."

"I don't think so." Raoul's gaze was steady on her face. "They're being raised by you."

"And they're growing up here." She saw Colin clutching a Royalist cockade the summer before last in Hyde Park. "It makes a difference." She tossed back another swallow of wine. "I thought I could find a way to help my friends without betraying Malcolm's trust. Yet here I am doing just that."

"Are you?"

"I'm telling you about his investigation. So you can help me stop it. But I very much fear—"

"What?"

She drew a breath and looked into her fears. "Malcolm is very, very good at what he does. If he's determined to ferret out French spies in London, I think he's all too likely to ferret out me."

"It's a risk." Raoul was never one to offer false reassurance. "Malcolm is clever. But so are you."

Her gaze flickered over his face. "Did you hear anything about the leak that led to the Dunboyne affair?"

Raoul's brows drew together. "I was in Dunboyne at the time, but I never heard the source of the leak."

She stared into the wine in her glass, bloodred in the candlelight. "Malcolm won't stop."

"Querida—" Raoul slid his hand across the table, then stilled it, inches from her own. "Whoever this man is who was behind the leak, he's in a position of power. He may not even have been working for the French. He could have had other reasons to help the United Irishmen."

"That hardly makes me less sympathetic to him." She could hear the passion in Raoul's voice when he talked to her about the United Irish Uprising.

"Perhaps not. But he could also have been driven by something other than Republican ideals. Ireland was never your fight. You don't owe him anything."

"Perhaps not." Her fingers twisted round the fragile stem of her glass. "Loyalty used to seem so much simpler. My family were gone. The cause came before everything. We had a war to win, and the choice between the sides seemed clear, even if our own was tarnished. Then I had a son. And a daughter. And a husband." She flashed a quick look at Raoul. "I know it sounds mad, but I realized early on I was loyal to Malcolm. Even as I betrayed him in myriad ways."

"I'm not laughing." Raoul took a sip of wine. "Your loyalty was quite apparent."

"But those loyalties didn't make the other loyalties go away. To the cause, to the people we worked with."

"Yet perhaps in this case the happiness of your husband and children comes first." How could Raoul's voice at once be so neutral and so gentle?

"But that's just it." Without realizing she had moved, she was gripping the edge of the table. "The man behind the Dunboyne leak has a life here as well. A family. People he cares for. If I help Malcolm expose him while doing my utmost to maintain my own secret and go on with my own comfortable life with my husband and children, then I'm the worst sort of hypocrite."

"My dear girl, in this life—"

"We do unconscionable things? Yes, I've long since accepted that." She released the table and sat back in her chair. "But not just to protect ourselves. One has to draw the line somewhere."

Raoul was silent for a moment. "No one could fault you for putting your children first."

"But I won't be much of a mother if I hate myself."

"You won't be much of a mother if—" He bit back the words. Even Raoul didn't want to look into the abyss.

Suzanne forced herself to face it. "If I'm arrested or thrown out by my husband?"

"I don't think one ever forgives oneself for abandoning a child."

It was her turn to probe his face, his turn to glance away. She tossed back the last of her wine and reached for her gloves and reticule. "I'm going to need your help."

"To do?"

She tugged a glove smooth on her left hand, covering her wedding ring. "To find the source of the Dunboyne leak before Malcolm does."

CHAPTER 8

"Cousin Malcolm." Chloe Dacre-Hammond ran across her mother's drawing room in a stir of white muslin and pale blond hair and flung her arms round Malcolm's waist. She had been born while Malcolm was in the Peninsula, yet for some reason he was a favorite of hers. He could still not quite figure out what he had done to deserve it.

"It's good to see you, poppet." Malcolm caught her up and swung her round in a circle.

Close on Chloe's heels, his cousin Aline's two-year-old Claudia toddled into him and threw her arms round his knees. Malcolm bent down to scoop her up. "I swear you've grown since Thursday, Claudie."

Chloe grinned. "Babies are always growing. You didn't bring Colin and Jessica?"

"Not this time. I'm just on my way back from Richmond, and I need to talk to your mother. But Suzette or I will bring them round soon."

"Careful, Chloe." Her mother's amused voice came from the sofa across the room where she was sitting with Aline. "It doesn't do to let a gentleman realize how eager one is to see him."

"Don't be silly, Mama. Malcolm isn't a gentleman, he's my cousin."

Malcolm moved to the matched violet-striped sofas in front of the fireplace, carrying Claudia, Chloe trailing after him. He hugged Aline, who had sprung to her feet, and bent to kiss his aunt's cheek. Aline's gaze darted over his face. For someone who lived much of the time in her head with numbers, she could read a great deal in faces. Odd to think that not so very many years ago he'd been thinking of her as the baby.

Chloe glanced between her mother and Malcolm. "Since Malcolm wants to talk to you and didn't bring Colin and Jessica this must be something Grown-Up. I suppose I have to go up to the nursery now."

"You can stay and have a cup of cambric tea," Lady Frances said. "But then, yes, I think Malcolm is here because he has something to discuss with me."

"I'll take you both up," Aline promised her little sister. "I can show you how to graph a puppy's tail."

Chloe plopped down on the sofa, mollified. A footman brought in a tea tray and Chloe chattered on about the greyhounds she'd seen in the park that morning, the new dress her mother had taken her to have fitted, and an upcoming expedition to the opera while Malcolm fed Claudia bits of jam tart and successfully kept his teacup out of her small fist. He mentioned to Aline that he had a manuscript to show her, but at present it was more urgent that he speak with his aunt. At last Aline took Claudia from Malcolm and reached for Chloe's hand. Chloe went without protest, though she gathered up two extra jam tarts.

"I'm not sure which she's more excited about, the opera or the dogs," Lady Frances said. "I'm afraid we're going to have to get a puppy."

"She's very happy." Malcolm retrieved his cup and took a sip of tea. "As a parent, I'd say that's an accomplishment we all strive for."

Lady Frances settled back on the sofa, cradling her own cup in one hand. Sometimes she looked so like his mother that his breath caught in his throat. It wasn't her physical appearance so much— her features were sharper and her hair a deeper gold—but the angle at which she held her head, the negligent way she lifted the teacup, the ironic amusement in the arc of her brows. "Chloe has a happy disposition," Lady Frances said. "Though I do think I'm managing rather better with her than I did with the older children. I was shockingly selfish in my twenties. And then Dacre-Hammond and I didn't get on. I don't know why that should have been a problem—plenty of couples in the beau monde despise each other and manage perfectly well—but realizing he wasn't the man I'd thought him to be was a sad distraction. Much easier when I accepted that the seemingly dashing soldier I'd married was rather dull and got on with my life." She tucked a strand of gold hair, which had only seemed to grow brighter through the years, behind her ear. "Aline appears to be making an excellent mother."

"Yes, it's hard to believe now she used to say she didn't want children."

Lady Frances took a sip of tea. "So did you as I recall. But you were both always excellent with the younger ones, despite having your heads in books. I wonder if it shows some sadly conventional streak in me to be pleased you're both happily married and enjoying parenthood. It's not that I think it's the only possible happy outcome in life, but it can be surprisingly agreeable. Not that I ever managed the happily married part myself." She regarded Malcolm with a shrewd blue gaze. "What does Carfax or Castlereagh have you investigating now?"

Malcolm returned his cup to the sofa table. "How do you know it's an investigation?"

"It has to be that or family business. There's nothing that I know of wrong with Gisèle or Edgar, and I know how you hate talking about the family."

Malcolm brushed at the jam tart crumbs Claudia had left on his cravat. "I wouldn't say—"

"About anything that touches on the personal."

She had looked at him in that same precise way when his mother died. As though she wouldn't dream of prying, but she could see through any denial he could make and was ready to listen to anything he might say. Though Malcolm doubted even Aunt Frances could be prepared for this.

"Actually it's a bit of both," he said.

Lady Frances raised her brows. He saw a flash of concern in her eyes. A concern she would never admit to. "Do, pray, enlighten me," she said.

Even now he hesitated to put it into words. Which was nonsensical. And others had already verbalized it, notably Carfax. But somehow to put it into words to his mother's sister—

"It appears Father's death may not have been an accident," he said.

Lady Frances's eggshell porcelain teacup tilted in her fingers, spattering Darjeeling on the lilac-sprigged folds of her skirt. "Dear God."

"I know you were never much fond of him, either," Malcolm said. "But I confess I can't help but feel a desire to learn the truth."

Lady Frances righted the teacup. The rattle of the china betrayed her shaking fingers. "And it's mixed up with politics?"

"It appears to be." Malcolm studied his aunt. She and his father had exchanged barbs for as long as he could remember. But while Lady Frances might have cordially disliked Alistair Rannoch, they had moved in the same circles. He could still remember her shocked face on learning of Alistair's death. He had actually seen her dash tears from her eyes. "Did Father ever talk to you about Lord Harleton?"

"Harleton?" Lady Frances pressed her handkerchief over the spatters on her skirt. "Good God, was he murdered, too?"

"Very likely."

Lady Frances set down the sodden handkerchief, got to her feet, and moved to the trolley by the windows, which held a set of decanters. She splashed whisky into two glasses, tossed down one of them herself, and refilled it. "Alistair and Harleton were at Oxford together. They were in a club. They were both founders."

"A club?" Would Alistair ever stop surprising him? "I never heard Father founded a club. I know he didn't share a great deal with me, but—"

"A number of people don't know about this." Lady Frances crossed back to him and put one of the glasses of whisky into his hand. "Their activities were—are—secret. So is their membership."

"But you knew." Malcolm regarded his aunt over the etched crystal.

"Some of the names of the members. And I can guess at their activities."

"Aunt Frances—" Malcolm looked into his aunt's uncharacteristically still face. Lines that were usually invisible stood out against her rouge and finely textured skin. "Are you telling me Father founded a hellfire club?"

"I imagine it was something of the sort." Lady Frances took a sip of whisky. "They used to have house parties at one or other of the members' shooting boxes. Needless to say, no ladies were invited. Though I suspect some ladies were present."

"What was it called?"

Her mouth twisted in unexpected amusement. "The Elsinore League."

Malcolm nearly dropped his whisky. "Father didn't even like Shakespeare." He could clearly recall Alistair's amused gaze and cutting remarks on more than one occasion when he found Malcolm reading the plays. Shakespeare was something Malcolm had shared with his mother, with his scholarly grandfather, with Raoul O'Roarke. With Simon and David and Oliver Lydgate at university. Now with Suzanne, with whom he often traded quotes. Something he anticipated sharing with his children. For some reason the idea that his father had taken any interest in the Bard felt like an invasion of his private sphere.

"Perhaps his aversion to Shakespeare was something he developed later because he didn't get on with your grandfather. Or perhaps the name wasn't his idea."

"Did you ever hear Father say anything about *Hamlet*?"

"Relating to the club? Not that I can recall." Lady Frances dropped down on the sofa beside him, with less grace than usual. "Why?"

"Harleton had a manuscript that appears to be an early version of *Hamlet* in his possession."

"Good God." Lady Frances pushed a curl into its pins, as though she could order her thoughts. "Have you sent for your grandfather?"

"I wrote to him at once at Aunt Marjorie's. Do you know who else was in the Elsinore League along with Alistair and Harleton?"

Lady Frances frowned over her whisky. "Lord Glenister. Theodore Bartlett. Archibald Davenport."

"What about Sir Horace Smytheton? General Cyrus? Lord Bessborough? Dewhurst?"

"I'm not sure. Bessborough would have been at Oxford before the rest. Why?"

Malcolm took a long drink of whisky. One of the few things he shared a fondness for with Alistair. Again, he hesitated to put it into words. *Ridiculous.* It was a fact, spoken or unspoken. "It looks as though Alistair and Harleton may have been working for the French."

He expected Lady Frances to drop her whisky glass, cry out, even faint. Instead, her eyes narrowed.

Malcolm stared across the striped Italian silk of the sofa at his mother's sister. "Dear God. Don't tell me you knew."

"Of course not." She took a drink of whisky. "The very idea is absurd."

"But?" Malcolm kept his gaze trained on his aunt's face.

Lady Frances set down her glass and spread her hands over her lap. "It had been apparent to me for some time that your father wasn't precisely what he appeared to be on the surface. Your mother and I discussed it."

"Mama—" Malcolm swallowed an upwelling of equal parts bitterness, regret, and longing. "You discussed that—what? That Alistair had some secret?"

Lady Frances reached for her glass. "Arabella always said she didn't care to talk much about Alistair. That he wasn't worth wasting time over. But once—it must have been five or so years after they married, you and Edgar were born but not Gisèle—I asked her where Alistair had gone, and she said he was with a woman. Or on some other business. And she sometimes thought the former was cover for the latter. When I asked her what she meant, she said Alistair was a man of secrets. That it might even make him interesting if he hadn't entirely lost his ability to fascinate her years ago."

Even now, after years away from home, Malcolm's parents were ciphers he doubted he'd ever decode. "Do you think the Elsinore League was connected to this?"

Lady Frances took a sip of whisky and seemed to let it linger on her tongue. "The time I referred to, he was at one of their gatherings. To own the truth, I often wondered if it was some sort of cover." She studied Malcolm. "Good lord, Malcolm, do you suspect the other men you named of spying for the French? Even Bessborough?"

"We suspect at least one of them of dealing in information." Malcolm told her about the Dunboyne leak.

Lady Frances listened with a gathering frown between her carefully plucked brows. "Damn Carfax for pawning this off on you."

"Yes, I know. But I need to learn the truth."

Valentin took Suzanne's bonnet and pelisse and informed her that Mr. Rannoch had asked her to join him in his study. Her talk with Raoul still swirling in her brain, Suzanne went down the passage to speak with her husband.

She found Malcolm at his desk, the baize-covered surface strewn with scribbled-over pieces of paper and two pages of the *Hamlet* manuscript, set beneath a sheet of glass in the light of a brace of candles. The curtains were still open, though the sky outside had darkened to a murky charcoal.

He looked round at her with an easy smile. "I'd lost track of the time."

"You've been longing for concentrated time with the manuscript." She didn't dare ask what secrets he might have unearthed. "Are you any closer to determining if it's genuine?"

"No, but I'd hazard a guess that the main hand that wrote the manuscript belongs to a man, and the second hand is a woman's." The fascination of the literary chase had eased the shadows round his eyes, but had not driven them away. "Tempting as it is to imagine Shakespeare writing out these pages with the Dark Lady making notes over his shoulder, I wonder if perhaps Eleanor Harleton's actor lover copied out an early draft of the play. There's quite a bit of underlining and some wording changes and notes on motivation in the Laertes scenes, and Crispin said that's the role he played in the first production."

"And you think the woman's hand belongs to Eleanor Harleton?"

"It makes sense. A lot of her notes involve the Laertes scenes as well. They wouldn't have been looking at this as a classic in the making, but a role that could advance his career." Malcolm flexed his fingers and stretched his back. "Of course that's all beside the point of the codes."

Suzanne drew a breath and willed it to stay even. "You've broken the code?" she asked.

"One at least. Crispin and I found a cache of coded papers Harleton had hidden. The code he was using is based on a scene between Hamlet and Laertes that isn't in the version of *Hamlet* we all know. It took a bit of time to sort that out, but once I found the scene it was easy enough to decode the papers."

"And?" There was no reason for her throat to be so dry. Nothing so far suggested Harleton had known anything about her.

"They seem to be from two different men. Most are brief notes containing dates and amounts."

"Payments from Harleton's handlers?" *Dear God, they could be from Raoul. Would Malcolm recognize his hand?*

"Perhaps. I don't recognize one of the hands, and the notes are so brief I'm not sure I could identify it even if it were someone I knew. But the other hand is Alistair's."

"You're sure?"

"Yes, because there's one note from him that's longer." Malcolm shifted papers to make room for her to perch on the edge of his desk. "It seems Alistair and Harleton were involved in more than spying together. I stopped in to see Aunt Frances on my way back from Richmond. Apparently Alistair and Harleton and some others—including at least some of the suspects in the Dunboyne leak—were part of a hellfire club."

Suzanne sat on the edge of the desk, as she had so often when helping him with a speech or a diplomatic memorandum. She remembered the first time, a few weeks into their marriage. She'd brought him a cup of coffee, cautious about intruding, and ended up staying far into the night and helping him draft a communiqué. Perhaps that was the moment their marriage had begun to change. "I thought the Hellfire Club ended a century ago."

"The original one." Malcolm leaned back in his chair. "It was founded by the Duke of Wharton in the heyday of gentlemen's clubs. Only this club admitted ladies."

"No wonder they had a reputation for sacrilege." She managed a smile that was almost genuine.

Malcolm grinned. "There were rumors they practiced black magic, but from what I've heard it was done in the spirit of mockery. Robert Walpole, who was Wharton's rival in Parliament, used the club against him. Walpole put forwards a bill against 'impieties' that was a thinly veiled reference to Wharton's club. Wharton lost his support in Parliament and the club disbanded. Rumor has it Wharton became a Freemason." Malcolm reached for the cup of coffee that stood amid the litter of papers. "But a number of other clubs sprang up, most notably one started by Francis Dashwood and Lord Sandwich, though it wasn't actually called a hellfire club until later. Rather more overtly bawdy than Wharton's. It was before Aunt Frances's time, but she says the caves at his estate at West Wycombe were legendary. The members addressed each other as 'brother' and the female guests were called 'nuns.' "

"So this club admitted women as members as well?"

"No." Malcolm caught hold of her right hand and laced his fingers through her own. "I gather the women at their gatherings were more likely to be hired for the evening."

"Not nearly so interesting." She forced herself not to clutch on to his hand as an anchor against the threatening storm. "That club ended as well?"

"Due to the members aging and a variety of scandals. But Dashwood's nephew started a club in his honor called the Phoenix Society. I believe it still exists."

"You haven't been invited to a gathering?" She summoned up another smile.

"Hardly." He looked up at her with an answering smile. From this angle, he looked particularly boyish. "You know my reputation. Or the lack of it."

She reached down and smoothed his thick brown hair back from his forehead. "From what I saw of your father it's not precisely surprising he'd have started such a club."

"No. Though the Shakespeare twist is something new. And Aunt Frances thought there might have been more to the club than met the eye. Apparently my mother suspected as much as well."

She heard the raw catch in his voice that came when he spoke of his mother. "Malcolm—" She tightened her grip on his hand. "You were a child. She'd hardly have told you about it."

"No, of course not." He carried her hand to his lips and released it. "It's just another reminder that I didn't really know either of them."

"Darling—Are you suggesting the club could have been a front for a spy ring?" It seemed best to confront the possibility head-on.

"It's hard enough to see one of these men as a French spy. It seems stretching belief to imagine all of them as such. But neither Aunt Frances nor my mother was given to idle fancy. And we do have Alistair and Harleton and perhaps whoever leaked the Dunboyne information connected to the club." He pulled a paper from the litter on his desk and held it out for her inspection. "Here's the plaintext of the longer note I decoded from Alistair to Harleton."

She studied the paper in the light of the candles.

> *I own the revelation of the Raven's identity holds particular dangers for me, but surely you realize that if I fall, you will almost certainly go down as well. We both have an interest in keeping that particular asset from British intelligence. Rather than circle round making pointless threats, I suggest we put our heads round the question of how to maintain the secrecy that has worked so well all these years. Whatever our past quarrels, we have mutual interests in common.*

"I haven't heard of the Raven before," he said. "I don't know if the Raven is the source of the Dunboyne leak, but I'm quite sure it's a code name for an agent."

Suzanne stared at her husband in the clean light of the wax tapers. The circle cast by the candlelight enclosed them in intimacy. A Mayfair couple at home in their jewel box of a house. But this simple piece of paper had increased the threat tenfold. She knew, but could not tell her husband, that the Raven was not the source of the Dunboyne leak. She had heard the name used more than once, though she had always deplored it as overly flowery and more worthy of a lending-library novel than the espionage game. Still it had stuck through the years in French intelligence circles. Better, Raoul had said, than using an actual name.

And Suzanne had to agree.

For the Raven referred to her.

CHAPTER 9

Harry Davenport slowed his horse to a walk along Rotten Row. The fashionable promenade in Hyde Park would be crowded with riders and open carriages at four o'clock on a spring day but was all but deserted at nine on a gray morning at the start of December. "Well, well. Who'd have thought the old man had so many surprises in him?"

Malcolm turned his head to look at his friend. Harry's face was even more strongly scored than usual with defensive lines of mockery. "Harry—"

"For God's sake, Malcolm." The sarcasm in Harry's voice cut as sharp as it had two years ago, before Waterloo. "You of all people should understand there's no sense in pretending to filial scruples when they don't exist. And Archibald Davenport wasn't even my father. Isn't even my father."

"He raised you."

"I was raised by a series of nurses, a collection of books, and my own imagination."

"Harry—" Malcolm glanced at the path ahead. The scattering of leaves on the gravel, the bare branches against the gray wash of sky. "I think perhaps the more detached one is from a person the harder it is to take such revelations."

"Spare me—"

"Because that's how it is for me with Alistair."

Harry's gaze fastened on Malcolm's face for a moment. "Sorry, old man."

"Thank you."

Harry turned and stared through the leafless tangle of branches. "Uncle Archibald never wanted children. He told me as much when he brought me home after the funeral. Bit odd for a man in his position, but there it is. Showed me my room and the library, said he wouldn't bother me if I didn't bother him. All things considered it worked out quite well for both of us. Save for the occasional dinner and a few trying occasions like the time he insisted on putting me up for membership at Brooks's, we scarcely saw each other. You should have seen the amazement on his face when I told him I was marrying Cordelia. I don't think he could imagine how a woman like that would look twice at me. Well, I couldn't imagine it, either." Harry's voice was steady, but Malcolm saw his gloved fingers tighten on the reins. "Not surprisingly, he was less than astonished when our relationship went sour. He did help me get my commission, I'll give him that. Probably because he was relieved to see me out of England. I was shocked to receive the occasional letter from him in the Peninsula. And he looks rather stunned to see me back in London now. Not to mention back with Cordelia." Harry was silent as their horses advanced a few more paces over the gravel-covered ground. "You'd do better asking Cordy for help. Uncle Archibald likes her better than me. But then she's prettier."

Malcolm studied his friend. Talking about his own feelings always felt like picking his way through a thicket. Trying to talk about such feelings with Harry was more like confronting the walls of a besieged city. "Harry—"

Harry let his horse, Claudius, lengthen his stride. "I'd be surprised to discover Archibald leaked the Dunboyne information or was an agent for the Irish or the French. I'd be surprised to discover he applied himself so much to anything. Though I can't say I know him well enough to really have an informed opinion. And you needn't worry I'd be devastated if it turned out he was the culprit. I think I expected rather less from him than you did from Alistair Rannoch."

"I never expected anything from Alistair Rannoch."

"No?" Harry's gaze turned lance sharp in that damnable way it sometimes did. "My mistake then. Now as to the other four suspects on your list—There I think I might actually be of help. Assuming you'll let me."

Malcolm grinned at his friend. "Thought you'd never ask."

"Good. Never thought I'd say it, but the scholarly life gets a bit quiet at times. Whom do you want to approach first?"

"It rather depends on whom we can find. But I was thinking of Cyrus. Apparently he's in the habit of sketching by the Serpentine most mornings. We may be able to catch him now."

"Sketching?" Harry shook his head. "Amazing the surprising sides one discovers to people in the course of an investigation. I was at Eton with his son if that's of any help. Can't say we were precisely mates. But then there are precious few about whom I could say that. Present company excepted."

Malcolm shot his friend a look. "I'm flattered."

"I never flatter, it's a waste of time. What have you done with the manuscript after the failed attack?"

"It's at Aunt Frances's now. Aline's going through it. But we're going to move it every day." Malcolm's fingers tightened on the reins. "We took an intolerable risk leaving it in the house with the children for as long as we did."

"Once whoever's after the manuscript saw that Simon hadn't given the original to the thieves, he'd assume you had it whether you did or not."

Malcolm forced his fingers to relax with a mental apology to his horse, Perdita. "You're annoyingly reasonable as always, Davenport. I thought I had things under control."

"And you did."

"Mostly. The damnable thing is I was more than passingly eager for the confrontation."

"No need to beat yourself up about that, you managed it as adroitly as usual."

"The man got away." Malcolm frowned at the trees ahead, seeing the greatcoated man swallowed up by the shadows of Seven Dials.

"But no harm came to Colin or Jessica or anyone in your household. First things first. You still have guards on the theatre?"

"And the Berkeley Square house and wherever the manuscript is. I may have been slow, but I learn my lessons." Malcolm watched a robin alight on one of the bare tree branches. "Harry—Have you heard of the Raven?"

"Let me guess. Another code name?" Harry steered Claudius round a branch that must have fallen in the wind last night. "One starts to think France's spymasters have a fondness for gothic novels. Or is this one English?"

"French apparently. I found a reference in a coded letter from Alistair to Harleton. Supposedly this Raven being exposed could cause problems for both of them."

"Do you think it's the Raven who was behind the Dunboyne betrayal?"

"Possibly. Not enough to go on yet." Malcolm gathered up the reins. "Let's see if we can find Cyrus."

Livia Davenport paused before the square plaque on Tower Green and stared at the list of those who had been executed there. "I don't see why they had to kill Lady Jane Grey. She didn't even want to be queen."

"She posed a threat." Cordelia was keeping a careful eye on fifteen-month-old Drusilla as she marched along the paving stones. "People might have rebelled in her name."

"Like Napoleon?" Colin looked up from tossing bread to the ravens.

"Very like Napoleon actually," Suzanne said, shifting Jessica on her hip.

"But Napoleon hasn't been executed," Colin said. "Even though a lot of people in France were. Like Marshal Ney." He scowled. Clearly he remembered how angry his parents had been over Ney's execution.

"Yes, they could have sent Lady Jane Grey to St. Helena or somewhere." Livia traced the inscription on the plaque. "It's not fair."

Cordelia smiled. "What would Daddy say?"

Livia looked up at her mother. " 'Life isn't fair,' " she said in a quite brilliant imitation of her father's acerbic tones. "I know. It doesn't mean I have to go along with it. Daddy would say that, too. It's not like she was a traitor or something." Livia frowned. "Not that I necessarily think traitors should have their heads cut off."

Colin tossed the last of the bread to an eager raven. "Which tower was Lady Jane locked up in?"

"I'm not sure." Suzanne looked at Cordelia, who also shook her head. "But perhaps that beefeater knows." She nodded at the guard across the courtyard.

"Come on." Colin tugged at Livia's arm.

Suzanne watched the children dash across the courtyard. If she focused on details like the weight of Jessica against her hip, the cool wind tugging at her bonnet ribbons with a promise of rain, the infectious glee of the children's laughter, she could pretend this was just another outing with her friend and their children and keep the recent revelations safely walled away inside her. She was good at walling things away after all. "A passion for history. Malcolm and Harry would be proud."

"They're so able to be happy in the moment," Cordelia said, studying the children as they peppered the beefeater with questions. "It's remarkable."

"A gift of childhood." Suzanne uncurled Jessica's fingers from a lock of her hair.

Drusilla had reached the end of the hedged walkway. Three months older than Jessica, she was much steadier on her feet. She stopped and looked at Cordelia in inquiry. "Back here, darling," Cordelia said.

After a moment's consideration, Drusilla moved back towards the adults. "It's so different now from how it was with Livia." Cordelia crouched down to Drusilla's level. "Then I felt I was making it up as I went along. Well, I still do, a bit. But it's different."

She glanced at Suzanne. "I didn't think I'd like being a mother, you know."

"Nor did I, precisely. That is, I didn't think I'd be very good at it, and I had no notion of how it would take over my life." Suzanne thought back to the girl she had been in Lisbon five years ago. That girl seemed like a different person, some sort of barely connected distant relative.

Cordelia caught Drusilla's hands as the little girl returned to her side. "I was afraid—We never really decided, you know. To have another one."

"It's hard to find the right moment." Suzanne smoothed Jessica's hair. Jessica, fresh from a nap, was in a snuggly mood, one arm hooked round Suzanne's neck.

"Quite." Cordelia's gaze was clear and candid. "Even under the best of circumstances. But it was different for me from how it was for you. I mean, there were added layers. Harry and I didn't talk about it. No, that's not quite true. Harry said it was entirely up to me. That's so like Harry. Some would say he doesn't have any delicacy or consideration, but the truth is he's painfully careful never to impose himself in any way." She took a few steps down the path in response to an insistent tug from Drusilla. "Part of me wanted to have another baby right away, the moment we were back together."

"I imagine a lot of people did after Waterloo."

"Yes, a way of grabbing on to life after so much death. You can see the results talking with other military families. But for me it was also a way to create a bond with Harry. To prove our mad reconciliation was real whatever the skeptics said."

"I can understand the impulse." Suzanne pulled her pearl earring from Jessica's exploring fingers and let Jessica take hold of one of the satin ribbons on her bonnet.

"And for the same reason I was terrified." Cordelia turned up the collar of Drusilla's pelisse as the wind picked up. "Because another child was one more person to be hurt if we couldn't—If I failed."

"I think Harry would say 'we.' "

"But it's always seemed more my failure." Cordelia swung

Drusilla up in her arms. Drusilla laughed with delight. "And then I decided anticipating failure was a poor foundation for happiness for any of us."

"Brave."

"I hope so." Cordelia kissed Drusilla's nose, then set her back down to explore. "I hope it wasn't selfish. I still can't quite believe—"

"That the life you live now is real?"

Cordelia nodded.

Suzanne swallowed because what Cordelia had described was so very like her own feelings in deciding to have a second child. Jessica turned her head and pointed as a raven squawked. How on earth, Suzanne wondered, had she ended up with a code name that was a type of bird associated with a place traitors were imprisoned?

Colin and Livia ran back across the courtyard. "She was in Number Five Tower Green. Over there, next to the Queen's House." Colin waved his hand towards the building.

"And her husband, Guildford Dudley, was in the Beauchamp Tower," Livia said. "You can see where he carved her name on the wall. Which is a bit odd when they only got married because their parents made them."

"Maybe they decided they liked each other anyway." Colin caught Livia's hand. "Let's climb the White Tower."

The injustice to Lady Jane momentarily forgot, Colin and Livia raced up the steep winding stairs of the castle's central keep. Cordelia and Suzanne stood in the cool stone of the entryway with the babies.

Cordelia released Drusilla so she could explore the steps and regarded Suzanne for a moment. "Do you want to talk about it?"

"It?" Jessica was wriggling and pushing against Suzanne's chest. Suzanne set her down beside Drusilla on the steps. "Da ba bo bo," Jessica announced as though she had just said something very important.

"Whatever you and Malcolm are investigating." Cordelia reached down to steady Drusilla. "I'm less clear on the details than I usually am when you embark on something, but I know something's in the wind. I understand if you don't want to talk about it. But I'm quite prepared to help if necessary."

"You're the best of friends, Cordy."

Cordelia flashed her a quick smile. "I'm a woman who loves her husband and children but could use a wider scope for her talents. Is it top secret?"

"Since when has that stopped us from appealing to you?" Suzanne watched her daughter grab the edge of the step and pull herself to a standing position with a crow of triumph, bouncing on her thin, black-stockinged legs.

"Is it something to do with the new version of *Hamlet* Simon Tanner is producing?"

Suzanne looked at her friend in surprise. "Did Simon tell you about it?" Simon and Cordelia were friendly, but Suzanne didn't think they'd seen each other recently without her.

"No, Caro did." Cordelia gave a wry smile.

Drusilla dropped down on the bottom step. Jessica plopped down beside her and stretched out a hand for Drusilla's face.

"Gentle." Suzanne bent down to pull Jessica's hand away. "Who told Caroline Lamb about the play?" she asked Cordelia.

"Caro made it her business to learn."

"Why—Because of Byron?"

"Precisely. I think she thinks the prospect of a lost Shakespeare play will intrigue him. And despite—or because of—all her denials to the contrary, Caro isn't the least bit over him. She asked me if I could get her into a rehearsal. I told Simon was very particular. I thought he'd prefer I said that than risk Caro causing a scene that could upstage even *Hamlet*."

"Very diplomatic." Suzanne watched Jessica and Drusilla, who were now waving their hands at each other and babbling back and forth.

Cordelia scanned her face. "So this does concern the *Hamlet* script?"

"In part. Someone attacked Simon when he was bringing it to our house two nights ago."

"Good God. They wanted the manuscript?"

"Or possibly something coded in the manuscript." Suzanne watched the girls clap their hands gleefully, then surveyed her friend. "Cordy, it may concern Harry's uncle."

Cordelia's eyes widened. "Archibald Davenport?"

"And Lord Bessborough."

"Good God." Cordelia put up a hand to the brim of her sapphire velvet hat. "One doesn't expect people one's known since one was a girl to be involved in anything cloak-and-dagger. Lord Bessborough was always just 'Caro's father' to me. And Mr. Davenport—" She touched Drusilla's hair, then glanced up the stairs from whence Livia's and Colin's shrieks emanated. "It would be woefully inaccurate to say he and Harry were ever anything approaching close. But he's the only family Harry has. Harry would laugh at the suggestion that he cares for his uncle. But then Harry often laughs at the things that matter to him most."

"Much like Malcolm with his father."

"Is Alistair Rannoch caught up in this as well?"

"I'm afraid so."

Cordelia watched Drusilla, who had found a raven's feather and was holding it out to Jessica. "I didn't see Mr. Rannoch and Malcolm together much. But I remember a party at Carfax Court when the Rannochs were staying there. One of Alistair and Lady Arabella's rare appearances together. I was about seven, so Malcolm must have been ten or so. I'll never forget the look on his face when the nursery party came in. Alistair could cut Malcolm with his gaze. And draw blood."

"I'm sorry." Suzanne looked at Jessica and clapped her hands. Jessica grinned and clapped back. "We've pulled you into something personal again."

Cordelia gave one of her brilliant, defiant grins. "I asked for it. And at least this time it doesn't involve one of my ex-lovers. I take it you want my help talking to them? Mr. Davenport and Lord Bessborough?"

"If possible."

"It's odd, they neither of them seem particularly political, for all Lord Bessborough is part of the Devonshire House set. Mr. Davenport is a Whig M.P., but he seems to spend most of his time going to parties at Carlton House. And ogling ladies. Which are much the same thing. Though I must say—"

"Yes?" Jessica took three careful steps over to Suzanne and grabbed her knees. Suzanne bent down to scoop her up.

Cordelia watched as Drusilla ran to the doorway. "I scarcely saw Mr. Davenport that first year Harry and I were married. The year we lived together. When Harry did mention him, his words were unusually dismissive, even for Harry. But after Harry and I—After he left." Cordelia swallowed. She had, she freely admitted, married Harry on the rebound from the loss of her childhood love, desperate less for a husband than for an establishment and a position in society. A year into her marriage, her old love had returned from the Peninsula and they had tumbled into an affair, though he too was married. Harry had discovered it, with disastrous consequences.

"When you were apart," Suzanne said.

Cordelia tucked a strand of hair beneath her bonnet. "I don't know why I should be shy to mention it. It's nothing you don't know after all. After Harry left, Mr. Davenport came to see me. Which was rather a surprise, as I was a distinct social pariah at that point. Even my own family looked at me askance. I fear I was rather inclined to pull the covers over my head and feel sorry for myself."

"You had reason." Suzanne set Jessica on the ground. Jessica toddled after Drusilla on stiff, careful legs, arms held out for balance. After four steps she dropped down and crawled the rest of the way.

"Well, yes, but it wasn't doing me any good. You'd have rallied much sooner. Not outside, darling." Cordelia turned Drusilla round before she could go out of the door and then crouched down to turn Jessica round as well. "Then Mr. Davenport arrived on my doorstep—earlier than I'd have expected him to be abroad—and said he might not know me well, but he'd seen enough of me to know I had too much bottom to be overset by a bunch of scandalmongers. When I said Harry might not thank him for taking an interest in me, he said he knew better than to get between a husband and wife, but I was still his niece. Then he insisted I put on my prettiest bonnet and go for a drive with him in Hyde Park. And of course since I was with him, people could not but stop and talk to us." She bent down to take a leaf from Drusilla's fingers and gave the baby her comb instead. "It saved me from receiving the cut direct. The next week he invited me to dine. The Duke of York and Lady Melbourne were among his guests. After that, though I lost my vouchers to Almack's and wasn't invited by the highest sticklers, I was no longer a social outcast." She cast a glance at Suzanne. "It sounds funny to talk about being an outcast after Waterloo and everything we've been through, but such things can matter. More than you think. More than they should."

"There's nothing odd about not wanting to be alone." Suzanne watched Jessica scoot back to her, one leg tucked under her, one hand held aloft. Jessica pointed a finger up at the ceiling. "Ma," she announced as though she'd made a great discovery.

"I appreciate life's complexities more now," Cordelia said. "But at the time such things mattered to me more than I care to admit. And it made life seem less cold. When Livia was born Mr. Davenport insisted on giving her christening breakfast." Cordelia touched Drusilla's hair and cast a quick glance up the stairs. "Though he must have known I couldn't be certain who her father was." She forced a smile to her lips, the smile with which Suzanne had seen her face down gossip. "I can help you talk to him. He's fond of the girls, I think. And more inclined to talk to me than to Harry. And I can talk to Caro about Lord Bessborough."

"You're a good friend, Cordy," Suzanne said, as Colin's and Livia's footsteps pounded back down the stairs.

Cordelia gave a crooked smile. "To own the truth, I've been growing rather nostalgic for our Continental adventures."

CHAPTER 10

"Cordelia, my dear." Archibald Davenport came forwards with a smile that lit his face and kissed Cordelia's cheek. He was a tall man, with strongly marked features. His hair was lightly powdered and his coat was cut in the style of the last century, which reminded Suzanne of Prince Talleyrand. As did the shrewdness in Davenport's blue eyes. "You're growing." He ruffled Drusilla's pale hair. Drusilla, in her mother's arms, grinned with delight. Davenport bent over Livia. "And you're turning into a young lady. As stylish as your mama."

"Thank you, Uncle Archie." Livia smiled and lifted her face for his kiss. Davenport swept a courtly bow and kissed her cheek.

"You know Mrs. Rannoch." Cordelia extended a hand. "And her children, Colin and Jessica."

"Quite a nursery invasion," Davenport said. But he smiled as he said it. "I believe there are some cakes in the kitchen. Let me ring and see what my staff can muster."

Livia giggled, obviously well at ease with her great-uncle. Davenport bent down, a little stiffly, and scooped her into his arms.

"We've been to the Tower," Livia informed her great-uncle. "Did you know Guildford Dudley scratched Lady Jane Grey's name on the wall of his cell?"

"Did he? Surprisingly romantic."

"Yes, especially since their parents made them get married. She was only eleven years older than I am. I'm lucky I have Mummy and Daddy for parents."

Davenport smiled at Cordelia over Livia's head, then looked back at his great-niece. "So you are, my dear, so you are."

A quarter hour later the children were settled round the fireplace with cakes and lemonade while Davenport poured glasses of a pale gold Tokay for Cordelia and Suzanne. "Now to business. Tiresome word that." He settled back in his wing-back chair, glass held negligently between two fingers. "I take it you are here because of some investigation you are engaged in with your husband, Mrs. Rannoch?"

"Uncle Archie." Cordelia opened her eyes very wide. "I didn't say anything about an investigation."

"Of course not, my dear. You're much too discreet." Davenport took a sip of wine. "But I could hardly fail to be aware of the swath the charming Mrs. Rannoch has cut through society in recent years. And contrary to the general opinion, I was not solely aware of her lovely person. Not that you aren't thoroughly noteworthy on that account, Mrs. Rannoch." Davenport gave Suzanne a smile that was an expert blend of the fatherly and the flirtatious.

"Thank you, Mr. Davenport. You're too kind."

Davenport lifted his glass to her and took a sip. "But though few would credit it, I do have a certain amount of political awareness. Enough to notice when spies are being ferreted out."

Suzanne regarded Harry Davenport's uncle over the rim of her wineglass. "Why don't you tell us what you know, Mr. Davenport?"

"What I know? Oh, nothing." Davenport leaned forwards and reached for the decanter. "What I infer? Why, that you and your husband are looking into the deaths of my friends Harleton and Alistair Rannoch and the source of the Dunboyne affair."

"How fascinating," Suzanne said with a bright smile. "What makes you think that?"

"My dear Mrs. Rannoch." Davenport topped off her glass. "I do have connections at Whitehall. Which doesn't only mean that I drink port with the prince regent, though I confess that is a large part of how I spend my time. But my interests are broader. As are my connections."

For the first time, Davenport put Suzanne in mind of his nephew. It was something about the bright hardness in his eyes and the mockery and challenge in the curve of his mouth. "Perhaps you should tell us what you surmise, Mr. Davenport."

"You think the source of the Dunboyne leak was at a certain dinner party, a dinner party more notable after the fact than at the time. Though I must say any dinner party at which someone is challenged to a duel is memorable, if perhaps in poor taste."

"Challenged to a duel?" Cordelia had been letting Suzanne do the talking, but this roused her to speech.

"Yes. In rather poor taste, as I said. I have the greatest admiration for the many attributes of your sex, but I hope you will forgive me for saying that one really shouldn't let a woman sully an evening of good port and billiards."

"Uncle Archie." Cordelia cast a glance at the children, who were building a fort out of the green silk sofa cushions, then leaned towards her uncle, hands in her lap. "Who challenged whom to a duel?"

"Harleton." Davenport took a sip of Tokay. "Never could hold his drink particularly well. And apparently also couldn't hold on to his women. And didn't have the sense to see that if one can't hold on to a woman, the best way to avoid embarrassment is to at least pretend that one doesn't care."

Suzanne watched her son put a steadying hand at Jessica's waist as she pulled herself to her feet, gripping the edge of the pillowless couch. "Whom did Lord Harleton challenge?"

Davenport set down his glass. "You're a woman of the world, Mrs. Rannoch. I don't expect you'll be shocked. Your husband's father. Alistair Rannoch."

Suzanne sat back in her chair. Always exciting when the puzzle pieces shifted, showing new patterns that might bring one closer to the solution to the mystery. But that excitement held a frisson of fear when the people involved were people close to one. And particularly close to one's husband.

"Lord Harleton and Alistair Rannoch were involved with the same woman?" She cast a glance at the children, but Colin was helping Drusilla run and Livia was clapping with Jessica and their cheerful squeals showed they weren't listening. Even if they'd been able to make sense of it, considering she herself was baffled by the affairs of the Glenister House set.

"Apparently." Davenport took a sip of wine. "Hardly unusual in our set." He too flicked a glance at the children. "I'm sure you're both too much women of the world to be shocked. In general, as I said, one either doesn't care or at least has the wit to pretend one doesn't. But of course it isn't always that tidy. One can have no concept of fidelity oneself and still feel possessive towards a lover. As my own past experience tells me."

"Who was the lady Harleton and Alistair quarreled over?" Cordelia asked.

"I don't know. I have a fair ear for gossip, but I hadn't heard anything. The first I knew of it was before dinner. We were about to sit down and suddenly I heard the sound of a fist smashing into a jaw. Harleton had drawn Alistair's cork. I must say Alistair was remarkably restrained. Got to his feet with a bloody nose, pulled out his handkerchief, and said perhaps he and Harleton could talk in private. Harleton said something along the lines of"—Davenport cast another glance at the children—" 'you upstart bastard, never could keep your hands off what wasn't yours.' Then he said"—Davenport frowned—" 'You'd steal it, too, if you could get your hands on it.' "

" 'It'?" Suzanne repeated. "Not 'her'?"

"No, he definitely said 'it.' " Davenport shifted in his chair, crossing his legs. "And the odd thing is that's when Alistair looked angry. More than that—alarmed, I'd say. He said, 'If you can't keep your women satisfied—,' but I'd swear he said it to provoke Harleton, to turn the conversation back to the woman in question instead of to whatever else Harleton had been referring to. And it worked. Harleton pulled off his evening gloves and slapped Alistair in the face. Alistair said he was delighted to meet him and strode from the room. Harleton followed shortly."

"That was why they both left early," Suzanne said.

"Quite." Davenport settled back in his chair. "Their idiocy kept them both from being suspected of the Dunboyne leak."

"What happened at the duel?" Cordelia asked.

"I don't know. Thankfully I wasn't called upon to be the second for either man."

"Did you ever hear anything more about the quarrel?" Suzanne asked. "About the lady or about the other matter?"

"No." Davenport frowned. "The odd thing is, the next time I saw Alistair and Harleton was at White's. They were in the morning room drinking port together as though nothing had occurred. I actually stared for a moment to make sure it was really them. Later I passed Harleton on the stairs and commented I was glad they'd patched things up. Harleton said—" Davenport frowned.

"What?" Cordelia asked.

Davenport took a sip of wine. " 'Best keep your enemies close.' "

Trees overhung the twisting waters of the Serpentine in a sodden tangle of bare branches with touches of lingering russet and gilt. The sky was washed gray. Few were abroad on this drizzly morning, but a man sat on a bench by the water's edge, wrapped in a greatcoat, a sketch pad in his lap, a charcoal in his hand. Malcolm sensed Hugo Cyrus was aware of his and Harry's approach from the moment they emerged from the tree line, but the man continued sketching and didn't look up until Malcolm and Harry dismounted and led their horses up beside the bench.

"Rannoch." Hugo Cyrus's pale blue gaze skimmed over Malcolm. "And Davenport."

"Good day, sir," Harry said. "Is Hugh well?"

"I think so. Haven't heard from him for a few weeks. My son keeps to the country and has a surprising affinity for farming. But we needn't waste time on niceties. I've been wondering when you'd seek me out."

Malcolm brushed a hand over the damp bench and dropped down beside him. "What made you think we'd seek you out?"

Cyrus gave an unexpected grin. "Come now, Rannoch. I have an ear to the ground. You've been talking to Carfax. You've been to Smytheton's beloved Tavistock. This *Hamlet* manuscript came from Harleton." His gaze shifted over the water. "When I left the house today I actually gave even odds on whether you'd seek me out. This seemed as good a place as any to talk."

"You come here often?"

"I like the view."

Malcolm glanced down at the sketch pad. It showed a half-finished charcoal of the river and trees, dark bold strokes, impressionistic and strong. "I didn't realize you drew."

"Not what one expects of a military man? Had to find something to fill the empty hours on campaign." He glanced at Harry. "I imagine you understand, Davenport."

"The need for distraction on campaign?" Harry murmured a command to the horses and dropped down beside Malcolm. "Quite. Also the need to create something of beauty in the face of numbing destruction."

"You're more poetic than I, Davenport, but perhaps there's an element of that as well." Cyrus squinted at the sky. "Most artists prefer to draw in the sunlight, but I've always liked the shadows. So much interesting hidden in them." He smiled at Malcolm and Harry as though the irony was quite lost on him, though Malcolm was sure it was not.

Malcolm turned on the bench to face Cyrus. "What do you know?"

Cyrus twisted the charcoal between his fingers. "I may not have your level of erudition, but I have enough wit to decipher that you're looking into the Dunboyne business."

Cyrus was an astute man, but it was quick for him to have arrived at this intelligence. "Have you discussed it with the others who were at the dinner party?" Malcolm asked.

"Would you believe me whatever I said?"

"I'd be interested in what you say regardless."

Cyrus gave a wintry smile and set the charcoal down in the sketch box beside him. "Smytheton came to see me last night. Said you and your lovely wife had been at the theatre, asking questions about the manuscript, and that it could lead to Harleton and then to Dunboyne."

"Why should the manuscript and Lord Harleton necessarily lead to the Dunboyne leak?" Harry asked.

"Harleton was at the dinner party where the Dunboyne information was uncovered."

"But he left before the information was taken," Malcolm said. "As did my father. And there's no reason any of it should be connected to the *Hamlet* manuscript."

Cyrus shrugged. "Smytheton always was excitable." He rubbed the charcoal from his fingers. "Couldn't figure out if he was warning me or seeking reassurance. Or both."

"Were you able to reassure him?"

Cyrus's smile deepened. "I told him if he had as little to do with the whole business as I did, he had nothing to worry about." He turned, stretching one arm along the back of the bench, as though laying claim to it. "But of course from your perspective, one of us must have had a great deal to do with it."

"It?"

"Don't play games, Rannoch, you're not pretty enough to pull off the coyness. The leak. The disaster at Dunboyne that took my brother's life." Cyrus's fingers tightened on the back of the bench. He'd missed a smudge of charcoal on the knuckle of his third finger.

"You must have wondered who was behind it," Malcolm said.

"Of course I wondered." Cyrus's voice rippled across the water. "Even without Carfax asking questions. Bungling drives me mad, but I own losing Thomas put it in a whole different key."

"I can understand that. I have a brother myself." Malcolm felt the weight of Edgar's wounded body when he lifted him in his arms after Waterloo. "And?"

Cyrus flexed his fingers against the wood. "I've never been the sort to claim my friends are saints. I've seen enough in war to know what the most seemingly honorable men can be capable of. But one still doesn't like to think—" He shook his head. "If there's one line one doesn't cross it's betraying one's fellows."

"Do you include my father and Harleton in that?"

"Your father was—" Cyrus broke off, the explanation dangling in the air like condensed breath.

"An outsider."

"No sense in wrapping it up in clean linen. At least he was an outsider when we met at university. By the time of the Dunboyne business, he'd come into his money and married your mother."

"But he was still an outsider."

"He was the Duke of Strathdon's son-in-law."

"And an outsider even to my grandfather."

"His relationship to your mother may have had something to do with that." Cyrus tapped his fingers on the back of the bench. "We were none of us lacking in funds at the time. At least I didn't think so." He cast a glance at Harry. "I always suspected your uncle's gambling debts were worse than he let on, despite his generous income. It takes deep play and lavish living to keep up with Prinny's set."

"He certainly lived lavishly," Harry said. "I can't claim to be privy to his finances. For what it's worth, he managed my inheritance rather well."

"Your uncle's no fool. Whatever he may let on. Always seemed proud of you."

Harry gave a short laugh. "I believe you were the one who said to spare the niceties, sir. Not to mention the out-and-out lies."

Cyrus stretched his legs out. "I don't waste time on niceties or lies, my boy. Certainly not the polite variety. I remember your uncle showing off an essay you'd written at Eton in the coffee room at White's."

The flash of surprise in Harry's eyes was quickly masked. "He must have been in his cups."

"No more so than usual. Have to admit I never felt the impulse to wave Hugh's essays round over the claret and beefsteak. But then I don't recall any of Hugh's efforts being particularly worth showing off."

"Tell us about the Elsinore League," Malcolm said.

He expected Cyrus to dismiss the club as undergraduate foolery. Instead, Cyrus's eyes narrowed. "What do you know?"

"My father and Harleton began it at university. You were all members. It was a sort of hellfire club."

Cyrus gave a short laugh. "Nothing like bawdy secrets to mask other secrets."

"What sorts of secrets?"

"You don't know? Interesting." Cyrus's gaze turned to the rippling water of the Serpentine again. "It was before the Revolution when all this started. Young men slipping over to the Continent for the Grand Tour. No one making too much of a fuss about what they brought with them when they returned."

"The Elsinore League were smugglers?" Harry asked.

A slow smile crossed Cyrus's face. "I think they saw themselves more as clever businessmen. Or agents who worked for themselves."

"Crates of brandy?" Malcolm said.

"And champagne. And works of art. Acquired by a variety of means. They had the art of looting down long before Bonaparte began to move across the Continent."

Malcolm recalled the Rubens portrait and Cellini bronze in Harleton's study. Crispin had said his father hadn't been an art collector. But Alistair had. An image of Alistair's study flashed into Malcolm's mind. Another Cellini bronze that served as a paperweight. The Titian portrait and Canaletto landscape that hung on the walls. The Venetian decanter and glasses. A world of art treasures that were now Malcolm's own. "For themselves?"

"For themselves and to sell. Your father had a taste for expensive works of art without the funds to support collecting, which I think is what started it. But they quickly realized it was lucrative. And a dangerous game. Dangerous games aren't only seductive in the bedchamber." Cyrus stretched his booted feet out in front of him. "I confess to having one or two pieces in my possession from that time. Off-the-record."

"Did it stop when we went to war with France?" Harry asked.

"On the contrary. The danger increased and so did the seduction. What could appeal to bored young aristocrats more than slipping into Revolutionary and Directoire Paris? A dangerous world where marriage had become passé and women went about without their petticoats. Smytheton and Dewhurst practically lived in Paris in the nineties, and we all visited. I'll own to some pleasant memories of my own from those days."

"Did it go beyond smuggling?"

Cyrus's eyes narrowed. "You mean did they smuggle information? Dewhurst and Smytheton were Royalist agents."

"Smytheton was?" Malcolm said, picturing the Tavistock's patron expounding on Shakespeare.

"Carfax didn't tell you?" Cyrus asked. "I daresay he had his reasons."

"Smytheton's an unassuming sort," Harry said. "Those can make for the best agents."

"And he got involved with that pretty actress of his. Pity when all that ended. Jennifer had some very lovely friends."

"Jennifer Mansfield?" Malcolm saw the auburn-haired actress who had prevailed upon Smytheton to take her out for lemonade during the break in the rehearsal. "I didn't realize she was French. Or if I did know I'd forgot."

"I daresay she didn't broadcast it, as we were at war with France when she came here," Cyrus said. "Took an English name. But when I first saw her across the footlights at the Comédie-Française, she was Geneviève Manet. Smytheton brought her here in the mid-nineties."

"And the others?" Malcolm asked, filing away this information about Smytheton and Jennifer Mansfield.

"You mean were any of them British agents?"

"That's one possibility."

"French agents?" Cyrus's brows rose. "Not that I know of. That would be . . . interesting." He drummed his fingers on the bench, seemingly more intrigued than shocked.

"Have you ever heard of the Raven?" Malcolm asked.

"Not that I recall." Cyrus's blue gaze betrayed neither recognition nor alarm. But then Cyrus betrayed little. "Is it a novel?"

"It appears to be a code name. I found mentions in my father's and Harleton's letters."

Cyrus snorted. "Very likely a name they gave to one of their women." His gaze sharpened. "Or do you think your father and Harleton were dealing in information?"

"One of their friends dealt in information by '98."

"So they did." Cyrus's gaze hardened. "Thomas had just been promoted to captain. I can still see him the day he found out." His gaze followed a leaf as it drifted to the water. "Of course I didn't know then that he'd volunteered for military intelligence. I'd have tried to talk him out of it for any number of reasons. Ireland was an ugly business."

"Did my father ever talk about it?" Malcolm asked.

"Ireland? Of course. Your grandfather had estates there. Alistair was worried about them. Alistair didn't have much use for rabble anywhere." Cyrus stirred a pile of fallen leaves with the toe of his boot. "I remember drinking with Alistair at White's when we got the news that Raoul O'Roarke had escaped to the Continent after the Uprising. Alistair swore." Cyrus cast a sideways glance at Malcolm. "O'Roarke was friendly with your family, wasn't he?"

"Yes, but more with my mother and grandfather than with Alistair." Malcolm kept his gaze on Cyrus's face, though he could feel Harry watching him.

Cyrus nodded. "Alistair had mentioned O'Roarke before. With venom verging on contempt."

"Why?" Harry asked.

"Because as I said, Alistair had no use for the rabble. And to his mind O'Roarke was the worst sort of rabble-rouser. So it wasn't so much the swearing when he heard of O'Roarke's escape that was unusual as the fact that his sangfroid was quite shattered. He snapped the stem of his glass and spilled claret all over the carpet. While the waiter was mopping it up, Alistair apologized to me and said he wasn't much of a believer in justice, but just once it would be nice to see the guilty punished."

"I remember my parents' quarreling during the Uprising," Malcolm said. "Not that it was unusual for them to quarrel. But in this case Alistair accused my mother of being a traitor to her class." It made Alistair the most improbable French agent. And perhaps therefore the best.

"Were any of the men at that dinner party sympathetic to the United Irish cause?" Harry asked.

"I wouldn't have said so," Cyrus returned. "But then, as you must know better than anyone, if they were good agents, they wouldn't have appeared to be sympathetic to the cause for which they were working."

"Quite." Malcolm studied Cyrus. He was shocked by how open the other man was being. He suspected Cyrus would only be so if he was hiding something. "When did you know your brother was part of the Dunboyne mission?"

Cyrus's mouth twisted. "When it failed and I got news of his death." He shot a look at Malcolm. "I know that makes me a suspect. Though I'd hardly have had to go through Dewhurst's things to learn military secrets." He shook his head. "It was a bloody mess. I'm not one to sympathize with revolutionaries, but I'll be the first to admit our own side didn't manage things well, either. I lost friends, including one or two among the United Irishmen. And then in the midst of all that I had to tell Anne about Thomas."

"Anne?" Harry asked.

"His fiancée. They'd been childhood sweethearts and had got engaged that summer. I can still see Anne's face when I told her—wanted to be the one to break the news and rode all night to her parents' house. She's always been pale—that sort of fair Irish complexion that's so dramatic with dark hair—but I'd swear every ounce of blood drained from her skin. I caught her as she fainted. For several months I wasn't sure she'd ever recover, emotionally if not physically."

"Did she ever marry?" Malcolm asked.

"Oh yes." Cyrus flicked a leaf from the bench. "She married me. The next summer."

Malcolm heard Harry draw in his breath. His own gaze was fixed on Cyrus.

Cyrus picked up another leaf and twirled it between his fingers. "Hugh's mother had died two years before. I could say the tragedy of losing Thomas brought Anne and me together. And it did in a way. But the truth is I'd loved Anne since were children. I only offered for my first wife because I knew I hadn't a prayer with Anne, for all she was still in the schoolroom. She didn't look twice at me until Thomas was gone. Even now I'm quite sure of the choice she'd make were Thomas to walk back through the door." He shook his head. "Not that I'm complaining. I have what I wanted. Which I suppose gives me a motive to have leaked the information to get rid of my brother. Save that I didn't know Thomas would be involved."

"So you say," Malcolm replied, holding Cyrus with his gaze.

"Oh, quite." Cyrus returned his gaze. "But then all of this comes down to what we each say, doesn't it? Until you find proof."

The smell of books always brought Suzanne comfort. Even at incongruous times, such as when, disguised as a parlormaid, she had slipped into the library of a Spanish commander in order to retrieve a coded document, full-well aware that the commander could walk into the room at any moment. Compared to that, today was child's play. All she was doing was stepping over the threshold of Hookham's Lending Library. Save that the knowledge that her husband was trying to unmask her reverberated through her.

She nodded to the bespectacled man behind the circulating desk. He inclined his head in response. She was a frequent visitor here, usually for purely literary reasons. She made her way past the aisle of novels she often browsed, past travel books, to a shadowed corner slightly mustier than the others, filled with volumes of classics. Harry Davenport would approve. And it wasn't as though she never read Latin or Greek.

She picked up a volume of Suetonius and turned the pages, though she couldn't force herself to go so far as actually to take in the words.

A whiff of sandalwood shaving soap alerted her to Raoul's presence before his shadow fell over the page.

"How bad is it?" he asked.

She looked up from the Julio-Claudian emperors and met the concern in his gray eyes. "Am I that transparent?"

"No, but you asked for another meeting after only a day."

She closed the book over her hand, hoping it would control the trembling of her fingers. "Do you remember when I went after the code in General Ribero's library?"

"I still get chills at the memory."

"You never said."

"That would hardly have helped the situation."

"When he came into the room, I pretended I was a maid caught borrowing a book. He was amused. And impressed that I could read."

"You still got the code."

"While I let him steal a kiss." She pulled her hand free of the book. "More was at stake than now. And less in some ways."

His gaze skimmed over her face. "What is it, *querida?*"

"Malcolm went to Harleton's Richmond villa yesterday. He found correspondence between Harleton and Alistair Rannoch mentioning the Raven."

Raoul bit back his curse before he uttered a sound, but she could feel the unvoiced words reverberating through the air. "How the devil did they find out?"

"Alistair referred to the Raven's identity creating problems for him. I think he knew it was his son's wife."

"But Malcolm doesn't know that."

"No, for the moment Malcolm thinks it may refer to the mole who betrayed the Dunboyne business. But—"

Raoul's fingers closed on her wrist. "Malcolm is brilliant, *querida.* But even brilliant agents can't uncover every secret."

"You're saying I can outwit him?" She could hear the tension in her own voice beneath the low murmurs and discreet rustles from the rest of the library.

"I'd be hard-pressed to bet on either of you. Save that you have one advantage in this over your husband."

"Your help?"

"Without question. But what I was thinking is that you know precisely how high the stakes are."

CHAPTER 11

The tapers on the dressing table wavered at the opening of the door. Suzanne's spirits lifted, as they always did, as her husband's image appeared in the looking glass. And then the memory of risk pulled taut beneath her corset laces and ruched bodice.

"You look lovely." He closed the door and leaned against the panels. "Though that dress has a distinct air of Yuletide about it. Must we begin celebrating the holidays already?"

"It's December now. And last year you admitted you enjoyed them." She fastened her second garnet earring, chosen to go with her gown of claret *gros de Naples*. The color and the gold cording at the waist did give it a holiday air.

"Last year I was basking in the glow of new parenthood and enjoying Colin's glee. This year we're back in the bosom of my family."

"You like your family."

"Some of them." He advanced into the room and shrugged out of his coat. "What is it tonight?"

"You're impossible." Warmth shot through her at the simple triviality of the conversation. "Who kept track of your engagements before you had a wife?"

"Addison." He tossed his day coat over a chairback and began to loosen his cravat. "But we were in Lisbon in the midst of a war. It was simpler."

"Tonight is Emily Cowper's rout."

He tossed the crumpled cravat after the coat. "Good, that should give me a chance to corner Dewhurst." He perched on the edge of the chair and regarded her. "Not an unproductive day so far. How about you?"

"The same." She swung round on the dressing table bench to face him. Their eyes met with the familiar challenge of a shared investigation. "You first."

"Hugo Cyrus claims the Elsinore League smuggled works of art out of the Continent. Which fits with what I saw in Harleton's study. And with Alistair's art collection." His gaze rested for a moment on the Boucher oil on the wall over her dressing table.

As with the Berkeley Square house, Suzanne knew Malcolm's conflicted feelings about his father had warred with his genuine admiration for Alistair's collection. "Even if they were acquired illicitly, you not keeping them would hardly have rectified the situation, darling."

"Quite," Malcolm said, though his tone betrayed the lingering bad taste in his mouth. "Cyrus also admitted that his wife had been betrothed to his brother Thomas. And that he'd long loved her, though she didn't look twice at him until after Thomas was killed at Dunboyne."

"Interesting. He didn't need to admit that last."

"No. It was confessed with a touch of bitterness that hinted at genuine guilt. But it could have been a clever feint. I suspect Hugo Cyrus is a very clever man." Malcolm began to undo his waistcoat buttons. "He also mentioned Alistair's distaste for the United Irishmen. Hardly a revelation, though it makes it even harder for me to reconcile Alistair as a French agent."

"Perhaps his distaste over the Irish rebellion was part of his cover."

"Perhaps. According to Cyrus, Alistair snapped a glass in two when he heard Raoul O'Roarke had escaped to the Continent after the Uprising."

"Of course," she said, keeping her voice steady. "If O'Roarke was friendly with your mother and grandfather, he'd have known your father."

Malcolm nodded. "I knew Alistair despised O'Roarke's politics, but I didn't realize how deep it went." A shadow flickered in his eyes, but whatever it was, he wasn't ready to discuss it with her. As she had trained herself to do, she bit back the questions that rose to her lips.

"In any case, we know it wasn't Alistair who was behind the Dunboyne leak," she said.

"Cyrus said none of the men at the dinner party were particularly sympathetic to the United Irishmen as far as he knew." His gaze flickered to her. "Harry went with me and was quite a help with Cyrus. He claimed—protesting a bit too much perhaps—not to be concerned by his uncle's possible role in the affair. And he said Cordelia would be better at talking to his uncle than he was."

"Cordy said much the same. She took me to visit Archibald Davenport. Along with the children, of whom Mr. Davenport is obviously quite fond. Cordy says he was very supportive of her after the scandal. He evidently cares for her."

"And?" Malcolm's gaze brightened with the scent of information.

"Apparently your father and Lord Harleton left the dinner party early because Lord Harleton challenged your father to a duel."

Malcolm let out a whistle. "Good work, Suzette. Over?"

"A lady with whom they had both formed a liaison. At least ostensibly. Mr. Davenport thought there might be more behind it. Apparently Harleton made some comment about Alistair taking 'it,' too, if he had the chance. In light of what Cyrus said, I wonder if the 'it' could be a piece of smuggled art?"

"Perhaps. Did Davenport know the lady's identity?"

"He claimed not to, and I don't think he was lying."

Malcolm frowned at his shirt cuff as he unfastened it. "Interesting. It could mean nothing. But anything that connects Alistair and Harleton is of interest. I'll talk to Aunt Frances again. God knows they didn't like each other, but they moved in the same set, and she's a keen observer." He grimaced.

"You hate poking into personal secrets," Suzanne said. It was a statement, not a question.

"With a passion."

"Difficult to separate the personal from the political in this world."

"And one often has to ferret out the secrets before one can tell the difference." He pulled his shirt over his head and went to take his shaving kit from atop the chest of drawers. "Time to get to work."

"Malcolm." David Mallinson touched Malcolm's arm as Malcolm emerged from the card room at Emily Cowper's. "I've been wanting to thank you."

Malcolm grinned at his friend. It seemed an age since they had spoken, though it had only been a few days. David's calm good sense was just the leavening Malcolm needed. "You're the most generous of friends. For what?"

"The men posted at the Tavistock." David scanned Malcolm's face. "How worried should I be?"

"They're likely to come after the manuscript again. I'd like to say we'll stop them, but of course I can't be sure. They may come to Berkeley Square instead of the Tavistock, though the manuscript isn't at either." It was in fact at his aunt Frances's, where Aline could work on it, though the plan was to move it every day.

"Good God," David said. "The children—"

"Trust me, we're prepared. And it would be a mistake to try to persuade Simon to stop the production."

David grimaced. "How did you know I was considering that?"

"Because it's what I would do if Suzette were the one in danger. And it would equally be a mistake."

David passed a hand over his face. "I know it. And it's not that I'd want him to. That is—A part of me would like nothing better than to pack up for Paris for a month."

"You and me both."

"You? You have an investigation again. You've come alive."

Malcolm gave a reluctant smile. "Perhaps."

David's gaze darted over his face. "I won't ask you what my father told you—"

"David—"

"No, it's all right, I know he tells you things he doesn't tell me. I don't envy you. It's difficult enough being his son, but he's even more ruthless as a spymaster than as a father. But is there any way he can turn this against Simon?"

Malcolm had been giving that possibility honest consideration from the moment Carfax had arrived on his doorstep two nights before. "I don't think so. But you can be sure I'll warn you if things change."

David nodded. "I need to find Simon. He's trying to charm Lord Thanet into giving the Tavistock money, and if I leave him alone too long he'll get too clever for his own good. Are you looking for Suzanne?"

"For Dewhurst actually. Have you seen him?"

"He ducked into the library."

Malcolm half-expected Dewhurst to be closeted in a secret meeting, but instead he found the earl alone with a copy of *Debrett's*. Dewhurst's ruddy face darkened to purple as Malcolm came into the room. "What the devil are you doing here?"

Malcolm dropped into a wing-back chair beside the one Dewhurst occupied. "Haven't you heard about my habit of escaping into the library at entertainments?"

Dewhurst's scowl deepened. "I hear you sought Carfax out at White's. Are we safe from you nowhere?"

Malcolm leaned back in the chair. "I thought if I called upon you at home you'd refuse me entrance."

"Damn right I would." Dewhurst slammed his book closed. "It's only respect for Emily that has me still sitting here."

"Precisely why this is where I sought you out."

Dewhurst snatched up the glass on the table beside him and took a long swallow of cognac, then set it down. "If Rupert sent you, I have no desire to listen to an emissary."

Was there a touch of hope beneath Dewhurst's acerbic tone? "Why would Rupert send me?"

"Because my son isn't speaking to me. Thanks to you."

Despicable as Dewhurst's actions had been, it was hard not to feel a twinge of sympathy for a father who had lost his son. "Lord Dewhurst—You credit me with too much influence if you think anything I did or said is responsible for your son's actions. Rupert is his own man."

Dewhurst reached for the glass of brandy. "If it weren't for you, Rupert would never have learned—never got such a pack of lies into his head. If it weren't for you—"

"Bertrand Laclos would still be presumed dead?"

Dewhurst's fingers tightened round his glass as though he wished it were Malcolm's throat. "In my judgment, Wellington and Castlereagh made a grave error forgiving Laclos for his crimes and permitting him to return to England. You can't tell me you didn't have a hand in that."

"If you mean I had a hand in Bertrand's name being cleared of wrongful accusations of treason, I'm happy to say I did."

"Arrogant puppy."

"Me or Bertrand?"

"Both of you." Dewhurst clunked down the glass. "What do you want, Malcolm?"

"It's odd, I've known you since boyhood, but I didn't realize you and my father were friends."

Dewhurst gave a short laugh. "We weren't, particularly."

"You were in a club together."

Dewhurst's gaze narrowed. Then he raised his glass and took a drink of brandy. "It was scarcely the sort of thing we'd discuss with children. Not uncommon for young men to form such societies at university."

"I understand the Elsinore League is still active."

"Perhaps. I haven't been involved for some time."

"You were at a dinner with a number of the members nineteen years ago."

Dewhurst stared at him for a moment. Then he clunked his glass down again, sloshing brandy onto the tabletop. "Out with it, Malcolm. What do you want?"

"Tell me what happened at that dinner."

"You know damned well what happened or you wouldn't be asking these questions. Papers were leaked that led to the regrettable blunder that was the Dunboyne affair. From my dispatch box, to my eternal shame. If you're asking about it now, new evidence must have come to light."

"We think we may be able to figure out who gave out the information."

" 'We'?" Dewhurst drew his handkerchief across his mouth. "Carfax sent you. I'd have thought he'd have had the wit to realize you aren't the best emissary. If there's one man in London I'm not inclined to talk to—"

"Sir—" Malcolm sat back and studied Dewhurst. "I think you'd rather talk to me than Carfax."

Dewhurst picked up his glass as though he wished it were a dagger. "Carfax told you to use the events of two years ago to get me to talk, didn't he?"

Malcolm regarded Dewhurst in the light of the tapers burning on the mahogany table between them. "You know Carfax."

Dewhurst tossed down a swallow of brandy. "And are you going to do so?"

"If I threatened you, would you believe me?"

Dewhurst looked up and regarded Malcolm with what might almost have been a hint of appreciation. "An hour ago, I'd have said you didn't have the guts. Now I'm not so sure. You're tougher than I thought, Rannoch. And God knows I already knew you could stab a man in the back." He leaned back in his chair and reached for his glass. "What do you want to know?"

"Did you see anything out of the ordinary that night?"

Dewhurst turned the glass between his fingers. "Do you know about the duel?"

"Father and Harleton, yes. Ostensibly over a lady."

"Ostensibly. Quite. I always thought there was more to it as well. Seemed to come out of nowhere. I did my best to make myself scarce. No desire to get caught up in their quarrel."

"You didn't wonder about it?"

"Not a great deal. Neither your father nor Harleton held a great deal of interest for me." Dewhurst took a sip of brandy. "Of course once we knew about the Dunboyne information being leaked it overshadowed everything else that happened that night. Carfax insisted on talking to all of us. I didn't know whether to be flattered or offended that Carfax thought the leak might have come from me."

Malcolm regarded him without speaking.

Dewhurst took a sip of cognac. "Given that you accused me of framing Bertrand Laclos as a traitor, I imagine you'd find a certain poetic justice in me being the culprit. But even granted I were entirely lacking in morality—which seems to be your opinion—why would I have risked my fortune and my family honor helping the Irish rabble?"

It was, Malcolm had to admit, a point, especially given the lengths Dewhurst had gone to perpetuate the family line. "The allure of risk? The challenge? Loyalty to your friends among the United Irishmen?"

"Any friends I had who joined the United Irishmen ceased to be my friends by doing so. I saw all too clearly in France that the Jacobins and their successors would bring about the end of our way of life. Unlike others who tend to romanticize them."

"My father would have agreed with you."

"Alistair was not without sense. You don't see that your sympathies are playing with fire, Malcolm. You never have. For God's sake, that rabble killed your wife's parents."

"Actually, French soldiers killed my wife's parents." French soldiers misdirected by his own hand, something for which he would never forgive himself. "But Suzanne is not consumed by revenge. Nor does she want to turn the clock back to before the Revolution." In fact, Suzanne's humanity when it came to viewing the Revolution and revolutionaries was one of the things he loved about her.

"She's a woman. They tend to be soft on these things."

"Have you met my wife?"

"Capable as Mrs. Rannoch is, she's still a woman. My daughter-in-law Gabrielle tends to take too soft a view as well." Dewhurst took another sip of brandy. "If Carfax is fool enough to put this investigation in your hands, don't waste time on me. Instead wonder about Horace Smytheton and what that French actress mistress of his got up to before she left France—and after. Not to mention how quickly he took in Manon Caret. That whole theatre is a nest of sedition. Oh, that's right. Forgot you were friends with Tanner. More and more nonsensical that Carfax trusted you with this."

"Smytheton got Jennifer Mansfield out of France?"

"Geneviève Manet. When she reigned over the Comédie-Française as Caret did later. Only La Belle Manet was working for the opposite side. At least supposedly."

Malcolm sorted through this barrage of new information. "Jennifer Mansfield—Geneviève Manet—was a Royalist agent?"

"Carfax didn't tell you? Odd when he told you so much. Perhaps he wanted to see how far you'd get on your own." Dewhurst got to his feet and moved across the room to a cabinet that held a set of decanters. "That's how Smytheton met her. He was working with the Royalists in the nineties. Along with me. I wouldn't precisely say we were friends, but we were colleagues. He has more wit than he lets on. Much like Harleton." Dewhurst unstopped a decanter and refilled his glass. "You know about Harleton working for the French?"

"Yes."

"We didn't then, of course. Smytheton and I were in and out of France, helping get Royalists out and funneling gold and advice to the counterrevolutionaries. Smytheton had a house in Paris, made a show of being part of society, while I did more of the reconnaissance."

"And Geneviève Manet?"

"Was giving information to the Royalists. We had a plan to try to break the king and Marie Antoinette out of prison." Dewhurst crossed back to his chair and dropped into it. "Didn't come to anything in the end, but Smytheton liaisoned with Manet. In more ways than one. Which fit with his cover, of course. English aristo besotted with a French actress. Then one night he came hammering on the door of my lodgings and said we had to get Geneviève out of Paris. The French were on to her."

"And he needed your help?"

Dewhurst smiled. "I was the one with the operational knowledge."

"So you helped them?"

"Oh yes. I had no reason at the time not to think of Geneviève as an ally."

"At the time?"

Dewhurst frowned into his glass. "I began to hear rumors not long before she fled to England. One of my contacts was exposed, a man only Smytheton and I should have known about. I wondered—" He took a swallow of brandy. "It would be a clever way to hide an agent in enemy territory. Get them to rescue her because she was supposedly spying for the other side."

"Did you talk to Smytheton?"

Dewhurst snorted. "He'd have called me out. The man truly was besotted, that was no pose. And then . . ." He hesitated, as though measuring how much to reveal to Malcolm. "We were sending a shipment of arms to the Royalist rebels in the Vendée. On a smugglers' boat. We'd used them before and everything had gone like clockwork. This time, French troops were waiting for us. I was on the boat myself. I barely escaped, had to hide out for a fortnight and pay a fisherman to sail me back to England. When we investigated, the leak was put down to Smytheton having let a letter go astray."

"But you think Geneviève took it?"

Dewhurst wiped a drop of brandy from the side of his glass. "Actually, I began to wonder if Smytheton wasn't Geneviève's dupe but her accomplice."

"You think Smytheton was a French spy?"

"I wondered. I wasn't the only one who did. I went to some efforts to look for proof, but couldn't find anything. In the end Smytheton retired from the business."

"Meaning he was forced out?"

"I think he realized it was prudent to focus on the theatre. Whatever he and Geneviève may have done, the rest of us judged they couldn't cause any problems now. Or so we thought. And then they took in La Caret."

"About whom nothing has ever been proved, either."

"Quite." Dewhurst gave a smile of satisfaction. "It's Carfax's problem, not mine, thank God. But I'd look into what's going on at the Tavistock."

"What about the others?"

"Bessborough and Cyrus and Davenport? They weren't British agents. As to whether any of them worked for the French, if I knew I'd tell you."

Malcolm sat back in his chair. "Cyrus says you were smuggling works of art out of the Continent, starting before the Revolution."

Dewhurst raised his brows. "Quick to admit his sins, our Cyrus."

"So you're admitting it?"

Dewhurst leaned back in his chair. "I'll admit the others were interested in filling their libraries and salons with old masters. And in the risk and adventure that went with it. I had more important things to do in Paris at the time."

"So you weren't involved in the smuggling?"

"Not seriously. I may have a piece or two."

"Apparently, the night of the dinner when they were quarreling over the lady Harleton asked my father what he had done with 'it.' Could that have been a work of art?"

"Possibly." Dewhurst reached for his glass. "But I know no specifics."

"Alistair went to Argyllshire to stay with Lord Glenister for a fortnight not long before he died. Was that a gathering of the Elsinore League?"

Dewhurst gave a short laugh. "No."

"You're very sure. Were you there yourself?"

"I was at my box in Perthshire. I stopped to see Glenister for a few days. Your father wasn't there."

Malcolm learned forwards. "You're certain? He didn't arrive later?"

"Glenister told me your father had asked him to cover for him."

"Where was Alistair?"

"Glenister claimed not to know, and Alistair certainly wasn't in the habit of confiding in me."

Malcolm studied Dewhurst. Much as he disliked him, he could not deny the other man had been at the heart of British intelligence for a quarter century. "Have you heard of the Raven?"

"Good God." Dewhurst set his glass down with a clatter. "Don't tell me the Raven is connected to this?"

"Why don't you tell me what you know about the Raven?"

Dewhurst leaned back in his chair. "According to a French foreign ministry clerk who was one of Fouché's agents and sold information to me, the Raven was a French agent under long-term deep cover."

"In England?"

"In the Peninsula."

"A British soldier?"

"Or someone attached to the army in some way. Fouché wasn't sure of the Raven's exact identity at the time and apparently was quite eager to uncover it."

Fouché, who had been minister of police for much for Napoleon's reign, had had his pulse on nearly everything in the empire. "Whom did the Raven report to?"

"I don't know. You should know better than anyone how byzantine intelligence networks can grow."

"You must have been curious."

"Of course. I mentioned it to Carfax, and we did more than a bit of investigating, but we were never able to uncover anything. As elusive as whoever was behind the Dunboyne leak."

"It didn't occur to you that they might be one and the same?"

"Not unless my source was misinformed. According to him the Raven was under deep cover, but only went back to 1810 or so. What makes you think the Raven has anything to do with the Dunboyne affair?"

Malcolm hesitated. "I found a mention in papers of Harleton's. Implying the Raven being exposed could hurt him."

Dewhurst tapped his fingers on the leather of the chair arm. "Interesting. Carfax was monitoring Harleton, but it didn't lead to the Raven. Unless Carfax didn't tell me of course. Quite a coup if you could unmask the Raven. Assuming you actually would."

"What's that supposed to mean?"

Dewhurst set down his glass. "Just that when it comes to rabble—in Ireland or France or here at home—you've always seemed to have trouble determining which side you're on." He leaned back in his chair. "Have you talked to Archibald Davenport?"

"Suzanne has."

Dewhurst gave a short laugh. "Never will understand your marriage. But if you're looking into Alistair and the tensions within our group at that dinner party, you might want to have a word with Davenport yourself. I doubt he'd have revealed this to your wife."

"Why?"

"Because it isn't the sort of thing gentlemen talk about to ladies." Dewhurst let his shoulders sink an inch deeper into the leather of the chair and reached for his glass. "Archibald Davenport was your mother's lover."

CHAPTER 12

"The Cowpers' marriage is a marvel," Cordelia murmured to Suzanne, looking across Emily Cowper's ballroom to where Emily, resplendent in peacock crêpe over white satin, her dark hair dressed in loose ringlets, stood between her husband and Lord Palmerston. "There's Emily conversing with her husband and her lover as though none of them had a care in the world."

"You don't envy her, do you?" Suzanne asked.

"Heavens no. I've had enough of juggling lovers—it's quite exhausting, and I shouldn't at all like it if Harry were a complacent husband. But I can't help but admire Emily's savoir faire."

Suzanne watched as Lady Cowper linked one white-gloved hand through her husband's arm and the other through Palmerston's. "And yet Lady Cowper and Lord Palmerston can't go about openly as a couple the way Dorothée did with Clam-Martinitz."

"Well, no, this is England. It's all very well for everyone to know one has a lover, but it can't be publicly acknowledged. On the other hand, I can't imagine Peter Cowper challenging Palmerston to a duel as Edmond Talleyrand did with Clam-Martinitz."

Emily Cowper touched her husband on the shoulder with her fan, smiled at Palmerston, and moved off on a third gentleman's arm. "I'm more impressed with the fact that she and Palmerston manage to maintain their affair despite the fact that it doesn't appear to be exclusive," Suzanne said.

"Yes, though I wouldn't say Palmerston is quite as complacent as Peter Cowper." Cordelia gestured with her fan towards Palmerston as he slouched along the edge of the dance floor, gaze fixed on Emily as she began to waltz with the third gentleman.

"To think I gave up a lost Shakespeare manuscript to squeeze through crowds in overheated rooms." Aline slipped between two young men gesturing enthusiastically with their champagne glasses to join Suzanne and Cordelia. "Suzanne, you quite ruined me. Before I lived with you in Vienna, I avoided parties whenever I could."

Suzanne smiled at her husband's cousin. "You realized parties could be interesting."

"Well, yes, but it takes a lot to compete with Elsinore. I must say, codes aside, the manuscript is quite fascinating."

"Do you think it's really by Shakespeare?" Cordelia asked.

"Not my area of expertise. I suppose I could construct a model to analyze word structure in Shakespeare's plays and compare it to the manuscript, but that would take time, and Malcolm has me looking for codes."

"I thought he found the code," Cordelia said.

"The one Lord Harleton was using. We'd need more documents to decode to learn more from that and just decoding's not that interesting. But Malcolm wants me to see if there's something else encoded in the manuscript, which is a much more intriguing problem."

"And?" Suzanne asked. The gleam in Aline's dark eyes reminded her of how she felt herself with a fresh mystery to solve.

"Nothing so far, but it's slow going. I have to look at the pages under glass because Claudia keeps wanting to touch them." Aline turned her head as Simon materialized out of the crowd to join them. "I can't wait to see what you do with the production. I keep getting caught up in the story and forgetting to analyze the manuscript."

Simon gave a wry smile. "We're at the stage of rehearsals where

I wonder at what I've bit off." He smiled at Suzanne and Cordelia. "Thank God for friendly faces."

"Did David drag you here?" Cordelia asked.

Simon twitched a fold of his immaculate neckcloth. "David knows better than to drag me places. I'm supposed to charm some possible funders of the Tavistock."

"That should be easy. You're very charming."

"But not necessarily on cue."

"No more trouble?" Suzanne asked him.

"None today. And the minders Malcolm sent blend in quite well as stagehands. David insisted on staying at the theatre all day as well, though I told him in the event of any violence we'd probably only get in the way of Malcolm's agents."

"Mr. Tanner." Lady Caroline Lamb swept up to them in a stir of feathery brown ringlets, gauzy white skirts, and *cocquelicot* ribbons. "I can't thank you enough for letting me attend the rehearsal this afternoon. I shall treasure the memory."

Simon's smile was genuinely kind rather than that of a playwright to a potential patron. He appreciated Caroline's eccentricities, Suzanne knew. And she suspected he also pitied her. "You're very welcome, Lady Caroline."

Caroline looked up at him with wide eyes. "I do hope I may attend again."

"We'd be delighted to have you."

"Simon. Ladies." David joined them.

"Isn't it exciting about the manuscript, Lord Worsley?" Caroline said.

"Quite," David returned, though Suzanne saw the concern at the back of his gaze. "Simon, Lord Thanet's asking for you. You said to keep an eye out for him."

"I did, didn't I?" Simon gave an ironic grin. "Forgive me, ladies. Duty calls."

Lord John Russell arrived to claim Aline for a promised dance. Caroline turned to Suzanne and Cordelia, her face alight with childlike delight. "Isn't it splendid? About the new *Hamlet*. I think I like it better than the usual version. Ophelia is much more interesting. I don't know why he changed it. Shakespeare, I mean. It must be authentic, don't you think?"

"I'm not a judge." Cordelia opened her reticule and took out a silver-backed mirror. "But it's certainly impressive."

"I want to attend more rehearsals so I can form a proper opinion."

Cordelia wiped a smudge of lip rouge from the corner of her mouth. "So you can write to Byron."

Caroline tucked a ringlet into her pearl bandeau. "I might mention it. He'd be interested, and we should be beyond petty disagreements now."

Cordelia snorted.

Caroline leaned a careless hand against the gilded molding. "I have the theatre in my blood. Sheridan was my mother's lover, you know. Dear Mama. She did pick interesting men. If only he'd given the script to her. Imagine, I might have been involved in bringing it to light."

"Sheridan?" Cordelia returned the mirror to her crystal-beaded reticule. "What makes you think he knew about the manuscript?"

"No, Lord Harleton." Caroline adjusted one of the knots of ribbon on her sleeves.

"Why should he—" Cordelia snapped her reticule closed. "Good God, I didn't realize."

"About Lord Harleton and my mother?" Caroline tugged the ribbon smooth. "Oh yes. Apparently it was quite intense for a time. Of course, I only learned about it after the fact. It was when I was quite young. Before Granville."

Granville Leveson-Gower, a handsome diplomat some dozen years younger than Lady Bessborough, had been her lover for over a decade. By the time Suzanne had met him in Paris, the affair had been long in the past and Granville was happily married to his former mistress's niece. It was, as Simon had once remarked, hard to create probable fiction when life was so fantastical.

Cordelia shot a look at Suzanne. Caroline had inadvertently given them an opening. Suzanne inclined her head.

"Caro—" Cordelia fingered the sapphire shot silk of her gown. "Was your father friendly with Harleton?"

"My father? I know the stories about the Devonshire House set, but I wouldn't say my father was *friendly* towards any of my mother's lovers."

"This might have been before," Suzanne said. "It seems your father was in a sort of club with Lord Harleton and Malcolm's father and some others."

"A club? Why should that matter?" Lady Caroline Lamb's wide dark eyes went wider. "Oh, good God, is this one of your and Malcolm's investigations? Why should you be interested in my father? He's never done anything remotely interesting."

"I sometimes wonder," Cordelia said with a smile, "how Colin and Livia and Dru and Jessica will talk about us and Malcolm and Harry when they're grown."

"Oh, that's different." Caroline waved a dismissive white-gloved hand. "You really have done interesting things. They'll recognize that. My father really is well . . . dull. He couldn't even keep my mother's interest much beyond the wedding."

"Sometimes—" Suzanne bit back what she'd been going to say.

Caroline studied her with a surprisingly sharp gaze. "Suzanne, are you going to suggest my father's utter lack of anything approaching romance or adventure might have all been a pose? It sounds like a novel, but I can't believe it. I *know* him."

Romance and adventure scarcely made for a good spy. In fact, the best agents often seemed—or even were—rather dull. But Suzanne could hardly say so to Caroline. Instead she said, "It's simply that your father may have relevant information. Information he may not even realize is important."

Caroline's delicate brows drew together. "I don't know about my father and Harleton. I don't recall seeing them together, and one would think Harleton would have had reason to avoid my father, though Papa never said anything about him much one way or another. But my father and Alistair Rannoch didn't like each other."

"Not surprising given what I know of Alistair Rannoch," Suzanne said. "Did your father tell you he disliked Mr. Rannoch?"

"Oh no. Papa hardly confided in me."

The waltz came to an end. Emily Cowper moved towards the windows and was quickly besieged by a quartet of admirers. Lord

Palmerston stood on the edge of the group, glowering. "Emily is just as bad as I am," Caroline said, studying her sister-in-law. "She just manages not to create scenes. And then she turns round and lectures me."

"Perhaps she should give you lessons instead," Cordelia murmured.

"Stuff. As if I'd take lessons from her."

"Precisely." Cordelia touched Caroline's arm. "Caro. What made you think your father didn't like Alistair Rannoch?"

"Oh, that." Caroline twisted her gaze away from Emily and her admirers. "It was late one night after one of Mama and Papa's parties. I sat up on the stairs watching the guests arrive, picking my favorite dress—the way we used to do at Chatsworth or your parents' house, Cordy. And even after my nurse got me back to my room, I couldn't sleep. I kept imagining all the people dancing and drinking champagne—it all seemed so much more glamorous in those days than later when we could actually go to parties ourselves."

"Yes, somehow in one's imaginings the gentlemen don't tread on one's flounce or reek of tobacco, the rooms don't smell of sweat, and the champagne never goes flat," Cordelia said. "And then? Did you overhear something from your room?"

"No, I sneaked downstairs when the party was over. I wanted to see if I could find any cakes left out before the servants finished tidying up. I was in the small salon. I confess I swallowed a leftover glass of champagne. I thought it tasted ghastly, but of course it was warm and flat. And then I heard voices from the antechamber next door—the door had been left ajar. It was my father's voice, and he was angry. At first I thought he was yelling at me. Then I realized he was talking to someone else entirely."

"Alistair Rannoch?" Suzanne asked.

"Mr. Rannoch. I'm sure of it. He has—he had—quite a distinctive voice." Caroline's eyes clouded at the memory of events not properly understood in childhood. "Papa was saying, 'You can't force me to do it.' And Mr. Rannoch replied, 'Need I remind you how much you owe me.' And then something about, 'It's little enough to ask.' Then Papa really seemed to storm about, and I think he might have thrown something. He said, 'It's monstrous.'"

And Mr. Rannoch said—" Caroline frowned. "Something about, 'It's the way the game is played.' Then he must have left. I think Papa threw something else. Then I heard the door slam. I waited the longest time until I heard the servants stirring, and I sneaked back up to my bed." She shook her head. "I lay awake the rest of the night trying to make sense of it. I didn't understand in the least, but somehow I sensed it was something it would be dangerous to talk about to anyone. Even you, Cordy." She darted a quick glance at her friend. "I know you say I overdramatize things, and I daresay I do, but—"

"No," Cordelia said, "this sounds dramatic enough."

Caroline's brows drew together. "I haven't thought of it in years. The truth is, Papa and his doings never interested me much. I got caught up in my own affairs, as one does when one grows up, and more or less forgot about it. Except for every so often when I'd take it out and worry it in my head as a dog does with a bone." She pleated a gauzy muslin fold of her skirt. "What on earth do you think it was about?" she asked, childlike concern breaking through her pose of worldly wisdom.

"I don't know," Suzanne said.

Caro's gaze darted over her face. "Ought I to have told someone sooner?"

"You couldn't have known whom to tell. And I doubt your not telling anyone caused problems." Suzanne squeezed Caro's thin hand. "But I'm glad you told us now."

"You won't—that is, I've never been particularly close to Papa, but he *is* my father."

In Caroline's breathy voice, Suzanne could hear echoes of Malcolm's and Crispin's responses to the revelations about their fathers. "It will be best for everyone to learn the truth," she said. Even as she spoke, she was aware of how very hollow her words sounded.

"Harry." Malcolm touched his friend on the shoulder. Harry was on the edge of the ballroom, arms folded with casual unconcern. "Is your uncle here tonight?"

"I think I caught a glimpse of him earlier." Harry shifted his shoulders against the paneling.

"You haven't spoken?" Malcolm asked. Dewhurst's revelation about Malcolm's mother and Archibald Davenport pressed behind Malcolm's eyes, a sharper surprise than it should have been, given what he knew about his mother's affairs.

"Cordy already found out everything she could from him."

"You might have reasons other than the investigation for talking to him."

Harry raised a brow. "Would you have sought Alistair out at a ball?"

"Alistair wouldn't have sought me out. But we did converse in public from time to time."

Harry shrugged. "My uncle was always rather distant. I remember once he came to Eton for speech day—"

"Your uncle came to Eton for speech day?" Malcolm said.

"Yes. Every year I was there as I recall. Used to take me to a pub in the village afterwards."

"I suppose there are different degrees of distance. Alistair never showed his face at Harrow on speech day. And my mother was absent as much as she was present."

Harry regarded Malcolm for a moment. "Put that way, I suppose my uncle could have paid a bit less attention to me. Especially since he didn't ask to be saddled with me. Not that I think either of us has any desire to live in the other's pocket. At a hazard, I'd try the card room if you're looking for Uncle Archibald." He hesitated. "Do you want my help talking to him? Not that I think I'd be of much use." His gaze drifted over Malcolm's face, with perhaps a glint of keener interest than he was willing to own to.

Malcolm paused, knowing he couldn't control what Harry would read in the pause. "Think I can manage this on my own, old man. But I appreciate the offer."

"Malcolm." Archibald Davenport looked up from his game of whist. "You look as though you've come to seek me out."

"If I could have a moment when you're done with your game, sir."

"No need for that." Davenport tossed down his cards on the green baize. "You've saved me from dipping even deeper." He pushed back his chair. "Gentlemen. Duty calls."

His friends responded with wry grimaces and some good-natured quips. Davenport returned the quips, reached for his walking stick, and jerked his head towards a door to the adjoining antechamber.

"I'm happy to talk to you, Malcolm, though I must say I quite liked it when you sent your charming wife to speak with me."

"I don't think Suzette would think much of the idea that I sent her anywhere." Malcolm pulled the door to. "But given the information I've just discovered, I thought it was best if I had a conversation with you myself."

"What information?" Davenport lowered himself into an armchair covered in a pale green damask that matched the wall hangings.

Malcolm leaned against the closed door and studied the other man in the light of the brace of candles. Perhaps it was a trick of the flickering light that gave Davenport's face a harder cast. "That you were my mother's lover."

Davenport went still for a fraction of a second. "Who told you that?"

"Dewhurst."

"That sounds like Dewhurst. He has no care for a lady's reputation."

"I agree. Though in this case, I think he was right to tell me. Given the implications about what it may have meant for your relationship with Alistair Rannoch."

"My dear boy." Davenport settled back in the chair. "Far be it from me to cast aspersions on anyone's parents. But surely you don't believe your father had any illusions about your mother's fidelity."

"That doesn't necessarily mean he was sanguine about it." Malcolm swallowed, aware of a tightness in his chest. "When did the affair take place?"

Davenport met his gaze, his own surprisingly gentle. "A decade after you were born. The spring and summer of '98."

Malcolm released his breath. He hadn't really thought it. He was fairly sure he knew who his biological father was. Still—

"She was a damned fine woman," Davenport said. "I think she meant more to me than I did to her, though in truth the affair didn't last long. You're old enough to know people can take these things lightly without it casting aspersions on those involved."

"So you were lovers at the time the Dunboyne information disappeared?"

"The affair ended shortly after."

"Alistair and Harleton fought a duel over a lady that night."

"A lady with whom they were both involved. I don't know her name. It wasn't your mother. By the time I knew her, Arabella claimed Alistair had no interest in whom she took to her bed."

"Did Alistair know about your affair?"

"I'm not sure. To own the truth, I preferred to give as little thought to Alistair as possible. And given the way he treated Arabella, it was hardly any of his business."

"Alistair never confronted you about it?"

Davenport crossed his legs and regarded the diamond buckle on his shoe. "My dear boy, are you asking if I killed your father?"

Malcolm advanced into the room and dropped into a chair, gaze trained on Davenport. "You think Alistair was murdered?"

"I didn't until you began asking questions about him and Harleton and the Dunboyne business. Then his and Harleton's deaths began to look a bit too coincidental. But even if Alistair had confronted me for cuckolding him—which he did not—my affair with Arabella would have given Alistair a motive to get rid of me, not the other way round."

"Unless you resented him for his treatment of Arabella."

"Resented him? I bloody well wanted to plant him a facer much of the time. In fact, now I think of it killing him wouldn't have been such a bad idea." Davenport smoothed a frilled cuff over his fingers. "Pity it never occurred to me."

CHAPTER 13

Malcolm stepped from the anteroom in which he had spoken with Archibald Davenport, his mother's face hanging in his memory, sharp as a pen-and-ink drawing. Even when she looked right at one, there had always been something elusive in her gaze. A familiar figure caught his eye across the passage, just moving off from a discussion with Lord John Russell. Malcolm went still. *How damnably ironic.* And yet though Raoul O'Roarke might not precisely be the person Malcolm was in the mood to face at present, O'Roarke's perspective on the United Irish Uprising was just what Malcolm needed. This was no time to start letting personal feelings interfere with the investigation.

O'Roarke turned, caught Malcolm's eye, then moved forwards after a hesitation that was so fractional Malcolm couldn't be sure he hadn't imagined it. "Rannoch. Your young friend Russell's just been talking about you with hero worship in his eyes."

Malcolm felt the wry twist in his own smile. "Johnny Russell is going to make a brilliant politician. But he's still young enough to believe change is only a few well-strategized votes away."

"He's not so very much younger than you." There was nothing patronizing in O'Roarke's tone. He'd never talked down, even when Malcolm was a boy of six grappling with concepts he could barely understand.

"But he wasn't in the Peninsula. Or at Waterloo or in Paris afterwards."

"True. And he never was an Intelligence Agent."

"That too."

O'Roarke met Malcolm's gaze for a moment. Working with the *guerrilleros* in Spain, he'd more or less been an Intelligence Agent himself. "But perhaps young Russell has the right of it. Perhaps one has to believe change is only a well-strategized vote round the corner in order to keep going."

"Is that what you did in Ireland?" Malcolm asked.

O'Roarke's gaze slid to the side. Malcolm caught a flash of the look he'd seen in the other man's eyes since boyhood when they discussed Ireland. A mixture of regret, anger, and something else that might have been longing. "I was hardly naïve at the time of the United Irish Uprising. I'd lived through the Revolution and faced the guillotine. But I don't think I'd have survived those months if I hadn't believed we had a real shot at winning."

Malcolm scanned O'Roarke's face. He'd always been direct with Malcolm. Malcolm owed him the same. "Carfax has me looking into something that's raised questions about the leaked information about Dunboyne."

O'Roarke's eyes widened, then narrowed. "My God. I should have known we hadn't heard the last of that."

"It was a disastrous blunder that cost the lives of British soldiers."

"And that almost certainly saved my own."

Malcolm studied his childhood friend. He wasn't used to thinking of O'Roarke as being on the opposite side. "I didn't realize you were there."

"I'd been in Wexford overseeing a guerrilla operation. I got to Dunboyne just a few days before the British attack."

"The United Irishmen had already been warned of it?"

O'Roarke hesitated a moment. "No. I received the warning the day after I arrived in Dunboyne."

Malcolm's gaze locked on O'Roarke's own. His childhood mentor and friend, the man who had helped them save Paul St. Gilles, had become an opponent. "Even if you knew whom the leak came from, I don't suppose you'd tell me."

O'Roarke's mouth lifted in a faint smile. "I don't suppose I would. But as it happens I don't know."

It was what Malcolm would have expected O'Roarke to say.

There was even a chance the other man was telling the truth.

Malcolm closed the door of the night nursery on the sleeping Colin. "Apparently Jennifer Mansfield—or rather, Geneviève Manet—was a British agent along with Smytheton and Dewhurst."

Suzanne looked up from settling Jessica at her breast. Her feet ached in their satin slippers from hours on the dance floor and the tenderness in her breasts told her it was time to nurse. But more than that, her mind ached from the strain of the evening. "Smytheton's personality is the perfect cover for an agent."

"Quite." Malcolm shrugged out of his coat. While he undressed, he relayed Dewhurst's account of Smytheton's work as an agent, Geneviève's involvement, their escape to England, and the suspicion that had fallen on both of them.

Suzanne shifted her arm beneath Jessica's kicking legs. "Carfax held a lot back."

"Not unusual for Carfax." Malcolm wrapped his burgundy silk dressing gown round him.

"So we go to the Tavistock tomorrow? Simon mentioned there's a rehearsal in the afternoon, and I don't think Sir Horace has missed one yet."

Malcolm nodded. "I'll call on Aunt Frances in the morning. Or as early in the day as I can count on her being out of bed. I want to ask her if she has any idea where Alistair might have been when he claimed to have been at Glenister's. As well as about the duel. And . . ." He hesitated a moment. "Folly to be squeamish about it. Apparently Archibald Davenport was my mother's lover at the time of the Dunboyne leak."

"Good God." Suzanne scanned her husband's face. "That is, I don't suppose it's surprising given the circles they moved in, but—"

"It's one more connection among the players. Almost too coincidental. And yet it doesn't give Davenport a motive to have leaked the Dunboyne information. And though Davenport clearly didn't think much of Alistair and went so far as to say it wouldn't have been a bad idea to have killed him, it doesn't make a lot of sense that he actually did. Especially so long after the affair."

Jessica was wriggling, gaze caught by the light of the tapers on the dressing table. Suzanne coaxed the baby's mouth back to her breast. "Apparently Caro Lamb has been attending rehearsals. Cordy and I talked to her tonight."

Malcolm dropped down on the edge of the bed. "About her father?"

"Not surprisingly, she doesn't know anything about the Elsinore League. But Harleton was her mother's lover for a time."

Malcolm let out a whistle. "Not necessarily surprising, either. But again almost too coincidental. Quite a web of connections."

"The web gets even thicker. Caro once overheard her father and your father quarreling." While Jessica squirmed in her lap, Suzanne repeated Lady Caroline's account of the exchange she'd overheard between Bessborough and Alistair Rannoch.

Malcolm listened in frowning silence. "My father was blackmailing Bessborough? Good God. This gets more and more byzantine."

"Do you remember anything about your father and Bessborough?" Suzanne asked.

Malcolm frowned in an effort of memory. "I remember the Bessboroughs at house parties at Dunmykel. At receptions here on the rare occasions I was in London. My parents were on the fringe of the Devonshire House set, for all Alistair's politics were resolutely Tory. But I have no particular memories of my father and Bessborough." He paused for a moment. "This fits with my father being a French agent and blackmailing Bessborough into stealing secrets for him."

"But Bessborough wasn't in the government. He's a Whig, and not even at the center of Whig politics."

Malcolm pushed himself to his feet and dug his fingers into his hair. "He's connected to powerful people. Lady Bessborough may have been the Prince of Wales's mistress. If Bessborough took the Dunboyne information, it's even possible Alistair blackmailed him into doing so. Though when I think of Bessborough's position on Ireland—Perhaps—" He shook his head. "We need more data."

Jessica released Suzanne's breast, sat up in her lap, and set loose a string of babble. "Do you want to talk to him?" Suzanne asked, jiggling the baby.

He turned and shot her a smile. "Yes, but Bessborough will let his guard down much better with a pretty woman. Even more so with two. You and Cordelia should talk to him." He frowned at the Boucher oil over the dressing table. "Dewhurst confirmed that members of the League were smuggling works of art out of the Continent. But it's difficult to see how that would have been enough for Father to blackmail his friends over. God knows Britain's great houses are filled with appropriated art treasures."

"Unless something happened in the course of acquiring one of the treasures," Suzanne said.

"It's a possibility." Malcolm dug a hand into his hair in the way he did when he was puzzling something over. "I talked to O'Roarke. About the Dunboyne leak."

Suzanne drew a breath and forced herself to release it slowly. She should have realized Malcolm would approach Raoul. "Did he know anything?"

"Yes, apparently he was at Dunboyne at the time. He says he might well have been killed if the rebels hadn't been warned." Malcolm's mouth twisted in a rueful smile. "One tries to keep the personal out of it, but I confess the thought of O'Roarke all but losing his life can't but color my view of the situation."

"The important thing is that you're aware your view is colored." She swallowed, hoping she wasn't being too deliberate. "Did you ask him about the leak?"

"He admits he was the one who received the information. And claims he doesn't know the source. But then I'd expect him to protect his source." Malcolm shook his head. "It's odd being on opposite sides. I'm used to thinking of him as an ally."

Suzanne's throat knotted with what might have been a laugh or a sob.

"Dewhurst had heard of the Raven," Malcolm added.

Jessica stretched out a hand for the silver gilt candlesticks. Suzanne pulled her back. Amazing her own hands weren't trembling. Out of the frying pan and into the fire. "What did Dewhurst say about the Raven?" she asked in a steady voice.

"He'd heard a mention from a source who was one of Fouché's people. Supposedly the Raven was a French agent under long-term deep cover in the Peninsula. And even Fouché didn't know the agent's real identity, at least at that point. But according to Dewhurst, his source was quite clear that the Raven only went back to 1810 or so. So I'm damned if I see how it connects to the rest."

Jessica let out a squawk and arched her back. "I know, but you're tired," Suzanne said, coaxing her back to nurse. "Perhaps the Raven had worked with your father and Lord Harleton and had information that could hurt them," she said, because some response seemed to be required.

"Though neither of them had direct connections to the Peninsula or to the army. Yet their paths must have crossed somehow." He frowned. "Dewhurst said the Raven wasn't someone recruited by the French but someone placed in deep cover. Difficult to do that with a soldier or a diplomat."

"You've created convincing backstories." Suzanne rocked Jessica against her. "You made Rachel Garnier look like a baron's daughter. And Talleyrand set Tatiana up as a Russian princess."

Malcolm nodded, his gaze thoughtful. "Easier perhaps for a woman, who is likely to be in a less official capacity." He moved to sit beside Suzanne on the dressing table bench and touched Jessica's hair. "I wonder if the Raven could be someone's wife."

CHAPTER 14

Rupert, Viscount Caruthers, walked beside a shaggy chestnut pony, steadying the small boy seated atop the pony's back, while Bertrand Laclos carefully led the pony along the path that wound along the bank of the Serpentine through Hyde Park.

"Stephen!" Colin called from his perch on Malcolm's shoulders.

Stephen looked round and waved. Rupert gave a wave as well, as did Bertrand.

"Didn't mean to interrupt." Malcolm lifted Colin from his shoulders and set him on the ground.

"Always glad to see you." Rupert grinned, in a way that recalled the undergraduate Malcolm had known at Oxford. He swung Stephen down from the saddle so he could run over to Colin.

Bertrand looped the pony's reins round his wrist and moved towards Malcolm. He wore the English gentleman's casual dress of buckskin breeches, Hessian boots, and an olive drab coat, but beyond that he looked at home here in Hyde Park. In a way that had seemed impossible when he first resurfaced in France. In a way that he hadn't even seemed at home as an émigré at Eton and Oxford. Heartening to know some things could turn out for the best.

"Was just reading the transcript of your speech on Habeas Corpus over morning coffee," Bertrand said. "Impressive."

"Probably futile."

"On the contrary. Someone has to make the argument or we're truly lost." Bertrand crouched down beside the boys. "Why don't we take Lancelot for a walk and find a place to sail your boat."

Colin and Stephen responded with cries of approbation. Bertrand gathered up the reins and cast a crooked grin at Malcolm and Rupert. "Looks as though you've got work to discuss. Glad to be out of that business."

"As am I, technically," Rupert said, watching his lover move off. "But as you warned me when I sold out of the army, one can never really leave off the intelligence game." He turned back to Malcolm. "I'm glad I decided to stand for Parliament."

"As am I. We could use more like you."

"I don't have your way with words, but by God it's good to have something to do with myself. God knows I don't miss the army, but I need an occupation. And it's not as though Father's going to let me help with the running of the estates." Rupert drew a breath. "Losing your own father. That can't have been easy."

"No." Malcolm stared at the Serpentine as a breeze rippled across the water. This was territory he didn't venture into with many, often not even in the privacy of his own thoughts. But Rupert's own history had opened their mutual scars to each other. And given Rupert's situation, he deserved a more complicated answer. "Alistair and I were on speaking terms, but barely. Just enough for Alistair to make his contempt of me clear."

Rupert cast a quick glance at him. "I'm sure—"

"That I'm misinterpreting? I'm sure a lot of sons do. But Father's contempt would be hard to miss." Malcolm watched a gilded leaf drift into the water, a remnant of autumn. "In some ways, because I scarcely knew him, I can't feel his loss. But in others—I think having so much unfinished business makes it harder to lose someone."

Rupert's gaze narrowed against the glare of the sun, or perhaps against the complexities. "You're saying I should swallow the past and speak to Father so it will be less difficult for me when he dies?"

"I wouldn't presume to say anything of the sort."

Rupert grimaced and looked away, into the shadows. "Bertrand thinks I should. He says no matter what, Dewhurst is my father and refusing to speak to him can't undo the past." His gaze settled on Bertrand and the boys up ahead. "Father tried to have Bertrand killed. Could you have spoken to Alistair if he'd tried to kill Suzanne?"

"I don't know," Malcolm said, though instinctive rage roiled through him.

Rupert scowled at a leafless tree branch trailing dark tendrils over the water. "It isn't even that, though, because Bertrand's right, not speaking to Father can't undo the past. I think I could bring myself to speak to Father, for Bertrand's sake, if it weren't for Stephen." Up ahead, the pony had his head down. Stephen was petting him. "I don't want my father's brand of hatred anywhere near my son."

Malcolm watched as Colin flung his arms round the pony's neck. "One wants to protect them from all hurts. It's almost unbearable to realize one can't."

"Perhaps not forever. But I can keep Stephen away from Father until Stephen's old enough for me to explain. Right now Stephen could be charmed all too easily. Because Father would dote on him. His heir." Rupert's mouth twisted.

"There's the difference. Alistair never showed much interest in Colin." But then there'd been no title at stake. And why should Alistair Rannoch have cared about the son of a son he doubted was his in the first place?

Rupert pushed his hair out of his eyes. "One day I'll have to show Stephen his heritage. But not yet. Let him enjoy childhood. As we were never really able to do."

Malcolm watched the boys run ahead while Bertrand gathered up the pony's reins. "It's a rare gift to give a child."

"I'm fortunate. Fortunate to have Stephen, as Gaby reminds me. Fortunate in so many ways. Two years ago I didn't think such happiness was possible." Rupert turned and they began to walk along the winding path of the river, at a more temperate pace than Bertrand and the boys. "Sometimes I'm almost afraid to breathe for fear I'll disrupt it."

"I know the feeling." Malcolm recalled standing in the nursery doorway that morning, watching Suzanne, her flounced skirts pooling round one of the tiny chairs, feeding porridge to Jessica and chattering in French with Colin. One of those moments he tried to hold tight to, afraid it would shatter in pieces.

Rupert shot a quick glance at him. "You don't have reason to feel guilty."

"You feel guilty because of Gabrielle?" Malcolm pictured Rupert's wife's laughing gaze and high color when he'd glimpsed her across the ballroom at Emily Cowper's. "She seemed in good spirits last night."

"She says she's happy." Rupert's gaze lingered for a moment on Stephen, as Bertrand knelt between the two boys and helped them set a red-painted boat to sail on the water. "She's been spending quite a bit of time with Nick Gordon. I'm glad. I want her to be happy. It's just . . . a bit of an adjustment."

"No one ever said feelings were logical," Malcolm said.

"No," Rupert agreed. "We're friends, that's what's important. And Stephen has both of us. And Bertrand." He frowned for a moment. "And I suppose he might have Gordon as well."

They walked on in silence for a few moments, the fallen leaves crunching beneath their boots. "Why did you want to talk to me, Malcolm?" Rupert asked.

Malcolm drew a breath, oddly reluctant to break the spell of a few quiet moments with his friend. "I talked to your father last night at the Cowpers'."

Rupert shot a look at him.

"I wanted you to hear about it from me," Malcolm said.

"Since I doubt you've developed a sudden desire for my father's company, I assume you sought him out. Which means he's involved in something you're investigating."

"Yes. It remains to be seen how deeply involved." Malcolm hesitated, unsure how much to reveal, both to reassure Rupert and because Rupert might have valuable information. "Your father and my father were in a sort of club together that goes back to their Oxford days. Called the Elsinore League."

Rupert grinned. "Sounds more like a name you'd come up with."

"You never heard of it?"

"No. But even when we were on speaking terms, Father and I were hardly confidants." He frowned. "Whatever you're investigating has to do with your father and mine?"

"And others."

Rupert stared down at the russet and gold leaves underfoot. "I thought it was odd at the time. But I didn't see any reason to tell you about it."

"What?" Malcolm asked.

"Last summer. It must have been early June. Not long before Harleton died. I took Stephen to play with my sister Clarissa's children. Clary seemed a bit distracted, but I didn't make much of it. She's always been something of a shatterbrain and with four children and a husband in Parliament she's constantly going a dozen different directions at once. Then, as we were coming downstairs after settling the children in the nursery, the library door opened, and I came face-to-face with Father."

"That can't have been easy."

"No." Rupert stopped walking, gaze moving over the tangle of bare branches overhanging the opposite bank. "It isn't easy for my sisters, for Clarissa and Henrietta, my not speaking to Father. I told them the truth. I felt I owed them that. But I don't think they can bring themselves to accept that it's true. At least Clary can't. Hetty told me she could understand how I couldn't forgive him, but she couldn't stop speaking to her father. I could understand that. I understand both of them. Mostly we just avoid talking about him, and they're careful not to invite us to their houses at the same time. But Father and his friends had surprised Clarissa." Rupert dragged the toe of his boot over the leaves. "She told me afterwards that they'd arrived on her doorstep an hour since and said they needed a place to talk. She looked at me with those big pleading blue eyes, the way she looked when she tried to explain how she'd taken out my hunter when she was thirteen, and said, 'I couldn't very well have said no.' Which of course was the case. I was only sorry she had to witness me cutting Father dead."

"Friends?" Malcolm asked.

"Yes." Rupert's gaze skimmed over his face. "Sorry, got caught up in the personal. His friends are why I brought it up. My father was with your father and Lord Harleton."

Malcolm kept his gaze steady on Rupert's face. "Do you have any idea what they were talking about?"

"No. I excused myself and went back up to the children. But from the quick look I got at their faces—I don't think it was a friendly discussion."

"Colin!" Chloe ran across her mother's boudoir and hugged her cousin. "Where's Jessica?"

"With Suzette," Malcolm said, bending down to ruffle his cousin's hair. "Colin and I've just come from the park. I need to have a word with your mother."

"So we have to go to the nursery?"

"Only for a bit. I'll come up before I go with some tarts or cakes."

Chloe reached for Colin's hand. "We're going to get a puppy," she said over her shoulder.

"The puppy isn't definite," Lady Frances said when her daughter and Malcolm's son had left the room.

"Liar." Malcolm dropped down on the sofa beside his aunt. "You wouldn't disappoint her."

Lady Frances twitched the skirt of her dressing gown smooth. She was seated at her dressing table, where she had been completing her toilette. Her rouge and eye blacking were applied and her hyacinth scent filled the room, but her hair was still in curl papers. "You know me too well." She reached for her coffee. "What else have you learned about Alistair? I take it that's what's behind this early morning intrusion."

"It's more a question of what I haven't learned." Malcolm helped himself to a cup from the coffee service on the sofa table. "About Alistair and Arabella. Did you know Mama had an affair with Archibald Davenport?"

Lady Frances raised her brows. "According to whom?"

"Lord Dewhurst and Davenport himself."

"Interesting." Lady Frances added more cream to her coffee. "They moved in the same circles, of course, but that's one love affair she didn't confide in me about. At least not to my recollection. My memory isn't what it was."

"Spare me, Aunt Frances. Your memory is as needle sharp as ever."

"Yes, my dear, but with the passage of years there is more to remember. It's difficult enough to keep track of my own amorous adventures, let alone Arabella's. Is this affair with Archibald Davenport important?"

"It may be. It happened about the time of the Dunboyne leak. What seems even more relevant is that Father disappeared for a fortnight not long before he died. The story was that he was at Lord Glenister's shooting box in Argyllshire, but I know that to have been a fabrication. Do you have any idea where he might have gone? Or whom he might have gone to see? Was he with the Elsinore League?"

Lady Frances drew a breath. The lines showed more than usual in her carefully tended skin, and the rouge she had just applied stood out on her cheeks and lips. "No."

"You know where he was? Because it could be important—"

"Malcolm, no." Lady Frances took another sip of coffee as though she wished it were whisky and set her cup aside with deliberation. "Odd how one can swear one will never mention something and then—"

"Father told you where he was?"

"In a manner of speaking." Lady Frances folded her hands in her lap. Her sapphire ring flashed in the sunlight. "Your father was in Devonshire for that fortnight."

"How do you know? If he told you—"

"I know because he was with me."

"What on earth were you—" Malcolm stared at his aunt. His mother's sister and best friend. "Good God. But—I thought you didn't even like Father."

Lady Frances lifted a hand to adjust her cameo necklace. "Liking has very little to do with it."

Both Alistair Rannoch and Lady Frances moved in circles where numerous lovers were commonplace. Where thoughtful hostesses placed their guests in bedchambers beside current lovers at house parties. Where even love affairs were hardly exclusive while they lasted. But still—"How long—" He bit back the words.

Her fingers trembled for a moment against the carved alabaster of the cameos, but her gaze was steady. "A house party in Derbyshire. The Beverstons. I don't know why I accepted, neither of them was the best conversationalist and they had a way of dampening the wit of the company. Alistair and I were both bored. We were having one of our quarrels, and then that night we were the last two to take our candles and go up to bed and one thing led to another. The next morning I was horrified. I don't pretend to anything much in the way of morality, but on sheer aesthetic grounds . . . And he was my sister's husband. I swore it would never happen again." She reached for her coffee cup and tossed down a sip. "But it did. The allure of the forbidden. The erotic side of anger. God knows."

"Did Mama know?" Malcolm tried to keep his voice even but couldn't quite succeed.

Lady Frances stared into the cup cradled in her hand. "I thought not. I went to elaborate pains to keep it from her, and I was wracked with guilt. A novel experience for me. Then at last one day we were driving in the park together and Arabella looked at me across the barouche and said she couldn't abide Alistair, but if I wanted to indulge myself with him that was quite my own affair. I had the grace to blush."

Malcolm took a sip of coffee. It burned his tongue, but that might be the effect of the revelations. "Did that—"

"End it? That would be tidy, wouldn't it? If no longer forbidden it ceased to be a thrill." Lady Frances looked into her cup as though seeking an explanation of her attraction to Alistair Rannoch in the dregs. "I must have sworn a dozen more times that it would never happen again. But then circumstances would throw us together or we'd grow bored—" She wrinkled her nose. "Hardly the stuff of romance. Though he did surprise me with this pendant several years ago." She pulled a chain from beneath the froth of lace at the neck of her dressing gown. A square-cut diamond set in white gold filigree. Malcolm had purchased enough jewelry for his wife to recognize the quality of the stone. It was also a piece he had seen his aunt wear a great deal.

Lady Frances released the pendant as though it singed her. "Not that it was ever anything approaching exclusive. Alistair at least understood that. Unlike some men, like Harleton."

"Harleton—" Malcolm stared at his aunt. "You and Lord Harleton—"

"Regrettably."

He stared at her. "You're the woman Harleton challenged Father to a duel over."

Her brows lifted. "How on earth do you know about that?"

"The challenge occurred at a gathering—"

"Good God. Of the Elsinore League?"

"I'm not sure. It was a dinner party at which a number of their members were present."

Lady Frances got to her feet. "I never knew how the challenge came about. In fact, I didn't know about the whole tawdry affair until after the fact. If I had, I might have felt compelled to try to stop it. Might." She moved to the drinks trolley and picked up a decanter. "One could make a fair case that both Alistair and Harleton deserved what they got."

"So they did fight?"

"In Hyde Park." She moved back across the room and splashed some whisky into his coffee and then her own. "It was swords apparently. Alistair was a better fighter, but Harleton managed to get him in the shoulder. That's how I found out about it. He winced when I was taking off his shirt."

Malcolm could have done without that particular image, but the information was useful. "Father and Harleton both continued to be involved in the club?"

Lady Frances settled back on the sofa with her coffee and whisky. "I presume they considered honor satisfied. Harleton was a great bore. I don't know why I ever wasted time on him. Well, he did have a good leg, and I was bored that season. And it was only that one time at the opera and then—" She broke off and laughed at Malcolm's expression. "Don't be a prude, my dear. Oh, very well, I expect I wouldn't have wanted to hear such details about my uncles and aunts, either. In fact, the thought is distinctly off-putting." She wrinkled her nose.

Malcolm took a fortifying sip of whisky-laced coffee. "Tell me more about Harleton. No, not that. Tell me your impression of him—outside the bedchamber."

Lady Frances frowned. "Is Harleton mixed up in this as well?"

"I'd rather get your impression of him first."

She turned her cup in her hand. "As I said, he was something of a bore. But—" Her gaze moved over the silk wall hangings, the white moldings, the pier glass, the Lawrence oil of her three eldest children, as though she was seeing into the past.

"What?" Malcolm asked.

"I sometimes had the sense he wasn't quite the fool he let on. There was one time we were lying in bed together—sorry, Malcolm, but that's where most of our interactions occurred—and he was blathering on about something. Before I could check my tongue, I blurted out, 'Oh, Freddy, even you can't be fool enough to think that.' And he got the oddest look on his face, as though he knew perfectly well he'd been talking like a fool and was afraid he'd—'gone too far' is the only way I can think to describe it. I spent the rest of the day trying to puzzle out why Freddy Harleton would have pretended to be a fool. Surely he couldn't have thought it would make him more attractive to women. Talk about foolery!"

"Anything else?"

"He didn't like Alistair. I think that's why he reacted in such a ridiculously overdramatic manner when he learned I was Alistair's mistress as well. I told him I'd been Alistair's mistress first, so even though I thought exclusive rights were something claimed by colonial powers, not mature adults, if he was going to get in a huff about betrayal he'd have to get in line behind Alistair and my husband, to name only two with a prior claim." She took a sip of whisky and coffee. "I'm afraid that didn't improve the situation."

"What else did he say to you about Father?"

"Dear God, Malcolm, it's centuries ago." She pushed her fingers into her hair with a careless abandon that brought a painful tug of memory of his mother. "One night at the opera he looked across the boxes at Alistair sitting with the prince regent and Brummell and said Alistair was an upstart, just like Brummell. That neither would be where they were without powerful friends."

"But in Alistair's case he didn't just mean the regent. One could hardly call Father a favorite of the prince's like Brummell."

"No." Lady Frances tossed back another sip. "I think he meant men like him and Bessborough and Glenister and others on that list you recited." She frowned. "I remember now. Harleton said Alistair wouldn't have got where he was if he wasn't willing to use information to force his friends' hands."

"He was saying Father was a blackmailer?"

"That was the implication. I didn't give too much credence to it at the time. Those sorts of men seem to be above scandal. And if it's true Alistair was a spy"—her voice caught, as though she still couldn't quite believe it—"he'd have been the one with the most dangerous secret." She lifted her gaze to Malcolm's face. "Good God, is that it? Was Harleton a French spy, too?"

"Apparently."

Lady Frances picked up the decanter and topped off both their cups again. "I knew it was a good idea to have this handy." She picked up her cup but closed her fingers round it without drinking. "Incredible. Yet it makes sense of Harleton's pose of the amiable fool, I suppose. Do you think Alistair was blackmailing him with the threat of exposure?"

"I hadn't until what you just said. But Harleton could have ruined Alistair just as easily."

"Why on earth—Harleton wouldn't have needed the money."

"No, it was Alistair who needed the money." Malcolm reached for his own cup. "For Harleton, I think it was the risk, the allure of adventure."

Lady Frances took a thoughtful sip. "Yes, I can understand that. It can be deadly dull, this life we lead, for all the excess and indulgence. Or perhaps because of them. One quite longs for some sense of focus and purpose at times. I wish I'd discovered my children could give me that sooner." She looked up at him. "I often think your mother—"

"Yes," Malcolm said.

Lady Frances smoothed a satin fold of her dressing gown. "Do you think Harleton's death—"

"Wasn't an accident, either? Yes. It seems he and Father were both murdered because of something they knew."

She shook her head. "It's incredible. This is Mayfair."

"A seat of wealth and power. Which can raise the stakes." He leaned forwards. "Aunt Frances—those last days you spent with Father. Did he seem afraid of anything? Worried about anything?"

"Alistair wasn't the sort to be afraid. It was one of his attractions. But—" She flicked a bit of lint from her skirt. "He was oddly keyed up those last days. Both intense and distracted. At one point he actually thanked me for our time together." She gave a faint smile. "Very unlike Alistair. But I can't credit that he thought—"

Malcolm could see his aunt going over those last days she had spent with Alistair Rannoch, details too intimate to be shared. "If I'd known that was the last time we'd spend together, if I'd had the least idea—" Her fingers closed round the chain of her pendant. She had either slept in it, Malcolm realized, or put it on first thing this morning. Did she always wear it, tucked into the neck of her gowns if it wasn't part of her toilette?

Malcolm stared at his aunt, struck by a blinding revelation that recast much of his childhood. "You loved him."

Lady Frances put up a hand to tuck the pendant back beneath her dressing gown. "Don't let it get about."

CHAPTER 15

"Oh, Malcolm. Glad to see you." Carfax looked up from the desk in his study, an oak-paneled room filled with books, papers, and well-worn furniture. "Amelia has the house turned upside down for our ball tonight. She spent breakfast fretting over the guest list. Seems afraid the Tories and Whigs will come to blows. Told her politics hadn't got quite that contentious. Though I'm not entirely sure I spoke the truth." Carfax pushed aside the papers he'd been reviewing. "Learned something?"

Malcolm pulled the door to behind him. "You didn't tell me Smytheton had been one of our agents."

Carfax set down his pen. "I was wondering how long it would take you to ferret that out. Glad to see you haven't grown rusty."

"And that he and Jennifer Mansfield are suspected of being doubles."

"Ah, yes." Carfax picked up the pen and twirled it between his fingers. "Well, that's why I didn't tell you. I wanted to see what you made of Smytheton and the Mansfield woman without putting suspicions in your head. I do value your opinion, you know, Malcolm."

"I'm flattered."

"You should be. Sit down, stop prowling about."

Malcolm dropped into a straight-backed chair across from the desk. "If you suspected Smytheton why the hell did you let him anywhere near the Dunboyne information?"

"Dewhurst claims to have watched him all night. He says he's nine-tenths sure Smytheton isn't the one who took it."

"But you didn't tell me—"

"Because on the one-tenth chance Dewhurst is wrong, I count on you to discover the truth." Carfax picked up his penknife and began to mend the nib. "I suppose Dewhurst told you all this."

"Yes. And of course he had an incentive to point my interest in another direction."

"Quite. Just as he may have done with Smytheton twenty years ago."

Malcolm studied Carfax. The spymaster had his desk positioned so anyone facing him had to squint into the light from the window behind the desk. Though the day was gray, a surprising amount of light leached through the clouds. "You think Dewhurst may have been a French spy?"

"I can't ignore the possibility." Carfax examined the mended nib as though he were inspecting a weapon. "He was also in love with Geneviève Manet."

"Dewhurst?" Malcolm began to recast his conversation with the earl.

"Or as in love as a man like Dewhurst is capable of being."

Malcolm shifted his chair to the side, scraping it over the floorboards. "Were they lovers?"

"I'm not sure. Nor am I sure if Smytheton knew. It's possible Manet was playing them off against each other. It's also possible she and Dewhurst were playing Smytheton for the fool he often appears to be."

Malcolm leaned back in his chair. "I suppose you also knew about the duel."

"Oh yes. Harleton and your father. Over—"

"My aunt Frances."

Carfax settled back in his chair, fingers tented. "Who told you?"

"Archibald Davenport about the duel. Aunt Frances that it was over her."

"Yes, Fanny would. I imagine that came as a surprise."

"To put it mildly. I always thought she and my father detested each other. But both Davenport and Smytheton thought Aunt Frances might have been merely an excuse for the duel. That there was some other issue between Alistair and Harleton."

"Interesting."

"Do you think Alistair could have been blackmailing Harleton?"

"I wouldn't put it past Alistair. But they both had the power to ruin each other."

"They were meeting with Dewhurst not long before Harleton died."

Carfax reached up to adjust his spectacles. "I didn't know about that. Though it's not surprising."

Malcolm sat back in his chair and leaned to the side, getting the best angle he could on Carfax's face. "Of course it's always possible it was to do with the Elsinore League."

Carfax released his breath with what might have been satisfaction. Or expectation. "So you learned about that."

"Something else you wanted me to ferret out?"

Carfax removed his spectacles and began to clean the lenses with a monogrammed handkerchief. "I wasn't sure if you already knew of it. Or even if—"

"I was a member? Good God, sir, you can't have thought I'd belong to any club Alistair had started."

"It didn't seem likely. And I don't think they've added members of the younger generation to their number. But they remain shrouded in mystery. After all, Alderson began the Phoenix Society in honor of his uncle."

"Alderson's relationship with his uncle must have been very different from mine with Alistair. Not to mention that I have to be the least likely member of a hellfire club in all Britain."

Carfax gave a dry smile, gaze still on the lenses. "Perhaps. Assuming they are a hellfire club."

Malcolm studied his spymaster and mentor in the wintry early afternoon light. It accentuated the sharp lines of Carfax's face and the chill in his blue eyes. "That's it, isn't it? The real reason you take such interest in this investigation. Why all this ancient history still matters so much. My father, Harleton, the manuscript, who was behind the Dunboyne leak. You want to find out about the Elsinore League."

"It's hardly the only reason. But I'll own to having been interested in them for some time. They've been shrouded in mystery from the first mentions I heard in my days at Oxford."

Malcolm studied the other man. Was it remotely possible Carfax had felt excluded from the exclusive club? It was not a way Malcolm was accustomed to thinking about his spymaster. "You were never a member yourself?"

Carfax hooked the spectacles back over his ears. "I'm hardly the likeliest member of a hellfire club myself."

For all Carfax's pragmatic approach to most ethical questions, Malcolm had never heard rumor of him so much as indulging in dalliance. In fact, he appeared genuinely devoted to his wife. Malcolm knew enough not to take devotion at face value, but still— "Cyrus says they were smuggling works of art off the Continent in the eighties and nineties. My father's collection and what I saw at Harleton's villa supports that."

"Interesting. But hardly enough to ruin men in their position."

"Alistair and Harleton were French agents. You suspect Smytheton and possibly Dewhurst. Could the whole Elsinore League have been a cover for a French network?"

Carfax drew in and released his breath. "I've wondered." He spread his hands flat on the desk and appeared to be studying his nails. "But I could never connect the dots further than Harleton and possibly your father. And if that many powerful men in Britain were French agents, surely—"

"They'd have won the war?"

"At least they'd have accomplished more."

"What does the Raven have to do with the Elsinore League?"

Carfax's head jerked up. "Where did you hear about the Raven?"

"In Alistair and Harleton's correspondence. Alistair implied the

Raven's exposure could damage them both. Dewhurst told me the Raven is a code name for a French agent under deep cover."

Carfax's brows drew together. "Yes. He brought me that report himself. We attempted to learn more. To no avail." He tapped his fingers on the ink blotter with frustration.

"Dewhurst said the Raven only went back to 1810 or so and was in the Peninsula. Not an English man or woman who was turned but someone set up with an alias."

Carfax nodded.

"You never found any connection to my father and Harleton?"

"No. I don't know that the Raven was ever even in England."

"What do you know about the Raven?"

"He appears to have been responsible for the French intercepting our tactical team at Burgos."

Malcolm leaned forwards. "Why didn't you say anything? That happened when I was in Lisbon."

"I had Tommy Belmont looking into it. I didn't need to put both of you on the matter."

"Are you so sure the Raven is a man? Because it occurred to me it would be much easier to plant a woman under deep cover."

"Interesting." Carfax turned his penknife over in his hands. "I wonder if that could be the source of the threat the Raven represented to your father and Harleton."

"You think she could have been mistress to one or both of them?"

"It's often the way women represent a threat to men."

"I wouldn't underestimate female agents, sir."

Carfax slapped the penknife down. "I never underestimate anyone. But it's often the way female agents represent a threat. Look at Tatiana Kirsanova."

Malcolm swallowed. Carfax couldn't know Tania had been his sister. And it was true in any case.

"But the French wouldn't have needed to set an agent to seduce Alistair or Harleton."

"Unless it was a way to keep tabs on them. Or perhaps the French were interested in the Elsinore League as well."

"You think the French knew about the Elsinore League? Assuming it wasn't a French spy ring?"

"Whatever games the Elsinore League were playing, they were powerful people keeping powerful secrets. Find out what they were up to, Malcolm."

Malcolm met the spymaster's gaze. Powerful secrets were the currency Carfax dealt in. His interest in the investigation now made perfect sense. What he would do with the information if Malcolm uncovered it was another question entirely.

Even an almost empty theatre had its own smell. Sawdust, the oil of rehearsal lamps, drying paint, the sweat of active bodies that could never quite be banished. After all these years, it still sent an indefinable thrill of magic through Suzanne. Jessica seemed to sense it from her mother, for she gave a crow of delight in Suzanne's arms and waved her hands. "Shush." Suzanne pulled her closer and cast a glance at Malcolm, wondering if they'd been wise to bring the children. Children were a great icebreaker, as Malcolm had said, but Jessica's shrieks when she got excited could be particularly piercing. Fortunately, she seemed to be growing out of her glee when she had first discovered how loud she could be.

Colin darted forwards and stopped midway down the aisle, staring transfixed at the stage. His mother's son.

A crowd of actors stood on the stage, clustered round Manon, who lay on the bare boards, covered with a black cloth. A fair-haired actor knelt beside her.

Brandon Ford watched from the side of the stage.

> *"What is he whose grief*
> *Bears such an emphasis? whose phrase of sorrow*
> *Conjures the wand'ring stars, and makes them stand*
> *Like wonder-wounded hearers?"*

Brandon ran forwards, announcing:

> *"This is I,*
> *Hamlet the Dane."*

He flung himself down beside Manon and the fair-haired man. The fair-haired man lost his balance and fell against Manon. Manon sat up with a yelp. "That was my arm."

"Sorry," Brandon said.

"Watch where you're going, will you, Ford?" The fair-haired man sat back on his heels and pushed his hair out of his eyes.

"You're supposed to be sitting by her head, Ned. You've got the blocking all wrong."

Manon shaded her eyes to look into the audience. "Simon, darling, I don't suppose there's any chance we could use a wax dummy for Ophelia's body?"

"Verisimilitude, love." Simon sprang up on the edge of the stage. "Ned, annoying as Brandon can be he's right in this case. You should be further upstage. We're running behind, and I want to go over the fight with the two of you. Besides, we have visitors."

"Sorry to interrupt," Malcolm said. "I was hoping for a word with Sir Horace."

"Good lord, with me?" Smytheton, who was again sitting in the audience, pushed himself to his feet. "Brought the whole family, have you, Malcolm? More about this investigation? Can't see what more I can tell you."

"Nevertheless, sir. If we could just speak with you for a few minutes?"

Roxane scrambled to her feet at the front of the house, where she must have been sprawled on the floor. "Can we play with Colin and Jessica?"

"They'd be thrilled." Suzanne walked forwards and put Jessica into Roxane's arms. Colin had already dropped down on the floor beside Clarisse and her coloring set.

Following the plan she and Malcolm had devised, Suzanne sat in the front row and watched the rehearsal while Malcolm and Sir Horace repaired to the Green Room. By the time Simon called a halt to the rehearsal and dismissed most of the actors for half an hour so he could work with Brandon and Manon on the nunnery scene, Colin was happily absorbed playing with Roxane and Clarisse. Jessica had climbed into Suzanne's lap and was tugging at her bodice in a way that indicated she wanted to nurse.

Jennifer Mansfield knelt on the edge of the stage with a friendly smile. "You're welcome to use my dressing room, Mrs. Rannoch."

Suzanne glanced at Roxane. "We're fine," Roxane said, with the ease of one who had been watching her little sister in theatres since the age of three. Colin grinned up at Suzanne.

"Thank you so much, Mrs. Mansfield." Suzanne got to her feet, holding her daughter. It couldn't have played out better. Really, children were a great asset in an investigation.

Malcolm and Smytheton repaired to the Green Room with its comfortably frayed sofas and chipped gilt paint. "Splendid about the play, isn't it?" Smytheton said, dropping into a chair. "The more I see of this version, the more I like it. A bit rough round the edges, but so many splendid shadings in Hamlet's relationship with Claudius just based on a few lines. Adds interest to both characters. Only I think Gertrude has a bit more to do in the official version. Wish we could add those lines back in, but Jenny told me not to fuss. Thought Jennifer should have been Ophelia, but she insists she's too old—lot of rubbish, she doesn't look a day over five-and-twenty, well, maybe twenty-six—and that she's always wanted to play Gertrude."

"Gertrude is a wonderful character," Malcolm said.

"Yes, I suppose so. Interesting layers and all that. Just can't credit Jenny as Ford's mother. Must say, La Caret's doing a quite creditable job. Talented girl that. What did you want to talk to me about?"

Malcolm perched on the edge of a straight-backed chair. "You hadn't heard of the script until Crispin and Manon took it to Simon?"

"Of course not. Think I could keep quiet about a lost version of *Hamlet*? In any case, how should I have heard of it?"

"You were friends with Harleton."

"Harleton? Friends?" Sir Horace snorted. "Hardly. We ran with very different crowds. Harleton had no appreciation of the theatre or the Bard."

Malcolm leaned forwards, hands clasped between his knees. "And yet you were in a club together."

For a moment, he would swear a shadow of unease crossed Sir Horace's face. Something infinitely more complex than his usual bluff good humor. "A club? Oh, you mean that Elsinore nonsense. Half the fellows in it didn't even know Elsinore was from Shakespeare. And I'd give even odds on if the others could name which play it's from." Sir Horace shook his head over the sad state of Oxbridge undergraduates. "Mind you, it was only the name that got me to join in the first place. Thought there might be some substance to it. Once I realized my mistake, I stopped attending events."

"Events?"

Sir Horace shifted on the sofa. "Parties. The usual sort of thing."

"It's all right, Sir Horace," Malcolm said. "We know it was a hellfire club."

Sir Horace coughed. "Had some gatherings at one hunting box or another. Made a token attempt at a Shakespeare theme but got the details all wrong. One was supposed to be Elsinore but full of references to the Forest of Arden and a second-rate soprano from the opera in a dampened petticoat singing Feste's songs from *Twelfth Night*. I ask you." He shook his head in outrage. "I think that was the last straw for me."

"My father was one of the founders," Malcolm said.

"Yes, of all the people to be abusing the Bard—No offense, my boy."

"None taken."

Sir Horace frowned at a print of the balcony scene on the opposite wall. "Of course Alistair actually was better versed in Shakespeare than others when he put his mind to it. Still, hardly a kindred spirit. In any case, found I was much happier hanging about the theatre. And then I met Jennifer." His eyes brightened at the memory.

Malcolm leaned back and crossed his legs. "You were at a dinner with seven of the Elsinore League members in '98."

"Was I? Were we?" Sir Horace frowned. "Can't remember what dinner parties I was at five weeks ago, let alone almost twenty years. Devilish dull things usually, and I can't bring Jennifer."

"There were no ladies present at this one. And the guest list seems to have been entirely members or former members of the Elsinore League. My father. Harleton. Archibald Davenport. Yourself. Lord Bessborough. Hugo Cyrus. Lord Dewhurst."

Again he thought he saw something shift in Sir Horace's gaze. Then Smytheton settled back against the sofa cushions with a smile of disarming lack of guile. "Now you mention it, I do remember something of the sort."

"What did you talk about?"

"Lord, how should I remember through the years? What do gentlemen talk about? The racing season. The ankles of the latest crop of opera dancers. Why does it matter?"

"Perhaps it will jog your memory if I mention that this dinner occurred shortly before the Dunboyne affair."

Once again, Sir Horace's eyes sharpened, then clouded over with bluster. "Dreadful business that. But what's that to say to—" The bluster faded. He slumped back against the faded red damask of the sofa like a man giving up a physical effort. "You know, don't you?"

"Know what?"

Sir Horace shook his head. "Shouldn't have tried to pretend. Jennifer says I always get myself in trouble when I try to act. But damn it, how was I to be sure you already knew about the business? I could have been the one giving away state secrets."

"Then let me assure you that I know information from Lord Dewhurst's dispatch box that night led to the Dunboyne mission being betrayed," Malcolm said in the same neutral voice. "How did you learn of it?"

"Oh, Carfax questioned us. Didn't tell you that? No surprise there, Carfax always was a secretive one to say the least. That damned sharp gaze of his is enough to make one sweat clean through one's linen. Couldn't tell him anything, though. I mean, didn't have anything to tell. Didn't see anything, and certainly didn't leak the information myself."

"Did you notice anything else that night?" Malcolm asked.

Sir Horace frowned at a spot on his cravat. "What sort of thing?"

"Anything in the least bit unusual even if it didn't seem to relate to Dewhurst's papers. I'm sure a man with your knowledge of theatre is an excellent observer."

Some of the tension left Sir Horace's shoulders. He drew a breath as though preening himself. "Come to think of it, Dewhurst looked a bit distracted. Came late, didn't take part in the usual ribaldry. Can't put my finger on anything in particular, just seemed a bit off. And before he arrived—" He swallowed, looked away, twitched his shirt cuff smooth.

"Harleton challenged Father to a duel?"

Sir Horace started. "Good God, man, one would almost swear you were there that night."

"You knew about the duel?"

"Yes, it was the damndest thing. Harleton challenged Alistair. Only I had the oddest sense they were fighting about something other than a woman. You know it was a woman?"

"Yes."

"And did Lady Fr—" He broke off.

"Yes, my aunt told me about the affair."

"Dashed fine woman, Lady Frances. If it weren't for Jennifer— not that she'd look twice at me. Lady Frances, that is. Still can't make out why Jenny does after all these years. I only knew about the affair because I'd stumbled into Lady Frances's box at Covent Garden at an inopportune moment when they'd neglected to lock the door. I expect that's why he asked me to be his second, because I was already in on the secret as it were."

"You were Alistair's second in the duel?"

"Yes." Sir Horace shook his head at the memory. "Had to meet with Cyrus—he was Harleton's second—and try to patch things up. Which was a bit hard, as we couldn't use Lady Frances's name, and I think we both had the sense that quarrel was really about something else."

"Do you have any idea what?"

Smytheton shook his head. "Your father and I were hardly confidants."

"What about the art treasures the League was smuggling?"

Smytheton blinked. "Who—"

"Cyrus told me."

"Should have known. Tried to warn him when you first started asking questions. Was afraid you'd jump to the wrong conclusions."

"Why don't you let me be the judge of what is and isn't relevant. Do you think the art treasures were behind Alistair and Harleton's quarrel?"

Smytheton folded his arms across his chest and appeared to give the question serious consideration. "It's possible. Alistair was a zealous collector. Harleton didn't seem to care much about it, save that he liked the idea of having more treasures than the others."

"There wasn't a particular piece they quarreled about? Archibald Davenport said he heard my father ask Harleton where he'd hidden 'it.' "

Smytheton frowned in a seemingly genuine effort of memory, then shook his head. "It's entirely possible. But I know of no particulars. Sorry I can't be of more help, Malcolm, but I was on the fringe to say the least. 'Fraid I've told you everything I know."

"You're too modest, sir. You couldn't possibly have done, considering you didn't tell me you'd been in the employ of the Crown."

Smytheton stared at Malcolm out of wide blue eyes, blinked, rubbed the bridge of his nose. Now that he knew the story of Sir Horace's past, Malcolm began to appreciate the man's capabilities. "My compliments," Malcolm said. "You're obviously a skilled agent."

"Wouldn't quite call myself that." Smytheton's smile was that of an amiable country squire. "Did the odd bit to help out while I was in Paris, don't you know. Kept an ear open, passed along what I heard, passed on the occasional piece of information."

"It's a fraught word, 'spy,' " Malcolm said. "It took me a long time to admit I was one myself."

"Not at all in your league, my boy. I've heard of the sort of thing you do."

"You underrate yourself. But I'm sure you wouldn't want to underrate Mrs. Mansfield. Or rather Madame Manet."

Smytheton drew a breath. "Jennifer is—"

"A brilliant actress. And a very capable agent." Malcolm leaned back in his chair. "It can't have been easy on either of you being suspected of betraying your comrades."

Something flashed in Smytheton's eyes. Anger? Calculation? Relief?

"I've heard Dewhurst's version of events," Malcolm said. "Now I should very much like to hear yours."

Smytheton's gaze slid to a framed playbill on the wall advertising Jennifer Mansfield in *The Merchant of Venice*. "Plots within plots within plots. Difficult now to think that Dewhurst and I once could have passed as friends. Although I suppose one could say the same of Claudius and Polonius."

Jennifer Mansfield's dressing room was tidier than Manon's, still crowded, but with the costumes hung from a clothesline or neatly folded, the hats and wigs on stands or in boxes, the jewelry mostly tucked into jewel boxes, the paints and powders contained. But the smell was similar—face powder, greasepaint, and lavender, mixed with the distinctive hyacinth and lily of Jennifer's perfume.

"Do sit down." Jennifer waved to the pale rose chaise-longue and struck a flint to light the spirit lamp. "And feed your daughter. I've fed both my own often enough in various dressing rooms."

Suzanne sank down on the sofa and settled Jessica in her lap. For the moment, Jessica seemed content to lean against Suzanne and look round, taking in the sparkle and shimmer of the costumes and studying Jennifer's face. "I didn't realize you had children."

Jennifer smiled as she set a kettle on the spirit lamp. "My older daughter must be about your age. She was five when we left Paris. She married last year and is expecting a baby. I can't say I'm looking forwards to being called 'Grandmama,' but I quite like the prospect of another baby to dandle." She took a blue-flowered tray with cups and saucers from atop the chest of drawers. "My younger daughter is eight. She's with her governess today, but she often plays with Roxane and Clarisse. Nice to have other children about the theatre." She set the tray on the table before the chaise-longue. "And yes, Horace is my younger daughter's father."

Jessica squirmed in Suzanne's lap, stretched her leg out, and grabbed her foot with one hand. Jennifer filled the teapot and set it on the tray to steep, then settled on a straight-backed chair beside the chaise-longue. "I didn't just ask you in for tea, as you must have discerned. I thought if we spoke in private we might be able to clear up some misunderstandings. Horace has a tendency to bluster and not realize when simply telling the truth would be so much simpler." She smiled. Her smile was dazzling and disarming and an infinitely more effective weapon than Sir Horace's bluff good humor.

"Mrs. Mansfield." Suzanne tilted Jessica in her arms. Jessica grinned up at her. "You must realize—"

Jennifer adjusted the heavy folds of the rehearsal skirt tied over her violet lustring gown. "I fully expect you'll share anything I tell you with your husband. I understand you work together. I applaud such a partnership. But Horace would make a fuss and get protective if I spoke with your husband. Much easier for the two of us to have a comfortable cose over tea."

Jennifer Mansfield could be a very dangerous woman. Suzanne liked her immensely already. Suzanne undid the flap on her bodice and settled her squirming daughter at her breast. "I should like nothing more than to hear your version of events."

"Splendid." Jennifer spread her hands over her lap. A sapphire ring that might just possibly be genuine rather than paste sparkled on her left hand. "I was already a successful actress by the time of the Revolution. And though like many I was caught up in the excitement at first, I was quickly appalled by the lengths to which things went. Besides, my elder daughter's father was an early victim of the guillotine."

"I'm sorry." Suzanne thought of how close Raoul had come to suffering the same fate.

Jennifer shrugged, appearing very French. "It makes a particular impression when one is young. In my case it was enough to push me beyond thinking about my own and my daughter's safety. I went to work for the Royalists. It didn't hurt that my next protector was a vicomte heavily involved in the resistance."

"As an actress you were ideally positioned to gather information."

"Quite. Milk or lemon?" Jennifer lifted the teapot.

"Milk." Suzanne adjusted her arm beneath Jessica as Jessica tangled her fist in the ribbons on her mother's bodice.

Jennifer set a blue-flowered cup in front of her. "Of course the vicomte was long gone—not to the guillotine, to a life of exile in England—by the time I met Dewhurst."

Suzanne froze midway through the delicate juggling act of lifting a cup of tea to her lips one-handed while cradling a baby in the other arm. "You were involved with Lord Dewhurst before Sir Horace?"

"Oh yes." Jennifer squeezed a wedge of lemon into her own tea and took a sip. "Dewhurst was running our network. Say what one will of him—and I could say a lot—he was a man of sense, unlike the many idealistic boys involved in the cause." She set her cup down. "I suppose that's what drew me to him. Well, that and a handsome fortune, I don't deny."

Suzanne returned her cup to the table with care. "You met him before Sir Horace?"

"He introduced me to Horace. Horace was to be my contact." Jennifer shook her head, stirring her burnished ringlets. "I confess at the time I wondered how he'd manage."

Jessica was squirming in Suzanne's lap. She let go of the breast, pushed herself to her feet, looked round and smiled at Jennifer, then buried her head in her mother's shoulder. "Sir Horace strikes me as being good at deception," Suzanne said.

"Yes, I should have seen it." Jennifer picked up a spoon and stirred her tea. "In general I pride myself on being a good judge of people."

Jessica bounced on Suzanne's legs, then dropped down on her lap. Suzanne adjusted the flap on her gown and settled Jessica at her other breast. "And then you and Sir Horace—"

"Oh no, not at that point. Dewhurst and I were still entangled, and though I've been known to juggle more than one lover at once, two lovers who were both Royalist agents seemed entirely too fraught." She took another sip of tea. "In fact, it was through Dewhurst that I met your husband's father."

Suzanne's fingers stilled on the folds of Jessica's muslin dress. "Dewhurst introduced you to Alistair Rannoch?"

"Not quite. Alistair Rannoch appeared in my dressing room one night demanding to know where Dewhurst was. I told him I hadn't seen Dewhurst in several days, which was true. Alistair cursed, said under other circumstances he'd certainly remain in my dressing room longer and that he hoped I wouldn't take his quick departure as an insult. After which he kissed my hand. The next time I saw Dewhurst—a few days later—I asked if his importunate friend had found him. Dewhurst laughed and said Alistair wasn't really a friend, more a colleague."

"By which you inferred Alistair was a fellow agent?" Suzanne asked, as Jessica released her breast and sat up in her lap.

"Oh, he was." Jennifer leaned forwards to refill the teacups. "He worked with us on several missions."

Jessica was fidgeting. Suzanne put her arm round her daughter to anchor her thoughts. "With the Royalists?"

"Naturally. He was clever, I'll give him that. Arrogant, but that can make a man intriguing. It even prompted me to break my rule about becoming entangled with more than one Royalist agent at once."

"You and Alistair Rannoch—"

"I don't think Dewhurst ever knew. I doubt it would have gone over well. Meanwhile I hadn't the wit to pay much attention to Horace, who still faithfully appeared in my dressing room most nights, supposedly to convey information. Though in retrospect, he was there even when there was no information that needed relaying. And then one night Horace insisted on seeing my daughter and me home from the theatre because there'd been some unrest in the city. One thing led to another, and I realized I'd quite underestimated him. In a number of ways. We settled into quite an agreeable routine—as routine as life can be for agents—until Horace came into my dressing room in the middle of the third act of *Barber of Seville* and said Paris wasn't safe for me anymore and he'd make all the arrangements." Jennifer squeezed another wedge of lemon into her tea. "Left on his own, I'm not sure Dewhurst would have got me out of France at all."

Jessica had gone from fidgeting to squirming. Suzanne set her on the floor where she could stand holding on to the edge of the chaise-longue. "And so you went to England."

"And Horace helped me find work at the Tavistock. It was run by old Mr. Ford then. Such a kind gentleman, we've been fortunate in our managers. Horace continued to go to France for a bit. Until the tiresome rumors about which Dewhurst has no doubt given your husband his own account." Jennifer set down her cup and met Suzanne's gaze directly.

The sound of Jessica's small hands pounding on the chaise-longue cushions punctuated the stillness. "And your account?" Suzanne asked.

"Horace isn't a traitor," Jennifer said. "Which leaves one other obvious source for the leaks."

"Did you have reason to think Dewhurst was a traitor?"

"I wondered when suspicion fell on me. I even broached it with Horace. But he said it was impossible a man would so betray his country." She shook her head in affectionate frustration. "Of course he was jealous of Dewhurst. I think perhaps he was over-compensating."

Suzanne reached down to steady Jessica as she grabbed hold of a chair and shook it. "And then?"

Jennifer shrugged, mouth curled as though with the determination to avoid bitterness. "There was no proof against Horace. Of course there was no proof against Dewhurst, either. And Dewhurst had more powerful friends. Horace said he was glad to be out of the plaguey business and he'd just as soon spend his time round the theatre. I must say I'm quite relieved to have him out of danger, though he does get underfoot a bit. But I think at times he misses the adventure."

Suzanne put her hand over Jessica's tiny one. Judging by her own experience, she was sure he did. "And that was the last of your espionage adventures?"

"Not quite." Jennifer smiled and caught hold of the hand Jessica was stretching out to her. "It had been so long I thought we were done with all that nonsense. And then in '98 we received an unexpected visit."

"From Dewhurst?"

"No. From Alistair Rannoch. Here, let me give you some fresh tea. You've scarcely had time to drink any dealing with the baby."

Suzanne accepted the fresh cup of tea without looking at it. "What did Alistair Rannoch want?"

"Horace's help. He—Alistair—came banging on our door late one night. He and Horace were closeted in Horace's study for over an hour. After Alistair left, it took me some time to get the story out of Horace, and I'm not sure I ever did get the whole of it. Because of course Horace was afraid I'd disapprove of him agreeing to help. Which I did."

Suzanne took an automatic sip of tea while steadying Jessica with her free hand. "Help?"

Jennifer settled back in her chair, and Suzanne had the oddest sense this was what the entire conversation had been leading up to. "Alistair wanted Horace's assistance in getting someone out of the country. Rather the reverse of my situation. Well, out of Ireland. Britain and Ireland weren't safe for many linked to the failed Uprising. Horace insisted he was helping because he didn't hold with the reprisals, that our own country was becoming as draconian in our way as the Jacobins had been in France. And that may have been it. It probably was at least part of it. But I saw the way he and Alistair looked at each other when Alistair left. I couldn't avoid the suspicion that Alistair had some hold on Horace. I asked Horace about it straight out. Horace denied it—with precisely the sort of bluster he gets when he's trying to avoid telling the truth." She shook her head, smiled at Jessica again, looked back at Suzanne. "I offered to help. If he was going to do it, I wanted to make sure he didn't get himself killed. But he refused to let me. Men can be tiresomely protective."

"I call those Malcolm's Hotspur moments." Suzanne caught Jessica's hands in both her own. "Fortunately, he doesn't have many of them."

"Yes, your husband seems to be free of Horace's more antiquated ideals about chivalry." Jennifer smiled in affectionate mockery. "For the next fortnight I lived in terror of Horace being arrested as a conspirator to treason for helping a traitor leave the country. I was ready to throw myself on Dewhurst's mercy, though I wasn't sure it would have worked. You can imagine my relief when Horace returned unhurt." She frowned as she reached for her teacup. "He never would tell me precisely what had happened, save that they got Alistair's friend safely to France."

Suzanne bent forwards to let Jessica drop to her knees, then pulled her up. Jessica gave a squeal of delight. "Did you ever learn the name of Alistair's friend?"

"Oh yes." Jennifer took a sip of tea. "It was Raoul O'Roarke."

CHAPTER 16

"Jen." Sir Horace looked up as Jennifer and Suzanne, cradling a now sleeping Jessica, stepped into the Green Room. "What on earth—There's no need—"

"There's every need." Jennifer closed the door and nodded to Suzanne. "I've spoken with Mrs. Rannoch, and we agreed Mr. Rannoch should hear this at once."

Sir Horace drew a breath and puffed out his cheeks. "I told you I'd handle it—"

"Which means you'd only tell Mr. Rannoch things in bits and pieces as he discovered them himself. As Mr. Rannoch is an exceedingly clever man—and Mrs. Rannoch is quite as clever—I have no doubt they would discover them. You'd only muddy the waters by making yourself look guilty when you aren't. Besides, I like the Rannochs, and I have no desire to slow their investigation."

"If you—"

"Horace, dear, I do adore it when you try to protect me, but in this case I assure you it is entirely misguided." Jennifer sat down beside Sir Horace and laid her hand over his own. Suzanne moved to a chair beside Malcolm, holding Jessica against her. Her mouth was dry, her brain whirling in a dozen directions. But what mattered now was Malcolm and how he reacted to the news.

Jennifer recounted the story she had given Suzanne about Alistair Rannoch's work in France with the Royalists and the mission in '98 to rescue Raoul O'Roarke.

Malcolm took it without obvious reaction until the mention of O'Roarke's name. His stifled "Good God" nearly woke Jessica. She buried her head in Suzanne's arm and subsided.

"Did my father say why he was helping O'Roarke?" Malcolm asked Sir Horace.

"No, and believe me I wondered as well." Now that the story was out, Sir Horace was matter-of-fact. "When I asked him why he wanted to help a man and a cause he'd always professed to detest, he merely said he had his reasons. Alistair wasn't a man one questioned. I went to Ireland and made the travel arrangements with a smuggler Alistair had found. It's an advantage to be thought something of a buffoon. People are always underestimating one. Alistair met us with O'Roarke."

"How did they seem?"

"About like Wellington and Napoleon might if one had helped the other. Save that I think the duke and Bonaparte had rather more respect for each other."

"This was after the Dunboyne papers disappeared."

"About six months." Sir Horace met Malcolm's gaze.

"Why did you help my father?"

"As I said to Jennifer at the time, the reprisals in Ireland went beyond the pale as it were. Didn't support the rebellion, but didn't hold with vengeance, either." He sat back on the sofa, arms folded across his chest. "If that makes me a suspect in the Dunboyne business, so be it. That's all there is to it."

It was said with bluster. And Suzanne was quite sure it was a lie.

Malcolm stared across the Green Room at Suzanne. Sir Horace had followed Jennifer back to the rehearsal, clearly eager to escape further discussion. "It doesn't make any sense. Every other piece of information has pointed to Alistair blackmailing and manipulating people. And yet here he is helping a man and a cause he detested."

Suzanne shifted the sleeping Jessica in her arms. For all the truths about Raoul she couldn't share with Malcolm, she had much the same questions. "The French were helping the United Irish-men. Perhaps your father was acting under orders from Paris."

"And his dislike of O'Roarke was all a pose?"

"Or his masters forced him to help a man he disliked. We don't know why he was working for the French—If he believed in the Republican cause or he was doing it for the money or for some other reason."

"In death as in life my father remains an enigma." Malcolm took a turn about the Green Room, frustration in the sound of his foot-falls.

Suzanne shifted her arm beneath Jessica's legs. "Jennifer thinks Sir Horace didn't tell her the real reason he helped Alistair. Having watched his response, I agree."

Malcolm nodded. "There's one person who may be able to shed light on this. O'Roarke himself."

Suzanne quite agreed. She just had to speak to Raoul first. "Dar-ling, Jennifer told me more. Apparently your father worked with Sir Horace and Lord Dewhurst and her helping the Royalists in the nineties." She recounted the rest of her conversation with Jennifer.

"With Royalist agent friends, it isn't surprising Alistair was act-ing as a double agent," Malcolm said.

"If Dewhurst or Smytheton was a double, two of the three of them were."

"Quite." Malcolm perched on the sofa beside her. "Smytheton was Alistair's second in the duel over Aunt Frances. Which he also thought was about more than the affair."

Jessica opened her eyes and stretched her arms over her head, arching her back. Malcolm held out a finger for her to grasp. "I have to meet David and Oliver at Brooks's about the machine-breaking bill. Then I'll see if I can track down O'Roarke. I'd like you with me when I talk to him."

Suzanne gathered her daughter up in her lap and looked steadily into her husband's eyes. "I'd be happy to do so, darling."

Suzanne slid into the chair Raoul was holding out for her as if this were a perfectly amicable meeting. Then, her back to the coffee-house, she slapped her gray doeskin gloves down on the table. "I know you don't tell me everything. I realize that now that I'm no longer your agent you tell me even less than you used to. But for God's sake, didn't it occur to you that it was relevant that Alistair Rannoch helped you escape Ireland after the Uprising?"

Raoul went still, his fingers curled round the back of his own chair. "Who told you?"

"Jennifer Mansfield. She had it from Sir Horace."

"Ah." Raoul let himself into his chair in one controlled motion. "I should have realized the risk when I heard Smytheton was part of this investigation."

"You still haven't said why you didn't tell me. Was Alistair Rannoch your agent?"

"My dear girl." Raoul poured a glass of wine and pushed it across the table to her. "No. I told you, I didn't have any notion Alistair Rannoch was a French agent."

She pushed the wine aside. "Then why on earth did you think he was helping you?"

Raoul filled a second glass, fingers steady on the bottle. In those few seconds, she saw a host of considerations race through his mind. One of those innocuous moments that contain the weight of a revelation that can change everything. "Because Arabella asked him to."

Suzanne's fingers curled about the stem of her glass. "Alistair's wife. Whom, according to Malcolm, Alistair disliked as much as she disliked him."

Raoul tossed down a sip of wine. "Malcolm was a boy at the time."

"His memories seem very distinct." Suzanne kept her gaze on Raoul's face. "You're saying that's not the truth about Alistair Rannoch and Lady Arabella's marriage?"

Raoul snatched up his glass and took a long swallow. "I'm saying that to explain the rest of this properly, I don't just need to talk to you. I need to talk to Malcolm."

"I left the children off at home and went to Hookham's, where I happened upon Mr. O'Roarke, so I thought I would ask him." Suzanne paused, aware that her voice sounded a trifle too breathless. She and Malcolm were walking along Piccadilly on the edge of Green Park. She had sent word to him at Brooks's, and he had met her at the corner of the park, since ladies were not to be seen on the stretch of St. James's Street that contained the gentlemen's clubs. Another of those absurd rules of the beau monde that were so hard to keep straight.

"And O'Roarke said he needed to speak with me when you asked him about Alistair and his escape from Ireland in '98?" Malcolm was frowning, but he didn't appear to question her story. She was overthinking things. Raoul had worked with them two years ago to rescue the St. Gilles family from Paris. Since then, she as well as Malcolm could reasonably consider him a friend and ally. Someone she might very well speak to on her own.

Suzanne nodded. She had to keep her persona straight without muddying it with details from her real life. "I don't understand his connection to your father, but it makes sense that whatever it is, he'd want to explain it to you instead of having me pass the information along."

Malcolm nodded. "He said Alistair assisted him at my mother's request?"

"Yes. Given everything you've told me about your parents, I was as surprised as you."

" 'Surprised' is scarcely a strong enough word." Malcolm was still frowning. She knew that look. It meant he was puzzling something out but wasn't ready to share it with her yet. "Where did you say we'd meet him?"

"At home." Still odd to be calling the Berkeley Square house "home." Still odd to have a home. "At four o'clock." She hesitated, aware of the tension in his arm beneath her gloved fingers. "Do you want to speak to him alone? I know you said you wanted me there, but if this changes things—" Given Malcolm's sensitivity about his mother, it seemed the obvious thing to say, though if he agreed she wondered how on earth she would ever get the truth from either him or Raoul.

He looked down at her with surprise. "Why? I don't have any secrets from you." A smile tugged at his mouth. "Well, at least I'm trying not to have any more than I already do."

She permitted herself a tiny sigh of relief, while the coming scene still tugged at her nerve endings.

They reached Berkeley Square to find the children in the square garden with Laura Dudley. Jessica was standing up, holding on to the edge of a bench, bouncing on the black kid–slippered soles of her feet. Colin was following Berowne, who was walking along the flagstones in a zigzag pattern. The cat was getting remarkably comfortable with his lead, though he didn't precisely walk like a dog.

Suzanne and Malcolm stopped and leaned over the gate to wave to the children. Colin scooped up Berowne and ran over to them. "He hardly ever just lies down and won't walk anymore."

Suzanne leaned over the gate to stroke the cat's head. "You're doing splendidly with him, Colin."

"Mamama," Jessica said. Suzanne still wasn't sure Jessica identified the sound with her mother, but Laura picked her up and carried her over to Suzanne and Malcolm. Suzanne took Jessica in her arms and kissed her.

"Do you want to come in?" Colin asked.

"For a few minutes," Malcolm said. "We have a visitor coming."

"Who?"

"Mr. O'Roarke."

"Perhaps he'll come to the park, too. I like him."

Suzanne touched her fingers to her son's head and willed them to remain steady.

For a quarter hour, Malcolm and Colin walked Berowne and rolled a ball while Suzanne nursed Jessica. Laura pulled out a book and pretended to be invisible, as she so often did. Suzanne was just doing up her gown, one-handed, while holding Jessica in her other arm, when Raoul strolled into the square.

"Mr. O'Roarke!" Colin sprang up from the pavement where he'd been playing with Berowne. "Do you want to play catch with Daddy and me?"

Raoul's smile gave no sign of being anything out of the ordinary, Suzanne noted, past the catch in her own breathing. After four years one would think she'd be used to such moments.

"Perhaps later, Colin. I need to speak with your parents. But I saw the throw you just made. You have a capital arm. As your father did as a boy. You also clearly have a knack with animals."

Colin grinned and dropped down beside Berowne, who had rolled onto his back and was expecting pets. Suzanne gave Jessica back to Laura and got to her feet. Malcolm was holding open the garden gate. "O'Roarke," he said. "It's good of you to come."

"Of course," Raoul returned.

The three of them crossed to the Rannoch house, where Valentin admitted them and they went through the maddeningly slow business of divesting themselves of their outer garments. Malcolm led the way to the library without further speech. The shadows slanting through the windows were deepening, so Malcolm lit the brace of candles on the library table. Suzanne realized belatedly that neither of the men could sit until she did so. She dropped down on the sofa. Malcolm sat beside her and gestured Raoul to one of the Queen Anne chairs.

Silence stretched through the room. Malcolm met Raoul's gaze. "Suzanne says Alistair helped you escape Ireland in '98."

"Yes." Raoul crossed his legs. "You're understandably surprised. Alistair hardly seemed a supporter of Irish independence."

"No. But then I didn't know he was a French agent, either."

"Good lord," Raoul said on a perfectly calibrated note of surprise.

"You didn't know?"

"Certainly not." Which was true, if one went back to before her own talk with him two days ago.

Malcolm rested one arm along the sofa back, not quite touching Suzanne's shoulder. "However, I'm more surprised by your assertion that he assisted you at my mother's request. Unless my mother's means of persuasion was to tell Alistair she'd like nothing better than to see you arrested."

Raoul gave a faint smile. "Yes, that might well have done the trick. But I don't believe it's the means Arabella used."

Malcolm's gaze locked on Raoul's own, gray eyes meeting gray. "What means did she use?"

Raoul leaned back against the red velvet of the chair and

crossed his legs. "I wasn't privy to their conversation. But my impression is that your mother had some leverage on Alistair that she employed to persuade him."

"Do you think she knew he was a French spy?" Malcolm asked.

"I didn't at the time. But given what you've told me—It's possible." Raoul leaned forwards. "Most of the leaders of the United Irishmen had been arrested in March when Thomas Reynolds betrayed us. Edward Fitzgerald and I escaped arrest—for some reason, Reynolds chose to warn us."

"And you were urged to leave the country."

"Government sources as good as told Fitzgerald they'd turn a blind eye," Raoul said. "They didn't want to arrest an Anglo-Irish aristocrat whose great-great-grandfather was Charles the Second. But Fitzgerald wouldn't use his position to escape when his comrades were under arrest." Raoul's mouth twisted. "He was a romantic idealist to the point of foolhardiness, but a good man. My own reaction was more tactical. I wasn't going to leave before the Uprising occurred."

"At that point you were unlikely to get French help," Malcolm said. "You have to have known the odds were against you."

Raoul sat back in the high-backed chair. "Oh yes."

"Speaking of romantic idealists who can be foolhardy."

"Your mother said something similar to me at the time. I maintain that I'm a pragmatist. Who's willing to run risks."

"That sounds the sort of thing a romantic idealist might say," Malcolm said. "Go on."

Suzanne said nothing. She had heard Raoul tell the story of the United Irish Uprising often before, but it was different hearing him relate the events to Malcolm.

"After the March arrests, martial law was imposed on most of Ireland. The country was seething. The pressure to act was enormous. It seemed as though if we didn't, all of us would be crushed. A matter of calculating the odds."

"You could have calculated the odds and decided you'd be safer in South America."

"I could have done. I didn't."

Malcolm gave a faint smile, his gaze not leaving Raoul's face. "As I said."

Was there just a trace of an echo in Malcolm's smile of her own hero worship? Raoul drew you in that way. It was the bone-deep commitment to a cause beneath the veneer of hardheaded pragmatism that made one willing to risk anything for him. After all, he was willing to do the same.

"I think you know how matters unfolded," Raoul said in a neutral voice. "Fitzgerald was again betrayed, this time by Francis Magan, and taken into custody only a few days before the planned rising."

"So you were the only leader not in custody by the time of the actual rising," Malcolm said.

"Hardly the only. The one with the most notoriety perhaps. And then, only an hour before the rising was set to begin, government troops occupied our planned assembly points in Dublin. Our men dispersed, strewing the surrounding lanes with their weapons." Raoul's eyes darkened.

"More informants," Malcolm said.

"Quite. I was outside Dublin at the time organizing support in the surrounding counties. I remember being not best pleased to be away from the heart of things, but that probably saved me from arrest myself. On 24 May the rising began. We actually got control of much of county Kildare for a time." A faint glow lit his eyes at the memory. The candlelight softened the lines in his face, and Suzanne had a sense she was seeing him as he had been at the time of the Uprising, not much older than Malcolm was now. "But we lost at Carlow and Tara Hill, and in Wicklow rebel suspects were massacred. Sir Edward Crosbie was executed for treason. We fought a guerrilla campaign at Wicklow that in many ways prepared me for Spain. I went back and forth between there and Wexford in the next few weeks," he continued, neatly sidestepping that his true loyalties in Spain had not been with the *guerrilleros*. He paused a moment. "After France, I could scarcely have been called a romantic when it came to rebellions, but any lingering illusions I had fled in those weeks. Perhaps it's folly to talk about degrees of brutality, but those months in Ireland were particularly savage. On both sides."

Suzanne had heard the stories, enough to shake even her hardened sensibilities. Both sides had burned prisoners alive.

"It was a waste. Brutality combined with incompetence. The blunders I've lain awake replaying—" Raoul's mouth turned grim. Suzanne well knew he hated incompetence and waste. "Finally in August we received help from the French. About a thousand troops landed at county Mayo. We had some success fighting with them, but we were soundly defeated at Ballinuck by government forces. And when a larger French force arrived in October, they surrendered after a naval battle without even landing in Ireland." Raoul passed a hand over his face. "I'm sorry. I'm giving you more detail than you probably wanted."

"No." Malcolm was watching Raoul as though processing details Suzanne couldn't quite understand. "It's good to have a full picture."

Raoul inclined his head in an odd sort of silent communication. "By October things were falling apart, though some guerrilla fighting went on for years. The French who were taken prisoner were packed back to France. But the Irish were considered traitors rather than prisoners of war."

"Because Ireland wasn't—isn't—acknowledged as a separate country," Malcolm said. "The source of the problem."

"Quite. So the rebels were executed as traitors. And because I'd been one of the original ringleaders, arresting me became a matter of some moment for the British authorities."

"As I've heard tell there were times you kept the rebellion alive in parts of Ireland by sheer force of will," Malcolm said.

Raoul shook his head. "No man—or woman—can really do that. Not without popular support. But I was a hunted man. I'd been wounded—not badly but enough to need treatment. Poor Fitzgerald had died of his wounds back in June when the British denied him proper attention. I managed to take refuge with a family in Tipperary, but I had no safe route to the coast, and it was only a matter of time before government troops found me."

"I remember," Malcolm said. "Mama's face was white. As it was when you were in Les Carmes during the Terror."

Raoul shifted slightly to the side, his face more in shadow. "Your mother was kind to be concerned for me. She came to see me in secret where I was hiding. She told me not to do anything foolish, that she could get me to France if I gave her a few days. I probably should have surrendered then to avoid letting her run risks, but as I said, I'm a pragmatist."

"Or you have respect for women's intelligence." Malcolm flicked a glance at Suzanne. "Go on."

"She returned with your father. I was as surprised as you were on hearing their plan. To own the truth I more than half-expected to be betrayed, but I had few alternatives at that point, so I went with them. Horace Smytheton had a smugglers' boat ready. Much to my own surprise, after an uneventful crossing, I found myself safely in France."

Malcolm sat watching Raoul. Suzanne would swear he hadn't moved a muscle during the last part of the story. "My mother risked a great deal for you."

"So she did. Arabella was a good friend."

"I remember seeing the two of you walking together. Watching you toss her up on her horse. Seeing her open your letters." Malcolm drew a raw breath. Suzanne had the sense he was hesitating on the edge of a precipice, aware of the irrevocable nature of the next step. It was oddly similar to Raoul's own hesitation before he admitted Lady Arabella's role in his escape.

Malcolm released his breath and leaned forwards. "Sir, are you my father?"

CHAPTER 17

Suzanne couldn't control her indrawn breath. Fortunately, Malcolm and Raoul were so focused on each other she doubted either was even aware she was in the room. She was a spectator to the revelations. And yet in some ways they could not have affected her more.

The rattle of carriage wheels from the street echoed through the stillness, though the air was so fraught she could almost have sworn the sound was the press of emotions hanging between the two men.

"That's a rather extraordinary question." Raoul settled back in his chair as though they were discussing chess moves or cricket play. "What makes you think so?"

"It's not so very extraordinary." Malcolm's voice was even and measured, though she could hear the tension that underlay it. "I've long suspected Alistair Rannoch wasn't my father. I think it first occurred to me when I was twelve. I was in London—one of my rare visits here—after winning a history prize at Harrow. My parents had dinner guests—hard now to remember they actually managed to give dinner parties together—and the schoolroom party came into the drawing room after dinner. One of Alistair's friends—I think it was Lord Bessborough—said he must be very proud of me.

And Alistair replied that he could take no credit for his heir's accomplishments."

Raoul's eyes remained steady on Malcolm's face. Suzanne caught a wince in the depths of his gaze. "That can't have been easy to hear."

Malcolm shrugged and gave a wry grimace. "To own the truth, it felt less like a shock than confirmation of something I'd known all along. It was almost a relief to be able to make sense of why my father—Alistair—had never much seemed to like me. Though to be fair he never seemed overfond of Edgar or Gisèle, either."

"Malcolm—" Raoul swallowed. "No one should have to grow up with that."

"It's hardly a unique burden. Most people know William Lamb is Lord Egremont's son. It's a fairly open secret in the family that only Aunt Frances's eldest is her husband's child. Judith and Christopher like to speculate that their fathers were royal. I never went so far as to voice my suspicions. Perhaps out of concern for my mother. But I could hardly be devastated that a man I didn't like wasn't my father."

"Very rationally put," Raoul said.

"But you think it's bluster? I've had a long time to consider it." Malcolm sat back on the sofa, mirroring Raoul's posture. "I saw my mother less than Aunt Frances's children saw her. I didn't know the names of most of her lovers. I tended to shy away from the gossip."

"Understandable."

"I should have suspected about you sooner," Malcolm continued in the same level tone. "You were always very kind to me. But you'd fled to France the autumn before I overheard my father's exchange with Bessborough. I think something stopped me from fully articulating the question, even to myself."

"Also not surprising."

"But I think I wondered all along about you without ever quite acknowledging it." Malcolm's words were still measured, but they tumbled from his lips more freely. Almost, Suzanne thought, as though it was a relief to finally speak of it. "The first I consciously voiced the question to myself was two years ago in Paris when you

helped us get the St. Gilleses out of France. And then, as with realizing Alistair wasn't my father, it was less surprising than like something I should have known all along. I learned then that my mother
had told you about Tatiana, a secret she jealously guarded. Now I
learn the lengths she went to to save you after the Uprising."

"There could have been a great deal between your mother and
me without my being your father."

"There could."

Malcolm's gaze locked on Raoul's own, gray eyes once again
meeting gray.

"You haven't answered my question," Malcolm said. "Are you
my father?"

Suzanne felt the breath tighten in her throat, as though she
could choke on the possible implications.

Raoul was silent for seconds together. The wind must have
shifted, because she could hear Colin calling to Berowne in the
square garden.

"Yes," Raoul said.

Malcolm released his breath in a rough sigh.

"Your mother . . . meant a great deal to me." Raoul seemed to
be searching through an infinite verbal landscape for the right
words. "As I think you know, your parents'—Arabella and Alistair's—marriage was problematic from the first. By the time your
mother and I were involved, they were openly estranged, though
they hadn't been married long. But there was no question of doing
anything but treating you as Alistair's son, of course. Your mother
was unconventional but not to that degree."

"And Alistair couldn't have disowned me without casting himself as the cuckolded husband."

"Quite." Raoul's fingers curled round the chair arm, his only indication of disquiet. "A few years later I married myself—an error
in judgment. Margaret and I were—are—spectacularly unsuited.
Your mother and I drifted back together. It wasn't what one would
call an exclusive relationship, but it endured."

"She was involved with Archibald Davenport in '98."

"Was she? I didn't know. But while I wouldn't say I was jealous,
I also wasn't precisely overeager to learn the names of her lovers."

Raoul hesitated. Suzanne saw his knuckles whiten. "I couldn't do a great deal for you. I certainly didn't do what a father should. But I was selfish enough to want some relationship with you."

"Your interest...meant a great deal." Malcolm drew another breath. "You were always kind to me."

"Malcolm—" Raoul's voice was rough, as though he had difficulty forming the words. "You deserved a great deal more."

"Many men would have done less." Malcolm still spoke in the careful voice Suzanne recognized as a sign that all his energy was being concentrated to keep a lid on his feelings. "One isn't considered to owe anything to a bastard child."

"Damn it, Malcolm." Raoul sat forwards, hands taut on the carved arms of the chair. "I won't have you using such words about yourself."

Malcolm leaned back on the sofa. "It's a statement of fact."

"You know better than to speak dismissively about someone based on his or her birth."

"I hope so. I learned as much from you."

Raoul gave a faint smile. "If you learned anything at all from me, I'm immeasurably grateful."

Malcolm's gaze flickered round the oak and gilt and marble of the library. "But it doesn't change the fact that by the rules of our world I'm illegitimate and have no right to my handsome inheritance."

"You know better than to give any credence to the rules of this world." Raoul's voice was even, but his knuckles showed white. "But if you did, the fact that your mother was married to Alistair Rannoch makes you his son."

"Something that never made either Alistair or me very happy." Malcolm glanced at the glass-fronted bookcase that held Alistair Rannoch's first editions. "Did he know?"

"That he wasn't your biological father? I think so. That I was? I'm not sure. He and Arabella—"

"Despised each other. That wasn't your fault."

"I'd have liked—" Raoul drew a breath. "I'd have liked to do more."

"And you were busy saving the world."

Raoul's mouth twisted. "Hardly that. Trying to make a difference round the edges. It seemed of all-consuming importance at the time. Looking back—I wonder about the nature of obligations and where one is needed most and owes the greatest loyalty."

Malcolm met Raoul's gaze in what seemed a moment of understanding. "In Brussels two years ago, it seemed vitally important to me to be there for the battle. Even though it wasn't really my fight." He turned his gaze to Suzanne for a moment. "I even told Suzette she couldn't ask me to stay back, and being Suzette she said of course she wouldn't. But in the midst of Waterloo, with my friends dying all round, I couldn't help but wonder if perhaps my greatest loyalty wasn't to her and Colin."

Raoul leaned forwards, hands clasped together. "Loyalty is never simple. I thought I was needed. But looking back, one could argue I didn't accomplish much."

To Suzanne's surprise, the gaze Malcolm turned on Raoul reminded her of the way he looked at Colin. So that for a moment it was as if he were the parent and Raoul the child. "You accomplished a great deal, O'Roarke. And in any event, you tried, which you always taught me is the important thing."

Something leaped for an instant in Raoul's eyes, quickly masked with a wry smile. "You're remarkably understanding. I wish I could make up for the past years."

"You needn't apologize." Malcolm had his armor well in place. "You didn't owe me anything."

"You can't mean that." Raoul's gaze flickered to the windows and the square garden. "I've seen you with your own son."

"But then I chose to be Colin's father. You were rather stuck with me."

"No." The word was quick and hard, like a hand slammed down on a marble table. Raoul swallowed. "I'm proud of few enough things in my fifty-some years, Malcolm. But when I read your speeches, I'm conscious of a pride I have no right to feel."

For a moment, Suzanne thought Malcolm's armor would crack. Then he said, "That's good of you."

"That's the truth."

Malcolm shifted on the sofa. "You said you weren't sure if Alistair knew you were my father. Not even after he helped you escape?"

"Perhaps particularly then. I've never seen someone so careful to give nothing away."

"And Smytheton?"

"Alistair brought Smytheton into it. Your mother wasn't happy about it, but Alistair said they needed his help and Smytheton wouldn't dare go against him."

"So Mama was blackmailing Alistair and Alistair was blackmailing Smytheton."

"So it would appear."

"Do you think Fa—Alistair was an Irish sympathizer?"

"I'm quite certain he wasn't. He said little to me on that voyage to France, but he did quite clearly say that at least we were getting my dangerous, subversive views out of Britain."

"But then he was a French spy."

"But I'd swear he wasn't a revolutionary at heart. Alistair had a conservative soul."

Malcolm inclined his head. "And you didn't learn anything else? Anything that could shed light on what Alistair was doing? Or Smytheton?"

"I've been thinking back over it in the past few hours. But no."

"Did you ever hear about a club called the Elsinore League?"

Raoul leaned back in his chair and crossed his legs. "Only vaguely, as a sort of hellfire club."

Malcolm nodded. "And the leak that led to the betrayal at Dunboyne?"

"I told you I didn't know where it came from."

"And I'm asking again."

Raoul gave a faint smile. "As I would in your shoes. But other than that it was obviously someone with inside knowledge of the operation, I don't know."

"You must have wondered."

"Of course. Further intelligence of that sort might have turned the tide for us. I made what inquiries I could in the midst of the rebellion."

"Even in the midst of a rebellion you're an intelligence expert, O'Roarke."

"I'm flattered. But regardless, I wasn't able to learn anything before circumstances forced me to run."

"Alistair didn't refer to it?"

"No, he—" Raoul frowned. "It was just before we set sail. Alistair said he wouldn't be such a hypocrite as to wish me luck, save that it was to both our benefits that I make it safely to France. Then he added that if it weren't for his friends things might have ended at Dunboyne."

The sound of the front door closing as Valentin showed Raoul from the house echoed through the stillness in the library. Suzanne touched her husband's hand. Shaken as she was, she had to remember he had endured the more soul-shaking revelation. "Darling—"

"I'm all right." He squeezed her fingers and gave her a quick smile. "It's a relief in a way. I can't say it cuts me free of Alistair, but it loosens the ties. I can't imagine someone I'd more like not to be tied to. And O'Roarke's right. To object to the term 'bastard' makes a mockery of everything I stand for."

"Words can sting even when one knows they shouldn't."

"If so, it's a sting I'll learn to live with." He carried her hand to his lips and brushed his mouth across her fingers. "Besides, I like O'Roarke. I always have. Not that—"

He broke off, as though whatever he felt about Raoul was still too personal to share. Perhaps because he was still sorting it for himself.

She tightened her fingers round his own, wanting to hold on to the warmth. "You never told me. That you suspected Mr. O'Roarke might be your father."

He glanced down at their clasped hands. "I suppose—I was still working it out for myself. As I said, the idea was formed in my head before I was even properly aware of it."

"And you weren't ready to share it. It's all right, darling. As I've said, marriage shouldn't wholly deprive one of privacy." Though it was so easy for emotional confessions to become proofs of love and secrets to seem barriers to it.

"I think perhaps I was afraid to make too much of it." Malcolm spoke slowly, as though picking his way through a verbal landscape, searching perhaps for the safest path, perhaps for the most honest one. "It shouldn't matter—who fathered me in the crudest sense of the word. It goes against everything I believe in to lay such stress on bloodlines. And yet . . ." He hesitated, as though afraid of what he might say next. "O'Roarke was more to me than just a biological sire. I don't have the words for quite what he was. I don't want to make it into more than it is in some sort of maudlin search for the father I've managed without for years. But I think perhaps it was far more than I understood at the time."

Thank God Malcolm had let go of her hand, because her fingers were chilled to the bone. Beneath her husband's matter-of-fact words was an undertone that might have been longing. And it sliced her in two.

"He went through hell in Ireland," Malcolm continued. "He risked everything for something he believed in. In a way I've never quite done."

"You've never had the same sort of cause. But you share a certain sort of loyalty." As they shared the color of their eyes—why, why had she been so blind to the similarities staring her in the face?

"Perhaps. I admire him. But—"

The question hung in the air.

Suzanne looked at her husband through the twilight shadows and flickering lamplight that filled the library. Outside the windows, the branches of the plane trees were a dark, twisted tracery against the pale gray sky. "But what?" she asked.

"But I'm quite sure there's a great deal he isn't telling us. Particularly about the Elsinore League." He turned to her with a smile that couldn't quite banish the ghosts in his eyes. "It shouldn't be a surprise. We've learned full well that liking a person and trusting them are two very different things."

She swallowed. "So we have."

Outside in the hall, the front door banged open and shut. High-pitched voices filled the air. Berowne meowed. Laura and the children returning from the square garden.

Malcolm stared at the door for a moment. "Not to give too much credence to biology. But this makes O'Roarke the children's grandfather."

Her hands locked together in her lap. "So it does."

CHAPTER 18

Malcolm got to his feet and moved to the library door. Colin and Jessica's grandfather. What an odd thought that the day's revelations tied Raoul O'Roarke not just to him but to his children.

"I need to feed Jessica before I dress for dinner," Suzanne said. "And we promised Colin a story. I can—"

"No, you nurse Jessica. I'll read to him." Malcolm opened the door to see Jessica taking tiny steps down the hall holding Colin's hands. Colin looked up at him. "She'll be walking by herself any day now."

Jessica gave a crow of delight and tugged her brother to walk faster. Malcolm grinned in spite of himself, swept into the comforting maelstrom of the child world.

Upstairs, the buttered toast and warm milk smells of the nursery were blessedly normal. Thank God Colin was still at an age where he'd cuddle. He snuggled up next to Malcolm on the window seat, and Malcolm was able to run his fingers through his son's thick hair as he read a chapter about King Arthur and Merlin. Talk about fathers and sons and surrogate fathers. This at least was unvarnished parenting. He was sure of himself, sure of his responsibilities, sure of his feelings and that they were returned. How odd he'd once thought he wouldn't know how to go on as a parent.

Suzanne was still nursing Jessica when they finished the chapter, so he saw Colin settle in for his supper with Laura and then went to dress for dinner and the Carfax House ball. Addison was in the bedchamber, brushing a black evening coat.

"I've laid out your things, sir." Addison's voice and gaze were as neutral as ever, but his eyes lingered on Malcolm's face for a moment. How much did his valet see? Malcolm wondered. Probably far more than Malcolm would wish, judging by the past. Addison had certainly sliced through the thicket of unvoiced emotions at the time of Malcolm and Suzanne's marriage.

Malcolm stripped off his day coat and began to undo the buttons on his waistcoat. The day's news wasn't really so earthshaking. As he'd told O'Roarke and Suzanne, he'd suspected for a long time. Today had merely brought confirmation. Alistair Rannoch was still the man who had given him a name and not loved him, Raoul O'Roarke was still the man who had been kind to him as a boy and sparked his curiosity about the world. He had learned how much his mother had cared for O'Roarke, but he had already known they were close. The oddest thing was Alistair's own role in rescuing O'Roarke. Which was puzzling and significant for the investigation but hardly something to turn his world upside down.

Malcolm paused, his shirt half over his head though he had no memory of removing his cravat. So why did he feel as shaken and cast adrift as when he'd been tossed from his boat on Dunmykel Bay? Because for an instant O'Roarke's words and the warmth beneath the cool gray gaze had struck a spark of warmth within him. Absurd and nonsensical. But for just a moment he had caught a glimmering of what it might be like to be sure of a parent's love.

"Darling?" Suzanne must have come into the room without him noticing the opening of the door. "Are you all right?"

Malcolm turned round. His wife was watching him with a concerned gaze, the nursing flap on her bodice still partially unbuttoned. Not only had she come into the room without his noticing, Addison had apparently withdrawn. "Quite all right." He smiled, rather surprised to find it didn't require an effort. "In fact, I think I may be better than I've been in some time."

Suzanne echoed his smile, but for an instant he thought he

caught a flicker of concern in her eyes. Then she stepped forwards and touched his face. "I'm glad. Colin asked if you could look in before we leave for Carfax House."

He grinned. "Of course."

Oddly, he'd never felt more like a father.

Malcolm had first visited Carfax House as a boy of ten, home from Harrow for a visit with David. It was one of the great houses of London, larger and grander than the Berkeley Square house, set back from the street with a handsome forecourt and its own ballroom at the back. Yet for all the grandeur and David's trepidation at facing his father, Malcolm recalled that the house had felt more a family home than his parents' house. Perhaps because Lord and Lady Carfax didn't detest each other. And they loved their children, whatever pressures they put on them.

Tonight he was climbing the same stairs he had first run up with David. This time in a black cassimere evening coat and white pantaloons rather than a schoolboy's jacket and dusty breeches. Instead of David beside him, he had Suzanne on his arm, trailing silver tulle, diamonds glinting in her hair. A sea of ball guests surrounded them. Malcolm felt a flash of affection for the boy he had been then. He would never have thought he could be as happy as he was now. Or so at peace with the truth about his father.

Lady Carfax stood at the head of the stairs, a petite woman with delicate features and a cloud of dark hair untouched by gray. "Malcolm. And Suzanne. How lovely. I count on you to help me keep the peace this evening. We have a positively alarming mix of Tories and Whigs in the ballroom. And I know it would be too much to hope that people will refrain from talking politics."

Malcolm kissed her cheek. *Odd that Carfax could be so devoted to a woman with whom he shared none of his work or the complex inner workings of his mind.* Malcolm couldn't imagine being satisfied with such a relationship. But then he couldn't really imagine being married to or at least achieving such a level of intimacy with anyone but Suzanne.

"Thank God." David moved to their side inside the ballroom doors. "I was afraid the investigation would keep you away."

"Ballrooms are excellent places to investigate," Suzanne said, leaning in to accept his kiss.

"I don't know what you said to Jennifer this afternoon," Simon said, kissing Suzanne as well, "but she was positively on fire at rehearsal after her talk with you. You could have cut the tension in her scene with Hamlet with a knife. Just what I wanted. Though Smytheton looked a bit distracted. We got through the whole scene—and a scene with Jennifer at that—without an interruption from him. My heartfelt thanks."

"Shakespeare's a good topic of conversation tonight," David said. "Excuse me. I promised my mother I'd keep Lord Holland and Sidmouth from coming to blows."

"The burden of being the heir and in the Opposition," Simon said as David moved off. "Lady Carfax is every bit as much a strategist in her own way as Lord Carfax, though she aims to smooth things over. In that David takes after her. They'd both prefer it if I kept my mouth shut. I can't help but wonder if it wouldn't be easier for him if I weren't here."

"I wouldn't think it for a moment." Malcolm squeezed Simon's arm. "Solidarity means a lot." He flashed a smile at Suzanne.

"But then Suzanne's a great deal more welcome than I am. She has a knack for saying what she thinks without stirring matters up."

Suzanne adjusted her pearl bracelet. "Perhaps because no one takes me seriously."

"In truth," Malcolm said, "I'm not sure the *Hamlet* manuscript is such a safe topic of conversation."

"So you'd rather I didn't talk about it?" Simon asked.

"On the contrary. I'd very much like it if you did. And note the reactions. Any trouble at the theatre today after we left?"

"Not so much as a whiff of anything out of the ordinary rehearsal chaos. No trouble in Berkeley Square?"

Malcolm shook his head. "It's odd, the first two attacks followed so quick on each other, I'm surprised we've gone this long without another attempt. I wonder—Allie. Geoff." He broke off as he caught sight of his cousin and her husband moving towards them. "Any new discoveries?"

"Sadly, no," Aline said, "though I'm finding the Hamlet-Claudius relationship fascinating. Geoff and I were debating whether the fact that Hamlet seems to suspect Claudius might be his father in this version would make him more or less likely to seek revenge for old King Hamlet's murder. I thought it might explain his trepidation, but Geoff—"

"Thought it could make young Hamlet that much angrier at Claudius," Geoffrey Blackwell said. "But then Hamlet seems to have loved old King Hamlet or least admired him, in this version as in the one we know."

Malcolm told himself it was only his imagination that Geoffrey's gaze seemed to rest on him for a moment. Geoff's gaze always appeared keen, after all. "A good point," Malcolm said. "Though in both versions there seems to be a good measure of duty mixed in with the love." Something Malcolm had never felt when it came to Alistair Rannoch. Perhaps a small rebellion against the social order even as a young child? Or a reaction to Alistair's complete lack of pretense at fatherly feeling. And yet—learning who killed Alistair did matter.

"A good point," Geoffrey said. "I've always thought of Hamlet as a Renaissance prince who comes of age in the twilight of the chivalric era. His father's era."

Simon grinned. "You could be quoting my speech to the actors before the first read-through. There's much left to interpretation in this version, as in the canonical version. But the subtext between Hamlet and Claudius in this version gives the actors some wonderful layers to play with."

"There's a lot to decode in Shakespeare even without hidden messages." Malcolm scanned the ballroom. "I see Aunt Frances. I've been hoping for a word with her. Easier sometimes to speak to one's relatives in a crowd."

He felt Suzanne's anxious gaze on him as he moved off. But this was a conversation he had to have alone.

"Malcolm." Lady Frances turned to greet him and extended her hand. "You've come at just the right moment. I was about to be cornered by Lady Gordon. I'm fond enough of my grandchildren, but I have no desire to while away a ball hearing about somebody else's."

"Actually, I was hoping we could speak in private. The blue salon?"

Lady Frances's gaze flickered over his face, but she merely said, "So long as we can bring champagne," and snagged two glasses from the tray of a passing footman.

There were advantages to having practically grown up at Carfax House. Malcolm steered his aunt through the crowd to an innocuous door in the white-and-gold paneling, which gave on to a small sitting room hung with blue-striped paper. A fire burned in the grate and a brace of candles flickered on the central table. Lady Carfax always had all the house ready for visitors.

Malcolm closed the door and surveyed his aunt. The clear blue of her eyes, the ironic curve of her mouth, the lift of her brows. So familiar through a childhood of uncertainties. "How much did you know?" he asked.

She sank down on a blue damask sofa, her filmy gray skirts pooling about her. "Is this more about the Elsinore League? Because I told you—"

"You know damn well it isn't. How much did you know about my real father?"

Her sapphire ring trembled against the stem of her glass, but her voice was steady. "Don't be melodramatic, Malcolm. You never liked Alistair. I should think you'd be relieved to learn he wasn't your father."

"I was in a way." He gripped the gilded arm of the chair across from her and let himself into it. "Though somewhat surprised to learn my aunt has known the truth for years."

She took a sip of champagne. A controlled sip, not a desperate gulp. "It wasn't my secret to share."

"So you'd have let me—"

"How did you learn?"

"I guessed. O'Roarke admitted it."

The name was out in the open. He saw that fact register in his aunt's eyes. "He meant a great deal to your mother. And she to him, I think." She smoothed her satin sash. "I was the one who wrote to tell him you'd been born."

"So you knew from the first?"

She nodded. "Your mother used to send him reports of you every week."

He gave a short laugh, sharp with the memory of long parentless stretches in Scotland. "I wasn't aware that my mother thought of me every week."

Lady Frances met his gaze. "I'd be the last to claim Arabella was a perfect parent, but she thought of you more than you realize. And then after—"

"After he went to France she continued to write to him?"

"Oh yes." Lady Frances took another sip of champagne. "But I was going to say that after Arabella died, I took to writing."

Malcolm stared at his aunt. "You're saying that all these years you've been sending Raoul O'Roarke reports on me?"

"You make me sound like one of your agents, Malcolm. I let him know how his son went on. Whatever my maternal deficiencies, I'm enough of a parent myself that I could understand him wanting to know."

"He wasn't—"

"Your father? I know you didn't think of him that way. But I'm quite sure that's how he saw himself. He was very concerned about you after Arabella's death. And then when—"

Malcolm stared at her, gripped by cold horror. "You told O'Roarke?"

"He deserved to know."

It was a wonder the stem of the glass didn't snap in his fingers. "You told him that I—"

"I told him that we would forever have cause to be grateful to David Mallinson and Simon Tanner for stopping you from slitting your wrists."

"They didn't stop me. They bandaged me up before I could bleed to death."

For a moment his aunt's gaze held a remembered fear that shook him. Aunt Frances wasn't a woman who was afraid of anything. "You can't tell me you wouldn't have wanted to know if it were Colin."

"Colin is my son."

"My point precisely."

Malcolm stared at his glass for a moment, then tossed down half the contents. "It's not as though there was anything he could do."

"Sometimes worrying is a parent's right," Lady Frances said in a quiet voice. "I know he was relieved when you went to the Peninsula. Because he thought it would give you a focus. And because he was able to see you."

Malcolm found himself tugging at his shirt cuffs. The scars were still there on his wrists, though so faint even Suzanne had never questioned them. Ironic that of all people it was Carfax who had come to his rescue, arranging his posting to Lisbon at David and Simon's behest. Malcolm, listless and sick of life, had gone along because it seemed easier than protesting. Carfax, to his credit, had not commented on Malcolm's situation but had calmly thanked him for his service to his country. Malcolm could still hear Carfax's dry voice and see him calmly fiddling with his spectacles on a day when any expression of sympathy would have undone Malcolm. Whatever he thought of Carfax, he knew he would be forever in the man's debt. "It's not as though—"

"Those were rather alarming months," his aunt said. "And one never stops worrying."

Malcolm stared at her. How had he never before glimpsed the worry behind her dry gaze? "My God. You're still afraid I'll try something."

"No." She put up a hand to tuck a curl behind her ear. "Not beyond the extent one always worries about one's children."

"So confident of my state of mind?" He could not keep the mockery from his voice.

"So confident of how seriously you take your responsibilities to your wife and children."

He bit back another retort. She was right. It was in part his very rootlessness that had driven his desperation. Whatever happened, with people dependent on him he would never seek that way out again.

"Did you know Mama got O'Roarke out of Ireland?"

Lady Frances nodded. "I told you, he was important to her. I don't much care for the phrase 'love of one's life,' and with Arabella it seems particularly problematic, but he was certainly central to her."

"Did you know Fa—Alistair helped?"

She was silent.

"Aunt Frances. This isn't just idle speculation about the past."

She spread her fingers in her lap, pressing down a snag in her skirt. "Arabella didn't tell me. But Alistair—He was in a temper. Normally we steered away from personal topics—I had no particular desire to hear about Alistair's preoccupations—but for some reason I teased him to tell me what was wrong. At last he said he'd never forgive Arabella for what she'd embroiled him in. When I asked what that meant, he said she'd compelled him to help a man who was out to destroy everything he'd achieved in life. He could care less that the man was her lover, but that men like O'Roarke would turn the world over to the rabble. Naturally I was surprised, and I said why on earth had he assisted her then. Alistair looked—" Lady Frances ran her fingers over the chain of the diamond pendant Alistair had given her. "I was going to say 'angry,' but it was more than that. He looked worried. I half-thought he wasn't going to answer, but I think he was afraid to stay silent out of cowardice. He said, 'Your sister isn't afraid to make use of information.' Which only made me even more intrigued. But I couldn't get him to reveal more, try as I might."

Malcolm stared into his glass for a moment. "Do you think he knew O'Roarke is my father?"

Lady Frances's fingers trembled against the white gold chain. "I wondered then, though I couldn't be sure. But—"

"He knew I wasn't his son."

Lady Frances drew a breath, then took a long sip of champagne. "What did he say to you?"

"Malcolm—"

"It's all right, he came close to admitting it to me."

"Then what he said to me shouldn't matter."

"Anything he said about any of this could relate to the investigation."

"This damned investigation of yours." She clunked her champagne glass down on a gilded mahogany table. "As if navigating the personal relationships in this family weren't difficult enough as it is."

"What did Alistair say to you?"

Lady Frances snatched up her glass and tossed down a sip. "It was the summer when you brought Suzanne and Colin to Britain for the first time. After the dinner I gave where he met Suzanne. When we—later that night—"

"When you spent the night together."

She gave a faint smile. "I was trying to spare your sensibilities. But yes, we were in my bedchamber. He said—" Again she drew a breath. "He said, 'People will remark on Malcolm's good fortune. But it's some comfort to know that one day he'll realize what it is to be betrayed by one's spouse.' "

"Is that all?" Malcolm laughed. "I'm not surprised he thought Suzanne would betray her marriage vows. He was clearly shocked she married me at all. But then I never cease to wonder at it myself."

Lady Frances touched his hand. "That's because you've always been woefully inclined to underrate yourself, my dear."

"Mrs. Rannoch."

The drawling voice pinned Suzanne where she stood, even before she turned round to meet his blue gaze and the smile that taunted with mockery. "Colonel Radley." She extended her hand. He was a nuisance, she reminded herself, a tiresome nuisance she had dealt with in the past. She had seduced Radley on a mission before she met Malcolm. Radley didn't know she had been a French agent, but he did know her past wasn't what she claimed it to be. He had tried to blackmail her over it in Vienna, but she had told Malcolm a version of the affair, which Malcolm had accepted without question. She had dealt with Radley then, she could deal with him now. It was only because of the other events of the day—of the week—that she felt as though she would shatter at the sight of him. "I thought you were still in Paris."

Radley bent over her hand. His mouth felt damp through the silk of her glove. "I'm on leave. Arrived in England last night.

Stewart said to come along to the party, and as Carfax and my father are old friends I thought they wouldn't turn me out."

Radley was close to Lord Stewart, Castlereagh's half-brother. Another tiresome thing about him. "I imagine a London ball seems tame after Paris."

"On the contrary." He retained hold of her hand, pressing it too tight. "It's good to see old friends. From what Stewart tells me you've become the toast of the beau monde."

Suzanne smiled into his mocking blue eyes. She wasn't going to give him the satisfaction of tugging her hand away. "Lord Stewart exaggerates." She doubted Stewart, who had made a crude pass at her in Paris, had said anything remotely complimentary about her.

Radley's gaze moved over her face. "It's different living here from being an expatriate. The English are so insular." Which was ironic, as he was a magnificent exemplar of that insularity himself. "I imagine you get a tiresome number of questions about your past."

She smiled at him. His heavy-handedness was a good reminder that she could run rings round him. "No more than I expected. Fortunately, Malcolm is wonderfully understanding about the difficulties, and that's really all that matters."

"Your husband is a very tolerant man."

"Suzanne." Cordelia swept up to them before Suzanne could answer and slid her arm round Suzanne's waist, solidarity in her touch. "Good evening, Colonel Radley."

"Lady Cordelia." Radley released Suzanne's hand without any sign of embarrassment. "Davenport. I heard you were living in London."

"And were shocked to find us still living under the same roof?" Harry inquired. "The world is quite turned upside down since Waterloo, you know."

"Always the jokester, Davenport."

"I find it helps to say cutting things first."

"Never could make head nor tail of what you said. But then I didn't go to Oxford. Ladies. I'm promised to Emily Cowper for the next waltz."

"Poor Emily," Cordelia said under her breath as Radley moved off. "I never could abide that man. Sorry we couldn't rescue you sooner, Suzie."

"I can take care of myself. Though the support is welcome."

"It's that sort of evening," Cordelia said. "Lady Carfax looked at me distinctly askance when we arrived. She's not a prude, but her own daughters are all so well behaved."

"I think she's generally nervous about any disturbance tonight because there are so many Whigs and Tories present," Suzanne said.

"I miss Paris. It's rather beastly to be where everyone knows one so well." Cordelia unfurled her fan. "Even at my worst I didn't actually cause scandals on the dance floor."

"No?" Harry asked, procuring glasses of champagne from a passing footman for the three of them.

Cordelia accepted a glass and took a meditative sip. "Well, there was the time Wetherby and Reggie Saunderson came to blows over whom I'd promised my next waltz to. But it was mild compared to the sort of insults Malcolm describes being hurled across the House."

Harry's gaze drifted round the ballroom. "Pity for the investigation you don't number any of the Elsinore League among your past conquests."

Cordelia smiled at him with the brightness of polished crystal, though Suzanne had a sense of what the exchange cost both of them. "Sorry, darling, I obviously wasn't thinking ahead enough. I don't suppose you want me to put my talents to use now?"

Harry lifted his glass to her. "I fear I'm not such a patriot. Or such a spymaster."

The word "spymaster" reminded Suzanne of her appointed task. She hadn't been sure Raoul would be here tonight, but she had glimpsed him a short time ago across the ballroom. She started to think up an excuse she could make to the Davenports when she saw that Raoul was making his way towards them.

"Mr. O'Roarke." Cordelia greeted him with a warm smile. Their adventure in Paris two years ago had made her think of Raoul as a friend and ally.

"Lady Cordelia. Davenport."

"It's good to see you, O'Roarke," Harry said. "I don't imagine you're particularly happy with either France or Spain these days."

"Quite. As often happens, one wonders what one was fighting for."

"I asked myself the same after Waterloo."

Raoul asked after the Davenport children, and then Harry led Cordelia onto the dance floor, leaving Suzanne and Raoul alone, without any need for subterfuge.

"I didn't realize you'd be here," Suzanne said. It was both helpful and disconcerting that she and Raoul could speak openly as friends in public now.

"I own I was surprised to receive the invitation. But as someone known to have fought with the *guerrilleros,* I'm considered an ally from the Peninsular War. Which apparently trumps my association with the United Irishmen in Carfax's eyes. Either that or he wants to keep an eye on me." His gaze moved over her face, carefully calibrated to reveal nothing more than polite interest. "I thought you might have matters you wished to discuss with me."

"How very prescient, Mr. O'Roarke." Her fingers tightened round the stem of her champagne glass with the press of the day's revelations. "There's an anteroom across the hall. Five minutes?"

He inclined his head.

She moved across the ballroom, reminding herself that it really didn't matter if anyone observed them. Even if there was gossip, Malcolm would just assume—correctly—that her conversation with Raoul was a follow-up to today's revelations. She stepped into the rose-papered room, swallowed the last of her champagne, and clunked her gilded crystal glass down before she could break it. Precisely five minutes later, judging by the gilt-and-porcelain clock on the mantel, Raoul came into the room.

Suzanne spun to face him the moment the door clicked closed, control worn to shreds. "Did you ever think about telling me?"

"Querida—"

She crossed to his side in two strides and gripped his wrists. "I told you Malcolm Rannoch had proposed to me. That I was thinking of accepting. Which would make him the father of the child I was carrying. The child you and I created. Did it occur to you to tell me the man I was considering marrying was your son?"

"It could hardly have failed to occur to me." His gaze stayed steady on her face, opaque, unfathomable. The familiar smell of his shaving soap washed over her. He made no effort to break her hold on his wrists.

"And?" She tightened her grip as though she could drag the answer from him.

"I did what I always do. Calculated the risks and rewards and decided not to tell you."

She released her hold on his wrists and slapped him across the face. "Damn you. Didn't it make any difference that Malcolm was your son?"

"Of course it made a difference." His voice was taut, but she could hear the roughness beneath. "I knew him. I'd watched him grow up. I trusted him."

"Trusted the man we both betrayed in every way possible—"

"Trusted him to be a good father to your child."

She took a step back and stared at the sharp bones of his face, as though his familiar collection of features belonged to someone she'd never seen before. "You can't seriously expect me to believe that was your foremost consideration."

"No." He met her gaze without shrinking from the fire. "We were at a crucial point in the war, and you could uncover invaluable information. Though ultimately you were the one who decided to marry him."

She flinched at the reminder. "Without knowing—"

"Would you have made a different decision if you'd known Malcolm was my son?"

"I—" She drew a breath, then felt the wind drain out of her. She dropped into a gilded chair, stomach roiling with self-disgust. "I don't know. Perhaps." She put her hand to her head, digging her fingers into the curls Blanca had so carefully arranged. "Oh, God, probably not. I was blind to the human equation, and I couldn't resist a challenge. The more impossible the mission the greater the lure." She fixed him with a hard stare. "But it should have been my choice to make."

"Granted." He dropped into a chair across from her and studied her for a moment with a cool gray gaze. A gaze so like Malcolm's. "I live with regrets that go back to before I met you, *querida*. Before you were born. One gets used to the taste of self-disgust. But my actions regarding your marriage to Malcolm are perhaps my greatest regret."

One of her diamond hairpins was slipping. She jabbed it back into place. "Would you do it differently if you had to do it again?"

He was silent for so long she wasn't sure he was going to answer. His gaze slid across the room to a pastoral print on the wall, then returned to her face. "I don't know."

"That's honest at least."

"Even I try to be honest upon occasion."

She dropped her head in her ivory-gloved hands. "And now I have to keep this from Malcolm as well."

"Which is precisely why I didn't tell you."

She drew a breath and lifted her head to meet his gaze. She wasn't yet ready to concede that he had any degree of right on his side.

"How did Malcolm seem after I left?" Raoul asked, in a voice that was a shade too carefully detached.

"Cautious." She rubbed at a smudge of eye blacking on her glove. "Unwilling to admit his feelings. Afraid to trust them to me or perhaps even to himself."

"He thanked me for paying as much attention to him as I did." Raoul's mouth hardened, then twisted. "For a moment I caught a glimpse—"

"Of?" She studied his face. It was a study of emotion held in check.

He hesitated as though perhaps he wasn't going to speak at all. Then, almost as though it was against his better judgment, said, "Of what it might have been like to actually have a son I could acknowledge. I didn't realize how much it would hurt." He gave a quick, self-mocking smile. "It's no more than I deserve."

"You might still have that. Malcolm is . . ." She hesitated. Why did she have this absurd urge to comfort Raoul? "I think Malcolm is happier than he'll admit to have found a father. I think he'd like more from you. And he may never learn the truth."

"But I know the truth," Raoul said in a low voice.

"And so you're punishing yourself?"

"If I were the sort to punish myself for my sins I wouldn't have done the things I've done. But nor am I capable of completely forgetting them."

The loss in his voice cut through to the place inside her that was a mother. "Raoul—" She stretched out a hand as she would to Colin. "I made the decision to marry a man and spy on him. That's on my head. I have to live with it."

" 'Living with it' being the operative words," Raoul said. "At the very least, we both owe it to Malcolm not to make this any worse for him than it is."

She pulled her shawl about her shoulders as a chill cut through her. "What this is for all of us may come down to a matter of luck."

"Then we'll have to do our best to make our own luck."

Her fingers tightened on the silk and cashmere of the shawl. "Malcolm told me he thinks the Raven might be a war bride. Easier to create a fictional past for a woman than for a soldier or diplomat."

Raoul gave a wry smile, though she saw the flash of concern in his eyes. "Yes, I thought he might think of that."

"You—" She stared at him. "Will I never get your limits?"

"It's an obvious question to ask. At least to a man of his understanding."

"And you know the way his mind works."

"That too. A bit like playing chess against a familiar opponent. There's no reason to think he'll guess it's you."

"Because he trusts me."

"Quite."

"A trust I built up under false pretenses."

"Not entirely false." Raoul straightened in his chair. "I put out information suggesting the Raven is a man. Malcolm or Davenport should uncover it in their inquiries."

She nodded, distaste sharp in her mouth.

"It's nothing we haven't done before."

"No."

Raoul regarded her for a moment. "I saw you with Radley. I almost intervened, but I thought that would only make matters worse."

"I can handle Radley."

"So you've told me." Raoul had been worried about Radley as long ago as when she first agreed to marry Malcolm. "Radley's a dangerous man. He's stupid enough one tends to discount him but clever and tenacious enough to cause problems when least expected."

She saw Radley's mocking gaze. It made her shiver. She wished it didn't. "Radley's just one more complication. God knows we have enough of them."

"*Querida*—" Raoul stretched out his hand, then let it fall to his side. "I can only imagine how angry you are at me. Take it out on me how you will. Stop talking to me if you must. But for God's sake, wait until we get through this investigation."

She felt a bleak smile twist her lips. "You're telling me I need you?"

"I'm pointing out that you have too keen an understanding to let personal feelings interfere with help in a crisis."

"It's a personal crisis."

"But not just yours."

She swallowed, seeing Jessica in her bassinet and Colin curled up with a book by the nursery fire when she'd gone in to say good night before she left for the ball. And Malcolm, smiling at her as they climbed the stairs at Carfax House. Perhaps it was unfair of her, but part of her fear of exposure was what the truth would do to Malcolm.

She looked into Raoul's steady gray gaze. "I know what I owe to my family. I'd accept help from the devil himself."

She saw her words settle in Raoul's eyes with what might have been relief. "You don't believe in the devil."

"No." She smiled again even as resolve hardened within her. "But I do believe in you."

CHAPTER 19

"Malcolm." Harry caught Malcolm on the edge of the dance floor when he emerged from his tête-à-tête with Lady Frances. "I've been looking for you." He stopped and scanned Malcolm's face. "You all right?"

For a moment the impulse to spill out the revelations about his parentage to Harry was so strong Malcolm could feel the words forming in his head. But though he discussed personal matters with Harry more than he did with most of his friends, it was usually by subtext rather than directly. And his own feelings were too unsettled to put them into words, even in his own head. "Just processing."

Harry watched him a moment longer, but being Harry, he didn't ask questions. "I've had some interesting results in my inquiries about the Raven."

Malcolm jerked his head towards a window embrasure. It was a relief to move to a part of the investigation that was removed from his personal life.

"I had a word this afternoon with a Spanish émigré who was one of my sources in the Peninsula," Harry said, when they'd reached the relative privacy of the embrasure. "He worked with the *afrancesados* during the war, but in fact was passing information to me. I helped set him up with a coffeehouse in Covent Garden after the war. He's still in touch with some former Bonapartists. He put out some inquiries. He didn't learn much, but according to two of his sources the Raven was definitely a man."

"Had these sources met the Raven?"

"Apparently one of them had. It's all second- or third-hand." Harry dug his shoulder into the gilded paneling. "But the interesting thing is that a third source told my friend he remembered hearing the Raven referred to as 'La Corbeau.' "

"Interesting."

"Yes, I thought so. Though it rather gets us back where we began."

"It proves how shrouded in mystery the Raven is."

"Whoever the Raven is, he or she has gone to earth since the war. By digging all this up, we're disturbing what may be a very peaceful existence."

Malcolm shot a look at his friend. "Are you suggesting we shouldn't dig it up?"

Harry shrugged. "Merely questioning the value. Perhaps I have a particular weakness for those seeking fresh starts. I know how difficult it can be. And how great the rewards." He gave an abashed smile. "In truth, I came home from my inquiries to be greeted by Livia and Dru rushing out of the library to hug my boots. As I scooped them up I found myself wondering if the Raven has a family."

Malcolm saw Colin turning the pages of a book and Jessica asleep when he and Suzanne looked into the nursery before they left for the ball. "If I'm right about the Raven, she—or he—had a family with someone she or he married under false pretenses."

"Which would mean the revelation would do all the more damage."

"But surely the Raven's husband or wife has the right to the truth."

"They might be happier not knowing."

"Living a lie?" It was the last thing Malcolm would have expected to hear from Harry, the epitome of the hardheaded realist.

Harry's gaze settled for a moment on Cordelia, waltzing with Simon. "I don't think Cordy will be unfaithful. Or I choose to believe it won't happen. But if it did again, I rather think I'd prefer never to know."

"You don't mean that."

"No?" Harry turned his gaze to Malcolm and lifted a brow. "You haven't been through the pain of your wife betraying you. Why in the name of God would I want to put us all through that hell again?"

In Harry's eyes, Malcolm saw memories of a bitter misery his friend wouldn't discuss directly. "It won't happen."

"You know better than to say anything won't happen, Malcolm. You aren't the sort to offer comforting lies. But I think that's the point. I'd prefer to believe the lie if I could. After all, as agents we spend enough of our lives telling them."

"And as agents we know how to spot them."

"Aye, there's the rub." Harry's gaze moved over the ballroom. "By the way, did you know Frederick Radley's in London?"

"Oh, Christ. Is he here tonight?"

Harry nodded and jerked his head towards an all-too-familiar golden-haired figure in regimentals waltzing with one of the Harley girls. "Cordy and I found him speaking with Suzanne. She was holding her own, of course, but he was making his usual nuisance of himself."

"Damnation. I should have been there."

"Probably just as well you weren't. Lady Carfax would never forgive you for coming to blows with one of her guests."

"I don't resort to such crude methods. Though I confess with Radley I'd be sorely tempted."

"I understand the impulse. But Suzanne had things well in hand."

"And wouldn't thank me for meddling. I can almost hear her telling me to focus on the investigation." Malcolm glanced about. "I don't suppose you've noticed if your uncle's here?"

Harry gave a faint smile. "He's in the card room as usual. I actually exchanged greetings with him earlier. Do you need to talk to him about the investigation?"

Malcolm hesitated, but really this, at least, did not need to be secret from Harry. He already knew O'Roarke was a family friend.

"My mother seems to have prevailed upon Alistair and Smytheton to help Raoul O'Roarke escape Ireland in '98. I want to see if your uncle knew anything about it."

Harry's gaze flickered over Malcolm's face. "You think Alistair might have told him? Or Smytheton?"

"I think my mother might have. Apparently she and your uncle were lovers."

Harry drew a breath. "Odd, as a child one tends to forget the adults in one's life have real lives. Uncle Archibald had good taste. Your mother was a very lovely lady. And quite brilliant." He studied Malcolm for a moment. "I'm sorry, old fellow, I don't suppose it's easy to hear."

"My mother had a number of lovers. And I rather think your uncle was a better man than many of them."

"Sometimes I wonder if I knew him at all."

Malcolm thought of his recent conversations with Lady Frances. "Sometimes I wonder that about all our parents' generation."

"I should engage your services, Malcolm. This is the second time in almost as many days you've rescued me from a bad hand and a dull game." Archibald Davenport surveyed Malcolm across the antechamber to which they had withdrawn. Similar to the one in which they had spoken at Emily Cowper's, save that the walls were cerulean blue instead of pomona green. "What else have you learned?"

"Is there something you're expecting me to learn?"

"On the contrary. But I assume you had your reasons for requesting this tête-à-tête."

"Did my mother say anything to you about Raoul O'Roarke's escape from Ireland?"

"Of course."

Malcolm took a quick step into the room. "What?"

"She was tremendously relieved. O'Roarke was a close friend. As of course you know."

"O'Roarke was her lover." No need to hide that, and Malcolm wanted to see how Davenport reacted.

"Yes, I know, she didn't make any secret about that. I think he meant a great deal more to her than I did." Davenport moved to a side table that held a set of decanters and poured a glass of cognac. "I'll say this for Carfax, he doesn't stint his guests." He held up the decanter to Malcolm.

Malcolm shook his head. "What else did she tell you about O'Roarke's escape?"

Davenport picked up the glass and took an appreciative sip. "Just something along the lines of 'thank God he's safe.' We were frank and had no illusions about each other, but she was tactful enough not to dwell on her other lovers."

"She didn't mention she'd had something to do with his escape?"

"Good lord." Davenport took another sip of cognac. "Arabella was a remarkable woman. Did she use friends of your grandfather's?"

"She blackmailed Alistair into helping her."

Davenport clunked his glass down on the polished walnut of the table. "Forgive me. I find it hard to credit Alistair helping O'Roarke, even given the blackmail."

"Quite. Which is why it's of some moment to learn what it was."

"Because you think it's to do with the Elsinore League and the Dunboyne leak?"

"Because it might be."

"Interesting." Davenport picked up his glass and turned it in his hand. "I can't imagine what hold Arabella could have had over Alistair. But then I can't imagine what Alistair had to do with the Dunboyne business. I never knew someone with such contempt for the Irish rebels."

"What about the art treasures you were smuggling?"

"Interesting idea." Davenport took another sip of cognac. "I've always suspected Alistair was willing to go to considerable lengths in appropriating them. There was little he'd cavil at."

"Including murder?"

Davenport met Malcolm's gaze. "You knew your—Alistair. Do you really think he'd have stopped at murder to get what he wanted? I think his only qualms would have revolved round what he thought he could get away with."

"And if my mother had had proof she might have been able to force Alistair to help O'Roarke."

Once again, Davenport's gaze seemed to soften. "It's only a theory, my boy. But it's an intriguing one."

So it was. And it would explain a lot.

Yet despite this, Malcolm was quite sure there was something Davenport wasn't telling him.

A figure slumped on a gold damask sofa in an embrasure between two pillars caught Suzanne's eye. When someone was hiding it was generally for an interesting reason. She scanned the light brown hair and bit of black coat visible.

As if aware of her regard, the man lifted his head. "Mrs. Rannoch. You've discovered me."

"Lord Harleton." Suzanne smiled at Crispin and took a step closer to the sofa. "Would you like me to give you cover?"

"Please do." His grin reminded her of Colin.

She positioned herself so the silver tulle folds of her gown hid him from view. "Whom are you hiding from?"

"My aunt Agatha. Or rather the series of eligible girls she keeps parading for me to dance with. Perfectly nice girls, but their prattle makes me feel ancient. I'm too old for eighteen-year-olds. Even twenty-two-year-olds."

"But your aunt wants to see you married."

"Has for years, but it's got worse since my father died. I'm supposed to ensure the survival of the great house of Harleton. Bit ironic, considering my father's actual legacy." Crispin sighed. "I used to enjoy parties like this. Now there doesn't seem to be much point without Manon."

And of course Lady Carfax would never receive an actress. Though she had received Suzanne with the warmest of smiles and Suzanne's past was even more scandalous. Manon had never been a whore. Hypocrisy was another of the sins to add to Suzanne's account book.

"Look here, Mrs. Rannoch." Crispin leaned forwards, then ducked out of view. "You're a friend of Manon's."

"I'm very fond of her, though we don't get much chance to talk." Suzanne chose her words with care, keeping the narrative thread of her fictional life firmly in mind.

"But she does talk to you. I can tell that. More than she talks to most people."

Crispin was a dangerously perceptive man. "We're both exiles in a way. It creates a bond."

"Yes, I can see how it would. Does she ever—" Crispin's gaze slid to the side, as though he was searching for the right words and perhaps was afraid of the answer. "Lately I've had the sense she's been pushing me away. I can't tell if it's because she's got some absurd sense that—"

"Your aunt Agatha is right?"

"No. Well, perhaps a bit. That somehow we can't be together. Or if it's because—" He swallowed, looked in Suzanne's face and into his fears. "Because she's growing tired of me."

Suzanne fingered a fold of her gown. "I'm not sure," she said. It was an honest answer, dragged from beneath layers of deception. "There's no denying Manon is mercurial. But I think perhaps she's afraid to let herself care for you, because she fears the pain when the affair ends."

"But why should it end?"

Suzanne saw the sort of white-gowned girl men like Crispin and Malcolm were supposed to marry. "Because I don't know that Manon would want to share you with your wife."

Crispin's brows drew together. "I told you, the girls Aunt Agatha throws at me—"

"But you're an earl. Sooner or later you'll marry." Not for the first time, Suzanne tried to picture the girl Malcolm would have married if he hadn't met her. For all his protestations to the contrary, she had no doubt he would have married eventually. He might not have Crispin's aunt Agatha, but with Malcolm's name and fortune young women were always being thrown in his way. Sooner or later he'd have come to the rescue of a girl left penniless or without protection, as he had thought Suzanne to be. But this girl would have shared his background. Would she have been too conventional for him? Or would he have found it easier to stay connected to his family and world? Or perhaps he'd have married someone he met on one of his missions, someone considered wildly unsuitable, like Rachel Garnier, who had worked as a spy in a brothel. He'd have caused a scandal, but his wife wouldn't have been a French spy. What really haunted Suzanne was whether he'd have fallen in love. The life she'd robbed him of would undoubtedly have been easier, but would it also have been happier?

Crispin was frowning over her claim that sooner or later he'd take a wife. "I always thought I'd marry. Eventually, at some date in the misty future. But now—Perpetuating the Harleton family honor seems a bit of a joke. And more important, I can't really imagine life with anyone but Manon." He looked at Suzanne a moment. "It's a rare thing, falling in love. To own the truth, I never really expected it to happen. Sort of sneaked up on me. Malcolm is lucky to have found you."

"I'm lucky to have him. Lord Harleton—" The urge to comfort fought the need for honesty, not to mention the need to conceal the extent of her friendship with Manon. "I know Manon is fond of you. Fonder, I think, than she realizes or would admit."

"Fond." His well-molded mouth curled scornfully round the word.

"As I said, I think she may be afraid to let it be more. Love makes one vulnerable."

Crispin dug a hand into his hair. "Don't I know it. That's why I envy you and Malcolm. You needn't fear losing each other."

"Malcolm and I are fortunate." That was true. She was more fortunate than she deserved. "But I don't think the vulnerability ever goes away." Her fingers tightened on the gauzy folds of her gown. So delicate. So easily rent. "There's more than one way to lose someone, Lord Harleton."

Malcolm caught Dewhurst as the earl was emerging from a tête-à-tête with Lord Sidmouth, the home secretary, in the drawing room, which Lady Carfax had given over to conversation. Dewhurst swept Malcolm with a gaze that made no pretense at civilities.

"I believe we said everything we could possibly say to each other at Emily Cowper's."

Malcolm positioned himself so Dewhurst was between him and an ebony-inlaid table. The earl couldn't slip away without attracting attention. "At the time. I didn't then realize that you had met with Alistair and Lord Harleton only a fortnight before Alistair's death."

Dewhurst fixed him with a stare like a pistol pointed between the eyes. "You've spoken with Rupert?"

"Rupert is a friend," Malcolm said. "I see him a great deal. But yes, Rupert reported that he encountered you and Alistair and Harleton meeting at Clarissa's."

"My God, Malcolm, I'd have thought you'd have had the delicacy to keep my family out of it."

"And I'd have thought you'd know better than anyone, sir, that delicacy has little place in intelligence investigations."

Dewhurst gave a short laugh. "*I* might. You used to have more scruples, my boy."

"In truth, I went to warn Rupert."

"And got the information out of him."

"I asked. Rupert isn't in a humor to keep secrets."

"No, not after what you and Laclos have done to him."

"You're as expert at constructing smoke screens as a theatrical machine, sir. What were you meeting with my father and Harleton about in secret?"

"Clarissa's library is hardly secret."

"But something made you meet there instead of at White's or one of your homes."

Dewhurst cast a glance round the drawing room. The buzz of a dozen different conversations reverberated off the white-and-gold ceiling. No one was looking their way. "If you must know, Harleton was concerned about that girl of his son's."

"Harleton was concerned about Manon Caret?"

"Don't act so shocked, Rannoch, you must have heard the talk about her work in France."

"But why in God's name would Harleton be making a fuss about a suspected French agent?"

"Perhaps as cover. Perhaps because whatever his own sins, he didn't want his son tainted by them."

"So what? He wanted to know what you and Alistair knew about her?"

"He wanted our help in ending the liaison."

"What did he try to use as leverage?"

"He didn't require any. He was appealing to us as members of the Elsinore League."

Malcolm stared at Dewhurst in the flickering light of the wax tapers. "You knew Harleton was a French spy."

"Suspected. He was still an Elsinore League member."

"What did you tell him?"

Dewhurst twitched his cuff smooth. "That I'd see what I could learn about Mademoiselle Caret that might put an end to Crispin's infatuation."

"You agreed—"

"Whatever Harleton's crimes, I saw no reason why Crispin should suffer. My own son may have shut me out, but I could help someone else's."

"How altruistic of you."

"We have to look out for our own. It wasn't just La Caret's questionable past in France. Harleton thought Crispin was a bit too fond of her."

"And you couldn't but be sympathetic to a man who thought his son was the victim of an inappropriate infatuation."

Dewhurst met his gaze with the cool of carved ice. "What father wouldn't be sympathetic?"

Malcolm folded his arms across his chest. "What did Alistair say to all this?"

"That Harleton was a fool if he thought he could control his son. As I recall, Harleton said he was a fine one to talk with a perfect set of grandchildren. Alistair snorted and said not to be taken in by pretty pictures."

Malcolm bit back a harsh laugh. "I'm sure he did. Why didn't you tell me any of this two days ago?"

"Because I knew anything I said about Alistair and Harleton

would only cause you to ask more questions—as you're doing now—and distract you from your investigation."

"How thoughtful of you."

"Believe it or not, I really do think it would be best for the country if you could learn who was behind Alistair's and Harleton's deaths and the Dunboyne leak. If you will excuse me, I need to speak to Castlereagh. The business of the country hasn't stopped for this investigation of yours."

CHAPTER 20

"Harry." Archibald Davenport approached his nephew, moving with an agility that belied his walking stick. "Good to see you attending entertainments more."

Harry met his uncle's gaze, at once indolent and sharp. He recalled some mild barbs in the early days of his marriage on his reluctance to go out. "Cordy enjoys society."

"Glad you're accompanying her. It may not be fashionable for husbands and wives to live in each other's pockets, but it can do wonders for a marriage. Speaking as a bachelor, of course."

For the first time it occurred to Harry that Davenport's barbs all those years ago might have come out of concern for his marriage rather than simply to make caustic conversation. "I hope I'm somewhat wiser than I was a decade ago."

"I make no doubt that you are. Besides, going out in society must be part of your work."

"You think I need to observe modern-day revels to write about the Julio-Claudians?"

"Perhaps. But I was thinking about your other work."

"I'm no longer in military intelligence."

"No?" Davenport turned the jeweled handle of his walking stick. "I assumed you were assisting Malcolm Rannoch. Or is it just

Cordelia who is assisting Mrs. Rannoch? I assume you know they came to see me two days ago?"

"Cordy said you were very obliging."

"Always happy to see Cordelia and the girls, and the Rannoch children are quite charming. As is Mrs. Rannoch. Also damnably astute. And I suspect more ruthless than her husband." Davenport flicked a bit of lint from the glossy black of his coat sleeve. "I confess I did find it interesting that you sent Cordelia instead of coming to see me yourself."

"I know you've always been fond of her."

"So I am. Though I would venture to say I'm more than passingly fond of you as well."

"You know what I mean, sir."

"That you haven't found me the easiest person to talk to?"

"No. That is—"

"I'm not offended, I assure you. I was hardly cut out to communicate well with a young boy." Davenport smoothed a lace frill that fell over his wrist. "Rannoch just spoke with me himself. Did he share that with you?"

Harry met his uncle's gaze. "You mean about you and Arabella Rannoch? I'm hardly shocked. From what I remember of her, she was a beautiful and brilliant woman."

"Interesting."

"That I'm not shocked or that I paid attention to Arabella Rannoch?"

"That Malcolm Rannoch trusts you with his family secrets. I don't think he trusts any more easily than you do. I'm glad you've found a friend."

A waltz sounded from the ballroom, something sweet and simple. Harry looked at his uncle's sardonic face, at once familiar and still that of a stranger. For the first time he considered what it must have been like for Davenport, at much the age Harry was now himself, to suddenly become the guardian of a withdrawn nine-year-old. "Talking with Malcolm recently, I was reminded that you were remarkably diligent about attending my speech days, sir," Harry said, a rare moment in which he spoke on impulse. "It was good of you."

Davenport gave a twisted smile. "It was little enough."

"I don't think I was properly appreciative."

"You'd just lost your parents, my boy. You had enough to contend with without trying to be appreciative. I'm sorry there wasn't more I could do."

Harry shot a surprised look at his uncle. "You didn't ask to be saddled with me. I imagine a nine-year-old boy was the last thing you wanted intruding on your bachelor existence."

"True enough. Though mostly because I wasn't in the least sure how to talk to you."

"All things considered, probably just as well we avoided each other."

"Harry—" Davenport surveyed him. "I never wanted to become a parent."

"Nor did I precisely." Hot shame washed over Harry at the memory of the years he'd more or less ignored Livia's existence. "And you at least gave me a home."

Davenport's gaze softened with what might have been understanding. "Cordy, fond as I am of her, put you through a great deal. I suspect you stayed away from Livia more because you weren't sure of your welcome and of her mother's wishes than because you didn't want to be a parent."

"Perhaps. But I should still—"

"You always were too hard on yourself, Harry."

It was not what Harry would have expected from Davenport. He was surprised his uncle had noticed. "I—"

"Your capacity for forgiveness with Cordelia is remarkable, my boy. Try a bit of that on yourself."

"Sir—"

Davenport touched his arm. "You're an excellent father, Harry. Far better than I could ever be. But I was going to say that little as I thought I wanted to be a father and imperfect as I may have been at it, I'm inestimably grateful that you gave me the chance to try."

"Oh, Malcolm, good." Carfax somehow materialized in front of Malcolm by the door to the supper room, blocking his egress. "Got a report for me?"

"I assumed you'd have other things on your mind tonight, sir."

"Nonsense, what's the point of entertaining if one can't gather information? Amelia couldn't have held this ball at a more advantageous time. I trust you've been making the most of the opportunities the night affords."

"Can you doubt me, sir?"

"I never doubt your abilities, only your point of view." Carfax folded his arms over the discreet blue brocade of his waistcoat. "What have you learned?"

Carfax's steady gaze and the blessed non-intrusive calm of his voice that day he offered Malcolm his diplomatic and intelligence position echoed in Malcolm's mind. Without the man before him he would never have met Suzanne. He wouldn't have Colin and Jessica. He might well be dead one way or another. But he knew full well how Carfax turned personal information to his own ends. It was one thing to share Alistair's secrets. Malcolm owed his putative father no allegiance. But now it was a question of his mother's secrets. And O'Roarke's.

"Dewhurst thinks Smytheton and possibly Jennifer Mansfield were French agents. Smytheton and Mrs. Mansfield suspect the same about Dewhurst."

Carfax adjusted his spectacles. "Interesting but hardly surprising. One of them is probably correct."

"Care to hazard a guess?"

"Guessing is a dangerous business, and if I knew, I wouldn't need you. What were you talking to your aunt about?"

"The duel," Malcolm replied without hesitation. "She can shed no light on it other than that she didn't have much use for either man."

"Astute woman, Frances. Pity I couldn't have set her to gather information on Alistair. Though I couldn't have been sure which way she'd jump. She always seemed a bit too fond of him."

"Jennifer Mansfield also told Suzette that Alistair was involved in Royalist missions."

Carfax frowned. "I knew Alistair dabbled in such activities. I didn't realize how deep it went."

"But the timing is wrong for him to have been the source of the leak that Smytheton and Dewhurst each blame the other for. Which leaves us with one of them."

"Or Mrs. Mansfield."

"Quite. Assuming she's been deceiving Smytheton all these years."

"It's been known to happen."

"Dewhurst claims Harleton asked to meet with him and Alistair to get their help ending his son's liaison with Manon Caret."

"Interesting. Do you believe him?"

"I'm not sure. At the very least, I think there was more to it."

"Harleton should have paid more attention to his own scandals. Though I can certainly understand the concern for a son and heir."

Malcolm stared at Carfax. Carfax stared back, as though silently daring Malcolm to bring up Simon's name.

After a long moment, Carfax said, "Anything else?"

"Not that's worthy of report," Malcolm said with only enough hesitation to indicate he was genuinely sifting through the information.

Carfax regarded him in silence for a moment. "Do you know I still remember the day I engaged your services, Malcolm? I can't say that about every agent. But I distinctly remember thinking you were going to be one of the best agents I'd ever employed. So long as your scruples didn't get in your way."

Malcolm met his mentor's gaze. It was not a coincidence Carfax was referring to the day Malcolm had gone to work for him. The ruthlessly unsentimental earl wasn't above emotional blackmail. "Are you saying I'm letting my scruples get in my way?"

"I'm saying it's not your job to agonize over those scruples. You collect the information and give it to me. I decide what to do with it. The moral compromises are on my head."

Neatly said. Assuming Malcolm trusted Carfax's morals. "Did you really think that would convince me, sir?"

Carfax's smile was ironic acknowledgment. "No, but I thought it was worth a try. You can't make everything your responsibility, Malcolm."

"No. But nor can I abrogate responsibility entirely."

* * *

Suzanne watched as Malcolm stroked his fingers against Jessica's cheek. Suzanne had put the baby in his arms when she finished nursing. Jessica's head flopped back against the burgundy silk of his dressing gown arm, and her small feet dangled over his other arm below the scalloped muslin hem of her nightdress. "Oh, to sleep so peacefully," Malcolm said.

"And to sleep whenever one wants." Suzanne did up the peach silk tie that closed the muslin frill at the neck of her own nightdress. There was something about nightclothes that was particularly decorous. She never felt she looked so wholly the demure wife. "When she fights falling asleep I want to tell her how fortunate she is."

"Quite." Malcolm smoothed the peach fuzz of Jessica's hair. "Harry told me Radley was at the ball." He lifted his gaze to Suzanne, his eyes dark with concern. "I'm sorry you had to deal with him alone."

Malcolm's understanding about the man he knew to be his wife's former lover summed up what an extraordinary man he was. And the secrets she was still keeping about Radley summed up just how much she had betrayed Malcolm and how precarious the state of their marriage was. "Cordy and Harry soon came to my rescue. And there's really nothing you could have done."

He gave a twisted smile. "Meaning I'm a fool to think I can try to protect my wife?"

"Never that, dearest. Your support is invaluable. Though satisfying as it would be to see you plant Radley a facer, I fear it would only complicate the situation."

"I said much the same to Harry. In theory I know better than to think violence would resolve the situation. But I confess I would have been sorely tempted."

"Precisely." The reminder of all the reasons she loved him brought a smile to her eyes and an ache to her throat. "Radley's unpleasant, but he can't really threaten me now that I've told you the truth." Which would be true if she had told him the whole truth.

"No. But I can't help but . . ."

"What?" Suzanne asked as he trailed off.

"Want to spare you unpleasantness." He gave a sheepish smile as he laid Jessica in her cradle.

Beneath the demure peach silk bow her heart turned over. "That's very sweet, dearest."

"But foolish." He slid his hands from beneath the sleeping baby and straightened up.

"That doesn't render it any less sweet." She moved to the cradle and settled a blanket—white and silver, a gift from Lady Frances—over Jessica's legs, where there was no risk of her pressing her face against it. She looked down for a moment at Jessica's even breathing, her long lashes veiling her eyes, her turned-up nose, the sparse hair clinging to her skull. So real, so warm. So vulnerable.

Suzanne turned, putting her back to Malcolm. "Could you undo the clasp on my necklace?"

Malcolm's fingers were cool against her skin as he undid the silver filigree clasp on her pearls. "According to Aunt Frances, Alistair was furious at having had to save O'Roarke. And he as good as admitted Mama blackmailed him into it." His breath brushed Suzanne's neck.

"Do you think she knew Alistair was working for the French?" It wouldn't do to avoid the obvious question.

"It's the obvious answer." Malcolm lifted the pearls from her throat and pressed a kiss to the nape of her neck. He'd been awkward at helping her undress when they first married, as though she were a china doll that might break, but now he was quite adept. The feel of his fingers dancing against her spine could be deliciously tantalizing, but now he was all business. Seduction was too simple an escape tonight. "In which case I wonder how long she knew."

Suzanne took the pearls from him and put them in their velvet box on her dressing table. "She probably saved Mr. O'Roarke's life, darling. She would have been putting the personal ahead of the political."

"Not necessarily a choice I disagree with." Malcolm adjusted one of the dressing table tapers that was tilting in its base. "Archibald Davenport claims not to have known Mama had anything to do with O'Roarke's escape. When I asked him if she might have used the art treasures as leverage, he said he wouldn't have been surprised by Alistair going to great lengths to acquire them. Including murder."

"Did he have someone specific in mind?"

"He didn't say so. But I couldn't help but think he was holding something back." Malcolm wiped a trace of wax from the side of the taper. "Apparently Aunt Frances also knew O'Roarke is my father."

Suzanne spun round to face him. "Darling—"

Malcolm's smile was at once sweet and defensive. "She said it wasn't her secret to share, which I suppose I can't argue with." He turned away and picked up her dressing gown from the bed. "According to her my mother wrote to O'Roarke about me. Weekly."

Suzanne heard Raoul's voice speaking about Malcolm at the ball with the sort of care that he would only employ to cover feelings too raw to touch. "He obviously took a keen interest in you, darling."

"It's not O'Roarke's interest that surprises me. It's my mother's. Aunt Frances said she went on writing to him after my mother died." He held out the dressing gown for her to slip on. "I feel a bit as though I've missed major chapters in the story of my own life."

She kept her arms steady as she slid them into the seafoam silk of the dressing gown. "I suppose everyone's life story appears different from their parents' perspective." God only knew what questions Colin and Jessica would have about their parents. She could only hope they would never know to ask the worst of those questions, yet it would always rankle that they didn't know the truth of who their mother was.

"And I'm not the only one to not know who his parents are," Malcolm said. "True enough, no sense in wallowing."

"You've had more to contend with than most."

"I saw you speaking with O'Roarke at the ball." There was no suspicion in his voice, only curiosity, held in check as though he was afraid to care too much or at least to reveal that he did.

"Yes." She pushed back the lace cuffs on her dressing gown.

"He sought me out. He wanted to know how much I thought the day's revelations had disturbed you."

Malcolm's mouth twisted, with bitter acknowledgment or perhaps at the irony of the situation. "What did you say?"

"That you couldn't but be disturbed. But that I also thought you were relieved to have a father you liked better than Alistair Rannoch."

Malcolm's gaze moved from the cradle to the door to Colin's room. "I can't imagine how unspeakable it would be to have a child one couldn't acknowledge was one's own. Not that O'Roarke would have seen himself as my father. But—" He turned away and moved to the chest of drawers, pausing to pet Berowne, who was curled up on their bed. "Harry had some news as well. A source of his claims to have heard the Raven referred to as a man."

"A reliable source?" She pulled the silk and lace of the dressing gown tight about her.

"Supposedly." Malcolm picked up the decanter that stood atop the chest of drawers (high enough to be out of range of small fingers). "But the same source had also heard others refer to the Raven as 'La Corbeau.' "

The night air bit into her skin despite her nightdress and dressing gown and the fire blazing in the grate. "Interesting."

Malcolm removed the crystal stopper and splashed whisky into two glasses. "I'm inclined to think this actually supports the idea the Raven is a woman and the rumors to the contrary are deliberate disinformation. It's what I'd have done if I were the Raven or her handler. Wouldn't you?"

She perched on the dressing table bench. "Very likely."

He set down the decanter. The crystal flashed in the firelight. "Is there anyone you can see as the Raven? You spent more time with the diplomatic and military wives than I did."

She tied the dressing gown's sash round her waist. The silk slithered between her fingers. "Does any of the women I took tea with and listened to gossip from strike me as a master spy? No," she said truthfully.

Malcolm stoppered the decanter. "It must be a hell of a life."

"Being a spy or being a military wife?"

"Perhaps both in a way." He put one of the glasses of whisky into her hand. "But I was thinking of being in deep cover, which by all reports the Raven is whether he or she is a man or a woman. The longest I've done it for is a few weeks. Five, I think. In a village near Burgos, posing as a priest to infiltrate a group of *afrancesados* and get information about the French garrison. Before I met you. And I had Tatiana and Addison with me, but Tania was playing an officer's wife and Addison was in the guise of a wine merchant, so I didn't see them for days on end. The feeling of being locked in a role—" He returned to the chest of drawers and picked up the second glass. "One begins to lose track of where one's self ends and the role begins. I remember missing the most obscure things. A good cup of tea, even though I'm quite happy with coffee in the general run of things. The boot polish Addison mixes. The social columns in the London papers."

"Hallmarks of the real you." She took a sip of whisky. Her throat hurt.

"A sad commentary on me if that is the case." He took a sip from his own glass. "But something familiar to latch on to." He was silent for a moment, leaning against the chest of drawers. "I always thought of myself as solitary. I'd have said it might well be easier to be alone than to deal with the burden of my family and sometimes even my friends. I never knew how truly alone one could feel. And what a challenge it was."

"A challenge you enjoyed meeting?" she asked without thinking, a genuine question.

"No. Yes. Perhaps. There's no denying the challenge of this damnable business."

She tasted the wine-sweet rush of triumph she sometimes felt to this day at managing a bit of deception. "There's nothing to be ashamed of in that, darling. Judge yourself for your actions if you must, not for whether or not you enjoy them."

His mouth twisted. "You always were much more practical, Wife." He took another sip of whisky. "Harry asked me if I was sure I wanted to disrupt the Raven's life. Whoever she or he is, the

Raven isn't causing problems now and may have a settled life. Perhaps even with a family."

"Though likely under false pretenses." She felt compelled to say it, for it seemed the logical response.

"Quite. I can't but think the Raven's spouse deserves to know, though Harry claimed in the same shoes he'd prefer to be in the dark. He said if Cordy was unfaithful again he wouldn't want to know."

"What did you say?"

"That she wouldn't be unfaithful."

"You can't know that, Malcolm."

"So Harry pointed out."

"And you say I'm the romantic."

Malcolm stared into his glass. "Beyond that, I think I can't resist wanting to get at the truth."

"I know, darling." Her fingers tightened on the glass, for she knew this might well be the undoing of both of them. "It's what makes you you. You might be able to bury a secret but not until you'd uncovered it."

"You make me sound like a dog with a bone."

"You share the tenacity. And the loyalty. But a rather more nuanced sense of the complexities of life. Fond as I am of dogs."

He gave a wry smile. "Carfax told me to leave the moral compromises to him."

"That sounds like Carfax. But even he should know you could never follow that advice."

"Oh yes. He even admitted it." Malcolm turned his glass between his fingers. The candlelight bounced off the Rannoch crest etched on the glass. "I refuse to believe moral compromise is inevitable."

Her heart turned over. "And so you can't trust Carfax?"

"If nothing else, Bertrand Laclos's story taught me to feel responsible for information I turn over. Besides, in this case—"

"It's your family?"

His brows drew together. "I don't feel any loyalty to Alistair. And one could argue my mother is beyond being hurt."

"Your grandfather and Lady Frances and Edgar and Gisèle aren't."

"No, that's true." He took another sip of whisky, as though debating the wisdom of saying more. "And then there's O'Roarke."

The breath stuck in her throat, choking her.

"His work in Spain with the *guerrilleros* gives him a certain credibility here," Malcolm continued as though quite unaware of how he had shattered her to the core. "But people haven't forgot the United Irish Uprising. This could bring it all up again."

She got to her feet. "Darling—"

His gaze shifted in that way it did when he pulled on his armor. "I've always felt a loyalty to him. It's not because—"

Her heart constricted. For in his gaze she saw that he'd found something today with the revelations about his parentage. Something he wouldn't have admitted—perhaps even now would still not admit—he'd been looking for. Which would make the unraveling of her past doubly painful. "Darling," she said again. She slid her fingers behind his neck. "Loyalty isn't something you have to apologize for. Whatever Carfax may say."

"Carfax would undoubtedly say I'm too squeamish to make hard decisions."

"Carfax is not the sort of man I want running the country my children are growing up in." Which rather justified her career.

He wrapped his arms round her waist. "Unfortunate. For that's exactly what he's doing."

"Which is precisely why we'd need men like you." Was that what her work consisted of now? Encouraging her husband? Something in her shied away from the thought, wanted to fight back.

"And women like you."

She smiled, despite the day's revelations, despite her fears for the future, despite her qualms about her role.

He returned the smile and lowered his mouth to her own.

CHAPTER 21

Cordelia tightened the blue velvet ribbons on her bonnet. "You're sure you want me here?"

"You know Bessborough."

"That may be a mixed blessing. I think half the time Bessborough looks at me and still sees a little girl who played dolls and rolled hoops with Caro. But the other half he sees an unfaithful wife who put her husband through scandal and made herself the talk of the town. All too like his wife and his late sister-in-law the Duchess of Devonshire." She tugged her gloves smooth. "Odd, when I was a little girl hanging over the stair rail to admire their ball gowns, I wanted nothing more than to grow up to be just like Lady Bessborough and the duchess. One never realizes how destructive childhood dreams can be."

Suzanne touched her friend's arm. "Cordy—"

"It's all right. I've faced far harsher censure than Bessborough's." Cordelia rang the bell.

A liveried footman conducted them into a study paneled in cedar and rich with leather and gilt. Lord Bessborough sat in a wing-back chair, his leg on a footstool. He reached for his walking stick to push himself to his feet at their entrance, but Cordelia hurried forwards and put her hand on his shoulder. "Don't get up,

Uncle B. We've never stood on ceremony. You know Mrs. Rannoch."

"Of course." Bessborough smiled at Suzanne. "You've cut quite a swath in town, my dear. Never thought Malcolm Rannoch had such good taste. Never seemed to be able to get his nose out of his books as a boy."

"Bookishness can be very attractive."

Bessborough ran a shrewd gaze over her. "Not the words I'm used to hearing from a beautiful woman. But then it sounds as if Malcolm has turned into more a man of action than I would have thought possible. Can't quite credit the stories I hear about his activities in the Peninsula, truth to tell. I suppose it goes to show you never can tell what people will grow into. Certainly wouldn't have thought my little Caro—" He coughed. "May I offer you anything? Tea? Madeira?"

"I'll get it." Cordelia moved to a table with decanters.

Bessborough watched her as she filled three glasses with Madeira. "I'm glad you're living with your husband again."

"For two and a half years now." Cordelia smiled brightly and put a glass of Madeira in Bessborough's hand.

"Good for you." Bessborough lifted his glass to her. His tone made the words at once an expression of approbation and an echo of doubt.

"I love him very much." Cordelia handed a glass to Suzanne, then dropped into a chair beside Bessborough. "It just took me a long time to realize it."

"Harriet and I reconciled." Bessborough held his glass to the light of the window and turned it in his hand as though seeing into the past. "More than once. Each time I thought we'd fallen in love again. I'd have sworn nothing could come between us."

Cordelia took a sip of Madeira. "I wouldn't swear nothing could come between Harry and me. I'm just going to do my damndest to make sure it doesn't."

Bessborough gave an appreciative smile. "Always were plainspoken." He eased his leg straighter. "What did you want to talk to me about?"

"I didn't realize you were a friend of my husband's father," Suzanne said.

"Alistair?" Bessborough snorted. "I'd hardly call us friends. Is this one of Malcolm's investigations?"

"You could say so."

For a moment Suzanne would swear she saw a shadow of unease cross Bessborough's face, much like with Sir Horace Smytheton.

"You and my husband's father were in a club together," Suzanne said. "The Elsinore League."

"Oh." Bessborough gave a hearty laugh, which changed midway to an embarrassed cough. "That."

"We know it was a hellfire club," Cordelia said.

Bessborough's brows snapped together. "You shouldn't know about such things, Cordy."

"Really, Uncle B. You know the world I grew up in."

"Not what one wants one's daughter to be part of. Besides, I wouldn't quite call it a hellfire club. Just a bit of an excuse for gentlemen to get up to their usual pursuits. I was always on the fringes."

"But it brought you and Alistair Rannoch together."

"In a roundabout sort of way."

"Uncle B." Cordelia moved into the conversational void with unerring instinct. "Caro says she heard you and Alistair Rannoch quarreling."

Bessborough clunkcd his glass down. "What the devil—" He gripped the arms of his chair.

"After a party in Berkeley Square. Some twenty years ago." Cordelia touched his hand where it lay on the arm of the chair. "Uncle B., was Alistair Rannoch blackmailing you?"

"Of all the damned—"

"We don't want to pry into your secrets—"

Bessborough jerked his hand away from hers. "What the devil do you call this?"

"It's important, my lord," Suzanne said. "Malcolm is looking into who leaked the information about Dunboyne among other things."

"Damnable business that." Bessborough glanced away, snatched up his glass and took a sip, clunked it down again. "It's no secret my finances haven't always been what one would wish."

"You and my father shared a love of cards." Cordelia's voice was at once sympathetic and matter-of-fact, not making an issue of it while she invited further confidences.

"Good old Brooke. Always played deep as well." A look that was half nostalgia, half regret drifted across Bessborough's face. "Not always easy being the Duke of Devonshire's cousin. Not to mention brother-in-law. It costs so much to keep up one's end of things. A London house, a country house, a carriage, hunters. And God help us when it comes to ladies' gowns and bonnets."

"Uncle B." Cordelia leaned forwards on the footstool, ivory skirts spread about her in a frothy layer, chin cupped in her hand. "Did Alistair Rannoch lend you money?"

Bessborough drew a breath, glanced at a hunting print on the wall, stared down into his Madeira. "Harriet and I had already had to go abroad. Had to leave the older boys in England. Then we'd had to move out of the London and Roehampton houses. Even then we couldn't seem to get matters under control. Harriet had her sister's head for cards. Don't think I ever got a proper accounting of her debts. Not that I'm one to cast stones, I suppose. Still, Alistair's offer of assistance seemed like the answer to our prayers."

"How did it come about?" Suzanne asked.

"We were sitting over cigars and brandy one night at Brooks's. Alistair wasn't a member, being a staunch Tory, but someone had brought him in. I was bemoaning the economies Harriet and I were forced to resort to. Later that evening Alistair touched me on the shoulder and said perhaps he could be of assistance. He was fortunate to have a large amount of capital and was looking for ways to put it to use. Far better to trust it to a friend than to sink it into a doubtful commercial venture. All sounded perfectly straightforward." He shook his head. "Should have known it was too good to be true. After all, Alistair and I had never been particularly friendly. But the more desperate one's straits, the less one is likely to question one's good fortune."

"What did Mr. Rannoch ask of you?" Cordelia inquired in a soft voice, her gaze trained on Lord Bessborough.

Bessborough shifted in his chair. "See here, my dear, no sense in dredging up a lot of nonsense from the past—"

"There is when it may be relevant in the present," Suzanne said.

"Can't very well—"

"I assure you, neither Suzanne nor I shock easily," Cordelia said. "Did he want you to steal something for him?"

"Steal something?" Bessborough's brows shot up in seemingly genuine surprise. "Why should Alistair have wanted me to steal something? He could buy most anything he wanted. No, he wanted—" Bessborough tossed down a swallow of Madeira. "He wanted me to keep Lord Derwent occupied for the evening."

Cordelia shot a look at Suzanne. "So he could—"

"What else would a man like Alistair want? So he could spend the night with Lady Derwent."

Cordelia sat back on the footstool. "How silly of me. Of course, what else would be of such moment among the Devonshire House set? But it can't be the first time one of your friends asked for your help with an amorous intrigue."

"But Derwent was my friend, damn it." Bessborough's fingers tightened round his glass. "A better friend than Alistair Rannoch. One doesn't poach on one's friends' wives. Well, at least one doesn't help another man do it. It simply isn't done."

Suzanne shook her head. The intricacies of the social and moral code of the beau monde continued to fascinate and baffle her. She doubted she would ever fully master it. She suspected one had to be born into it to do so.

"So you refused," Cordelia said.

"Naturally. Impertinent puppy."

Alistair Rannoch had been Bessborough's junior, but the dismissal was less that of a younger man than of a man who, whatever he had attained in life, had been born with a less exalted name and a distinct lack of fortune. For a moment, Suzanne felt the smallest twinge of sympathy with her late father-in-law.

"And?" Cordelia asked.

Bessborough shifted in his chair as though he could edge away from the memory. "Alistair didn't have the decency to see he'd overstepped. Threatened to call in the loan. He knew damn well I couldn't raise the money to pay him back. If I'd been in a position to do so I wouldn't have needed his money in the first place. There was no way round it."

"So?" Cordelia's voice was gentle.

"What else was I to do? I kept Derwent busy for the night. Played cards with him and lost more money as it happens. Still ashamed whenever I think of it. Of distracting Derwent, that is."

"It was very wrong of Mr. Rannoch," Suzanne said. "Did he ask other favors of you?"

"From time to time. Of the same sort." Bessborough's mouth twisted. "One begins to grow disgusted with oneself. The worst was Anne Cyrus."

"Hugo Cyrus's wife?" Suzanne leaned forwards. "One of your fellow Elsinore League members?"

Bessborough nodded. "That seemed to make it worse. We'd sworn an oath of brotherhood for God's sake."

"Did Cyrus ever find out?"

"He'd have called me out if he did, I expect. Man is besotted with his wife, even if she was his brother's love first."

"And the debts?" Cordelia said.

"Oh, Alistair was good about those. Didn't press when I was late with payments. Even came up with a bit more when I needed it for Caro's marriage portion."

"So Malcolm inherited the obligations?" Cordelia asked.

"No, it was never so formalized." Bessborough swallowed the last of his Madeira.

"Then?"

Bessborough set the glass on a table beside his chair and wiped a trace of Madeira from the side. "I suppose you could say the debts died with Alistair Rannoch."

Suzanne slid into a chair beside Malcolm and the children at a pastry cook's that had become a favorite stop near Madame Tussaud's. And an excellent place for their parents to talk. "Your father loaned Lord Bessborough money to settle his debts. Quite a bit of money."

"And Alistair used it as leverage?" Malcolm asked. In his lap, Jessica stretched out her arms to Suzanne.

"Yes. To get Bessborough to assist Alistair in romantic intrigues." Suzanne took Jessica from Malcolm. Ridiculous how comforting it was to have one's arrival greeted with such a radiant smile. Nothing like small fingers gripping one's collar to anchor one to reality. "Including with Anne Cyrus."

"Good God."

"Bessborough didn't think Cyrus knew. But if he did—"

"It gives him a motive to have got rid of Alistair. But not Harleton. And we can't sound out Cyrus without betraying Anne Cyrus."

"You're wonderful, Malcolm."

"I have no desire to destroy a woman's reputation or marriage if we can help it." Malcolm shook his head. "His friend. His fellow Elsinore League member. I will never get Alistair's limits."

Colin set down his mug of milk. "What did Grandpapa do?"

Malcolm and Suzanne exchanged a glance. They were going to have to start watching what they said in front of Colin. "Grandpapa had a complicated life," Malcolm said. "And a lot of secrets."

"And you need to understand them?" Colin carefully conveyed the last bite of his tart to his mouth. He always made it a point to make his food last.

"Normally people's secrets are theirs to keep," Malcolm said. "But in Al—your grandfather's case, those secrets may affect other people. So we need to understand them."

Colin nodded. "And you're good at finding out secrets."

"More or less."

"It's what spies do, Daddy." Colin took another sip of milk. "Don't worry, I know I'm not supposed to say anything about you and Mummy being spies."

Malcolm exchanged a look with Suzanne. "Do you know what that word means, darling?" Suzanne asked, pressing a kiss to Jessica's nose.

Colin swallowed the last of his milk and set down the mug. "You pretend things. To get information and solve problems."

It was in many ways a more honest—though perhaps overly charitable—definition of spying than many would give. "Well put," Malcolm said. "Shall we walk back through Green Park?"

While Colin ran ahead to dart through the trees and Jessica surveyed the leafless branches from her baby carriage, Malcolm returned to the previous topic. "Did you get any sense that Alistair had used his leverage to get Bessborough to do more than assist with romantic intrigues?"

"Such as steal information? No. I asked straight out if Alistair had had him steal anything and Bessborough said why would Alistair need to steal anything. He didn't seem to have the least suspicion Alistair was anything more than a wealthy man with a fondness for dalliance and few scruples. Of course it's possible Bessborough's a very good actor."

"We seem to come back to theatre one way or another, don't we?"

Suzanne turned her head to regard Malcolm from beneath the velvet brim of her bonnet. The gnarled branches cast a tracery of shadows over his face. "It does give Bessborough a motive to have had Alistair killed. A fairly powerful motive."

"And Harleton had been his wife's lover."

"Do you think he knew?"

"He gave no sign of it. His regret over what his marriage had come to was palpable. But from Cordy's stories, Bessborough could hardly blame that solely on Harleton."

Malcolm nodded. "Even assuming Bessborough decided to seek vengeance on his wife's lovers, Granville would seem a far likelier target than Harleton. Although in Harleton's case there was the added fact that they were in the Elsinore League together."

"That seemed to bother Bessborough when it came to Anne Cyrus. He said they'd sworn an oath of brotherhood. If—"

Jessica stretched a hand upwards as a robin hopped from branch to branch. "Ma."

"Yes, that's a bird," Suzanne said, in the bright voice she used automatically with her children. "If Alistair loaned money to Dewhurst for leverage, I wonder who else he may have loaned it to."

Malcolm swung his head round to look at her. "Excellent question, Suzette."

A few minutes later they turned into Berkeley Square. A gust of wind stirred the branches of the plane trees.

Colin, who had run ahead, stopped on the pavement. "Our door's open."

The polished mahogany door was indeed flung open. Michael and Valentin were maneuvering a large trunk up the stairs. Malcolm's brows snapped together, but he merely said, "It appears we have a visitor. Let's go and see."

They climbed the steps and stepped through the doorway under the fanlight just as Michael and Valentin set the trunk down. Another trunk and a stack of bandboxes littered the black-and-white marble tiles. A tall man with graying hair stood in the center of the hall removing a pair of York tan gloves.

Suzanne felt Malcolm's stillness a split second before her mind registered who their visitor was. Malcolm drew a breath and then released it with the evenness of iron control. "Grandfather."

CHAPTER 22

"Oh, there you are, Malcolm." The Duke of Strathdon glanced up with a careless nod as he removed his second glove. "Glad you're back. Suzanne, my dear. Young Colin. You've grown."

Colin cast a glance up at Suzanne and at her nod took a step forwards and bowed. "Great-Grandpapa."

"Nicely done. Your mother has you well trained." Strathdon cast a glance round the hall. "Hope I haven't put you out too much," he said, in the tone of one who all his life had been welcome anywhere. After all, he was a duke.

"Not at all." Suzanne stepped forwards, shifting Jessica against her shoulder. "Valentin—"

"His Grace's valet is already in the guest suite," Valentin said. "We'll take the rest of the bags up."

"The rest—Of course. Thank you."

"And the groom took the carriage and team round to the stables," Michael added.

"I do hope you'll be comfortable." Suzanne moved to the duke's side. Jessica, who had been studying him gravely, her head tucked against Suzanne's shoulder, lifted her head and made a grab for the duke's cravat. "Da ba." It might have been an attempt at "Grandpapa" or simply gibberish.

"Querida." Suzanne reached out to detach her daughter's sticky fingers from the pristine linen. The duke had struck Suzanne as distinctly ill at ease with babies when they'd been in Scotland over the summer.

Strathdon studied Jessica as though she were a recently discovered manuscript. "My word, how she's grown. One forgets." He twitched his cravat smooth, casting the briefest glance at the small jammy fingerprints on the linen. His mouth twitched with what might have been either disapproval or the faintest smile.

"We'll have your room prepared directly, Your Grace," Suzanne said. "Valentin, perhaps you could have refreshments sent to the library."

With her usual knack for appearing at the right moment, Laura Dudley came down the stairs to take the children. Jessica squawked and dug in her fingers when Suzanne started to hand her over, and the tightness in her breasts told Suzanne why. "I'll join you presently," she told the men.

"No need to run off," the duke said.

Suzanne shifted Jessica against her shoulder. "I need to feed her."

"Oh." Strathdon held his gloves out for Valentin to take. "Well, no need to run off to do that. We're a very broad-minded family." The duke stepped towards the library.

Suzanne met Malcolm's gaze. Her husband's look said clearly, *Don't abandon me.* So when she had seen Colin off with Laura, Suzanne followed her husband and his grandfather into the library.

She had met the duke twice, on her and Malcolm's first visit to England three years ago and again the previous summer. He had seemed vaguely pleased Malcolm had taken a wife and equally vaguely pleased to see his great-grandchildren, provided they didn't disrupt his routine. The duke rarely left his estate in Scotland. According to Malcolm, he came to London occasionally to attend the theatre or to consult with other Shakespearean scholars but preferred it if they came to see him.

Suzanne sank into a chair by the windows, discreetly removed, and unfastened the flap on her nursing bodice.

The duke settled himself in one of the high-backed Queen Anne chairs before the fireplace. "I like what you've done with the house, Suzanne." He ran his gaze over the curtains and window seat coverings. "It looks more comfortable."

Malcolm gave a faint smile as he moved to the drinks trolley. "I didn't think you noticed comfort, sir."

"It is perhaps something we tend to overlook. I don't think your mother and father gave a great deal of thought to it, but then I fear their lives were not very comfortable, so why should their house be? I'm glad to see you're doing better."

Suzanne saw the shock of surprise in her husband's gaze as he poured two glasses of whisky. "You are a constant source of surprises, sir." He put one of the glasses in his grandfather's hand.

"Lucky thing your letter found me at Marjorie's. Surely you realized that if anything would bring me to London it would be the mention of a new version of *Hamlet*."

"Possible new version."

"All the more reason for me to see it." Strathdon settled back in his chair, whisky glass cradled in his hand. "Is it genuine?"

"I'm no expert."

"You're well versed in Shakespeare."

It was, Suzanne knew, huge praise from the duke. She saw that fact register in Malcolm's gaze, but he merely dropped into the chair across from his grandfather and took a sip from his own glass. "It looks authentic to me. I'm eager to have your opinion." Malcolm explained his theory that the manuscript had been copied by Francis Woolright and that Woolright and Eleanor Harleton had made notes on it.

"That's plausible," Strathdon said. "Woolright apparently had a good ear for the language. There are stories—perhaps apocryphal, perhaps not—of Shakespeare asking him for feedback. If he wanted to study the role of Laertes in particular, he might well have made his own copy and shown it to his mistress." Strathdon took another sip of whisky. "Shakespeare seems to have been working on *Hamlet* in 1599. An interesting year. The Chamberlain's Men had thrown up the Globe from the timbers of a dismantled theatre and finally had a home of their own. The Irish were rebelling, Elizabeth's relationship with Essex was falling apart. Shakespeare also wrote *Henry V, Julius Caesar,* and *As You Like It* that year. Not surprising they all deal with deposed rulers one way and another." Strathdon curled his fingers round his glass. "But I don't suppose historical details are what's caught your interest. What aren't you telling me?"

"I beg your pardon?"

"My dear boy. I can see it in your face."

Malcolm cast a glance at Suzanne. Jessica gave a squawk as though aware of the adults' disquiet. "It appears there may be a connection to Alistair," Malcolm said.

Strathdon's brows rose. "What on earth would Alistair have to do with a manuscript of *Hamlet*? He had no use for Shakespeare."

"Did you know when he was at Oxford Alistair founded a club called the Elsinore League?"

"No." Strathdon frowned for a moment. "Or if I did, I forgot. I made it a point to forget as much as I could about Alistair."

"An understandable impulse. I wish I could do the same."

Something shifted in Strathdon's eyes. They held a look that might almost have been called tenderness. For a moment, Suzanne thought he was going to say something about Malcolm's relationship with his father. But instead the duke took another sip of whisky and said, "Whatever the name, somehow I doubt this club of Alistair's was for the purpose of analyzing the finer subtleties of iambic pentameter."

Malcolm turned his glass in his hand. "The official story is that it was a sort of hellfire club."

"And the unofficial?"

Malcolm wiped a trace of liquid from the side of the glass. "It may have been a cover for French spies."

The Rannoch family did not often show shock. Even so, Suzanne expected to see the words register in the duke's gaze like the thunderclap they were. Instead, Strathdon's face went blank as an empty stage. With total shock. Or perhaps recognition.

"My dear boy. Are you suggesting your father may have been a Bonapartist agent?"

"Oh, my God." Malcolm sat back in his chair. "Don't tell me you knew, too."

Strathdon took a sip of whisky. "Do you imagine I'd have kept quiet if I knew my daughter's husband was betraying Crown and country?"

"It might have disturbed your research more to say something than to keep quiet."

A gleam lit Strathdon's eyes. "A palpable hit. In general you're quite right to see me as self-absorbed, but as it happens I believe I would have said something about out-and-out treason."

"And yet?" Malcolm's gaze remained fixed on his grandfather's face.

The duke shifted in his chair. "I don't shock easily. But I own I was shocked when Alistair asked me for your mother's hand. Or rather when he told me he already had Arabella's consent. Even then I didn't believe she'd agreed to it until I asked her myself."

Malcolm went absolutely still. Suzanne felt the jolt of tension that shot through him, half-wanting an answer, half-fearing it. "What did she say?"

Strathdon's gaze clouded with memory. "That Alistair Rannoch was the man she wanted. To which I replied, not surprisingly, I think, 'Why?' "

"And?"

Strathdon turned his glass in his hand. "She said it was time she was married and Alistair could give her what she wanted. And wouldn't ask for anything she wasn't prepared to give."

The words held an echo of Malcolm's phrasing when he'd proposed to Suzanne. Suzanne tightened her hold on Jessica. Jessica arched her back with a cry of protest.

Strathdon cast a brief glance at his great-granddaughter, though he seemed to be looking into the past. "Arabella could have had her pick of men that season or any other. Half the single men—and a fair share of the married ones as well—at any ball were head over heels in love with her."

"But Alistair wasn't," Malcolm said.

"No," Strathdon agreed. "I think that was what appealed to her.

He wouldn't make emotional demands. She didn't have to worry about disappointing him. She didn't want to run the risk of falling in love."

"Again," Malcolm said.

The gazes of grandson and grandfather locked across the library. The oak and gilt of the room carried echoes of the revelations of three years ago at the Congress of Vienna. Lady Arabella's trip to the Continent with her father when she was seventeen, her unhappy love affair with the older, married Duke of Courland, the birth of her illegitimate daughter, who grew up in secret in France.

"Yes," Strathdon said, and though his voice was quiet the regret beneath the neutral tone was palpable. "I fear Arabella never got over her disappointment. She didn't want to love again. She didn't want to be in a situation where she would even risk it."

"Perceptive," Malcolm said. "But then you do spend your time studying Shakespeare. Who understands the intricacies of the human heart better?"

Strathdon gave a faint smile. "You flatter me."

"So you gave your consent?" Malcolm asked.

"Not immediately." Strathdon watched the winter sunlight bounce off the crystal of his glass. "I was always of the mind that my children would do better making their own decisions than with me hovering inexpertly over them. And for the most part I believe that's proved true. Marjorie seems surprisingly happy and Frances has done well enough, for all Dacre-Hammond wasn't the most imaginative choice. But I . . . mistrusted Alistair. And I still blamed myself for Arabella's predicament. So I made some inquiries into my prospective son-in-law."

"And?" Malcolm's voice was tight with strain.

Strathdon smoothed a crease from the glossy superfine of his sleeve. "Much of what was apparent on the surface. Alistair was ambitious. Suffered at school for being there on charity. Made friends with his wealthier school fellows and was all too aware of the differences between them. Was undeniably clever. Came into an unexpected legacy from a distant cousin in Jamaica as he was finishing up at Oxford, made some shrewd investments, and built a tidy fortune. Save that the money didn't come from that cousin in Jamaica."

"Where was it from?" If Malcolm's voice had been rope it would have frayed from the strain.

"I couldn't discover. The illusion that it was from his cousin was quite elaborate. Documents, funds routed through the cousin's bank. The cousin had made Alistair his heir. At least a will existed, naming Alistair, though it may have been a forgery. But the cousin died in debt."

"Did you ask Alistair about it?"

"Oh yes. He said the accusations were nonsense and I couldn't possibly prove any of it. Rather contradictory. Then I went to Arabella."

"And?" Malcolm's gaze was locked on his grandfather's face.

Strathdon's brows drew together. "Arabella said she already knew."

Suzanne saw Malcolm's fingers curve round the chair arms. "Did she say she knew where the money had come from?"

"She wouldn't tell me one way or another. She said if it didn't concern her, there was no reason for me to concern myself with it." Strathdon frowned into his whisky glass.

Malcolm leaned forwards as though he would spring from the chair. "And you simply stood back—"

"There wasn't anything simple about it." Unwonted fire flashed in Strathdon's eyes. "I said I've made it a point to let my children make their own decisions, especially since their mother died. Some would say it was selfishness. Others might call it an acknowledgment of my singular lack of ability to guide them. It seems to have turned out all right for Fanny and Margie. But I've often wondered if when it came to Arabella, I should have—" He shook his head. "I didn't, and there's an end to it. Arabella was set on Alistair Rannoch. She threatened to elope. And I confess I feared one of her depressions."

"And so she married Alistair." Malcolm's voice was flat as a sword blade.

"And so she married Alistair." The duke took a sip of whisky, deeper than was his wont. "To the day of the wedding I wondered—But that's water under the bridge now. And without it, she wouldn't have had you and Edgar and Gisèle."

Malcolm drew a breath, then released it. When he spoke it seemed to be something different from what he had first intended. "Did you ever—"

"I had a man sending me information about Alistair through the years. Don't look at me like that, Malcolm. I may not be a trained agent like my grandson, but being a duke has its privileges."

"And?"

Strathdon shifted in his chair. "There was no record of Alistair receiving other mysterious payments. Of course by that time he had little need of money. He'd invested his supposed inheritance well, and he had—"

"Mama's marriage portion."

"Quite. Though most of your mother's money was tied up for her and for her children."

Malcolm's gaze remained trained on his grandfather's face. "He didn't receive more mysterious payments, but—"

Strathdon shifted his shoulders against the high chairback."He disappeared from time to time despite the best efforts of the quite competent man I employed to watch him."

"To France?"

"To the Continent."

Suzanne saw Malcolm's knuckles whiten round his glass. "Did you ever wonder—"

"To own the truth I suspected he was involved in smuggling." Strathdon took a sip of whisky as though sifting through the past. "But being a French agent would certainly fit the facts as well."

"You're very calm, sir."

"I've seen a great deal in my life, Malcolm. I have few illusions when it came to Alistair Rannoch. Far fewer than you."

"I don't—"

"My dear boy, he was your father. You couldn't help but have illusions about him."

Malcolm swallowed. Suzanne felt his unvoiced pain cut through her. "I scarcely knew him."

"All the harder, I think. You never had the chance to resolve matters with him."

"That wouldn't have happened if Alistair had lived to be one hundred." Malcolm spoke in a voice from which all feeling had been hammered. "I didn't like him very much."

"I know. You really should stop blaming yourself for it."

Malcolm's head snapped up. "Damn it, sir, you're supposed to be above noticing such things."

"You flatter me, my boy."

Malcolm pushed himself to his feet. "He betrayed his country."

"You already knew you disagreed with him on political matters. Is his being a French agent so much more shocking than his being a Tory?"

Malcolm stopped in the midst of the Aubusson carpet and stared at his grandfather. "For God's sake, sir—"

Strathdon lifted his brows. His gaze was mild and yet at the same time the gaze of one accustomed from the cradle to not having his word questioned. "Surely you can't be surprised that I've never taken Crown and country as seriously as some. I'm not saying I'd commit treason myself. But I don't find it as shocking as you. Of course I've never been an agent."

Malcolm opened his mouth to speak, then bit back the words and dug his fingers into his hair. "It's no secret I disagree with much of what our government stands for at home and abroad. Looking back at what we did in Spain and what the French did, it's difficult for me to argue we were clearly in the right. That's a large part of why I left the diplomatic service and stood for Parliament. David could tell you about my impassioned letters. Suzette could tell you about my tirades after diplomatic dinner parties." He flashed a smile at Suzanne.

The duke regarded his grandson with a surprising combination of steel and gentleness. "But you take your loyalties seriously. And you may not yet have realized how complicated loyalties can be."

Suzanne wondered if Jessica could feel the pounding of her heart through the velvet-edged merino of her gown. She seemed to be asleep. Suzanne put her lips to the baby's head and forced her fingers not to clench on the pintucked muslin of Jessica's dress.

"Alistair used to accuse me of being a Jacobin," Malcolm said.

"If you worked for the French," Strathdon said, "I rather think you'd do so openly."

"Alistair was one of the most anti-Bonapartist people I've ever met. Either he was a master at deception or—"

"He was only in it for the money."

"Quite."

"Knowing what I do of my late son-in-law, I'd be more inclined to believe the latter. Though God knows I'm not the best judge of character." Strathdon turned his head. "You're very quiet, Suzanne. What do you think?"

"I scarcely knew Mr. Rannoch." Her voice, somehow, came out sounding something approaching normal. A testament to years of training.

"But you were in Britain during the last months of his life. And you strike me as a good judge of character."

She shifted Jessica carefully in her arms. Jessica burrowed into her with the abandon of sleep. "I own I was shocked to hear he was working for the French." That much was true. "But he struck me as a man who wasn't loyal to much of anything. Not his family, not his friends. So then it's hard to believe he was particularly loyal to his country or to any set of beliefs."

Strathdon inclined his head. "You made an excellent choice when you married her, Malcolm."

"One of the few sensible things I've done in my life. But if Alistair was motivated solely by self-interest, it's hard to fathom why he'd have run the risk of working for the French once he no longer needed the money."

"The truth could have ruined him," Suzanne pointed out in a carefully calibrated tone. Not for the first time, she realized how lucky she was Raoul had let her go. He could have used the threat of revealing the truth to Malcolm to force her to work for him indefinitely. "And then there's the lure of the game. Perhaps that's the one place you take after Alistair, darling."

"I don't—"

"You miss it, Malcolm. Don't deny it. Much as you may like to pretend you're grown-up and above it. I could see it in your eyes when Simon appeared over our windowsill. Because I was feeling much the same myself."

A rap at the door echoed through the room. Valentin came in with a tray of tea and cakes. Suzanne moved to the settee between the two chairs, cradling the sleeping Jessica. Malcolm poured her a cup of tea.

"Did Mama ever say anything to you that might have indicated she knew?" Malcolm asked the duke, offering him a cup of tea.

"I told you, I didn't know it myself." Strathdon waved aside the tea.

Malcolm filled a cup for himself to a precise quarter inch below the silver rim. "Did she tell you Raoul O'Roarke is my father?"

Strathdon's gaze shot to his grandson's face. Malcolm set down the teapot. "You knew."

"No." Strathdon took a sip of whisky. "Arabella hardly confided in me in that way. I wondered."

"Why?"

"I'd seen how close they were."

"You mean you knew they were lovers."

"Suspected. One doesn't like to dwell on such questions about one's daughter. But then there was the interest O'Roarke took in you. And Alistair's—"

"Lack of interest."

"To give the man more charity than he deserves." Strathdon took a sip of whisky. "I always liked O'Roarke. Dabbled—more than dabbled—in dangerous waters, but he was a good man. Is a good man. And clearly fond of you."

"You read a lot in the situation."

"Contrary to what some think, I take more than a passing interest in my children and grandchildren. O'Roarke tried not to make his relationship to you too obvious. He was concerned for you. And for Arabella."

Malcolm inclined his head. "I'm sure you want to see the manuscript." He'd obviously said as much as he was prepared to about Raoul.

A smile lit Strathdon's eyes. "I thought you'd never ask."

Malcolm set down his cup. "We move it every few days. Right now it's at David and Simon's. Allie's there working on it. I'll take you round. We're going to a performance at the Tavistock this evening—one of Simon's plays. You're welcome to join us if you can put up with a non-Shakespearean evening."

"I'd be delighted. Always been an admirer of Tanner's work." Strathdon swallowed the last of his whisky. "Er—is Mademoiselle Caret in it?"

"She's the lead," Suzanne said.

"Splendid." Strathdon pushed himself to his feet. "Talented young woman that. Saw her as Cleopatra but didn't get the chance to meet her."

Suzanne exchanged a look with Malcolm. With the Duke of Strathdon, meeting Manon did not mean crowding in with the throng that customarily overflowed her dressing room after a performance. Suzanne shifted Jessica in her arms and got to her feet. "I'll stop by the Tavistock and see if I can arrange for Manon to save time for us after the performance."

Malcolm nodded. "I'll check if Harry's left a message for me and meet you there. We can walk home together."

"It won't be that late, darling. I'd be perfectly fine walking on my own."

"But this gives us another quarter hour together."

Suzanne smiled at him with affectionate mockery. "Of course. Hotspur."

"Have there been more attempts to take the manuscript?" Strathdon asked.

"Not since the night after Simon brought it to us." Malcolm exchanged a look with Suzanne.

"It's almost as though whoever was after the manuscript has given up," she said.

"Which doesn't make sense given how determined he was," Malcolm said. "Unless—"

"Unless recovering the manuscript doesn't solve his problems anymore," Suzanne said. "If there's something he's worried about in the words themselves, simply getting the manuscript back wouldn't protect him. It's common knowledge by now that the Tavistock is presenting the play. All the actors have scripts."

"So he might have decided further efforts to go after the manuscript would only draw our attention to whatever he's trying to conceal," Malcolm said.

"Interesting," Strathdon said. "The question would seem to be what that is."

CHAPTER 23

"Rannoch."

Malcolm bit back a curse at the drawling voice. Why in God's name did Frederick Radley have to frequent this coffeehouse? One would have thought there were entirely too many newspapers rustling and pens scratching to suit him. Malcolm and Harry used the coffeehouse off Piccadilly to pass messages. Malcolm had ducked in after taking Strathdon to David and Simon's lodgings in the Albany, where Aline was working on the manuscript. By the time he ascertained that Harry had not left a message for him, Malcolm looked up to see Radley moving towards him. Radley's slicked-back blond hair gleamed in the lamplight, and his blue eyes were alight with a mockery and self-assurance that took Malcolm right back to Harrow and the sort of fellow student who would always see himself as superior simply by virtue of being who he was.

"Good day, Radley."

Radley dropped into a chair across from Malcolm without waiting for an invitation. "Didn't have a chance to speak with you at Carfax House the other night, though I saw Suzanne. She was looking lovely. I understand she's become quite the toast of London. Remarkable how things turn out."

Malcolm took a sip of coffee, resisting the urge to fling it in Radley's face. "I don't think anyone who knows my wife would find that remarkable."

Radley lifted a finger to signal a waiter. "That would depend upon whether or not they knew about her past."

Malcolm's fingers tightened on his cup. It was a wonder the handle didn't snap. "I haven't the least idea what you're talking about, Radley."

"No?" Radley at least had the grace not to say more while the waiter approached. Or perhaps the colonel was just enjoying Malcolm's discomfort. Radley ordered a glass of claret from the waiter and then sat back in his chair with a sense of ownership. "Your tolerance is quite remarkable, Rannoch. Whatever men will put up with from their wives after they have an heir, most wouldn't tolerate the revelation that the woman they married had a lover before they put a ring on her finger." He crossed his legs. "Assuming of course that she really did tell you. I've always wondered. I'd give even odds on her merely bluffing."

"Then you'd have underestimated my wife."

"Well, well. Isn't this civilized. It's not many men who could share a drink with their wife's former lover."

If he could, Malcolm would have thrown his cup, upended the table, and smashed his booted foot into Radley's smug face. But Radley was the one who wanted a scene. So Malcolm took a slow, deliberate sip of coffee and set the cup down with barely a clatter. "You must know that the only reason I haven't called you to account is that I abhor dueling."

"Because I besmirched your wife's honor?"

"Whom my wife slept with before she married me is quite her own affair. But you took advantage of a young woman left penniless and without protection."

Radley gave a short laugh. "Believe me, Suzanne was well able to take care of herself even then."

"That doesn't excuse your actions."

The waiter set a glass of claret on the table in front of Radley. Radley lifted it, sniffed the bouquet, and took an appreciative sip. "She was hardly an innocent when our affair began. Or to put it more bluntly, I wasn't her first lover. And I'm not talking about the French soldiers who ravished her. Her—shall we say skills?—told of a different sort of relationship in her past."

Malcolm willed his face to reveal nothing and shut his mind to any questions. Everything he stood for insisted that he not respond. And it wasn't completely a surprise. The fact that Suzanne had entered into the affair with Radley at a time of crisis had made Malcolm wonder if the colonel had perhaps not been her first lover. "That's her business."

Radley twirled the stem of his glass between his fingers. "Don't care that your wife is damaged goods?"

"I don't consider her past any more damaging than my own."

"You do take your Radical nonsense to extremes, don't you, Rannoch?" Radley took another sip of wine. He was enjoying this far too much. Malcolm reminded himself again not to sink to the other man's level. More than anything, he wanted to wipe the self-satisfied smirk off Radley's face. "Especially given that Suzanne had tête-à-têtes with not one but two of her former lovers at the Carfax House ball. Of course when it comes to me our involvement is strictly in the past. But I couldn't swear the same about the other ex-lover she spoke with. They looked very cozy."

Malcolm willed his face not to betray surprise and his hands to stay steady. "My wife has a number of friends."

"As do many ladies of the beau monde and what they do with their friends is anyone's guess. But Suzanne slipped off to meet this particular friend in León five and a half years ago. I saw them embracing. Of course, being so open I expect she's told you all about it." Radley took another sip of wine and regarded Malcolm over the rim of the glass. "Or hasn't she?"

The coffee turned bitter in Malcolm's mouth. Fears he could not yet quite articulate stabbed his brain. Part of his mind screamed to leave it, but the other knew he could not. He took a sip of coffee. It was lukewarm, but it scalded his tongue. "You're a good story-teller, Radley. Who's the subject of this particular tale?"

"She hasn't told you? Interesting." Radley tossed off the last of the claret. "In León, your charming wife was exceedingly close to Raoul O'Roarke."

Malcolm's impulse to laugh aside anything Radley said warred with the persistent, gnawing tug that this was something more, something not easily explained away. He shifted in his chair, his impulse to move away from the words that had been spoken. Suzanne had been in León. O'Roarke could have been there. When she first met Malcolm, she'd been concealing her relationship with Radley. She might have neglected to mention O'Roarke for the same reasons. When one began with a lie it could be difficult to go back and confess the truth. He'd been in that situation. He took another deliberate sip of coffee. "Hardly surprising that she encountered O'Roarke in Spain."

Satisfaction thick as clotted cream spread across Radley's face. "So she didn't tell you. I thought as much. She more than encountered O'Roarke. Unless she was in the habit of bestowing clinging kisses on every man she encountered. Always possible I suppose."

Anger shot through Malcolm. Along with something else he wouldn't yet put a name to that danced along his nerve endings. He wanted to deny any interest in the sordid story and walk away. But he had to know. He had to know how dangerous the information made Radley. And he had to know for himself. "You saw my wife and O'Roarke embracing?"

Radley lifted a finger to summon the waiter again. Malcolm was obliged to wait while the waiter brought the bottle and refilled Radley's glass. "In a doorway. To own the truth, I'd begun to wonder if the fair Suzanne was more than she seemed, and I followed her. The doorway was shadowy, but it was plainly them. Their embrace conveyed what can only be called familiarity."

Malcolm pushed aside the questions crowding his brain for later. "Did you ask her about it?"

"No. It was time to end the affair in any case."

"To abandon her."

"Call it what you will." Radley took an appreciative sip of claret. "I didn't know who O'Roarke was at the time as it happens. Our paths never crossed in the Peninsula. It was only when someone pointed him out to me at the ball last night that I realized who it had been." Radley settled back in his chair, the stem of his glass held between two fingers. "Thought you should know, Rannoch. After all, whatever our differences, we're both Harrovians."

Malcolm pushed through the coffeehouse door and turned down Piccadilly, only dimly aware of the artists and tradesmen he brushed past. He could scarcely remember what he had said when he left Radley at the table, save that he knew he'd refrained from planting the man a facer.

Suzanne had known O'Roarke in the Peninsula. A friend of her parents? Could the embrace Radley exaggerated actually have been more paternal? Or perhaps they had been lovers. He'd accepted that she'd had lovers before Radley. She hadn't known Malcolm then and certainly hadn't known O'Roarke's connection to Malcolm. O'Roarke wouldn't have known she would end up married to the man he had fathered. Malcolm wouldn't have expected O'Roarke to become the lover of an unmarried girl and then abandon her to her own devices, but perhaps there was an explanation in the chaos of war. O'Roarke had a wife in Ireland. He couldn't have married Suzanne. God knew people could behave irrationally. Perhaps—

Fragments of memory swirled in his brain, slashing through the scenario he attempted to construct. Aunt Frances quoting his father—*People will remark on Malcolm's good fortune. But it's some comfort to know that one day he'll realize what it is to be betrayed by one's spouse.* "La Corbeau." Alistair's letter to Harleton—*I own the revelation of the Raven's identity holds particular dangers for me.*

The pieces shifted, broke apart, re-formed into an unmistakable scenario.

Malcolm walked full tilt into a woman carrying a basket of turnips. The turnips scattered over the pavement. He gathered them up and murmured an apology, scarcely aware of the words he framed. The woman moved on, mollified.

Malcolm took a half-dozen more steps and paused, gripping the black metal of a lamppost. The metal was cold even through the York tan of his gloves. He knew how to gather and sift information and follow it to its logical conclusion, however surprising. However unwelcome. The image formed by those fragments hung before his mind, inescapable, unavoidable.

His wife had been the Raven. And the man who had fathered him had been her spymaster.

Somehow he let go of the lamppost and walked down the street without stumbling under carriage wheels or knocking over other pedestrians. Of course, of course, of course. So much seemed so obvious now. The papers for Count Nesselrode that had disappeared from his dispatch box in Vienna. The British code that had found its way into French hands on the eve of Waterloo. The way O'Roarke had suddenly known in Paris two years ago that they needed help rescuing the father of Tatiana's son. The instinctive sympathy between Suzette and Manon Caret.

He remembered a glimpse of his wife in the theatre yesterday, Jessica in her arms, bending over Colin as he played with the Caret girls. He had stopped for a moment to drink in the sight. In the midst of the investigation and the torrent of revelations about his parents, he'd reminded himself of what a truly fortunate man he was.

He'd never been one to use terms like "happiness." Perhaps because he'd thought of himself as possessing a worldly wisdom that regarded such words as trite and oversimplistic. Or perhaps because it had seemed to be tempting fate. But he saw now that he had been happy. Beneath the everyday ups and downs of his life had been a solid, steady core of contentment. Built on everyday trivialities. His son's babble over breakfast in the nursery. His daughter's arm curled round his wife's breast as she nursed. His wife applying blacking to her lashes or unpinning her hair.

He'd been happy. Simply. Wholeheartedly.

Blindly.

He stopped walking, seconds before he smashed into another lamppost. His hands had curled into fists. He gripped the lamppost with shaking fingers. One couldn't really know another person. He knew that better than anyone. Should know it. Should have known it. He'd long since accepted that he'd never fully understand either of his parents. Tatiana remained an elusive mystery, dancing just out of reach, even years after her death. Edgar had closed down all but the most rudimentary lines of communication between him and Malcolm after their mother's death. Gisèle had grown up without him. Even Aunt Frances, who he would have sworn was beyond her ability to surprise him, had shocked him with the revelation of her affair with Alistair.

But Suzette—

He'd been cautious when he'd married her. Afraid of hurting her, of offering more than he was capable of giving. But if he was honest, he'd been protecting himself as well. Afraid to take the risk of emotional intimacy with a woman he was convinced was only marrying him as a way out of her predicament. Why else would she choose him? How odd that he'd been right, though for all the wrong reasons. Were it not for her circumstances, Suzanne would certainly not have married him.

When had he changed? When had caution and prudence and a practical recognition of the limitations of human relationships given way to blind idiocy? In Vienna he'd still been so careful of his feelings that Suzanne had been convinced Tatiana was his mistress. His guilt over misleading her bit him in the throat now, an irony so sharp it sliced to the bone. Even at Waterloo he'd been cautious enough he hadn't told her where he was going when he slipped off to the château the night of Julia Ashton's death.

Was Waterloo when it had changed? Saying good-bye to Suzette at the Duchess of Richmond's ball, knowing he might be kissing her for the last time? In the blood and smoke of the field, wondering if he'd got his loyalties hopelessly muddled and should have put staying with his wife and son above the call of Crown and country? In the aftermath, the horror of the battle stamped on his imagination, Edgar and Harry fighting for their lives, when he had clung to her as though to his last vestiges of sanity?

Or had it been in Paris, his views diverging seemingly inescapably from Castlereagh's and Wellington's, the White Terror making a mockery of any vestige of belief that they'd been fighting for anything but the preservation of the status quo, the search for Tatiana's child bringing his guilt over her death welling to the surface? Suzette had been his touchstone, the one constant he could rely on. He'd said things to her about his family, his feelings, his conflicting thoughts on his work and future that a year, even a few months, before would have been unthinkable.

And then there was the morning the following spring when she'd told him she wanted to have another child. A further bond between them, consciously created. His fingers tightened round the lamppost. Why in God's name had she done it? What had she had to gain from another child? Had it been some sort of insurance against what might happen if he ever learned the truth?

Images of the night of Jessica's birth sliced into his brain. Holding Suzanne's hand, her fingers a vise round his own. The wriggling baby sliding into Geoffrey Blackwell's arms with a reassuring squawk. Placing her on Suzette's chest. A tiny hand gripping one finger. Showing her blanket-swaddled form to Colin. Perhaps the best night of his life.

And then there had been the night he'd formally resigned from the diplomatic corps and written to David saying he'd stand for Parliament. He could see Suzanne's steady dark gaze, glowing with the light from the brace of candles on their dinner table, when he told her. Feel the reassuring pressure of her hand on his own. He'd never have felt strong enough to face the demons of his past without her beside him. But even then some barriers had remained, stronger perhaps when he'd returned home and confronted his family and his relationship—or lack of relationship—to them.

Until Alistair's death and its aftermath had smashed the last of the barriers. Malcolm flinched as his raw sobs echoed in his ears, as he felt again the force of Suzanne's arms round him. The seduction had been complete. He'd held nothing back. And so now he had no defenses left. No refuge to hide in because the refuge he had learned to rely on had proved to be a painted sham.

A gust of wind cut down the street, rattling the gold-painted key of a locksmith's sign overhead. He took one hand from the lamppost and dug his fingers into his hair. He'd lost his hat somewhere. Probably when he bumped into the woman with the turnips.

Once he'd taken it for granted that he faced everything alone. He was going to have to do that again.

Because though his world might be in wreckage, he needed answers more than ever.

CHAPTER 24

Suzanne heard Malcolm's footsteps in the shadows of the wings and moved across the stage to meet him. "Darling? Manon was charming about saving the evening for the duke. Everyone just left to get ready for the performance this evening. I'd have left myself if you hadn't been so insistent about walking me home. Really, if you haven't got more important—"

Something checked her before she could even see into his eyes. The tension in his footfalls? The quality of the silence? "Malcolm?" She moved towards him. "What is it? Something about your father?"

Malcolm had gone stone still, his gaze fastened on her face. The thick yellow light from the rehearsal lamps slanted across him, leaving his eyes in shadow, but the quality of his gaze at once singed her and chilled her to the bone.

And she knew. Before her brain could form the thought, the sick certainty settled inside her. It seemed inevitable, something that had always been as sure to arrive as Christmas or a birthday or a change of seasons. Yet at the same time so unthinkable she seemed to have been robbed of the power to speak or move or even formulate a thought.

His gaze held her own for what might have been seconds or

minutes. Long enough for a marriage to shatter like shards of crystal, never to be re-formed.

"When you married me," he said, "how long did you think it would last?"

"Darling—" Somehow it was the first word that broke from her lips.

"Don't." His voice was like the slap of a sword blade on rock. "There've been enough lies."

"That's not a lie. It's how I think of you."

How had she never realized the way his gaze changed when it rested upon her? The particular quality, half-ironic, half-vulnerable, at once intimate and a little removed, as though he could not quite believe the bond between them. She wouldn't have been able to describe it before. But it was so clear to her now it was gone.

"My first thought," he said in a strangely detached voice, "was that you must have been blackmailed into it. Not for money. Through a threat to a family member or someone you loved. I had myself convinced of that."

"Malcolm—"

"But then I realized you're much too strong. You'd have found a way out. Or told me the truth eventually. Odd. I obviously don't know you at all. Yet I'm sure enough of you to know you aren't a victim."

She swallowed. "It's true. I'm not proud of what I've done, but I did it freely."

"You haven't answered my question," he said. "About what you expected when you married me." She'd never credited those who called him cold, but now his voice could freeze raw spirits.

The unthinkable had come to pass. Like pregnancy or illness or a natural disaster, something one could barely contemplate went from unimaginable to stark reality. All these years. The fear that had been a pressure behind her eyes, a tension coiled in her chest, a nightmare vision dancing on the edge of her consciousness. You'd think she'd have planned, strategized, had a dozen speeches written in her head, a score of contingencies planned for. Instead she was living the actor's nightmare, onstage without knowing her lines or even the plot of the play in which she found herself.

"When I married you, I was mad enough to think I could walk away in a few months or a few years." Her voice came out flat and strangely under control. When a mission went wrong, one answered as simply and straightforwardly as possible and didn't elaborate.

He stood watching her in the shadows, tension writ in the lean angles of his body. "I suppose you didn't realize the extent of the information you'd be able to uncover."

"I didn't have the least understanding of you. Or of myself."

"Was it all a plan?" His voice cracked, the dead cold breaking open to reveal an abyss of pain. "Did you have the whole thing in mind from the moment we met?"

"You're an agent, Malcolm." It seemed, somehow, important to remind him of that. "You know one can never foresee the twists and turns of a mission so accurately. One has to improvise in the field. I didn't expect you to take me to Lisbon. I was calculating how long I could afford to stay there and continue my masquerade when you proposed."

"And in doing so played right into your hands."

She could see the same images in his eyes that ran through her own head. The cool, moonlit wrought-iron balcony where he'd proposed during a ball at the British embassy. The airless sitting room in which they'd taken their vows. The bedchamber smelling of lavender and spilled champagne in which they'd spent their wedding night.

"I was shocked," she said. "Shocked that you asked me to marry you."

"You underestimated your talents."

"I underestimated your kindness and determination to take care of those in need."

"You think that's why—"

"You married me to protect me, Malcolm. I've always been grateful."

His harsh laugh carried through the theatre. "You're probably less in need of protection than anyone I've ever encountered."

"That doesn't change my gratitude."

He took a step closer, gaze trained on her face. "You're good,

I'll give you that. Probably the best agent I've ever encountered. I can scarcely comprehend the extent of what you've done. And I obviously don't know you at all."

"Malcolm—" She put out her hand, then let it fall to her side. "I think you know me better than anyone."

He laughed again, a sound that cut through the dusty air of the theatre. "Don't, Suzette. Don't add more lies. As two seasoned agents, we should be able to be honest with each other."

Her throat ached with the impossibility, not just of trust but of any sort of honest communication between them. "I don't expect you to believe it. But the fact that you know me is perhaps the truest thing about me."

"In Vienna. In Brussels. During Waterloo." Once again she saw memories chase through his mind, but this time they were of the two of them talking, debating, devising strategies, drafting memoranda. Of his dispatch box sitting on the dressing table in their shared bedchamber. Papers left out when he took her in his arms as they undressed after a party. Malcolm was careful, but he'd come to trust his wife implicitly.

"I remember how Davenport looked when he first came to the Peninsula," Malcolm continued, in the flat, detached voice of one speaking about distant acquaintances. "As though the curtains had been ripped down in his world to reveal a hollow comedy. I understand that now. In a way I never thought I would."

She sank down on the bottom step of the rehearsal stairs where Hamlet confronted Ophelia. She wasn't sure she could stand any longer. "Ask me what you will. We'd better get this over with."

He turned, pinning her with his hooded gaze. "Whom are you working for now?"

"No one. I stopped after Waterloo."

"Why? There are plenty of Bonapartist plots still."

She kept her gaze locked on his own. "I decided whatever I worked for I'd do it openly as your wife."

"You expect me to believe that?"

"No. I'm not sure I would in your place. But it happens to be the truth."

"And yet you stayed."

She linked her hands round her knees. Her fingers, predictably, were trembling. "I told you. I realized I couldn't walk away. Because of the children. Because of how I feel about you."

"You can't expect—"

"I'm not nearly as nice a person as the person I created for you, Malcolm. But the core of me is the same."

"Don't, Suzette." He strode across the stage as though his thoughts would not let him be still. "I can admire the skill of the woman who pulled off what you've accomplished. But such emotional appeals make me ill."

"Yes, I know. Which is why I wouldn't have said it if it weren't the truth."

His face was in shadow now, but she saw her words bounce off the armor in his eyes. "Obviously your family didn't die in the French attack on Acquera."

Her fingers tightened, pressing against the bones of her hands. "No."

"Did you know Tania's and my intelligence had been responsible for misdirecting the French to Acquera?" He paused a moment. She could feel the pressure of his gaze, like a sword point beneath her chin. "Or did O'Roarke?"

He knew about Raoul. In the dead cold of his voice, she knew that more than just their marriage had shattered. Whatever fragile, unvoiced thing he and Raoul had discovered was broken as well.

"Yes, I know about O'Roarke," Malcolm said. "Frederick Radley saw the two of you embracing in León."

A bitter sound broke from her lips. She could not have said whether it was a laugh or a sob. "Dear God. I underestimated Radley."

"He didn't have the least idea what he'd really seen. He was trying to convince me O'Roarke was your lover. Which I presume was the case. Is the case."

"Was." The word tumbled quickly from her lips. Probably folly to care so much about drawing certain boundaries round her crimes. "It ended . . . a long time ago."

"Given that our marriage was a sham, it's hardly any concern of mine whom you slept with when. But once Radley told me about the incident in León the rest of the pieces fell into place. The criminal thing is that I didn't see it sooner."

"Malcolm, you couldn't—"

"Oh, but I could." His voice was flat, his gaze unyielding. "If I hadn't been willfully blind. If I hadn't let my guard down in the worst way possible. If I hadn't been so very bad at my job and you hadn't been so very good at yours."

"You had no reason to suspect—"

"I can think of a dozen reasons now, but I overlooked them all." He moved upstage and dragged a straight-backed chair towards her. "You haven't told me if you knew about my role in the Acquera tragedy when you invented your backstory." He dropped into the chair, facing her like an interrogator.

She saw the dusty cottage in which she'd met with Raoul to plan the details of her mission to intercept British diplomat Malcolm Rannoch. The smoke from the open fire in the center of the floor had turned her stomach. She'd been more than two months pregnant, though she hadn't realized it yet. "Raoul knew about Acquera. He thought—"

"That connecting your supposed family tragedy to Acquera would make me all the more sympathetic to you. Perhaps even get me to offer you marriage."

"I told you your proposing wasn't part of the plan."

"Not part of your plan. I wouldn't put it past O'Roarke. He's obviously a master chess player." He sat back in his chair and spoke in a tone of examining an obscure footnote that might or might not be of interest. "Did you know O'Roarke was my father?"

She swallowed, aware of the mines they were treading round. One could argue she owed Malcolm the truth. But then there was the question of what she owed Colin. "No. I learned when he admitted it to you yesterday."

"That must have come as a shock." He tilted his head back. "What did Alistair have to do with orchestrating our marriage?"

"Nothing." She leaned forwards, appalled at this thought. "We didn't even know about your—Alistair."

"You're asking me to believe my wife, my biological father, and my putative father were all French spies and each didn't know what the other was doing?"

"Alistair must have learned about me at some point, given those comments about the Raven in his letter to Harleton. But I didn't know about him, and Raoul says he didn't, even when Alistair helped him escape Ireland. I'm far from believing Raoul in everything, but in this case I think I do."

"And you expect me to believe you?"

"I don't expect you to believe anything I say, darling. But it happens to be the truth. You know how fragmented intelligence operations are. It isn't safe for agents to know the names of other agents and it often isn't practicable, either. I've heard you bemoan the duplication of information often enough." She sat back, drained by recognition of the futility of trying to get him to understand anything. "I was as shocked as you when Crispin told us about Alistair. And horrified."

"Why horrified?"

He probably wouldn't believe anything she said, so she might as well tell him the truth. "Because I didn't like the idea that I was anything like Alistair."

Malcolm gave a short laugh. "I suppose one could say Alistair married my mother under false pretenses as well, though not to spy on her. He certainly put less effort into being a husband than you did into being a wife. I doubt O'Roarke and Alistair would have much cared for the thought they had anything in common with each other." He stared at her for a long moment. His gaze was at once hard and cold and unbearably remote, as though he had already moved an unbreachable distance from her. "O'Roarke is Colin's father, isn't he?"

The silence in the theatre seemed deafening. Dust motes danced in the air. Her throat ached with unbearable loss. "Malcolm—"

"Don't." He shot his arm out to silence her. "I may have been appallingly slow where you're concerned, but I can still work some things out. You weren't raped by French soldiers who attacked your family at Acquera. So that isn't why you were pregnant. O'Roarke is the obvious candidate. Though I assume there were others."

"Yes. But not—"

"You told me it couldn't be Frederick Radley, but I suppose you might have been lying about that as well."

"No." The truth, bitter as it was, was better than furthering the web of lies. "That is, I know who fathered Colin. You're right, it was Raoul."

He hadn't been quite sure. She saw the bitter weight of the revelation settle in his eyes. "Putting us all in the midst of a cross between a Greek tragedy and a Jacobean drama."

"He didn't know," Suzanne said. "When he sent me on the mission, he didn't know I was pregnant. I didn't know myself. I wasn't giving enough heed to such things."

"But he knew when he told you to accept my proposal."

"He didn't tell me to accept you. He left it up to me." She saw the gray sky that December day in the plaza in Lisbon. Raoul's cool, veiled gaze and carefully detached voice. She paused, then added, "I'm not sure what I'd have done if I'd known the truth."

"That's an honest admission. Amazing we have any honesty left between us." His hand curled round the edge of his chair. His fingers were shaking. "Is Jessica—"

"She's your child, Malcolm. In every sense of the word. You may not believe me, but you can see it in her face."

"Given my relationship to O'Roarke, that doesn't really prove anything."

"Raoul and I didn't—We weren't lovers after I married you. As it happens, there wasn't anyone else after I married you."

He stared at her. His eyes were like those of a wax figure at Madame Tussaud's. Or a dead man. "You really expect me to believe that?"

"No." She leaned forwards, bracing her hands on the step behind her. "But if you won't take my word, look at it like an agent. It's true 'fidelity' wasn't really a word in my vocabulary when I married you. To own the truth, even after I came to care for you, what mattered to me was that fidelity was important to you, that I owed it to you out of respect. But you know the longer one is on a mission, the more deeply one has to enmesh oneself in a role, Malcolm."

I was playing the part of a faithful, supportive wife. Sleeping with another man would have been completely at odds with the role."

"Playing." Bitterness danced through the word.

"In the beginning."

His gaze moved over her face as though he was looking for hidden messages in a deciphered code. "Fidelity in the service of a larger goal. I can believe that. You're a good enough agent. And obviously ruthless enough. You sacrificed a great deal to marry me."

She could see it in his eyes, the memory of their wedding night and all the nights that had followed, the realization that the woman he'd taken to bed had been playing a part even when they were at their most intimate. So much couldn't be mended, but it would mean something if she could at least make him believe this. "I'd be lying if I said I'd never even thought of another man in that way since I met you. One doesn't stop noticing. I'm sure you haven't stopped noticing beautiful women. But it was no sacrifice."

He gave a short laugh. "You can stop pandering to my ego. That isn't part of your job anymore."

"Darling—" She sprang to her feet and crossed to his side. She would have taken his face between her hands, but he jerked back. "You can't believe it was all pretense."

"I'd have sworn not. But I'd also have sworn I knew you, Suzette. Any faith I had in my own instincts is entirely destroyed." He pushed his chair back, scraping it over the boards of the stage, and stood to face her. "You made yourself into the perfect wife."

"I've never been in the least—"

"Not the perfect wife in general. The perfect wife for me. The man who never thought he'd marry. You anticipated my every need, without letting me realize how much you catered to me. You shared my adventures. You helped draft my memoranda and dispatches, God help me. Do you have any notion how many people lost their lives—"

"It was war."

"*And that excuses it?*" He closed the distance between them and seized her by the arms.

The last time they'd been this close they'd been moments away from a kiss. Probably their last. Oddly, as she confronted the full force of his anger in the grip of his hands and the fury of his gaze it was easier to maintain her resolve. "I'd never claim my actions were excusable, Malcolm. But in war no one's hands are clean. If my actions took British lives, they also saved French lives."

She saw the flinch in his eyes. "Is that how you justify it to yourself?"

She didn't let herself jerk away from his touch or the anger in his eyes. "I have nightmares, Malcolm." She could feel the comforting pressure of his fingers on the nape of her neck in the dark of the night. "As you know better than anyone."

"Are you asking me to believe your nightmares are real?"

"I'm hardly in a position to ask you to believe anything. But as it happens they are."

He was still gripping her arms but not quite so tightly. For all his anger, he was trying to puzzle it out. How very like Malcolm. "So you're saying people would have died in any case?"

"That's a gross oversimplification. But I suppose in a way I am."

"And that you were acting in the service of your country as I was of mine."

"That's what agents do."

"Except when they're taken in and betray their own people through their blind idiocy." He flung himself away from her and stepped back. "Whatever may be on your conscience is now doubly on mine."

She'd always known Malcolm would never be able to forgive her if he knew the truth. She saw now that it was much worse. He would never be able to forgive himself. "Malcolm—" She took two steps towards him, then checked herself. She had no right to touch him. But she had to find a way to reach him. "Direct your anger where it belongs. At me."

"Believe me, I feel no lack of anger."

"Because it's folly to blame yourself."

His gaze clashed with her own. "Meaning that I'm a dupe who had no hope against you?"

"Meaning the circumstances were entirely stacked against you."

She swallowed. "You're a brilliant agent, Malcolm. But I think you're too honest a person to suspect this level of duplicity."

"The perfect mark. How fortunate for you." He stared at her for a long moment, as one might contemplate a lost illusion. Then he turned on his heel without another word and strode from the theatre.

CHAPTER 25

The stage door slammed shut, echoing through the wings. An exclamation point, marking the moment the unthinkable had come to pass. Suzanne stared at the greasy light on the boards of the stage, the crumpled folds of her gown, her bonnet, pelisse, gloves, and reticule lying forgot on a chair.

The door creaked again, the stage manager returning. Through the sick tumult, thoughts began to form in her brain. That was the thing about the unthinkable. The world didn't stop. It might shift and crack, but one had to stumble on through the wreckage. And so she shook out the folds of her skirt, moved to the chair, put her bonnet on her head and managed to tie the ribbons in a bow, slid her arms into her pelisse and did up the frogged clasps, pulled on her gloves, and slipped her reticule over her wrist.

One thing at a time. That was the only way she would get through this. She made her way the mercifully short distance back to Berkeley Square, even managing to stop and exchange greetings with Henry Brougham on the edge of Green Park. She smiled at Valentin in the entry hall, relinquished her bonnet, pelisse, and gloves, and climbed the steps to the nursery.

Blanca looked round at the opening of the door to the night nursery. She was beside the chest of drawers, pinning a nappy round a wiggling Jessica, who was bouncing on the balls of her feet, clutching Blanca's shoulder. "You're just in time," Blanca said with a smile. "I'm almost done changing her."

Suzanne closed the door and leaned against the cool panels. "There's something I need to tell you."

Blanca went still for a moment, then adjusted the last pin and lifted an insistent Jessica to the floor. "More threats?"

"Worse. Malcolm knows."

The stunned silence was broken by a shriek from Jessica, the sort of gleeful way she announced her presence, as she crawled across the nursery carpet, one leg tucked under her, one hand held aloft clutching a stray sock. "You told him?" Blanca asked.

"He discovered it."

In Blanca's gaze, Suzanne saw her friend's world shatter much as hers had done. But Blanca merely nodded. "We always knew it was a risk."

Jessica caught Suzanne's skirt in her fists and pulled herself to her feet. Suzanne automatically reached down and lifted her daughter into her arms. Jessica pressed her face against Suzanne's throat and wrapped her arms round Suzanne's neck. Suzanne tightened her hold, wanting to lose herself in the fresh baby smell and resilient baby laugh. "I'm not sure when Malcolm will be back. You should tell Addison as soon as possible."

Blanca's gaze locked on Suzanne's own. "You know that Addison and I—"

"I'm not blind. Neither is Malcolm."

Blanca jabbed a strand of hair behind her ear. "It was always Addison who wanted to be discreet. It isn't the done thing for valets and ladies' maids to have lives of their own. But a fortnight ago—He asked me to marry him."

"Blanca—" Happiness, grief, and guilt washed over Suzanne in quick succession. Jessica had looped one arm round Suzanne's neck and seized Suzanne's pearls in her other hand. "I'm so sorry. I dragged you into this. I locked you into a role and into a set of lies. You shouldn't have to pay the consequences for my sins."

Blanca lifted her chin. "No one forced me to go along with it. I wanted to fight the British as well." Blanca's family had been killed during the British retreat after Corunna in which Suzanne had also lost her own family, though they hadn't known each other at the time. "And later I wanted to keep the secrets to preserve my relationship with Addison just as you did with Mr. Rannoch. I made my own choices."

"If I hadn't married Malcolm—"

"I wouldn't have had a chance to become Addison's lover." Blanca shook her head. "It took long enough to get past his scruples."

Jessica wriggled in Suzanne's arms. Suzanne set her on the floor.

"How many others know?" Blanca asked.

"No one that I know of." Suzanne watched her daughter crawl over the pastel carpet, crab-style, one leg tucked under her, the other foot flat on the floor, a silver rattle in her hand now instead of the sock. "I don't know what's going to happen. I don't think we'll have to flee the country. Obviously, you'll always have a home wherever I do."

Blanca picked up the towel spread over the chest of drawers and shook it out with a crisp snap of her wrists. "Mr. Rannoch isn't going to turn you over to the authorities or throw you out."

"Mr. Rannoch is never going to forgive me." Malcolm's rage echoed in her head.

"Right now he's been felled by a boulder. Even he can't know what he'll be feeling in a few hours, let alone days or months. But he won't want the scandal—"

"Malcolm doesn't care about scandal."

Blanca folded the towel and dropped it in the clothes hamper. "He won't want the scandal for the children."

Jessica was engaged in one of her favorite games, pulling out the contents of the rubbish bin and strewing them over the floor. Suzanne wanted nothing more than to catch her daughter up in her arms and hold her tight. She glanced towards the door to Laura's room. Colin would be doing lessons with Laura in the adjoining day nursery. "He won't—"

"Whatever he does or feels, he won't take the children from you," Blanca said. "And you won't take them from him. Everything may have changed, but I don't see us going anywhere."

Jessica had pulled a note card from the rubbish bin and was turning it over in her hands, examining it with great interest. "Malcolm has never confronted anything like this before. It's difficult to know what he'll do."

"Difficult but not impossible."

"I don't—"

Blanca crossed the room and seized Suzanne's hands. "Stop wasting time worrying about what you do or don't deserve and think about what you need to do for your children. Not to mention your husband."

Jessica was now gnawing on a corner of the note card. Suzanne forced herself to look into the torn wreckage of her life. "What might be best for Malcolm is to be free of me."

"Rubbish, but even if you think that way Colin and Jessica come first."

That was true. It was what was going to get her through this. That and her own instinct for self-reliance. She wanted to barricade herself in the house that might not be hers anymore and hug her children to her, but that wasn't what was called for at present. She squeezed Blanca's hands. "Laura can watch Jessica so you can speak with Addison. I need to go out."

"To look for Mr. Rannoch?"

Where had Malcolm gone? Folly to repine on that. "No, he wouldn't speak to me right now." Suzanne waved at Jessica, who had heard the words 'go out' and was waving good-bye. "To warn the other person whose life has been turned upside down. I need to speak to Raoul."

Malcolm pushed his way through the stage door of the Tavistock, grateful he was at least gone before Simon or any of the others returned, and walked blindly, the buildings a blur of brick and plaster and ironwork, the sounds of bridles jangling, horse hooves clopping, and ironbound wheels rolling over the cobblestones a dull cacophony that could not drown out the relentless deluge of his thoughts. Fortune's fool indeed. No, his folly was owed not to fortune but to his own stupidity. Had he been so eager to believe a woman like Suzanne—or the Suzanne he thought he'd known—

could love him that he'd been willfully blind? Because there must have been clues. And it was his training to pick up on such clues. To weigh, to sift, to never take things at their face value.

Suzanne had betrayed him. But it had worked because she was brilliant at her job and he had woefully failed at his.

His pace quickened. His chest was tight with the sort of exertion that came from running from a foe, as though he could outpace the hell the revelations had unleashed. He gave no thought to where he was headed until he found himself in Marylebone, before a shiny blue door with a neat brass knocker and late primroses in a brilliant yellow spilling from the window boxes. He stared at the door in surprise for a moment, thinking he should turn and leave. But perhaps it made sense. He rang the bell.

Gavin, the manservant, a cheerful man of middle years with receding hair and a wry gaze, admitted him with a friendly smile and waved him towards the back of the house. "She's in her study."

Malcolm stepped round a stack of books, a tumble of brightly colored blocks, a tangle of wool scarves and boots, a dog's ball, and a skein of yarn that looked like a cat toy. The smell of paint drifted down the stairs from Paul St. Gilles's studio two floors above.

"Malcolm." Juliette Dubretton turned round at her desk when he knocked at the door of the study. "Are Suzanne and the children with you?"

"No, just me this time." The answer came easily from his lips, seconds before the reality slammed into him that Suzanne would never again be such a natural, automatic part of his life. How long would it be before the new reality smashed the old one to bits and became settled fact? It had taken him a long time to adjust to being married, to remember that his life was bound up with another person's and he had obligations to her. Would it take an equally long time to adjust to his marriage being over? "I found myself in the neighborhood and thought I'd stop in."

"I'm glad you did. Paul's upstairs painting and the children are in the garden." Juliette gestured towards the window in front of her desk. Redheaded ten-year-old Pierre was pushing Rose, a three-year-old with her mother's dark hair and strong features, in the swing that Malcolm had helped Paul hang from the old oak tree.

Eight-year-old Marguerite, fair-haired like her father but with Juli-ette's sharp blue gaze, threw a stick for Daisy, an energetic King Charles spaniel.

"You must tell Suzanne how much I appreciate her notes on my latest draft," Juliette was saying. "She has a wonderful eye for clarity."

"Yes, she's remarkable at editing my speeches." Malcolm man-aged to keep the grim edge out of his voice.

"And for a woman with a remarkably happy marriage, she has a keen understanding of the potential pitfalls of matrimony."

"My wife is a woman of many talents." Hard to avoid the irony, but perhaps he only heard it because it fairly leaped from the con-text.

Juliette turned her chair round and waved him towards a frayed blue velvet armchair. "Is it true that Simon Tanner's discovered a lost *Hamlet* manuscript?"

Malcolm sank into the chair, relieved at the shift to safer con-versational ground. "He's certainly discovered a manuscript that's an alternative version of *Hamlet*. Whether or not it's by Shake-speare remains to be determined."

Juliette's blue eyes lit with the same sense of magic Malcolm re-membered feeling when he first heard of the manuscript. "I confess it gives me chills."

"I'm sure Simon would be happy to have you stop by a re-hearsal. And I'd welcome your thoughts on it."

"I'll be sure to take you up on it." Her gaze shifted over his face. "It's more than a Shakespeare manuscript, isn't it?"

"It may be."

"Knowing you and Suzanne, I imagine that's a mixed blessing. Not that your lives aren't complicated enough, but I can't but think you've both missed having something to investigate."

"How well you know us." The words again came automatically. It was what he would have said in response to her comment a few hours before. Now it brought a reminder that even Juliette, for all her skill at reading people, didn't know the real Suzanne. Unless— No, he couldn't start jumping at shadows.

"I won't pretend I'm not intrigued, but nor will I tease you to reveal things that aren't your secrets to share. It goes without saying that Paul and I will do whatever we can to help should our assistance ever prove useful."

"You're too kind."

"We owe you a great deal." She grinned. "And you aren't the only one who misses adventure. Though I can't claim ever to have experienced it on your level."

"The events you lived through in France were their own sort of adventure."

"Though not one I'm eager to repeat." Juliette got to her feet. "Come out into the garden. I'm at a stopping place, and the children would like to see you."

The day was cool, but a hint of sun peeped through the gray clouds and the children seemed undimmed by the weather. Marguerite ran over to give Malcolm a hug, Daisy frisking at her heels. "Oncle Malcolm. Where are Colin and Jessica?"

Malcolm touched his fingers to Marguerite's bright hair. "I'll bring them next time."

"Jessica gets bigger every time I see her. Is she walking yet?"

"Not quite steadily. To her endless regret. And frustration." He blinked away the image of Jessica taking careful steps holding Suzanne's hands. He bent down to pet Daisy, who was nuzzling his boots.

"She will be soon. Rose walked just after her first birthday."

Pierre carefully brought the swing to a stop and lifted Rose, who was crowing with excitement, into his arms. Rose wriggled to be put down and ran over to throw her arms round Malcolm's knees.

"It's good to see you, Oncle Malcolm." Pierre crossed the garden at a more dignified pace and reached out for Malcolm. At ten he was, blessedly, not too old for hugs.

Malcolm embraced his sister's son and then looked down into the blue eyes that were so like Tania's it still stopped the breath in his throat.

You have the mind of a brilliant agent, Malcolm. Tania's voice echoed in his head. *But not the temperament. You haven't learned that collateral damage is inevitable. Sometimes there are no good choices. Merely a choice of which is least damaging. And whom to try to avoid hurting. You do so much better in this business if you can accept it's a game.*

What would Tania have made of Suzanne? Malcolm wondered, his hand on her son's head. Close on the thought came his sister's voice again, speaking words she'd never spoken but that he knew instinctively were what she would say to him now. *Shocked, Malcolm? Hurt? She's beaten you at your own game. You always claimed to admire ability in women. Or is it that you thought she loved you? But you knew she didn't when she married you. Are you angry with yourself for being deceived into thinking there was something real between you?*

"I'm learning the St. Crispin's Day speech," Pierre said. "Tell Tante Suzanne. She helped me choose it. She said she'd coach me before speech day at school."

"I'm sure she will." He saw Suzanne sitting in the Berkeley Square library with Pierre, bent over a book. Had that only been last week? In the St. Gilles family's escape from Paris two years ago, she'd saved Pierre's life. That hadn't been part of her mission.

"Tante Suzanne taught me how to pick a lock." Marguerite looked up from petting Daisy. "I've been practicing on the garden shed. She's going to show me how to do a more complicated one next time, like the front door. I want to be like her when I grow up. And like you, Maman."

"Diplomatically spoken. I think you've been taking lessons from Oncle Malcolm." Juliette smiled and bent down to scoop up Rose.

"Tante Suzanne doesn't let people tell her she can't do things because she's a girl," Marguerite said. "She doesn't need to be afraid because she can take care of herself. And other people—she was splendid with those armed men who wanted to take Pierre. That's the sort of person I want to be."

"Someone who picks locks?" Pierre asked.

"Someone who has adventures and doesn't let people tell her what to do and has children and still gets to wear pretty clothes and jewels and curl her hair."

"You don't ask for much, do you, *chérie?*" Juliette said.

Marguerite scratched Daisy between her ears. "I don't see why I can't have all those things."

"Nor do I, *ma chère,* nor do I. Perhaps you should write my next book."

"What if your husband doesn't want you having adventures?" Pierre asked his sister.

"Pierre!" Marguerite sprang to her feet and stared at him in outrage. "Are you saying you'd try to stop your wife—"

"No, of course not. But some men would. That's what Maman writes about."

"I'll marry a man like Oncle Malcolm or Papa."

"Men like Oncle Malcolm and your father are rare and precious, *ma belle,*" Juliette said.

"I'll find one. They have to be on the lookout for the right women." Marguerite looked at Malcolm. "You wouldn't want a boring wife who didn't want to have adventures, would you, Oncle Malcolm?"

"Perish the thought," Malcolm said. And it was true. He couldn't imagine being married to a woman who didn't share his work. *But you thought you had the best of both worlds.* He could hear the words Tania might have spoken again. *An agent wife who became an agent to assist you. Not an agent in her own right, with her own loyalties and priorities and moral compromises. A phantom she created to take you in. The real woman is probably a great deal more interesting.*

Perhaps. But then the real Suzanne was someone he didn't know.

Rose wriggled in Juliette's arms. "Story," she said.

"That," Malcolm said, "is one request I can comply with."

The coffeehouse was the same. The dark, scarred woodwork. The faded hunting prints in chipped frames on the walls. The smell of strong coffee and sharp red wine and newsprint that hung in the air. Just as it had been on a score of occasions in the past two years when she had met Raoul at the Crystal Heart. The setting was the same, but everything else was different.

This time Raoul had got there first. The urgency of her communication must have come through. She dropped into the chair across from him, gloved hands gripped tight on the tabletop to hold on to some semblance of sanity. "He knows."

Raoul's gaze flickered over her face. "You told him?"

"He put it together himself."

A dozen thoughts and emotions raced through Raoul's gray gaze, but he merely said, "Impressive." He picked up the bottle of wine on the table and poured a glass.

"Apparently Frederick Radley saw us together in León five years ago."

"Damn it." The wine sloshed as Raoul set down the bottle. "I knew Radley was a danger. Why the man couldn't have had the decency to fall at Waterloo—"

"Decency's never been much in Radley's line. He told Malcolm you'd been my lover. Malcolm put the pieces together."

"A hellish coincidence." Raoul put the glass of wine in her hand.

She pushed the glass aside. "We probably should have guessed that he'd put it together eventually."

"Hardly." Raoul's voice was taut but level. Faced with the unthinkable, they'd both fallen back on their training. "For all Malcolm's talents. I doubt he would have done without the current investigation. Drink some wine. You're two shades paler than usual."

She pulled her gloves from her numb fingers and managed a sip of wine. Malcolm's bleak gaze in the shadows of the theatre reverberated in her memory. "I think Malcolm is cursing himself for a fool for not guessing sooner."

"*Querida*—I'm sorry." He reached across the table and gripped her free hand. "Sorrier than I can possibly say."

For a moment, the desire to spring up from the table and run to him and bury her face in his cravat in a way that had nothing to do with the passion that had once been between them was almost overmastering. She forced a smile to her lips and another sip of wine down her throat. "I went into my marriage knowing it wouldn't last forever after all. One could say I got far more out of it than I deserved. We none of us had any illusions our goal in life was personal happiness."

"I'd have given anything to spare you this," he said in a low voice.

Something in his tone shook her. Why now, of all times, should she be sure he spoke the unvarnished truth? "I'm still better off than those in France who face execution." She drew a breath. She felt chilled and numb at the same time. "He knows about you as well. And about Colin. I'm sorry."

Raoul's mouth tightened. "From what you said about Radley I assumed so. It makes it worse for all of you."

"No. I mean I'm sorry for what you've lost."

She saw his defenses flash into place in his eyes, just as Malcolm's did. "My dear girl, when it comes to Malcolm I could hardly be said to have had anything to lose."

"You had the memories of his childhood. And what you'd recently shared."

Raoul's gaze shifted to the side. "Malcolm learning about his biological parentage hardly made me a father."

"No." She kept her own gaze trained on his face. "But I think perhaps his recasting the past did, on his side. On yours, I think you may have been his father all along."

"Sentimental twaddle, *querida*." His voice was still level but rougher than usual. "Whatever I've lost, one could say it's no more than I richly deserve."

"Aren't you always saying it would be a sad world if we all got what we deserved?"

His mouth twisted. "One could make a fair case that I deserve more than most."

"Then one could certainly say the same of me. I'm still safer than many of our friends." She pulled her hand from his own, because she couldn't give way to the need for comfort, and took another sip of wine. "I'm not sure where Malcolm has gone. I'm not sure what he's going to do. You should consider leaving England while you can."

Raoul poured a second glass of wine and took a sip. "He can't betray me without betraying you."

"What makes you so sure he won't betray me?"

"What I've seen of the two of you over the past five years."

"What you saw was an illusion that ended this afternoon. Malcolm now knows the woman he thought he loved never existed."

"Malcolm is too sensible a man to think that."

"He'd be right. I'm not sure who I am anymore."

"I don't think you have cause for alarm on this score, but if you do—Do you want me to help you leave?"

She curled her hands round her glass and shook her head. "I can't take the children away from him. And obviously I can't leave the children." Her fingers tightened round the glass. "Make no mistake, if Malcolm goes to Carfax or tries to throw me from the house, I'll fight to protect myself. I'll fight to keep the children. I actually found myself thinking of what leverage I have to use against him. That's the depths I've sunk to. Or perhaps the depths at which I've always existed. But I won't be the one who breaks up the family." She took a drink of wine and set the glass down, willing her fingers to be steady. "I've let myself go soft these past years. I need to remind myself I'm good at coping with the unexpected."

"Suzanne." Raoul reached out and closed his hand over her own again. "I can do little enough for you. God knows I've done little enough in the past save complicate your life. But I can be someone to whom you can openly admit your feelings. You have few enough people who can offer you that. I know because it's the same for me." He met her gaze across the table. "If it helps, I'll admit that losing the brief flicker of what I almost had with Malcolm is cutting me in two."

She swallowed again, but this time the torrent of feelings came welling up. "Damn you, must you always be right? Of course it hurts like hell. Of course I feel as though my soul's been ripped out and shredded in pieces, and I'll never be whole again. And I know I haven't any right to feel that way, to mourn the loss of something that was only mine through false coin, but that doesn't make the feelings go away. I never thought I was supposed to be happy, I never thought it was possible, but I was, and there's no way to capture it again. He'll never look at me in the same way because I'm not the person he thought I was. And I don't even know who I am anymore." She drew a breath, throat raw with unshed tears.

"Feel better for having said it?"

She tugged at the brim of her bonnet. "I'm wondering how I can even be thinking about myself when I've smashed Malcolm's life to bits."

"And your own."

"But I knew what I was doing. And now I'm wallowing. I hate wallowers."

"You don't have to worry about how you look with me. You never did."

She jabbed her side curls back beneath the brim of the bonnet. "I underestimated the human element. I was blind to the pain I was causing—or at least I didn't give it enough weight."

"That rather sums up my own feelings."

"But it doesn't make the other elements go away." She stared into her wineglass, forcing herself to confront the ugly, gnawing truth. "For all my wallowing, I can't say I'd act differently."

"Nor can I."

"Which makes us hypocrites."

"Which makes us aware of conflicting loyalties. The question is what we do about them."

"Damn it, Raoul. I've seen you weigh the odds and sacrifice an agent as though he or she was a pawn."

"My dear girl. You know how badly I sleep. I assure you it hasn't got any better."

"But you knew where your loyalties lay. You'd accepted the necessity of betrayal in the game we were playing."

Raoul picked up the bottle and refilled her glass. "Loyalties conflict every day. Causes, countries, friends, comrades, lovers. It's often impossible to be loyal to all. One has to make choices."

"And that's it? There's no right and wrong?"

He set down the bottle and wiped a trace of wine from its neck. "You know nothing in our world can be neatly classified as right and wrong."

"No. But one can't use that as an excuse to say anything is justified. I've seen people like that, people like Fouché. Perhaps it's self-delusion, but I can't believe we've sunk to that level."

"One's still bound by one's own conscience and what one can

live with." Raoul's gaze rested on her face like the brush of finger-tips. "You have to learn to forgive yourself, *querida*. If you don't owe it to yourself, you owe it to your children. And your husband."

Malcolm's gaze in the shadows of the theatre cut into her. "Even if he can't forgive me?"

"How can you expect him to if you can't forgive yourself?"

"I accepted long since that we have to make compromises. That our work isn't easy or pretty. But with that surely we have to give up the hope of a happy ending."

"Oh, my darling girl, surely you know better than to believe in endings." Raoul twisted the stem of his glass between his fingers. "The board shifts, the game changes, and one moves on. And makes the best of where one was left standing. And if one has a scrap of sense one snatches happiness where one can."

"Are you saying that's what you do?"

He looked into the glass as though seeing into the past. "I snatched some with you, I snatched some with Malcolm when he was a boy. I snatched some in Paris two years ago when we all worked together. Or yesterday seeing Colin and Jessica in the square." He took a quick drink of wine. "Arabella was one of the most unhappy people I've ever known. Whether it was flirting or shopping or breaking codes, she constantly had to be doing some-thing. If she stopped for a moment one could see the desolation in her eyes. I wouldn't wish that on anyone. Or on anyone's children."

"I'm not—"

"No, you aren't, thank God. Your belief in the world is too strong."

She gave a short laugh. "Dear God, Raoul, after all these years do you know me so little?"

His gaze moved over her face with that look that never failed to warm her. "I know the spark inside you that the most appalling events couldn't quench. You may not think you can be happy, but at least you acknowledge happiness is possible."

"Malcolm said something similar once. But of course he was talking to a woman he didn't really know." She snatched up her gloves and closed her fingers tight round them. "I may have sunk into a dream these past years where I was deluded enough to believe happiness was possible. That I could get by with nothing worse than living with the fear of discovery. That I could make it up to Malcolm by actually being the woman he thought he'd married." She tugged the gloves onto her cold fingers. "But that dream ended today. It's folly to think about happiness. I need to focus on survival."

CHAPTER 26

Malcolm climbed the stairs at Mivart's Hotel. The fashionable hotel in a terraced house at the corner of Brook Street and Davies Street was only five years old, but he remembered climbing similar steps in another London hotel as a small boy, holding his mother's hand, to visit her friend Mr. O'Roarke. He rapped once at the door of room 212. His fingers felt numb beneath the York tan of his glove. The December chill had settled deep inside him.

O'Roarke opened the door. He wore a paisley silk dressing gown over an immaculate white shirt. The dressing gown also held memories from that childhood visit and country house parties. The same one? Or something similar?

O'Roarke's gaze flickered over Malcolm's face for a moment before he stepped aside. "Rannoch. Do come in."

Malcolm strode into the room and turned round, one hand gripping a chairback. The air smelled of cedar and paper and ink. Familiar smells. There had been hunting prints on the walls in that other hotel as well and mahogany furniture, though the upholstery was red and white striped where twenty years ago it had been green damask.

O'Roarke surveyed him in the flickering light of the single brace of candles that burned against the late afternoon shadows. Malcolm had seen that look in the eyes of senior diplomats gauging the extent of a diplomatic breach. Though perhaps beneath it was something else. Something Malcolm wasn't prepared to think about at present.

"Sit down," O'Roarke said, waving his hand towards one of the red-and-white-striped chairs. He picked up the gray coat strewn over the other chair. "I've just come in myself."

"I imagine Suzanne sent word to you."

O'Roarke met his gaze. Malcolm was quite sure O'Roarke knew, but of course the other man wasn't going to admit anything without being sure of the extent of Malcolm's knowledge. "What makes you think Mrs. Rannoch would have wanted to speak with me?" O'Roarke asked, laying the coat over the escritoire.

"To warn you your cover had been blown. Or perhaps to ask for help escaping."

Their gazes locked. O'Roarke still wasn't going to be the first one to step over the precipice.

"It must have been quite an advantage," Malcolm said. "Knowing what you did of me from boyhood when you set one of your agents to marry me. I make you my compliments. As one agent to another, it was a brilliant plan."

"Malcolm—" O'Roarke stretched out his hand, then let it fall. "I would say you had every right to call me out save that I know what we both think of dueling."

"How far in advance were you planning it?" Malcolm heard his voice, crisp, even, detached, taut as a bowstring. It sounded as though it belonged to someone else.

"Believe it or not I was more shocked than anyone when Suzanne told me you'd asked her to marry you."

"Did you know she was pregnant?"

"Not when she first went on the mission. I don't think she knew it herself."

"Yes, that's what she said as well. What a lucky accident."

O'Roarke drew a harsh breath. "Malcolm—I make no pretense that what I've done is anything other than unforgivable. I won't even attempt to defend the choices I've made. But you can't think Suzanne and I would trivialize Colin as convenient."

"No? You were quick enough to make use of him."

"A palpable hit." O'Roarke tightened the belt on his dressing gown and took a turn about the room. "Ask me whatever you will."

Malcolm stared at the man he had trusted since boyhood. "Why should I believe anything you say?"

"I don't suppose you will." O'Roarke came to a stop in front of the windows, the gray light at his back. "But at least you can evaluate my answers."

The heat from the fire in the grate choked the air. Malcolm shrugged out of his greatcoat and tossed it over one of the chairs. "Whether or not you planned it, you must have been pleased when you saw how neatly my chivalry played into your plans."

"Pleased?" O'Roarke gave a short laugh, then bit back whatever he had been about to say. "No, I wouldn't precisely say I was pleased."

"Yes, there is that, I suppose." Malcolm watched as O'Roarke's gaze slid away.

"What?"

"I may be the most gullible fool since Malvolio, but it's quite apparent to me that you're still in love with my wife."

O'Roarke's gaze shot to Malcolm's face. For a moment Malcolm would swear he'd caught the other man off guard. "Don't romanticize things, Malcolm. If you had any illusions about the sort of man I am, today's revelations should have destroyed them."

"I don't see why there should be any correlation between the ability to betray and the lack of ability to love."

"Spoken like a true idealist."

"Spoken like a man who has no illusions about the ennobling power of love."

O'Roarke moved to the other striped chair and dropped into it. "Don't confuse your own feelings for her with mine."

"I'm not." Malcolm pushed aside the folds of his greatcoat and sat in the chair opposite O'Roarke, keeping his gaze trained on the other man. "What did it cost you to let her go?"

O'Roarke settled back in the chair, legs crossed with an appearance of nonchalance. "Obviously not a great deal considering how readily I did it."

"On the contrary." Malcolm began to remove his gloves, tugging at the York tan finger by finger. "I know how much you're willing to sacrifice for the cause. I think this may be proof of just how far that goes."

"Don't lapse into lending library language, Malcolm."

"I have eyes."

O'Roarke was silent for a moment. "Odd the things one can deny with impunity. And the things one can't bring oneself to deny." He pushed back the cuff of his dressing gown and stared at it, as though unfathomable secrets lay in the twists of black silk braid. "What was between Suzanne and me ended with your marriage."

Questions he would never be able to answer and that shouldn't matter in the light of everything else sliced through Malcolm's brain. "She told me that as well."

"But you don't believe it."

"I'm not sure." Malcolm slapped the gloves down on the table beside his chair. "Either way, ending being lovers doesn't end being in love."

O'Roarke drew a breath, looked away, drummed his fingers on the arms of the chair. "Suzanne would rake me over the coals for making excuses for her. And I'd be the first to say we all make our own choices and have to live with them. But she didn't have the least idea what marrying you truly meant."

Malcolm bit back the instinct to tell O'Roarke not to presume to talk about Suzanne's feelings. One could make a fair case that O'Roarke was in a better position to do so than Malcolm himself. "You're saying she didn't know what it meant to me?"

"Oh yes. She herself would admit she didn't realize how seriously you took it. But I was thinking more that she didn't know what it meant to her."

Malcolm saw his wife sitting on the steps in the theatre, refusing to make excuses for herself. "Clearly not a great deal. Though I suppose there's always a risk an agent will take a role too seriously."

O'Roarke drew a breath, the rough breath of one picking his way round ground strewn with explosives. "She'd also never forgive me for implying she was ever mine to lose. Which is true. We'd never made any promises that gave each other those sorts of rights. But I remember when I knew it would never be the same between us. I met her in the church of St. Roque in Lisbon on a cold December morning. A few days after your marriage. She was as contained as always, but her hands were like ice. She said it wasn't at all as she'd expected. That it meant more to you than she'd realized."

Where had Malcolm himself been that day? Was it the afternoon he'd come back to their rooms to find her hanging prints of Lisbon on the walls? Or the day she'd met him for dinner at the embassy, cheeks bright with color from the cold air, the pearls he'd given her round her throat? "That doesn't necessarily mean it meant anything to her."

"No. But I can read subtext."

"Now who's putting a romantic gloss on things?" Bitterness welled up on Malcolm's tongue. "You can't expect me to believe marrying me was anything other than a tactical decision for her."

"Not at the time." O'Roarke stared down at a book left open on the table beside the chair that he must have been in the midst of reading. "When I met Suzanne she'd lost everything."

"Meaning what? She obviously wasn't the daughter of the Comte de Saint-Vallier." The blank that was his wife's past yawned before him. Everywhere he looked there were more layers to the deception.

"No, though her father was French and her mother Spanish."

"Good cover story strategy. Always good to use what truth one can."

"Quite. Suzanne's father had a small traveling theatre company that moved between France and Spain."

"Let me guess. They performed Shakespeare in translation. Though her father must have taught her the plays in English. Did you tell her she'd catch my eye if she could cap my quotations?"

"I imagine I did, but thanks to her father she already quoted Shakespeare freely. Though I believe she's actually named after Figaro's Suzanne."

"Of course." Malcolm felt his mouth twist. "She named Colin's stuffed bear Figaro. I found it charming that she was far from anti-Republican, despite her family having fled the Revolution. I imagine her father was a fervent Revolutionary?"

"At least a Republican who supported the Revolution at the start. I think playing a Royalist was the hardest part of her masquerade. Or the part furthest from her real self."

Malcolm studied O'Roarke. Part of him didn't want to tread on personal territory, but he needed to know. "What happened to her parents?"

"Her mother died in childbirth when Suzanne was seven."

"She has a sister? Or a brother?" The moorings of the past had been cut from beneath him. He'd always thought of his wife as an only child. For all he knew, Colin and Jessica had a passel of uncles and aunts and cousins.

"She had a sister. Rosalind."

Unease coiled through him. "Had?"

"In December of 1807, her father's company was performing in Spain on the northern coast."

"Good God. In the middle of Moore's retreat?" Sir John Moore's forces had been driven from Spain in late '07 and endured a disastrous retreat after the battle of Corunna. The commissariat had not been able to keep up and the starving troops had left a trail of destruction in their wake.

"My thoughts when she first told me. Apparently her father thought they could stay out of it. They had friends on both sides."

"And then?" Malcolm was almost afraid to ask. Strange he could fear any revelations after the truths that had already been revealed this day, but he shied away from what he could sense coming.

"The village the theatre company was staying in that Christmas was attacked by a band of English soldiers."

O'Roarke's voice was flat. For a moment, Malcolm entirely understood the effort it took the other man to keep it that way. He met O'Roarke's gaze in the candlelight and shadows that filled the room. "That part of her cover story is true as well, isn't it? Soldiers attacking her family—" He couldn't quite say the rest.

O'Roarke nodded. "I've only heard the story in bits and pieces through the years. She saw a bullet strike her father in the head.

Through the window of the house where they were staying. Then soldiers burst in. She and her sister were dragged into the plaza."

"And raped." He wouldn't have thought the story of Suzanne's past could be worse than what he already knew.

"Yes." O'Roarke's fingers, Malcolm noted, were curled into fists on the arms of his chair. "I'd known Suzanne for two years before she admitted she'd crawled round the plaza afterwards and found her sister bleeding to death, tossed in a pile of rubbish. Rosalind was eight."

For a moment Malcolm thought he was going to be sick. His children's faces swam before his eyes. And then his wife's face. She'd been scarcely more than a child herself. At fifteen, his sister Gisèle had barely left off playing with dolls.

"So in sum it was much like her cover story," O'Roarke continued in the same flat voice. "Save—"

"That the soldiers were British, not French."

O'Roarke loosed his fingers from the chair arms as though by conscious effort. "Acts of brutality are committed by both sides during a war. In the Peninsula both sides—all sides—were particularly savage."

It sounded logical. It didn't erase the images of redcoated soldiers and his wife holding a dying child in her arms. "She must have hated—she must hate—the British."

"I don't think that was the only thing that drove her. But yes, that was part of it."

Malcolm drew a breath, forced air into his lungs. "And then?"

O'Roarke stared at a patch of candlelight on the carpet. "She went to León with some of the actors who had survived. But the friends of her parents she'd thought she could stay with had fled north and by the time she realized it the actors were gone."

"And she was alone in a strange city."

"She lived by her wits for a time."

"On the streets?"

O'Roarke nodded. "Picking pockets. She had light fingers even then."

"Where did you find her?"

"In a brothel."

Malcolm felt his chin jerk up.

"Someone caught her picking his pocket and told her she was too pretty for the streets. She'd been there for a few months when I met her." O'Roarke paused. "I don't know why I should feel impelled to say this or why you should believe me, but I was there in search of information. About a *guerrillero* leader who frequented the brothel. Suzanne not only supplied the information, she offered to obtain more. Her quick wits and keen understanding were obvious."

"She wasn't even sixteen. Why the hell didn't you—"

"Send her off to safety? She'd have gone mad. She didn't want to be safe, she wanted to fight. She needed a focus for that anger."

"And you saw the makings of a brilliant agent."

"That too. I make no pretense of disinterest." O'Roarke flipped the book closed and rested his fingers on the gilt-embossed cover. "Her father had raised her on Paine and Rousseau and Godwin. She claimed to have stopped believing in anything, but it wasn't hard for the ideals she'd been bred up on to reawaken."

"The same ideals I was raised on."

O'Roarke regarded him for a moment, gaze dark and still in the candlelight. "In many ways. Yes." He pushed his hair back from his forehead. "She was a quick study. By that autumn she was ready for her first mission." He drew a breath. "I tell you all this not to rouse your sympathy or make excuses, but to try to explain who the woman you married is. For Suzanne more than others, the cause was all."

"The cause or the game?"

O'Roarke's mouth twisted in a bleak smile. "Perhaps both. It can be difficult to differentiate. I don't think she let herself think of the future. And she saw the human element as a distraction."

"Except for you?" Malcolm tried to keep the bitterness from his voice but could not quite succeed.

"Oh no. To own the truth, I don't think she ever let herself fully trust me. Which was probably wise."

"She loved you." Malcolm said it as a statement of fact.

"One can love without being lost in love." O'Roarke's fingers moved over the gilt-embossed book cover. "It was Colin who changed things for her, though he didn't make her old loyalties go away."

Malcolm met O'Roarke's gaze. "Colin is my son."

Part of him felt he shouldn't have needed to say it, while another part of him felt it was imperative that he did.

"Of course."

"Whatever happens between Suzanne and me."

"I knew that the moment you married her."

"Did Suzanne know it?"

O'Roarke hesitated, fingers tapping the tooled leather. "Suzanne was perhaps more caught up in the needs of the moment. She was younger. She didn't take as long a view."

"She thought she could leave me and take Colin with her."

"If so, she quickly realized her mistake. After he was born and she saw what he meant to you."

"And you? If you thought she couldn't leave, what the hell did you think would happen?"

O'Roarke was silent for the length of a dozen heartbeats. Or pistol shots. "I knew that eventually the war would end, one way or another."

"And Suzette would have no need to stay with me."

"I rather thought by then she'd want to."

Malcolm gave a laugh that scraped against his throat. "You can't be serious."

"It was fairly obvious how she felt about you after a few months. And the signs of what might happen between you were there sooner."

"Next you'll be saying you orchestrated the whole thing for our sakes."

"No. I took advantage of circumstances and both your feelings to gain tactical advantage in a war we were trying desperately to win. By most standards what I did was unforgivable. But I wasn't unaware of the feelings of those involved."

"Colin—"

"We pick and choose our loyalties. I chose loyalty to a cause— so inextricably bound up in love of the game I'm not sure where one left off and the other began."

"Over being a father."

O'Roarke met Malcolm's gaze, his own at once unusually open and unfathomably barricaded. "In a nutshell."

"If it had been Frederick Radley who had offered to marry Suzette and give a name to her child, would you have encouraged her to accept?"

O'Roarke's mouth curled. "Frederick Radley never would have offered his name and protection to a woman in trouble."

"But if somehow he had? An officer who is friends with the British foreign secretary's brother. Suzette could have gained valuable intelligence from him. And I flatter myself he'd have been easier to deceive than I was. If he'd offered for her—"

"You damn fool, what do you think?" O'Roarke slammed his hand down on the book. "I'd have done everything in my power to stop her short of kidnapping. Possibly not even short of that."

Malcolm folded his arms across his chest. "Interesting."

"Don't make too much of it."

Malcolm leaned forwards. Beneath the layers of betrayal, there were hard facts he had to ascertain. "Who else knows?"

"Knows?"

"Who else knows Suzette was an agent?"

"It's not—"

"Damn it, O'Roarke, I can't protect my wife if I don't know who was aware of her activities. We may not agree on much, but I don't think either of us wants to see Suzanne accused of treason."

A slow smile spread across O'Roarke's face. "I told her as much. She wasn't at all inclined to believe me."

Malcolm stared at Suzanne's spymaster. His father. "What did she think I'd do? Turn her over to Carfax?"

"I think she wonders. She knows you're loyal."

"Not to Carfax."

"To Britain."

"Not blindly. Who else knows my wife was a French spy?"

O'Roarke's mouth tightened. "I did my best to keep her identity secret from as many as possible. But unfortunately two years ago she discovered Fouché knew."

"God in heaven." Malcolm sifted back through the events of two years ago. "Did he try to use it to get her to stop my investigation into the Laclos Affair?"

"Your mind is as quick as ever. Yes."

Malcolm's fingers curled inwards with the—probably laughable—impulse to protect his wife. "You stopped him?"

"I tried. Fouché called my bluff. I think Suzanne fully expected Fouché to expose her."

"What happened?"

"Talleyrand intervened."

"Tall—My God, does he know, too?"

"Talleyrand has a way of knowing everything."

"Alistair. You. Talleyrand. Is there anyone who helped shape my childhood who doesn't know the truth about my wife?"

"Carfax, I would hope. Your aunt Frances. Your grandfather."

"So Talleyrand knew what Suzanne was doing in Vienna? He was representing the Bourbon government. Suzette, I assume, was working for Bonaparte."

"He'd have suspected. He's fond of her, I believe. Grateful for what she's done for Dorothée."

"And being Talleyrand, he found it useful to have a foot in both camps."

"That too. One can never be sure what Talleyrand will do with his back against a wall, but I think his instinct would be to protect you and Suzanne. Fouché doesn't wield a great deal of power these days, but in any case Talleyrand will keep him in check."

"There must be others who know. Former agents. Some of whom must be in England."

"There are. Suzanne will always live with risk. As will you. Whatever—"

"Becomes of our marriage?" Malcolm pushed himself to his feet. "That's for me to discuss with my wife."

"Malcolm. Thank goodness you're home." Aline appeared in the library doorway as Malcolm walked into the entry hall of the Berkeley Square house.

It took a moment for Malcolm to remember the life he'd had before the day's revelations. The investigation. The *Hamlet* manuscript. His grandfather and Aline's work on the code.

Aline's gaze flickered over his face. "Are you all right?"

"Splendid, love." Malcolm forced himself to smile into his cousin's bright gaze and took her hands. "You've learned something?"

"I think we have. That's why we came here from David and Simon's, only then neither of you were home at first." Aline drew him into the library. "We've just been telling Suzanne."

Malcolm stepped into the library to see his wife standing beside his grandfather. Their eyes met for an instant, heavy with the day's revelations. Malcolm jerked his gaze away and glanced round the room. The marble library table was stacked with scribbled-over sheets of paper. Strathdon got to his feet and came forwards. In the light of the brace of candles on the table, Malcolm caught a gleam in his grandfather's eyes that was very like Aline's.

Aline cast a glance at her grandfather, but Strathdon inclined his head. "Go ahead, my dear. It's your discovery."

"It's both of ours, really." Aline reached for a sheet of paper. "It's Hamlet's letter to Ophelia. We don't think Shakespeare wrote this version of it."

Malcolm glanced down at the paper Aline had pulled forwards. "So you don't think Shakespeare wrote the manuscript?"

"No, just this speech. It stands out from the rest. 'Doubt that my blood is fire, /Doubt the raven for a dove, /Doubt the sea to be a mire, /But never doubt I love.' The scansion is off and the imagery doesn't really make sense."

"Shakespeare uses the raven and dove comparison in *Midsummer*," Suzanne pointed out. "When Demetrius wakes up in love with Helena. 'Who would not change a raven for a dove?'"

"Yes, but here it's juxtaposing two different things—I mean it's logical to doubt a raven for a dove, which is the exact opposite of what the text is supposed to be saying."

"Brandon Ford pointed out that Shakespeare knew the sun didn't move, either," Malcolm said. "But at least one could argue that there were people who thought it did, whereas I don't think there's any point in history where people have confused doves and ravens."

"Precisely," Aline said. "Even if Shakespeare was trying to make Hamlet sound like a typical love-struck undergraduate, these lines seem too clunky. Also, an earlier version of the speech has been crossed out. There's a lot of smudging, but from what we can tell, the crossed-out lines seem to be the ones in the version of the play we all know or close to it. We think someone else crossed it out and wrote the new lines in." She exchanged a look with Strathdon.

"So then of course we began to ask why," Strathdon said. "Allie?"

Aline drew a breath. "We think it's a code. Or rather a clue. The language is strained enough that whoever wrote the lines seems to have had reason to work in those particular images."

Suzanne cast a quick glance at Malcolm. "Do you think the new lines were added to the manuscript recently?" she asked.

"We thought about that," Aline said, "but though we can't tell for a certainty, the manuscript seems to be old and the ink on the new lines looks as old as the rest. I don't think this has to do with spies and this Elsinore League thing. If Malcolm's right that Francis Woolright copied the manuscript and he and Eleanor Harleton made notes on it, we think they wrote this version of Hamlet's letter."

Strathdon grinned. His face had the delight of a little boy. "I'd hazard a guess we're looking for sixteenth-century treasure."

CHAPTER 27

Suzanne moved into the bedchamber and dropped down on her dressing table bench. A habitual action in a life that had been cracked asunder. Aline had left to go home and Strathdon had gone to his room to dress for dinner. As they did every night, Suzanne and Malcolm had looked in on the nursery, where Colin and Jessica were having their supper. Suzanne and Malcolm had sat at the nursery table and she'd nursed Jessica while he answered questions about the Essex rebellion. The Lady Jane Grey questions on their visit to the Tower had started Colin off on a fascination with the Tudor dynasty. It had almost felt normal save that Suzanne and Malcolm had avoided meeting each other's eyes.

When they left she'd walked down the passage past the night nursery to their bedchamber because it was what she always did (why had she never realized how much she had become a creature of habit?) and because she did need to dress for dinner. She hadn't been at all sure Malcolm would follow her, but now he appeared in the bedchamber doorway. "I saw O'Roarke."

She spun round on the dressing table bench and met Malcolm's gaze. "I'm glad. That is, I don't know if it helped, but—"

"There were things I could only say to him directly. And he to me. If nothing else, I think one could say we both understood each other better at the end of the interview." Malcolm pushed the door shut and advanced into the room. "We need to be careful of what the servants might overhear."

With a pang Suzanne realized they could no longer talk easily in their own house. Not that they'd ever been able to do so completely, given the nature of their work, but they'd moved into entirely new territory.

"I understand you saw O'Roarke yourself this afternoon," Malcolm said.

"I owed it to him to warn him. I know that probably sounds mad given what he's done, but—"

"Not mad given your history."

"I advised him to leave Britain. He chose not to."

"Did you consider leaving yourself?"

She lifted her chin. "No. At the least I owed it to you not to run."

"But you thought I might turn you over to Carfax, according to O'Roarke."

"I wondered. I couldn't be sure of what you might do in circumstances like these."

He stared at her with a gaze like polished granite. "I can't believe I'm saying this, but after five years of marriage how in God's name could you know me so little?"

"Darling—"

She saw the recoil in his eyes.

"Malcolm, you've been pushed beyond what anyone could be expected to bear. One can't be entirely sure what anyone will do under those circumstances."

He studied her, not with the anger of this afternoon but as though she were a new-met acquaintance he was trying to take the measure of. It was, she realized, a pang sharp in her throat, the way she was going to have to get used to him looking at her. "You may have been pretending all these years, but you can't be so blind to who I am. You're the mother of my children."

She swallowed. "That's not in question."

"And I couldn't do that to you. To them." He dug his fingers into his hair. It was a gesture that always put her in mind of what he must have looked like as a schoolboy. He looked so unutterably weary that she longed to put her arms round him. "I'm not sure how far I'll be able to go. I don't know that I'll ever get past being angry. But for Colin's and Jessica's sake we have to find a way to co-exist. After all, I was a diplomat for almost a decade. I learned how to dine with the enemy."

Some of the tension drained from her chest and left a gaping hole she knew would never heal. "That's far more than I deserve."

"It's not a question of deserving. It's a question of how we can go on living." Malcolm continued to watch her. Something had shifted in his gaze, but she couldn't put a name to it. "O'Roarke says I should blame him rather than you."

"That sounds like Raoul." She folded her arms over her chest and realized she hadn't done up the buttons properly on the nursing bodice of her gown. "I know you wouldn't be so foolish as to believe him. I'm responsible for my own actions."

"I don't think O'Roarke would deny that. It's a matter of perceptions." Malcolm advanced into the room and shifted so the light was at his back. "He also told me what happened to your family. I didn't realize you had a sister."

She couldn't control her flinch. "Rosie wasn't part of my cover story."

"No. But your cover story was rooted in reality. Save that the soldiers were British rather than French."

"Don't, Malcolm." Her fingers dug into her elbows. "Don't make excuses for me or turn it into something so simple. I wasn't striking out at the British out of some sort of blind vengeance. I know what I believe in. I chose my side."

"I didn't suggest otherwise." His voice was level, but there was a softness beneath that threatened to undo her. "But I don't see how it could help but weigh in the scales." He paused, as though searching for the right words. The pressure of his gaze on her face was different. If not tenderness, it held compassion, which threatened to undo her. "I can't tell you how sorry I am."

She steeled herself against the tone and the words. It would be unforgivable to use Rosie's tragedy to ask for sympathy. "It's worse because it was English soldiers rather than French?"

"I feel more responsible." He dropped down on the edge of the bed, on a level with her. "And I know what it's like to lose a sibling. I think it must be that much worse when the sibling is younger."

She swallowed. She tried to shut her mind to the memories, but they welled up like blood from a fresh cut. The bullet smashing into her father's head. Hands pulling at her. Her sister's screams. "I keep going over the events of that day. Rosie and I were having a stupid fight when the soldiers broke in. I was trying to mend a tear I'd got in the hem of my costume the night before when Romeo stepped on it—I was playing Juliet for the first time—and Rosie wanted me to help her build a dollhouse beneath the table from bits and pieces she'd taken from the costumes and props. I wasn't very patient. I keep thinking—"

"One always does."

She nodded. She met his gaze in more understanding than she would have thought possible between them a few hours before.

"And then you were alone. You didn't have Blanca with you then?"

"Raoul and I found her on a mission the spring after I started working for him. Her family had been killed in the retreat after Corunna as well. She lived with her uncle who ran a tavern that was a meeting place for *guerrilleros*. Blanca had to dodge her uncle's blows and the wandering hands of the customers. She was all too happy to help us outwit her uncle. And having done, of course she couldn't stay there. Even if she'd wanted to."

"And of course Blanca is an agent, too." He made it a statement of fact, something he had just worked out.

"Blanca wanted to fight the British. But it was my choices that trapped her in our masquerade. She warned me how difficult it would be. She warned me I'd care too much. And that you would."

"Did she foresee that she would herself?"

Suzanne's breath caught. "I think she'd begun to care for Addison, even then." She pressed her fingers into the fabric of her sleeves. "This afternoon I told Blanca to tell Addison the truth."

She saw the flinch in Malcolm's gaze at what that talk would mean to his valet. "Before I could intervene? I wouldn't have denied her that. I wouldn't have denied it to Addison. He deserves to hear the woman he loves explain her actions. For better or worse."

Suzanne hadn't seen Blanca since her own return to the house. She shivered at the thought of her friend's life being smashed as badly as her own.

Malcolm studied her as though he was sifting through lies for shreds of truth. "You were younger than Gisèle when you lost your family. A child."

She tightened her arms over her chest. "After that day I wasn't a child anymore."

She saw the reality of it settle in his eyes. He pushed himself to his feet and took a quick step forwards. "Suzette—"

She put out a hand to forestall him. "Don't, Malcolm. I'm not the loyal wife you thought me. I'm also not the tragic victim of war. Don't build up another false image of me. I made choices. Limited choices at times, but still choices. Which I can't honestly say I regret."

He stared down into her eyes. "You must have been so angry."

"It seemed such a waste. How could I believe in anything? Raoul changed that."

"He gave you an outlet for your anger."

"He gave me a glimpse of a chance of making the world a better place. He read the same writers as my father—Paine, Rousseau, Locke, Beaumarchais. My father was a dreamer while Raoul was a hardheaded pragmatist. Yet beneath it was still the dream of a world in which there was some respect for the rights of men—and women. Where children didn't starve in the streets, where printing presses weren't summarily shut down—"

"Where Habeas Corpus wasn't abruptly suspended?"

Suzanne met her husband's gaze. She had helped him write a speech urging the repeal of the suspension of Habeas Corpus only a fortnight ago. "Quite."

"You're saying you're fighting for the same things I am."

"I wasn't saying that precisely. But . . ." She hesitated. Was she making excuses for herself or trying to make him understand? "I saw that in you from the first. How else do you think I could help you write your speeches? I can stretch to a lot, but I don't think I could have penned Tory diatribes."

"So the ends are all that matter and damn the means?" The words had a bitter edge, but he made it an honest question.

"You think it's better to argue within the system? A system that itself is so circumscribed it gives the illusion of choice while keeping whole viewpoints out of the discussion? Or creates the illusion that arguing with the foreign secretary over a glass of port gives one a say in the course of the country?"

Malcolm swallowed. "Point taken."

"I didn't mean—"

"You're right. Why else did I leave the diplomatic service after all?" She unclenched her hands and pressed them against the folds of her skirt. "Having Colin changed things for me. I had ties outside my work. I had ties to you. I could stand outside the game and see its flaws. But"—she drew a breath, searching for the right words—"in a way it also made me more committed than ever. Because the world we live in—Castlereagh and Wellington's world—isn't the world I want for my children. Despite how privileged they are. Or perhaps because of it."

"My world."

"The world you were born into. The world you've spent most of your life rebelling against. In your own way, you're far more subversive than Lord Byron, darling."

He gave a sudden, unexpected laugh. For a moment she was looking at her husband and partner of the past five years. "To think that I'd ever be called more extreme than Byron. And yet you've also claimed I'm a British gentleman underneath."

"You are." She studied him, chest tight with all the reasons she loved him and all the reasons they couldn't be together. "It's the paradox of who you are, darling."

He was silent for a long moment, and she had the odd sense he was examining himself rather than her. "British gentleman or not, I don't want that world for my children, either. But if I can't offer them a world with personal loyalty, then it renders all other loyalties a mockery."

"You have a way with words, Malcolm. You've just summed up the difference between us."

He watched her for a moment, his gaze appraising but no longer filled with anger or guilt. "O'Roarke said he found you in a brothel."

"Did he tell you he was there on a mission?" Somehow she felt she owed it to Raoul to make sure Malcolm knew that.

"He mentioned it."

"He didn't—There wasn't anything between us until I asked him. Raoul's made his share of compromises, but he has his own sort of honor."

Malcolm gave a wry smile. "He's quite obviously in love with you."

It was her turn to laugh. "I don't know what's funnier—the idea of Raoul in love or the idea of you talking about love."

"Don't play games, Suzette. I'm not excusing what he did. I'm not saying he's not a manipulative bastard who played dice with both of us. But I can see it in his eyes when he looks at you. If I hadn't been so willfully blind I think I might have seen it before I knew the truth. He's a good actor, but that sort of feeling is hard to deny."

"Raoul is the epitome of putting personal feelings before the cause. And yet—"

"You admit he cares about you?"

"I was going to say, 'And yet he obviously cared about you.' Until these past few days, I hadn't realized he could care in that way."

"But he put the cause first. At the cost of manipulating both of us."

"Yes." Myriad conflicting emotions twisted in her chest.

Malcolm's gaze drilled into her. "You loved him."

"He gave me a sense of purpose, a way to fight, a role to play. How could I not love him? But I couldn't let myself become lost in that love. Because I knew the cause came first with both of us."

"For someone who talks eloquently about competing loyalties, I think you're overemphasizing O'Roarke's ability to only feel one thing."

Her mind shot back six years. She'd been taken prisoner by the splinter group of *guerrilleros* she'd infiltrated. Logically Raoul should have left her there. She could have held out long enough to let him cover his tracks before she told them anything. Instead he'd rescued her at considerable risk to himself and the three operatives he'd brought with him. When, half out of her head, she'd asked him if he'd been afraid she'd break, he'd replied, *No, I was afraid they'd kill you before you broke.*

Her fingers dug into the lace that edged the sleeves of her gown. "Perhaps. But you can't think—"

"I think O'Roarke is an inveterate schemer who isn't afraid to use those closest to him. I think he's ruthless. And I think giving you up cost him more than he'll admit to anyone. Perhaps even himself."

She shook her head. "You don't—"

"Know him as you do? Very true. But I have known him longer." He watched her a moment, as though again sifting through information. "You care about him."

"Of course. That is—He'll always be important to me. He was my only family for a long time." And he was still the only person with whom she shared a certain side of herself. She struggled for the right words. Perhaps it was a fool's quest, but suddenly it mattered very much that Malcolm understand. "But it shifted when I married you. I think he saw that before I did. I know you probably don't believe it—"

"Oh, I believe it. Circumstances changed your relationship."

"That's not what I meant."

"No. But there's a truth beneath what you meant." He leaned against the bedpost, arms folded over his chest, and watched her a moment longer. "Explain it. Make me understand."

"What?"

"Why you did what you did."

She looked into his eyes and saw challenge but also genuine entreaty. "I don't think you could understand, Malcolm. That's the irony. Your empathy makes you a good agent. And plays merry hell with your conscience. It's part of why I fell in love with you. But I don't think you could put yourself in my shoes. I don't think I'd want you to. I don't want you to see the world that way."

"Rubbish, Suzette. That's taking the easy way out. You're not too horrible to explain yourself. And I'm not too innocent to understand."

"I put my goal first. And I told myself it was worth the damage. That without that ruthlessness nothing would be accomplished."

"And if you didn't stop to consider your own feelings why consider anyone else's?"

"I look after myself. I'm no martyr."

"But you also put the goal ahead of what you might want." He moved to the door to the adjoining dressing room. "I'll change in the dressing room tonight. We should be able to talk to Crispin in the interval."

She blinked at the change in subject. "About—"

"Allie and Grandfather's discoveries. If the manuscript holds the key to something hidden in the sixteenth century the answer lies with the Harleton family."

So. Whatever else had changed, they were still investigative partners. She tried to speak and found her face hurt. "Malcolm—"

"We're in the midst of the investigation, Suzette. We have to finish it." He turned the door handle. "I'll see you at dinner."

Malcolm stepped into the dressing room and pushed the door to behind him. Since they'd moved into the Berkeley Square house he'd done little more than pass through this room. He and Suzanne had begun sharing a bedchamber out of necessity in his cramped Lisbon lodgings. By the time they had a house, they shared a room by choice. At least his choice. God knows what Suzette would have truly preferred, as so much about her was shrouded in mystery. A good deal of the time they dismissed Addison and Blanca when they were dressing or undressing so they could discuss their latest investigation or diplomatic or political affairs. He grimaced. More chances for Suzanne to gather information.

The door from the passage opened and Addison stepped into the room, three freshly starched cravats draped over one arm. The two men regarded each other. In many ways they knew each other better than anyone else, yet they rarely spoke of personal matters. Because that wasn't the sort of man either of them was. And, Malcolm acknowledged, because that wasn't what happened between masters and valets. Now the air was heavy with the weight of secrets both knew the other knew though they had never spoken of them to each other.

"Sir." Addison's voice had a scrupulous neutrality that reminded Malcolm of his own tone when he was making a massive effort to control his feelings.

Malcolm met his valet's gaze across the room. He felt sick at what the other man was going through, yet in Addison's gaze he saw sympathy. And fear. Fear for what this was doing to Malcolm himself. Malcolm's fingers clenched.

"I've spoken with Bla—Miss Mendoza."

Malcolm swallowed. Circumstances had forced Addison and him to wade into the personal waters they had so carefully avoided in their decade together. "I'm sorry. That can't have been easy. It's an impossible situation, yet I am uniquely suited to say I do perhaps have a sense of what you're going through."

"Quite." Addison tugged a gleaming shirt cuff that had already seemed perfectly aligned. "As you no doubt realized, Miss Mendoza and I have grown close. Closer than is customary for two people in service together."

"Your private life is your own affair, Addison. I'm sorry the circumstances of your employment don't afford you more privacy."

"That's very good of you, sir." Addison laid the neckcloths out on the dressing table, twitching them smooth. "I'm aware that our relationship would be frowned upon in most households."

"We are not, thank God, most households."

Addison gave a fleeting smile. "And I'm also aware that my behavior with regards to Miss Mendoza could rightfully be termed less than honorable."

"As Shakespeare would say, 'honor' is but a word." Malcolm could hear Suzanne reminding him of as much.

Addison pressed a wrinkle from one of the cravats. "But a word with the ability to do harm, particularly to a woman."

Malcolm recalled the way Addison and Blanca had looked at each other and the discussions he and Suzanne had had about the progress of the relationship. "Were it not for your scruples, I imagine your relationship would have progressed more quickly."

"Perhaps." Addison twitched the other, equally immaculate shirt cuff straight. "A fortnight ago I asked Blan—Miss Mendoza to marry me."

"My dear fellow." Somehow the words came out as both congratulation on the original proposal and commiseration on what it must now mean.

"I should have told you sooner, sir." Addison moved to the wardrobe and took out a black evening coat. "I was waiting because I know it would be highly unusual for Miss Mendoza and me to remain in service after our marriage. I would not lightly leave my employment, sir." He draped the coat over a chairback and smoothed his hands over the shoulders. "It has meant a great deal to me."

For a moment the years fell away and Malcolm was slumped in a chair, Addison helping Simon bandage his torn wrists. "To me as well. But there's no need—There would be no need—"

The revelations yawned before them. Knitting them together, forcing impossible choices on them both that could end a relationship that stretched back to before either had met the women in their lives.

"I don't know about you, but I could do with a drink." Malcolm strode to the chest of drawers and poured two glasses of whisky. He put one in Addison's hand and dropped into a striped damask chair. "Do sit down, my dear fellow."

It was hardly the first time they had shared a drink, though customarily such occasions had been more celebratory. The nights Colin and Jessica were born, when Malcolm had been elected to the House, when they got the news from Waterloo. Suzanne's and Blanca's faces that night shot into Malcolm's mind. What must they have been going through, surrounded by British celebration? His fingers tightened round his glass.

Addison moved carefully to a chair across from him. He took a sip of whisky. A deeper sip than he usually indulged in. "I can't imagine what the news about Mrs. Rannoch must have meant to you, sir." The words were out, the unacknowledged secret fully acknowledged. "Thank you for allowing Blanca to tell me. It was best

I heard it from her. And I imagine you don't find it easy to share it with anyone at all."

"I'd trust you with my life, Addison."

Addison met his gaze for a moment. "Thank you, sir."

And, Malcolm realized, with this information he had trusted Addison with Suzanne's life. Or at least with her safe existence in Britain.

Addison turned his glass in his hand. "I would imagine it's worse for you. It's your work—"

"Yours as well."

"I suppose that's true. But I think being an agent is more central to who you are. Then too, it was Mrs. Rannoch who made the decision to—"

"To marry me to spy for France." Malcolm took a long drink from his own glass.

Addison met his gaze. He might be reserved, but he wasn't one to hide from hard truths. "While by the time my relationship with Blanca began she was locked into the masquerade as it were." Addison took another drink. "I say all this to explain—I don't know what you mean to do, sir. How you and Mrs. Rannoch will resolve things." His knuckles whitened round the glass, as though he knew the step his next words constituted. "But I've told Blanca I still wish to marry her."

"My felicitations." The words came from Malcolm unbidden.

Addison clunked his glass on the table beside his chair. "You can't mean that."

"I assure you, I do." Malcolm had surprised even himself.

"I'm fully aware that there are any number of reasons you might not wish Blanca or me to continue in our positions in the household," Addison continued. "If you wish us to be gone at once I entirely understand."

"Don't be ridiculous. After everything we've been through—"

"We've never been through anything like this."

"In a sense I got you into this. The least I can do is help you through the aftermath."

Addison met his gaze steadily. "And Mrs. Rannoch?"

Malcolm stared at the Rannoch crest etched on his whisky glass. "I don't know what's going to happen between Suzanne and me. But we have two children. For their sake, we have to go on living under the same roof one way or another."

Addison nodded. He reached for his whisky and stared into the glass. "I said being an agent wasn't as central to me as it is to you. But it means enough that I can understand the allure of a mission. And how in the midst of it one confronts choices one hadn't thought could be possible. Loyalties can be muddy."

"One could say Suzanne made a great sacrifice for her cause." Malcolm wouldn't have put it that way until now. But it was, he suspected, what Tania would have said.

Addison looked up quickly and met his gaze. "I saw rather a lot of Mrs. Rannoch in Lisbon, sir. I'd swear whatever else was going on, her feelings were not unengaged."

"But then Mrs. Rannoch is obviously a consummate actress." Malcolm took a sip of whisky. He doubted the bitter taste would ever leave his mouth.

"Yes. But I've more than once been complimented on my skills at reading people."

"You pick now of all times to forego your usual modesty?"

Addison turned his glass in his hand. "Do you remember the mission to Burgos? You were delayed and I wound up in the city for a fortnight posing as a wine merchant?"

"I'm still in your debt for that."

"Not in the least. But I learned then what a lonely place it can be, trapped in a masquerade with no notion of when it may end. I don't imagine it was easy for Mrs. Rannoch. Particularly at Waterloo."

Malcolm saw again Suzanne's smile in the midst of the hugs and toasts with champagne after the news of the Allied victory at Waterloo. How much had it cost her to maintain that smile? And then he felt the weight of his friend Canning, dying in his arms that day. "No," he said. "I don't imagine it was."

Addison took a careful sip of whisky. "One could of course claim Blanca is a romantic—though Blanca would strenuously deny it— but she says it was obvious to her that Mrs. Rannoch loved you a few months into the marriage."

"Blanca is understandably loyal to Suzanne."

Addison met Malcolm's gaze without blinking. "But she's a remarkably keen observer herself." He drew a breath. "I'll understand whatever you decide to do, sir. And it goes without question that you will have my support in whatever decision you take."

Malcolm returned Addison's gaze. "That means a great deal to me." He tossed off the last of his whisky. "You and Blanca must of course remain here as long as you are both willing to do so."

"That's very—"

"That's a necessity as far as I'm concerned. You'll need a suite of rooms. I'm sure we can work something out. I'll speak with—I'll speak with Mrs. Rannoch about it."

Suzanne stared into the dressing table looking glass, willing her fingers to be steady as she lined her eye with blacking. A host of details drifted through her mind. Simply juggling the day-to-day business of life was complicated enough, particularly this time of year. She'd ordered Jessica's birthday dress, but she needed to take her in for one last fitting. She had to sit down with Mrs. Erskine to finalize the details of the dinner—Jessica was quite good at feeding herself cooked broccoli. . . .

A year. Her baby girl was going to be a year old. Pulling herself up, teetering on the brink of walking, bravely facing the world, wholly unafraid. Suzanne turned round on the dressing table bench. She had brought Jessica into the bedchamber while she dressed. Her daughter was taking careful steps holding on to folds of the coverlet. Unafraid, but cautious enough to know she might fall if she let go. Entirely secure in her world. That in itself was enough miracle and adventure to stop Suzanne in her tracks and drive the breath from her lungs.

She'd sent off Christmas parcels to her friends Dorothée and Wilhelmine on the Continent, but she'd barely started shopping for Colin and Jessica, and then there was Cordy's family, Paul and Juliette and the children, David and Simon, Isobel and Oliver and their family . . . She should do something for Roxane and Clarisse. She needed to organize parcels for the servants. And Malcolm. She hadn't the least idea what she was going to give Malcolm.

She froze, the eye-blacking stick dangling from her fingers. It hardly mattered now. He'd scarcely welcome a gift from her. And yet—They were living in the same house. The children and the servants would notice if she didn't give him something. And it wouldn't feel like the holidays if she didn't. Not that it was going to feel like the holidays in any case. Dear God, when had she started to care about the holidays?

Somewhere, at some point, in the midst of the pretense, in the midst of living within the shell of a persona, she'd become someone entirely different. No, not entirely. But different enough she wasn't sure who that person was herself. So how could she possibly explain to Malcolm?

She'd given him a first edition of Ludlow's memoirs for their first Christmas. And a watch for their second. Engraved with a quote from *Romeo and Juliet: My bounty is as boundless as the sea, /My love as deep. / The more I give to thee, the more I have / For both are infinite.* Overly romantic perhaps. But it had seemed to fit the woman she was pretending to be. And it had summed up feelings she hadn't been able to put into words. Not then.

And now she had lost the chance that he would ever believe them.

CHAPTER 28

Harry and Cordelia were already seated in the Rannoch box at the Tavistock when Malcolm, Suzanne, and Strathdon arrived. Suzanne felt the keenness of the Davenports' gazes beneath their welcoming smiles. Could they tell something was wrong or was it just her over-active imagination? God knew both Harry and Cordy were sharp-eyed observers.

Harry got up to pull out a chair for Suzanne at the rail beside Cordelia. "You look lovely," he said.

That settled it. Suzanne sank into the chair, flashed Harry a smile, then kept her gaze on her skirt as she settled the folds, a web of black net over champagne satin. Harry definitely knew something was wrong. Compliments were not at all in his usual line.

"All this talk about the *Hamlet* manuscript has given me an appetite for the theatre," Cordelia said, voice just a shade too bright.

"Indeed." Strathdon dropped into a chair beside Harry.

"You actually deign to attend plays written in this century, Duke?" Cordelia asked with a smile.

Strathdon returned the smile. He might have his head in his books most of the time, but he was not above noticing a pretty woman. "I've known Simon Tanner since he was an undergraduate. Always was clever. And he has a gift for language. Acknowledges

Shakespeare as an inspiration as well. Good to remember the theatre is a living, breathing thing and not remain mired in the sixteenth century."

"Much as I like *Hamlet,* I'm rather glad tonight is a comedy." Harry dropped back into his chair. "Much-needed leavening if we can manage to laugh."

"And you have a chance to look at Manon Caret," Cordelia said.

"I don't know what you're talking about," her husband returned, straight-faced but a gleam in his eyes.

"It's all right, dearest. I don't mind your looking."

God. Harry and Cordy could actually joke about infidelity. It seemed impossible to imagine being at that point. Suzanne heard Malcolm settle himself in the chair beside Harry.

"Ah, to be young," Strathdon said.

"My grandfather may claim to be immune," Malcolm said, "but he got Suzanne to arrange a private interview with Mademoiselle Caret after the performance."

They had got through dinner by leaving the talk primarily to Strathdon. Fortunately, the manuscript and his and Aline's discovery provided plentiful food for conversation. How much, if anything, Strathdon sensed had been difficult to tell. He was the sort who might choose to ignore personal undercurrents even if perfectly well aware of them. The easy facility of his commentary on the Tavistock versus Drury Lane and favorite *Hamlet* productions at both perhaps indicated that he knew something was required to fill the void. Or perhaps simply indicated that *Hamlet* was on his mind.

Suzanne lifted her opera glasses and turned her gaze to the other boxes. Looking and being looked at. The way of the world in the beau monde. Caroline and William Lamb had just come into a box across the theatre. Lady Caroline was leaning eagerly over the rail to speak to someone in the next box, the lilac ribbons on her filmy gown fluttering in her enthusiasm. William stood at the back of the box speaking with Lord John Russell. The distance between the Lambs was palpable, far greater than a few feet of velvet and gilding. Was that how she and Malcolm would now appear in public? Or did they have sufficient skills to carry off what was probably the greatest masquerade of both their careers?

The curtain rang up. The theatre was as close as she had to a childhood home. Usually, whatever crisis they were in, she could capture at least a small bit of that magic when the lights dimmed. Tonight the words swept over her and the actors were a blur. It was *The Invalid Marriage,* one of her favorite of Simon's comedies, but perhaps not the play for her to focus on tonight. Difficult to see the humor in anyone's marital difficulties. She managed to keep her gaze fixed on the stage, to laugh and clap at the appropriate moments. She was vaguely aware that Manon was giving a particularly exhilarating performance. Sometimes a crisis could bring out the best in an actor.

The curtain came down on the first act. The stir of getting up and moving into the salon at least provided distraction. Malcolm moved off, in search of Crispin, she knew. Strathdon was detained by Lord Holland. Harry went to procure champagne. Suzanne both welcomed and dreaded being alone with Cordelia, but Simon stopped beside them before either was forced to speak.

"Dearest Simon." Cordelia leaned forwards to kiss him. "It's a splendid play."

"You're too kind, Cordy. Nothing like listening to Shakespeare all day to make a writer face his own inadequacies."

"I was actually thinking that hearing *Hamlet* recently makes me realize how wonderfully you use language."

"Shameless flattery, my dear, but I'll take it."

"Your insights into marriage amaze me." Suzanne realized something was required of her. "Of course, to all intents and purposes, you've been married longer than any of us."

"I worry about Daniela and Trevelyn every time I see the play," Cordelia said.

Simon flashed a smile at her. "Then I've done something right. Normally with this sort of comedy audiences are comfortably assured of the happy ending. After all, that is what fiction is. At least this sort of fiction."

"Your characters transcend the genre," Suzanne said.

"There's a lot to be said for a hard-won happy ending." Simon's gaze lingered on her face for just a trifle longer than one would have expected in the normal course of interaction. Then he excused himself and moved off, with the slightest press of Suzanne's hand. That show of comfort was ridiculously warming; at the same time it set off alarm bells in her head. Simon always did see too much.

Cordelia regarded her for a long moment after Simon left. "You needn't talk about it. God knows I won't tease you. But I know you well enough I can't help but notice something's amiss."

Suzanne swallowed. For a moment, the desire to unburden herself to Cordelia was almost overmastering. Her skills at dissimulation must be slipping. Of course, she had remarkably sharp-eyed friends. Out-and-out lies would only leave Cordelia wondering and speculating. And would somehow cheapen their friendship. "I should have known you'd realize. Malcolm and I—Something's come up from the past."

"Frederick Radley? I couldn't but be concerned when he turned up at Emily Cowper's."

Suzanne adjusted the steel strap of her reticule over her wrist. "Not precisely. That is, Malcolm already knew about Radley. At least part of the story. But more recently he's come to realize I'm not the woman he thought I was."

Cordelia spun round, her back to the salon. "Rubbish, Suzie. I don't know what your past holds, but no one seeing you and Malcolm together could think he doesn't know the woman you are."

Suzanne looked into her friend's bright blue gaze. Cordelia had the remarkable knack of being wholly herself for better or worse. "Perhaps what you see isn't the real me, either."

Cordelia shook her head. "I used to think Harry didn't see the real me. He himself would admit he didn't when he proposed to me. Even after Waterloo, when we were living together again, I thought, 'He'll realize I'm still the woman I used to be and leave.' Then I realized I wasn't that woman anymore." She tucked a ringlet into her pearl bandeau. "Harry's the first to admit he had a completely false image of me when he offered for me. He fell for my face, though one would expect better of Harry, and conjured all sorts of impossible virtues or attributes behind it."

"I think perhaps he saw the vitality behind it."

"Perhaps. Or the loneliness. But he didn't understand me, any more than I understood this broody scholar wrapped up in his books." Cordelia wrinkled her nose. "But then the truth is I don't suppose one can ever really know another person inside and out. It's a bit like trying to piece together a picture of the past from odds and ends in the historical record. One can only approach it by approximation. Harry's and my approximation of each other is rather better now. And I say yours and Malcolm's of each other is as close as one can come."

"That assumes you know us."

Cordelia's gaze was shrewd as it flickered over Suzanne's face. "As well as I know anyone."

Suzanne smoothed the folds of her shawl, moss green and black silk and cashmere from Turkey. A gift from Malcolm her birthday before last. The urge to confide washed over her again. Was it going to be like this from now on? The secrets she had kept buried for so long now seemed to constantly well up in her throat. "I don't think it's unusual for men to idealize the women they love, even if they see themselves as hardheaded pragmatists. I'm quite sure Malcolm idealizes me." *Or rather used to do so.*

"Perhaps. But not as much as Harry. He isn't as much of a romantic." Cordelia's gaze drifted round the salon to settle on her husband in the crowd round the bar. "That was one of my mistakes about Harry. It took me years to realize only a desperate romantic can become as bitter and cynical as he did. But I finally realized whoever I am, I'm more than the person Harry sees. Just as you can't define yourself by what Malcolm sees."

For years Suzanne had defined herself as a French agent. Now that that was gone—

Cordelia touched Suzanne's arm. "Don't torture yourself, Suzette. Whatever you think you've done, it can't be nearly the mess I made of my life."

Suzanne's fingers closed instinctively over her friend's own. "I think most women would envy what you have now."

Cordelia gave a wry smile. "I've made such a mockery of fidelity I can't really expect it or offer it. But I don't think the fact of betrayal makes fidelity impossible." She fingered the ebony sticks of her fan. "I'm not saying I'm certain I can live up to it. I'm not saying I'm certain Harry can—though I'm more confident of him than of myself. But I do believe in trying. And I'm rather more confident in myself than I was." She unfurled the fan and waved it with what might have been defiance. "But then I've always been something of a gambler. My father was an inveterate one after all."

"In this case I'd say the odds favor you rather than the house."

"I hope so." Cordelia ran a finger over the painted silk of the fan. "It's odd when I think about Julia."

"Odd how?"

"First we learned she betrayed her marriage vows. Which one wouldn't think would have shocked me, but I always liked Johnny. Then we thought she was a French spy. Yet in the end we learned she wasn't spying for the French at all, she was working for England. For our side. She wasn't a traitor, but in the course of her work she betrayed her marriage vows. One type of betrayal instead of another."

Whereas Suzanne had betrayed her own husband politically but not in bed. She could not have failed to note the difference during their investigation into Julia Ashton's murder. "Are you weighing them in the scales?"

"I can't help but wonder if the fact that she slept with other men in pursuit of a higher purpose makes her infidelity any easier for Johnny to bear. Or if he'd find it easier if she betrayed Britain rather than him. Of course I can't ask him any of it. And I certainly wouldn't want to now that he and Violet seem to be getting on so well. But it makes one wonder."

"Which loyalty is strongest?"

Cordelia nodded at Henry Brougham. "And which betrayal is worst."

Suzanne looked at her friend. Cordelia looked back at her. She could find no clue that Cordy suspected. And yet—

"I don't suppose there is an easy answer," Cordelia said. "One can't rank betrayals like officers or the line of succession. There are simply different sorts and each carries its own particular sting. A sting which endures."

Despite everything, Suzanne's impulse was to comfort her friend. "Cordy—"

"It gets easier," Cordelia said. "But I don't expect it will ever really go away. After all, I long ago learned life isn't about fairy-tale happy endings that tie things up in a neat bow. There's always an 'after.'" She adjusted her fan, as though to shield them. "Of course much of the time I don't think about such things at all. I'm too busy making sure the girls get to the park and ordering dinner and supervising lessons and scribbling notes on a monograph. The minutiae of day-to-day life. I often think focusing on that is the secret to surviving. And what knits a couple together."

For five years, focusing on those details had preserved Suzanne's sanity. And helped her forge a bond with Malcolm without really realizing it. She should have simply nodded her head at Cordelia's words, but instead she found herself saying, "Those ties can't stand up to everything."

"Suzie. If there's anything Harry or I can do—"

Malcolm was waving to her. Both a welcome distraction and an unwelcome interruption. "Thank you, Cordy. I need to go talk to Crispin. Investigations don't stop for anything."

Malcolm leaned his shoulders against the paneling in the sitting room to which he, Suzanne, and Crispin had removed. He had just finished recounting his grandfather and Aline's theory that Hamlet's letter to Ophelia in the manuscript had been written by someone else and offered clues to a person or place. "Does it mean anything to you?" he asked Crispin.

Crispin had been frowning, but at this he nodded. "Perhaps. Eleanor Harleton. The sixteenth-century Lady Harleton, the one with the actor lover. Her husband was caught up in the Essex revolt. He was in the Tower and eventually went to the block and was attainted. The estates were confiscated—his nephew who inherited got them back under James the First. But a famous set of emeralds that had been in the family since the Wars of the Roses disappeared and was never recovered. There were always rumors that Eleanor hid them."

"You think that's what this is a code to?" Suzanne asked.

"Eleanor Harleton and her actor lover concealed the emeralds somewhere? It fits with Malcolm's theory that Francis Woolright copied out this version of the manuscript and Eleanor made notes on it."

"There are notes in both hands on that particular speech," Malcolm said. "Does the wording mean anything to you, Crispin?"

Crispin carried the paper Malcolm had given him with the speech copied onto it over to a brace of candles and studied it. "There are family stories about a secret hiding place at the Richmond house, though we've never been able to find it."

"Do you think it would make sense if you were there in person?"

Crispin gave a faint smile. "One can only hope. Are you suggesting a treasure hunt, Malcolm?"

"Tomorrow if possible."

"Done. Manon will probably be relieved not to have me hovering over rehearsal."

"Perhaps you should take Harry," Suzanne suggested. "He'd be good at it."

Malcolm met his wife's gaze. She was, he realized, giving him a way out of spending the day in her company. "I think we should invite Harry and Cordelia," he said. "The more heads we have focused on this the better."

"Bring the children as well," Crispin suggested. "I'll bring Roxane and Clarisse. We can pack a picnic. Might as well make it a day of fun."

"How lovely," Suzanne said. Her voice was like silver polished so bright it blinded one to the wear.

CHAPTER 29

"Harry." Malcolm touched his friend on the shoulder as the second interval started. They were standing in the anteroom of their box. Suzanne and Cordelia had been besieged by admirers in the box and Strathdon had gone to speak with Lady Frances. By the time Malcolm and Suzanne had finished talking with Crispin, the second act had been starting, so this was his first chance to speak with Harry.

Harry raised a brow, but behind his look of inquiry was a concern all the sharper for being veiled. Harry knew, Malcolm realized with a sick shock of surprise. If not all the details—how could he?—he knew that something had gone wrong between Malcolm and Suzanne.

"How do you fancy a spot of treasure hunting?" Malcolm asked.

Harry's eyes narrowed. "Looking for more manuscripts?"

"Looking for something from clues in the manuscript." Malcolm explained about his grandfather and Aline's discovery and Crispin's theory about the jewels being hidden at the Richmond house.

Harry gave an unexpected smile. "Cordy will like this. She's always been good at party games and riddles. And it will be good for the girls to have a day in the country." Harry's gaze went to the curtains to the box. Cordelia's laughter carried through, followed by the murmur of several male voices, but Harry's eyes held no hint of jealousy.

Malcolm surveyed his friend. "You're happy."

Harry met his gaze and gave a wry smile. "The shock in your voice speaks volumes."

"I'm sorry." Malcolm shook his head. "That isn't what I meant at all. Though I suppose anyone being happy is something of a feat."

"And I used to sneer at the very possibility."

"You had good cause."

"I found it easier to sneer than to attempt to make something of my life."

"We're all shaped by the past." Malcolm struggled for the right words that would neither offer insult nor reveal too much about his own wife's secrets. "What I marvel at is how you've—"

"Forgot my past?" As usual, Harry knew precisely where Malcolm was headed. Malcolm wondered if there was any chance he'd ultimately be able to keep Suzanne's secrets from Davenport. "But I haven't. I know it would be impossible. And I'm not even sure I'd want to. The past is my first glimpse of Cordelia across the Devonshire House ballroom, the way the candlelight gilded her hair, and the wonder of her agreeing to dance with me. The day she agreed to be my wife, the first time she laughed at one of my jokes, the glee on her face when we discovered a bit of Roman pottery on our wedding journey. All those are as much a part of the past as the quarrels and silences and finding her in George Chase's arms and the endless gossip that followed me to the Peninsula. In the end the real challenge wasn't realizing I could live with the past, it was persuading Cordy we both could do so. She was sure one day I'd look at her across the breakfast things and hate her."

In the carriage driving to the Tavistock, Malcolm had looked over at Suzanne, hair perfectly coiffed, the blacking round her eyes, her familiar scent filling the air, so much his wife and such a stranger. Anger had welled up on his tongue like blood from a sword slash.

Difficult to imagine that anger ever wholly dissipating. "And you haven't?"

Harry raised his brows.

"I'm fond of Cordy," Malcolm said. "But she did—"

"Betray me? True enough." Harry glanced again at the curtains to the box, then leaned his shoulders against the wall, putting his back to the curtains. "No, I don't look at Cordy and hate her. I don't think I ever will. I think the risk is more that she'll hate herself."

Malcolm saw Cordelia's brilliant, defiant gaze. "I think Cordy's too strong for that."

"Yes. It's one of the reasons I love her." Harry regarded him for a moment. "When I step back from the situation instead of looking at her as my wife, I find it isn't nearly so clear-cut where the blame falls. We both made choices. We both made mistakes. If I'd seen Cordy properly, I'd never have put her in the situation where she was torn between hollow marriage vows and George Chase. And in the end if the past hadn't happened, we wouldn't be where we are today."

"Harry—" Malcolm frowned at the candle sconce on the wall opposite, glittering against the gold damask wall hangings with cool fire. "Did you ever wonder why you did it?"

"It?"

"Intelligence work."

"Oh, that's easy. It was my job."

"It wasn't a job you needed."

"Define 'need.' Perhaps I didn't need it financially, but I needed something to keep me from going mad, hitting my wife's lover again, or crawling to her on my knees begging her to take me back on any terms."

"You could have gone to dig up antiquities or buried yourself in an archive."

"The war had made Continental travel problematic. And I was in the mood to bash something. The army had its appeal."

"So you could have worked for the French just as easily?"

"Certainly, if I'd been French." Harry stooped to pick up a hairpin that had fallen on the carpet and set it on a marble side table. "And I'll own there were more than a few times in the Peninsula when I wondered if the French weren't doing more good than we were."

Malcolm recalled a Spanish advocate he'd met in the course of a mission who'd detailed the progressive legal changes under Joseph Bonaparte and the stories of how in Lisbon the French government had found work for the poor cleaning the city. "I'll own I did at times myself." He frowned at the shadows the candles cast on the carpet. "God knows I don't share Wellington's and Castlereagh's vision of the world. In the end I couldn't take more of advocating policies I didn't agree with across the diplomatic negotiating table. Only last month when I made my speech urging the repeal of the Habeas Corpus suspension one of the Tory backbenchers called me a traitor. It wasn't the first time I've been called that."

Harry grinned. "Badge of honor."

"In a sense I saw it that way. I've certainly never gone in for talk about Crown and country. But—It has to mean something."

"It? England? You're a Scotsman."

"Britain. But I didn't mean the country so much as loyalty itself. Or perhaps it's simply the idea that there's something one's working to perfect. One can walk away, but one doesn't betray it."

"One could make a fair case that one can't walk away. At least Carfax would argue that."

"Perhaps it's simply the idea of making a commitment and sticking with it."

"In the course of which one cheerfully betrays the other side." Harry met Malcolm's gaze for a long moment. "By the time of Waterloo, I was fighting for my friends. And to stay alive."

The remembered smell of blood and cannon smoke welled up in Malcolm's memory. "That's what it came down to for me as well in the carnage. And yet I felt I needed to be there, even though it wasn't really my fight."

"You also told me you found yourself wondering if your first loyalty shouldn't have been to stay with Suzanne and Colin and stay alive for their sakes."

It was true. Ironic that his first loyalty had been to his French agent of a wife. And yet one could say he too understood divided loyalties.

"I'm glad to be out of it," Harry said.

"You just said we couldn't really be out of it."

"True enough. I'll even confess a part of me wouldn't want to be entirely. But we can pick and choose assignments more." He gave a grin. Malcolm had the oddest sense Harry was trying to cheer him. "I'm quite looking forwards to Richmond tomorrow. Nothing like a treasure hunt."

"Thank God." David ducked into the anteroom of the box. "Mind if I seek refuge?"

"Difficult night?" Malcolm asked.

David grimaced. "Family dinner. Family and a few select friends. They sat me next to Lady Mary Cranford. Mother's latest attempt at finding a wife for me, carefully vetted by Father. Simon, needless to say, wasn't invited. Just as well, as he'd probably have stalked out. Lady Mary is a perfectly agreeable girl. Out for a few seasons so rather more rational than the eighteen-year-olds they sometimes throw at me."

"And looking for a husband," Harry said.

"Quite. I hope tonight didn't give her any ideas about my intentions. I tried to be careful, but Bel said my attempts to be polite could be misread." David gave a wry smile. "It isn't easy. Not being able to be one's self. Or at least keeping large parts of oneself hidden."

Malcolm stared at his friend and realized his hands had gone still at his sides. "I don't think I ever realized quite how difficult it is."

"Didn't mean to whinge on about it. But it's hard, knowing what I owe my family."

"You're responsible to yourself first."

" 'To thine own self be true?' Not anymore. Not since I became heir to the title." David twitched his shirt cuff smooth. "I thought it would get easier when the ladies left the table, but then Father started going on about the uprisings in the north. Calling them treason. And Lady Mary's father said the MPs who spoke out in support of the protesters were traitors as well. As if there's no difference between attacking injustice and spying for the French."

"And yet there are times at least one could make a case the

French were doing a better job of fighting injustice," Harry said. "Certainly some Spaniards reached that decision. Many of the more enlightened ones."

"That's different. They were fighting for what they thought was best for their country. We're Englishmen. One can criticize one's country, but once it commits to a course of action one supports the action."

"Does one?" Harry asked.

"It's what we did when Bonaparte escaped from Elba. I spoke out in the House against war, but once war became inevitable we had no choice but to support our country."

Malcolm thought back to some discussions in Brussels. "I'm not sure Simon would agree."

David frowned. "One has to draw the line somewhere. Simon and I just disagree sometimes about where the line should be drawn."

"The line?" Harry asked.

"Between treason and supporting one's country."

"And if our country declares war on the protesters?" Malcolm said.

David's brows drew together. "That would be declaring war on Englishmen."

"So that's what matters?" Harry inquired. "Whether they're English or not?"

"You have to admit a quarrel among Englishmen is different from defending one's country against a foreign opponent. Whatever insults we hurl across the House, we're all Englishmen."

"Actually, Rannoch's Scots," Harry said.

"And a quarter French thanks to my mother," Malcolm added. And a quarter Irish and Spanish thanks to Raoul O'Roarke, he realized.

David grinned. "It's the same island. I wish my father understood that."

"That Britain is one island?"

"That too, to hear him talk about the Scots and the Welsh. But I meant that we both love this country. That whatever our quarrels with each other, we stand fast against our enemies."

"Such as French agents?" Malcolm asked.

"Those are more in your line than mine. But yes."

"So if you knew who was responsible for the Dunboyne leak you'd expose them?" Harry asked.

"My God, of course."

"Even though it's in the past?" Harry persisted.

David stared at him. "English—British—men died."

"People died on both sides," Malcolm said.

"Yes, but—Malcolm, surely I don't have to remind you what country you belong to. One has to—"

"Draw the line somewhere?"

"Quite."

"Mademoiselle Caret." Strathdon swept a bow with the courtly grace of the last century, neatly contriving to avoid a collision with any of the wigs, masks, and costumes that littered Manon's dressing room. "A charming performance. Quite touching at the end. Made me realize the surprising complexities beneath the surface of the story."

Manon smiled and extended her hand. She might have been a duchess receiving guests in her drawing room, Suzanne thought, standing back with Cordelia and Harry. Manon still wore the spangled gown that was her last-act costume, and her hair—she hadn't worn a wig in the play—spilled about her face in a riot of ringlets. "Do tell Simon that. Working on *Hamlet* has him fretting about his own play."

"Already told him. Said false modesty didn't become him."

"Simon was grinning ear to ear." Malcolm leaned against the closed door of the dressing room. "He has the greatest respect for your opinion, sir."

"Good to know you were all paying a bit of attention as boys."

"Do sit down." Manon waved a hand towards the settee and chairs. "When Suzanne said they were bringing you round I told them I wouldn't receive any other visitor this evening. I'm so looking forwards to a sensible discussion of theatre rather than the usual undergraduate prattle."

"Most of your admirers are considerably older than under-graduates," Crispin said.

"But their behavior isn't. Roxane, Clarisse. Come and make your curtsies to His Grace."

Roxane and Clarisse came in from the adjoining sitting room and made careful curtsies to the duke. The daughters of a Republican agent curtsying to an English aristocrat. Suzanne wondered how Manon felt about the irony. The girls went back to Berthe in the sitting room. Suzanne, Malcolm, Strathdon, and the Davenports settled themselves about the dressing room. Crispin opened a bottle of champagne and filled the glasses Berthe had set out on a wicker hamper.

"I was privileged to see you as Cleopatra," Strathdon said, settling back in his chair with a glass. "I don't think I'll ever see anyone your equal in the role."

"You're very kind, Your Grace." Rather than the artifice she usually displayed receiving post-performance compliments, Manon seemed genuinely flattered.

"Not in the least. I speak the unvarnished truth, at least as I see it. France's loss is undoubtedly England's gain. You have a gift for interpreting our greatest writer."

"The verse makes it easier to remember English words. And at the risk of offending the country of my birth—not that I care for that—there's more real-life messiness in the verse and in the characters than in Racine or Corneille. One is constantly surprised, by the meter and by the plot."

Strathdon's gaze warmed, like that of a man looking at a beautiful woman, though in this case Suzanne suspected it had more to do with Manon's words than with her physical attributes. "Well put, mademoiselle. Hope you know what you have here, Harleton."

"Indeed, sir." Crispin dropped down on the settee beside Manon and reached for her hand. "Always liked Shakespeare," he added. "Wasn't the best student, but the thing is they're cracking good stories. Couldn't decide as a boy if I wanted to be Prince Hal or Hotspur. And then there's the family connection."

"Francis Woolright has always intrigued me," Strathdon said.

"Forgive my abysmal ignorance," Cordelia said, "but who is Francis Woolright?"

"One of the original actors to create Shakespeare's characters." Strathdon took a sip of champagne, warming to the subject. "There's a bit of a mystery about Francis Woolright. As the story goes, Woolright joined the company comparatively late for those days. He was in his early twenties when he turned up at the Chamberlain's Men, as the company was called then, and asked for an audition. Burbage was going to send him packing, but Shakespeare was intrigued by his brazenness and agreed to hear him read. According to legend, Woolright launched into Richard the Third's opening monologue. Apparently Burbage cursed him for doing it better than he did himself and hired Woolright on the spot."

"What's known about Woolright's background?" Crispin leaned forwards to top off Strathdon's glass. "I've never heard."

"Nothing. He seemingly had no history. There were rumors even then. Everything from a bastard half-brother of Shakespeare to a bastard son of Mary Queen of Scots to a former King of the Underworld. I've always suspected the truth was probably much more prosaic, but Woolright knew the value of good publicity."

"Some things never change," Manon murmured.

"How did Woolright meet Eleanor Harleton?" Suzanne asked Crispin.

"I've no idea, though I've always assumed it must have been a performance at court."

Strathdon set down his champagne glass. "No idea when she and Woolright met, but the Chamberlain's Men performed at her betrothal ball." Strathdon set down his champagne. "They dusted off *A Midsummer Night's Dream*."

Crispin whistled. "Wonder how far back the affair went. So you think it makes sense that they made notes on the *Hamlet* manuscript?"

"It's certainly plausible." Strathdon took a sip of champagne. "Woolright is thought to have played Laertes when *Hamlet* was first performed. That would have been before the Essex rebellion and before—"

"Eleanor ran off with him," Crispin said cheerfully. "I'm glad they found a bit of happiness."

"You can't know they were happy, *chéri,*" Manon murmured.

"Unlike Eleanor and her first husband, they had no reason to stay together if they weren't."

"She actually married him, didn't she?" Strathdon said. "Quite a love story. Odd she left the manuscript behind."

"She probably had more pressing things on her mind," Malcolm said. "Her husband attainted, the estates forfeited. And her own family may not have been best pleased she was running off with Woolright."

"Though she did manage to keep her Harleton daughter with her," Crispin said.

"She didn't have any sons with Harleton?" Suzanne asked, absurdly comforted by the thought that Eleanor Harleton had not lost custody of her child.

"No, they just had the one daughter. At the time of Harleton's death there was no estate or title to pass on, but Harleton's younger brother's son eventually got both restored. Eleanor Harleton and Francis Woolright had a son and two more daughters, I believe."

"I confess it sounds on the surface as though they had an agreeable life," Manon said. She took a sip of champagne. "But of course we all know appearances can be deceiving."

Jessica stretched and opened her eyes as Suzanne bent over her bassinet in the night nursery. She smiled in anticipation of her late-night feeding, a spit bubble forming on her lip. Malcolm smoothed the covers over Colin and tucked his stuffed bear, Figaro, back into the crook of his arm. Laura Dudley would have been listening for both children from her room next door, but she discreetly never bothered Suzanne and Malcolm at night when the children were sleeping. Suzanne hoped Laura was asleep herself.

Suzanne carried Jessica through the door into their own bedchamber. Once again she wasn't sure what Malcolm would do, but he adjusted the tin shade on the night-light and followed. Suzanne settled in the worn green velvet armchair, unfastened her net overdress, and undid the strings that held the nursing flap on her gown in place (Jessica's birth had necessitated a whole new wardrobe). First things first, and it was for Malcolm to speak.

Malcolm lit the Argand lamp, just as he always did when they returned from an evening out. The hiss and flare of light brought the comfort of the familiar and the ache of its loss. "Addison's going to marry Blanca."

She nearly gripped Jessica too tightly as relief coursed through her. "Thank God." Blanca had been bright-eyed and surprisingly cheerful when she had helped Suzanne dress for the evening. She must have been waiting for Addison to tell Malcolm before she shared the news with Suzanne. Suzanne studied her husband. The futures of so many different people depended on him. "Do you—"

Malcolm shrugged out of his coat. "I want Addison to do what makes him happy. God knows he's been tailoring his life to suit my humors long enough. I've told him we'll find rooms for them. Perhaps we can rearrange the guest suite. I thought you'd have a better idea about that than I would."

"Malcolm—" Suzanne stared at his shadowed eyes in the wash of lamplight. "You want them both to stay here?" Even without the recent revelations it was an unorthodox arrangement.

"I think at this point it's a question of both of them or neither." He kept his gaze on his cravat as he unwound it. "Did you think I'd revert to aristocratic type and refuse to have a valet who was married? Or that I'd refuse to allow Blanca to continue under this roof when you're here?"

"No." She cradled Jessica closer. "That is—"

He met her gaze, a bitter challenge in his eyes. "You weren't sure. Once again I find myself wondering if you knew me any more than I knew you."

"Addison and Blanca were unsure enough that they put off their betrothal."

Malcolm tossed the cravat down. "Addison takes the forms seriously. But then as a valet he has to." He started on the jet buttons on his waistcoat. "Even granted I'm the prisoner of my world that you think me, I don't think I'd ever have been so barbaric or so shortsighted as to tell Addison and Blanca they couldn't marry and keep their employment."

Her heart turned over. "No. I do realize that, darling."

He tossed the waistcoat after the coat and cravat. "I probably should have realized Addison would have these scruples and have told him straight out they were ridiculous. But that would have meant stepping onto personal ground Addison and I avoid." He unfastened a shirt cuff. "Addison's ability to see the situation from Blanca's viewpoint is remarkable."

Jessica was still suckling industriously, though her eyes were closed, her arm curled over Suzanne's breast with comforting familiarity. "Blanca was swept into the masquerade along with me. She never meant to entrap Addison. Addison saw where to place the blame."

"That's much what he said." Malcolm pulled his shirt over his head and quickly wrapped himself in his dressing gown, as he would have done in the early days of their marriage, when they were still physical strangers. "But not the part about placing the blame. In fact, I'd say he saw the situation from your perspective better than I did. Of course he wasn't wallowing in his own stupidity."

She swallowed. "Malcolm, if I could—"

"I doubt it." He tied the belt on his dressing gown and leaned against the bedpost. "I doubt you'd do anything differently. You're too good at your job. At least Addison's going into his marriage with his eyes open. And it's what he wants. I owe it to him to do my best to help him make it work."

"Thank you." She swallowed. How could a few feet of their bedchamber seem an uncrossable gulf? "That is, I know you didn't do it for me, of course, but I'm very happy for them. You know how much they both mean to me."

He looked at her for a moment, his gaze not so much angry as remote. "No, I don't really. I know you've seemed fond of them, but then you've seemed a lot of things. I'm still adjusting to the fact that I don't know you at all."

Jessica stirred in her sleep and threw her head back, kicking her legs. Suzanne coaxed the baby's head back to her breast. "Sometimes I'm not sure I know myself."

"I can well imagine it after living a lie for so long." Again it was a statement of fact rather than an accusation. Which somehow cut deeper than a dagger thrust.

"Darling—Malcolm—You can't think it was all—"

"I think you made yourself into the perfect wife for me." He crossed his arms over his chest, turning the burgundy silk of the dressing gown into armor. "Who knew just what I needed, just what I would respond to." He glanced round the room, the sconces with crystal girandoles she'd chosen, the gray and cream wall hangings, the moss green and burgundy embroidered silk coverlet she'd purchased in Lisbon, the theatrical prints she'd hung on the walls. "You created the perfect home." His gaze went to the door behind which Colin slept. "The perfect nursery—"

"You can't think the children are part of it." The words were stung out of her.

"The children are at the heart of it." He looked at Jessica in her arms, then studied Suzanne herself as though she were a text written in code. "You used me. You used yourself. That's what spies do. But you dragged Colin into the game before he was even born. What in God's name were you thinking?"

"Of the spring campaign." She could feel the insistent tug of Jessica's mouth on her nipple and the weight of the baby's arm across her breast. "How vital it would be to the course of the war. I could barely think ahead to June, when he'd be born."

"That's no way for a parent to think."

"No." She looked down at Jessica's profile. In the warm lamplight, the bones of her face stood out beneath the baby softness, showing the woman she would grow into. God knew what that woman would think of her mother. "I wasn't a parent then. And even now I still sometimes think like an agent. In many ways I'm not a very nice person."

"Don't, Suzette." His voice was like a shock of cold water.

"Don't what?"

"Take the easy way out." He watched her a moment longer, the way he'd look at a code when a pattern began to form in his head, but the data remained tantalizingly out of reach. "All right. With Colin you responded tactically. I can even perhaps understand that.

But what in God's name were you thinking when you told me you wanted to have Jessica?"

Instinctively she pulled the baby closer. Miraculous, the boneless way they melted into you. "That I wanted another child with you."

He gave a harsh laugh, then stared at her. "So I'd be tied to you? Because you thought you owed it to me? So Colin would have a sibling?"

"I'm not sure."

His gaze shot over her face, hard and level. "Well, that's honest at least."

"I think I wanted—" She stumbled, picking her way through an unfamiliar landscape. "A child that we created together. That wasn't part of past deceptions."

He gave a rough laugh that bounced off the freshly painted plasterwork. "Christ, Suzette. Everything between us is mired in past deceptions. And always will be."

She smoothed a tuft of Jessica's hair that curled up at the back of her head. "I know I wanted Jessica. For reasons that had nothing to do with being an agent."

"You can't possibly be sure of that." He glanced away, then looked back at her face. "But it's hard for me to quarrel with events that gave me Colin and Jessica. I just want to be sure they don't suffer for our sins."

"My sins."

"And mine, at least of omission. If I were halfway good at my job, I'd have had the wit to see what was going on." He grimaced. "I knew I wasn't cut out for marriage. I told myself you needed me"—he gave a wry laugh—"and that gave me license to try."

"Malcolm, no." She leaned forwards, then checked herself because of Jessica and because she saw the recoil in her husband's eyes. "Whatever I've done to you, don't doubt yourself. You're a wonderful husband. And father. Don't let me prevent you from caring for others."

"Thank you. I think you can leave it to me to manage my personal relationships." He watched her for a moment as though he were looking through a telescope at an object receding into the distance. "I was going to move my things into the dressing room, but

I don't want to alert the servants to anything being amiss between us. The next thing we know there'll be talk and ten to one it will get back to Carfax. So we'll have to muddle through in the same room."

"I've never objected to sharing a bed." She wondered when, if ever, he'd touch her again. After all, anger and lust were far from mutually exclusive. But with Malcolm, passion had always been inextricably linked to tenderness.

His look told her it would be a long time. "For Colin and Jessica's sake, we have to find a way to live together without hating each other. I've seen what it does to children to grow up with parents with nothing but contempt for each other. I'd give anything to spare Colin and Jessica that fate."

"I could never hate you, Malcolm. But I don't know that you'll ever be able to stop hating me."

He released his breath and she saw some of the tension drain from him, leaving a void that made her ache for his loneliness. And her own. "I don't hate you, Suzette. A part of me can admire how well you did your job. Another part of me is horrified that you caught our children up in it. But I'd be a hypocrite not to recognize intelligence is a slippery slope. And God knows I can understand your reasons for entering into that world after what O'Roarke told me. In the end, you, like me, are left tied to a marriage that wasn't of your choosing."

Their daughter was warm and secure in her arms. Her husband was as closed to her as the walls of a fortress. "I don't expect you to believe this, any more than I expect it to make a difference. But if I didn't choose it then, I'd choose it now."

He didn't laugh her words off. It might have been better if he had. "You can't possibly be sure of that, Suzette. After so many lies how can you be sure of who you are, let alone what you want?"

She swallowed as the cut struck home. "I'll own at times I feel I don't know what trace of me is left under the trappings of the world we live in." She shifted her arm, suddenly aware of the way her nursing corset bit into her skin over the goffered muslin of her chemise. "But you can't think it's all pretense."

A stranger stared at her out of his familiar gray eyes. "I think a good agent builds a persona to fit the demands of the mission. Tweaks and tailors it to whoever is the mark. I think you're a brilliant agent. And you've had years to build your persona."

She stared at him, aware of just how insurmountable the gulf between them was. For how could she expect him ever to recognize the real her when she wasn't sure she'd recognize that person herself?

She thought back to a moment three years ago on the beach at Dunmykel Bay. Malcolm had had Colin on his shoulders. She'd removed her shoes and stockings so the sand could squish round her toes. Malcolm had just capped one of her Shakespeare quotations, and she'd looked into his eyes and been sure—"I know it sounds mad, but there are times when it seems you know me as no one else ever has."

He looked in her eyes, his own dark with what might have been pity. "My darling, if that's true I think it only means you've come to believe your own deceptions."

CHAPTER 30

Colin looked up at Laura as she put on her bonnet. "Why aren't you coming to Richmond with us?"

"Because it's her afternoon off." Suzanne Rannoch was coaxing a wriggling Jessica into her pelisse.

Colin blinked and looked from his mother to Laura. "Where are you going?"

Laura smiled. He was a very grown-up four, but he still quite failed to understand that adults might have lives outside the time they spent with him.

"That's her business." Mrs. Rannoch got Jessica's second arm into a sleeve. Jessica's attention was on her stockings. She had one half-off and was staring at the black merino toe with great concentration as she tugged it.

"To see a friend," Laura said. It wasn't precisely the truth, but it was closer to it than some of the things she said. Though she often felt hopelessly compromised, she tried at least to be honest with the children.

Colin smiled at her. "Have a pleasant afternoon."

"I'm sure I will." Laura tightened the ribbons on her bonnet and bent to kiss his cheek, something she wouldn't have done a year ago. She straightened up and turned to Suzanne. "I should be back by five."

"Stay out for the evening if you like." Suzanne gave Jessica a hairpin to hold and managed to get the stockings in place with that distraction. "I don't know what time we'll be back from Richmond, and Malcolm and I don't have plans this evening."

"Thank you, Mrs. Rannoch." Laura looked at Jessica. The pelisse was on and the stockings were more or less in place, at least for the moment. "Do you want me to help you get her shoes on?"

"No, I'll manage." Suzanne reached for the shiny black shoes. "Go and enjoy your day off."

Laura smiled at Suzanne, touched her fingers to Jessica's cheek, picked up her gloves and reticule, and whisked herself out of the room.

Suzanne Rannoch had seemed pale lately, lines of strain showing about her eyes, but she looked better now that she was with the children. Laura had glimpsed the same tension in Mr. Rannoch's face last night when the couple came into the nursery for supper. Perhaps it was the investigation they were in the midst of, but Laura had seen them involved in investigations before and she'd swear this was something different. She'd almost say the tension was between the two of them.

Laura shook her head at herself as she reached the ground floor hall. Dangerous for a governess to care too much about her employers. Particularly dangerous for someone in her other line of work. She should know better than anyone what a downfall personal entanglements could be.

She tugged on her gray doeskin gloves, smiled at Valentin, and stepped through the front door he was holding open for her.

A crisp wind cut across Berkeley Square, tugging at the ribbons on her bonnet. The day was gray, but the air had a bracing chill with none of the damp promise of rain. She walked at a brisk pace, grateful for the distraction of the cold and the exercise. Her dark blue pelisse, trimmed with black braid, and plaited straw bonnet with blue satin ribbons were her best going-out clothes, chosen because the household would expect her to wear them on her afternoon off, but still dark and anonymous. The habit of a governess made for an excellent disguise. No one looked at governesses. If she was doing her job well, a governess blended entirely into the background.

She thought for a moment of the black net and champagne satin Suzanne Rannoch had worn to the theatre the night before. Mostly Laura would have said she was resigned to her lot in life. That her past was buried so deeply it was like a dimly remembered foreign country. And of all the things she missed from her old life, Laura wouldn't have said clothes were high on the list. But there were times. . . .

She went into a bakeshop and ordered tea, drank half a cup with the careful sips of a governess savoring a rare moment alone, then got to her feet, teacup still on the table, and went behind the screen to the ladies' retiring room. He was already there, in the shadows. She could smell his citrus shaving soap before she made out his form. "Right on time as always."

"A governess needs to be punctual. There's little room for spontaneity. Though the Rannochs aren't as strict about nursery schedules as some families."

"You like them." It was neither censure nor praise.

Laura swallowed. Perhaps she should have put sugar in the tea. It left a bitter aftertaste. "I can't afford to like them."

"As a governess?"

"Among other things."

It was too dark to make out his expression, but she could feel his gaze moving over her face. "What do you have to report?"

Jessica had taken three more faltering steps, a fortnight after the first set, before deciding crawling was safer. Colin could sign his name and was autographing every paper he could get his hands on, including one of his father's draft speeches. Berowne had got off his lead in the square garden, and Laura had had to climb one of the plane trees to get him down, with the children calling anxiously to her from the ground. But of course that wasn't what he'd been asking about. "The Rannochs are involved in an investigation. I don't know the precise details, but it centers round this new version of *Hamlet* that the Tavistock Theatre is putting on. Mr. Tanner came to see them about it late one night. He was injured, according to Valentin."

"The footman?"

"Yes." One would think he could make the effort to keep the servants' names straight. She'd been reporting to him on many of the same people since Paris. "I think someone was trying to steal the manuscript. The next night someone set fire to the kitchen and tried to break in. There hasn't been trouble since. I assume they've moved the manuscript." She paused. Not the first time her impulse had been to hold something back. But she knew that way lay disaster. "Also Raoul O'Roarke's been to the house."

She felt his attention quicken as though he had scented something on the wind. "Interesting. Because of the investigation?"

"Or something connected to it. Mr. and Mrs. Rannoch . . ." She hesitated, fingering a fold of the serviceable kerseymere of her pelisse.

"What?"

The words stuck in her throat, an intolerable invasion of privacy. *Damn it.* This was what came of letting people in under her guard. First it was Colin's small hand in hers, then it was Jessica's smile echoing her own, next thing she knew she was caring about their parents. "Something's . . . shifted . . . between Mr. and Mrs. Rannoch."

"They've quarreled?"

"Not that I heard. Not that there's been any servants' gossip about. They're faultlessly polite with each other. But I can feel the constraint between them."

"When did it start?"

Laura gave the question honest consideration. "She's seemed under strain for some days now. But the first I noticed something wrong between them was when they came into the nursery last night to have supper with the children."

"Do you think he has a mistress?"

Laura blinked. "I can't imagine—"

"Your incredulity is touching, Laura, but he is a man after all."

"You know I'm anything but a romantic. But I'm also a good observer. If you'd seen the way he looks at her—"

"Mooning about after one's wife is no guarantee."

"It's not that. He's one of the least romantic men I've met. And yet—He looks at her as though she holds the secret to his soul." The words tumbled out without thinking. She braced herself for his derision. Instead, she sensed his appraising gaze.

"Perhaps she's the one who was unfaithful."

Laura frowned, unease prickling the back of her throat. Somehow that seemed more plausible. "She loves him."

He gave a low laugh. "I'm sure she'd say she does."

Laura tugged at her braided cuff. "A love affair is the obvious explanation when there's trouble between a couple. But with Mr. and Mrs. Rannoch, the obvious explanation is rarely the correct one."

"You have a point." He shifted as though trying to see her better in the shadows. "How did O'Roarke seem when he visited the house?"

"Polite."

"How did he seem with the Rannochs?"

"They were all serious."

"Any unease from any of them?"

Laura cast her mind back. O'Roarke talking with Colin and Mr. Rannoch. Suzanne Rannoch nursing Jessica, her gaze on the men. "They were friendly enough. Even took time for the children. But no one was in what I'd call an easy humor."

"Interesting."

"You don't think O'Roarke—"

"Raoul O'Roarke is a complicated man. With a complicated relationship to the Rannochs."

Laura scanned his face. As much as she told herself she was better off not knowing details, it was difficult not to search for clues. Natural curiosity. But more than that. The Rannochs intrigued her, but they had also got their hooks into emotions she had thought safely suppressed. "Mr. Rannoch knew Raoul O'Roarke as a boy."

"Indeed."

"But there's more?"

"Not that you need to know."

She felt the ribbons on her bonnet tighten as she lifted her chin.

"Surely I can gather information more ably if I have more to work with."

"As I've said in the past, you can do your job better without distractions."

Frustration rose up in her throat. For a moment, the temptation to turn and walk away was almost overmastering. They wouldn't be able to find her. Surely they wouldn't look that hard. She could start again. Not an easy task for a woman on her own, but she had been taking care of herself for a long time. She could feel the satisfaction of staking out her independence ripple through her. But only for an instant. Because then the memory of everything she had to lose coursed over her, rooting her to the ground. She swallowed her anger and her thirst for autonomy. "Are you implying O'Roarke could be connected to Suzanne Rannoch? That he could be her lover?"

"What do you think?"

She checked an instinctive denial. She had few illusions about fidelity, but she'd seen the bond between the Rannochs. And yet Raoul O'Roarke's visits were connected to the start of the constraint. An image lingered in her mind as O'Roarke and the Rannochs crossed from the square garden to the house. Mr. O'Roarke's gray-gloved fingers extended and then checked as though he had pulled himself back, inches from the mulberry velvet folds of Mrs. Rannoch's pelisse. Sometimes restraint could tell far more than an open display of affection. "I think Mrs. Rannoch loves her husband."

"So you've said. Love doesn't preclude infidelity."

The urge to protect (often a traitorous urge) warred with the need for honesty. She dragged herself back to the rules of ruthless practicality that had served her so well in the past. "You're right. His relationship to the Rannochs is complex. What else?"

"Who's been to the Berkeley Square house besides O'Roarke?"

"The usual people. Mr. Lydgate and Lady Isobel and the children. Colonel Davenport and Lady Cordelia and their children. Simon Tanner and Lord Worsley."

"To talk about this play?"

"I assume so. I'm not privy to their conversations."

"You bring the children into the drawing room after dinner. I know full well the Rannochs spend more time with their children than many couples. And I know how good you are at gathering intelligence."

"They're trying to verify the authenticity of the play. Mrs. Blackwell is helping. And the Duke of Strathdon."

"Ah, yes. I heard he'd come to stay. Impressive this brought him to London."

"One can imagine him being drawn in by a Shakespeare manuscript. He went to see Mr. Tanner this morning."

"And Mr. Rannoch?"

"Of course he's spending time with Mr. Rannoch."

He took a step closer to her. His breath smelled of coffee. "Don't play games, Laura. It doesn't become you. How are they getting on?"

"They would hardly quarrel in front of me."

"But?"

She swallowed. "Family relationships are usually complicated."

"And you've proved excellent at decoding them. It's part of what makes you such an effective asset."

Her fingers twisted in the skirt of her pelisse. *Ruthless practicality.* "I believe Mr. Rannoch and the duke have been discussing his parents. The investigation seems to have opened questions about Alistair Rannoch's death. Mr. Rannoch now wonders if it was an accident."

"Damnation."

Laura stared at him in the shadows. "You mean it wasn't? Good God, did you—"

"Don't be stupid, Laura. Why would I—we—have wanted Alistair Rannoch dead?"

"I haven't the least idea why you want anything."

"You're a tough woman, Laura, but you've lived with them for some time." His voice held an odd sort of sympathy, which was somehow worse than derision. "And the Rannochs can both be very disarming. You've seen them *en famille,* playing with their children, being kind to their staff. They're really quite ruthless."

A laugh escaped her lips unbidden. "Remarkable coming from you."

"It takes one to know one. I know Suzanne Rannoch seems like the perfect wife and mother—"

"Actually, what I like about her is that she's well aware that she's not perfect."

"—but you have no idea what she's capable of."

Laura saw Mrs. Rannoch coaxing Jessica into her pelisse. "Doing it much too brown. Just because she's not a milk and water miss—"

"Suzanne Rannoch is a great deal more than that. She's not what she seems."

"No, she's much more capable and less decorative. Men always talk this way about a woman who can think and act for herself." And yet certain memories sprang to mind. Meeting Mrs. Rannoch in the upstairs passage in the middle of the night in Paris. Mrs. Rannoch had been dressed as a groom. Easily enough explained by her investigations with her husband. As was the time Laura was quite sure there'd been bloodstains on the triple-flounced skirt of Mrs. Rannoch's morning dress. But there was one occasion she was quite sure Mrs. Rannoch had climbed in through the breakfast parlor window and Mr. Rannoch hadn't had the least idea about it. Laura had kept silent of course. Because that was what a governess did. And because her sympathies were directed towards Mrs. Rannoch.

"Suzanne Rannoch has a great deal to lose and that makes her dangerous," Laura's companion persisted. "Rannoch has a few more scruples, but even he's done things you'd cavil at. Don't waste your sympathies on them."

"I don't waste my sympathies on anyone."

"You're a clever woman, Laura. But you have more compassion than you admit, perhaps even to yourself. If you don't take care, it could be your undoing." He reached out and touched her hand.

Laura jerked away from his touch. "I always take care."

"It's those with the most confidence in their abilities who make mistakes." The floorboards creaked faintly as he shifted his weight from one foot to another. "Does Carfax share Rannoch's suspicions about Alistair Rannoch?"

"I'm not sure. I don't think Mr. Rannoch fully trusts Lord Carfax. But I do know Mr. Rannoch is asking questions about the League."

She felt the jolt of tension that ran through him. "And?"

"For the moment he seems to think it's a hellfire club."

He gave a short laugh. "God knows there's an element of truth to that. One can only hope there's enough smoke to distract him."

"Mr. Rannoch has a way of unearthing the truth. So does Mrs. Rannoch."

She felt the pressure of his gaze on her face. "Just remember the consequences for all of us if they unearth this particular truth."

She drew her reserves about her. It would never do to let him see her shiver. "You've reminded me of it often enough."

He nodded. "Next week. The same time."

She tugged on her gloves. Her hands were clammy.

"Laura," he said in a soft voice.

She looked at him in the shadows.

"I don't need to remind you of the consequences if you have any foolish thoughts about confiding in the Rannochs, do I? If I told them the truth, it would ruin any trust they have in you. Not to mention other repercussions."

She tugged her second glove, breaking a stitch, and nodded. It was damnably hard to maintain one's autonomy when one was playing a wretched hand.

Crispin scowled at the pilasters that flanked the library fireplace at the Richmond villa. "I had such high hopes for those birds. They look like ravens."

Suzanne studied the carved birds that topped each pilaster. "I think they may actually be hawks. We were looking for ravens." Ravens seemed to be everywhere these days.

"In any case, there's nothing hidden behind them." Malcolm pushed himself to his feet. He had been kneeling in front of the pilaster, tapping to look for a secret panel. Harry was doing the same with the other pilaster.

Happy shrieks came from the window seat, where the children were bouncing. Suzanne glanced over, but the capable Roxane had things well in hand. The five adults moved to the central library table. Crispin leaned against the gleaming oak, brows drawn together. "It looks as though we have to move on to another room. I was so sure this was where Eleanor Harleton would have hidden something. It's the heart of the old house. And the story is that it was her favorite room."

Excited young voices bounced off the fretted ceiling. The children were marching towards the fireplace now the adults had moved on. Jessica, Suzanne noted, was walking holding Livia's hands. "I think we've checked every possibility for a hidden compartment," she said. "Perhaps—"

She broke off because out of the corner of her eye she saw Jessica's foot catch on a corner of the hearth rug. Suzanne was already running across the room before Jessica stumbled. Livia caught her, but the rug slipped and both girls landed on the floor in a tangle of muslin, merino, and lace-edged petticoats. When Suzanne reached Jessica, her face had the stillness of breath being drawn for a scream. Suzanne snatched her daughter up just as Jessica let loose a full-throated howl.

Suzanne pressed her lips to her daughter's head. "I'm here, *querida,* it's all right," she murmured. *She's fine,* she mouthed to Malcolm, who had run across the room after her, the other adults close behind him.

Livia looked up at Suzanne and Jessica with stricken eyes. "I'm sorry. I thought I was holding her steady."

"It's all right, sweetheart," Suzanne said. "You just slipped."

Cordelia moved to touch her daughter's hair.

Clarisse was peering at the floor. "Did Jessica hit her head? It looks like there's blood."

Colin plopped down on the floor and touched his fingers where she was pointing. "It's just a bit of stone," he said, relief in his voice.

As she was occupied stroking Jessica's hair, it was a moment before Suzanne made the connection. She glanced at Malcolm. He had already dropped down beside Colin. The square before the fireplace, which had been covered by the hearth rug, seemed to be inlaid with a pattern. Malcolm tugged at the rug. "It seems to have been nailed down," he said. "Then a corner came free. Do you have a hammer somewhere, Crispin?"

While Crispin went in search of a hammer, Suzanne and Cordelia took the children to the kitchen and settled them under the watchful eye of a kitchen maid with lemonade and cookies. Jessica, enthusiastically breaking off pieces of cookie, had long forgot the fall and even Livia seemed to be over her worry about it.

Suzanne and Cordelia returned to the library to find Malcolm pulling up the last nail. He rolled the hearth rug back to reveal an image of a dragon with a sword between its teeth.

"Good lord," Crispin said. "It's the Harleton crest. I never knew it was there."

"The hearth rug had been carefully positioned over it," Malcolm said. He touched the carnelian that formed the dragon's eye. "Bloodred. The copper of the sword hilt could be called fire."

"The tip of the dragon's tail looks like onyx," Cordelia said. "Raven black."

"And the sword blade is mother-of-pearl," Suzanne said. "Not exactly dove gray, but—"

"Poetic license." Harry dropped down beside Malcolm. "The aquamarine in the hilt is obvious for the sea, but what about the mire?"

"There's the bronze on the dragon's spine." Cordelia knelt beside her husband. "At least unpolished it looks sort of muddy, like a mire."

Malcolm pressed his fingers against the carnelian, the copper, the onyx, the mother-of-pearl, the aquamarine, and last the bronze. The central square tilted beneath his fingers. He pressed again. Hinges creaked and the square of floor with the Harleton crest slid to the side to reveal a shallow compartment.

CHAPTER 31

Crispin released a breath of wonder. "My word. It really does exist. Half of me thought we were on a wild-goose chase."

"That's the thing about investigations," Harry said. "One often has to put in a damnable amount of time before one knows if there's anything to it."

Crispin studied the plain brown box in the compartment before them. "Of course I haven't a clue where the key might be."

"I wouldn't worry, Lord Harleton," Cordelia said. "You have quite a collection of proficient lock pickers present."

In the end it was Malcolm who went to work on the box once they had carried it into the library and set it on a table by the mullioned windows, with the added light of a lamp. Suzanne watched her husband's long fingers go through the familiar motions with his picklocks. It was an old lock, and from the tension in his neck and shoulders she knew picking it was harder than he made it look. The kitchen maid had taken the children to the garden. The children's gleeful shouts carried through the windows, a counterpoint to the quiet tension of the adults in the library. Her two worlds colliding. Or two of her many worlds.

"There." Malcolm sat back in his chair. "Do you want to do the honors, Harleton? It's your family's treasure."

Crispin hesitated a moment, then moved to the table. For all the layers of deception in the room, Suzanne felt the thrill that ran through the company. She and Malcolm and Harry might be hardened agents, but the prospect of unearthed treasure awakened something in them as young as the children scampering on the lawn outside.

Crispin pushed back the lid of the box. Two drawstring bags, one of brown wash leather, the other of black velvet. Crispin picked up the leather bag first and tugged at the drawstring. A necklace, bracelet, coronet, and earrings spilled onto the chamois cloth Malcolm had spread on the table. Emeralds sparked in the sunlight, undimmed by the years. The setting was gold, aged to a fine luster, the design suggested the fifteenth century. Crispin drew a breath of wonder. "So she did hide the jewels away."

"You're sure that's what these are?" Cordelia asked.

"Oh yes. I can show you a painting in the stairwell of Eleanor Harleton wearing them. And they all seem to be accounted for. Which makes me wonder about the other bag." He reached for the velvet and tugged the string. Loose stones spilled onto the chamois cloth, glittering with fire against the dark fabric.

Harry let out a whistle. "In addition to the emeralds, your ancestors seem to have hidden a fortune in diamonds."

Crispin frowned. "Odd."

"If the family was attainted, they'd have wanted to hide away whatever they could," Malcolm said.

"Yes, but I never heard any talk about diamonds being missing. Surely jewels on this scale couldn't have gone missing without attracting notice."

Suzanne studied the sparkling stones. "And these were broken up, which makes them seem less like a family heirloom."

"Perhaps the Elizabethan Lord Harleton received them as payment from Lord Essex," Cordelia suggested.

"Difficult to imagine Essex handing over such a fortune," Malcolm said. "These must be worth far more than the emeralds." He reached for the black velvet bag. "And this doesn't look anything like two hundred years old. I wonder if the diamonds were hidden far more recently."

"By my father?" Crispin asked.

"That would be likeliest."

"So he found the emeralds but kept them hidden?"

"Perhaps as insurance against needing to make a quick escape," Harry suggested.

Crispin's face darkened. "You think the diamonds were payment from the French?"

"Even were Lord Harleton the best asset imaginable, that would be an incalculably large payment," Suzanne said.

Malcolm met her gaze and nodded. Sometimes it was best to brazen things out.

"We don't know what secrets my father gave up," Crispin said, a grim edge to his voice.

Malcolm watched through the diamond panes of the window as Crispin swung a giggling Clarisse in the air.

"He's so good with them," Suzanne said.

"Remarkably. Of course, as I well know, one can become a father in a number of ways," Malcolm said. Outside Crispin bent down to acknowledge Jessica, who was tugging at his boots. "It will cut him in two if Manon leaves him."

Suzanne swung her gaze to Malcolm. "I was thinking of what it will do to Manon when he marries."

Malcolm looked down at his wife. "Whom would Crispin marry?"

"A girl from a good family cut out to be a baron's wife." She paused for a moment, then added, "Much the same sort of girl you'd have married if I hadn't contrived to stumble across you."

Malcolm looked into the sea green eyes of the woman who had changed his opinion about marriage. "On the contrary. If it weren't for your predicament—what I thought was your predicament—I wouldn't have married at all."

Her gaze had the wry, wistful quality of one remembering something long ago, like a lost love. "My predicament was real enough, even if the circumstances weren't what you thought them. And I know you always say you wouldn't have married, dearest, but if I hadn't got past your scruples, someone else would have. I know how sought after you were—it's plain from the hostility of the matchmaking mamas to whom I'm an interloper. You can't help but—"

"Damn it, Suzette, if you say once more that I'm a prisoner of being a British gentleman—"

"I was going to say you can't help but do everything in your power to take care of people. There'd have been some other girl you'd have felt impelled to take care of."

A series of faces flashed through his mind. David's cousin Honoria Talbot, lovely, blond, self-possessed. The girl many had assumed Malcolm would marry and whom he might even have offered for if he hadn't been sure he'd make a hash of both their lives. Dark, elfin-faced Evelyn Mortimer, a poor relation who had grown up in a great house but lacked a dowry. She had cried on his shoulder one summer, and in the end he'd helped find a living for the equally penniless curate she was in love with. Elegant Jane Murchison, left on the shelf after a childhood bout with smallpox left her scarred. He'd wondered, home on leave one Christmas, if marriage to him would be preferable to spinsterhood. But in the end he'd decided it would make them both unhappy. Which was abundantly the case, as Jane had later eloped with the estate manager with whom she'd apparently been in love for years. "I doubt it," he said.

"You take care of everyone, Malcolm."

The tender mockery in Suzanne's voice scraped him raw. "But inevitably I'd have calculated the odds and decided whoever it was, was better off without me."

"And my case was so extreme you didn't think I would be?"

"On the contrary. I was terrified I was taking advantage of you. If not, I'd have proposed far sooner. It was only when Stuart pushed me—"

"Into doing your duty?"

Malcolm saw the ambassador's face that afternoon in Lisbon. "It was only when Stuart started insisting we had to find some solution for you that I realized I was more terrified he'd push you into someone else's arms than that I'd make a mull of things." He looked at his wife's clear eyes, her winged brows, the curve of her mouth, and remembered the first moment he'd seen her in the Cantabrian Mountains, face smeared with dirt and blood, eyes brilliant with life. "The truth is I wanted you. Your predicament gave me an excuse for my selfishness in offering you a marriage built on Spanish coin."

He saw a spark in her eyes—relief? triumph? fear?—quickly suppressed. "Eventually you'd have wanted someone else."

"No. Not in this way. Not to the point of throwing caution to the wind. If I hadn't met you I'd be alone." And he wouldn't have the children, either. "I suppose one could even argue I have cause to be grateful for your deception."

"No one would claim that, darling."

He dragged his gaze away. Outside the window, Crispin was on his back, with Colin and Livia sitting on his chest and Clarisse tugging at his hair, while Roxane held Jessica and Drusilla. "Crispin could marry Manon."

Suzanne's sharp laugh cut the air. "Don't be silly, darling. Men like Crispin don't marry actresses. Even Sir Horace hasn't married Jennifer Mansfield."

"Some gentlemen marry actresses. Some even marry courtesans. Henri Rivaux married Rachel Garnier."

Who had worked in a brothel. And Malcolm had helped create a cover story for Rachel to mask her past. "Henri was remarkable. And it meant a great deal to me that you helped them. But—"

"What?"

"You wouldn't have married me if you'd known the truth of my past."

He bit back the instinctive defensive quip. "I wouldn't have married you if I'd known you were a French spy. At least not if I'd known you intended to go on spying."

"And if you'd known I was a whore?" She flung the word out like a glove tossed down in challenge.

He forced himself to look honestly at his thoughts and motives. "I don't know."

Her gaze had softened. It was almost pitying. "It's not that I think you'd have considered the idea and rejected it, darling, so much as that I think it wouldn't have even occurred to you. You wouldn't have seen me as in want of protection. Not that sort of protection."

"I think you do us both a disservice. Your child would have still been in want of protection. And I'd have still—"

"Wanted me? Well, if you'd known the truth, you'd have known you could have me without marriage."

"Don't, Suzette. I wouldn't—That cheapens both of us. And no matter what, that's not a way I'd ever have seen you."

She looked at him a moment longer. He might now know she was a stranger, that she had been his enemy, but it didn't kill the tug of desire.

"Did you work with Manon Caret during the war?" he asked, drawing on his defenses, reminding himself of who his wife was and what she'd done.

He felt Suzanne's hesitation. He kept his gaze steady on her. "You're hardly betraying anything. I already know she was a French agent."

Suzanne swallowed but didn't look away. "I first met her in 1809 when I was fresh from my first mission. Later she probably saved my life when I stole some documents from the ministry of police."

"You were working against Fouché?"

"As we've discussed, intelligence alliances are complicated things."

He watched her for a moment, thinking of the friendship that had seemed to spring up so easily between his wife and the actress, and the way Suzanne had introduced Manon to Simon. "You helped Manon escape from Paris two years ago, didn't you?"

This time she didn't even hesitate. "Yes."

"With O'Roarke."

"Yes. I owed her my life, Malcolm. More than that—I owed something to all my former comrades who were hunted by Fouché's agents while I danced and dined with the victors."

He inclined his head. "I can understand that."

"Can you?"

"I understand loyalty."

"I wasn't sure you'd believe I was capable of it."

"You were loyal enough to your cause that you went into an arranged marriage for it." He studied her for a moment, this woman who had betrayed him in so many ways. "That's where you and O'Roarke met the Kestrel, isn't it?" The Kestrel had been Bertrand Laclos's nom de guerre when he rescued victims of the White Terror.

"Raoul had found him, though he didn't know the Kestrel's true identity."

"So without your rescue of Manon Caret we might not have been able to rescue Paul St. Gilles. And Bertrand might still be presumed dead and might never have been reunited with Rupert."

"Ironic the way things can work out."

"I can hardly quarrel with saving anyone from the White Terror." He turned back to the window and smiled as Crispin sat up on the lawn with all six children climbing on him. "I think you're not giving me enough credit, though, in your certainty I wouldn't have married you. And not giving Crispin enough credit when it comes to Manon." He was silent a moment. Crispin lifted a giggling Jessica overhead. "We should start thinking about Jessica's birthday," Malcolm said abruptly.

Her first birthday. Suzanne swallowed and pushed a strand of hair behind her ear. "I've started planning a party with Cordy. I'll find an excuse to cry off."

"No need. We won't let the investigation disrupt it."

"No, but—"

"It's her first birthday. We can manage to sit down to dinner with our friends." He shifted against the wall. "Have you bought her presents?"

"A stuffed cat and some blocks. And I've ordered a new dress. She'll be more interested in the paper and ribbon, if I remember from Colin's first."

Malcolm nodded. "We have a couple of birthdays before she's dictating what she wants. I ordered a strand of pearls from Asprey's. Small ones. She can wear them now on special occasions and have them as she grows."

"She'll chew on them."

"Very likely. But I wanted her to have something she could keep as she gets older. I meant to tell you. I did it when I ordered your— Your anniversary present."

She swallowed. "Fortunately, Asprey's is good about returns."

He gave a wry smile. "Having gone to the trouble of picking it out, I'd just as soon you had it."

Her throat constricted. "Malcolm—"

He gave a smile that was somehow at once honest and distant. "After all, you are still my wife."

CHAPTER 32

Suzanne slipped into the back of the Tavistock. They were in the midst of the "get thee to a nunnery" scene onstage. A relationship collapsing in the midst of treachery and divided loyalties, a woman set to spy on the man she loved. Poor Hamlet and Ophelia didn't stand a chance. Suzanne sat at the back and let the words wash over her until Simon called a break.

Manon stretched her back. "In either version, whether Hamlet is trying to protect Ophelia or disentangle himself from a spy, he could manage it more adroitly. Oh, Suzanne, thank goodness. Do come to my dressing room for a cup of tea. I've been round actors all morning."

Brandon threw a wadded-up piece of paper at her. "All morning isn't very long considering when you get up."

Manon pulled a face at him, then grinned. "So nice to have a leading man one can tease," she murmured to Suzanne as they went down the passage to her dressing room. "He's less arrogant and has a keener understanding than most." She gathered up her flounced skirts to step round a basket of props. "I understand you had a very interesting visit to Richmond yesterday. Though even after listening to Crispin talk half the night I'm not sure what it all means."

"I don't think any of us are yet."

"Crispin had me try on the emeralds. I must say they're quite lovely." Manon opened the door of her dressing room. "Tea, thank goodness. I have a headache."

Suzanne pushed the door of Manon's dressing room to and leaned against it. "Malcolm knows."

Manon spun round, the kettle in one hand. Her gaze acknowledged the fear they both lived with and went past it in the same instant. "What's your escape plan?"

"Who says I have an escape plan?"

Manon set the kettle on the spirit lamp. "An agent always has an escape plan."

"But I'm not an agent anymore. I'm a former agent who hoped to go on living quietly with her husband and children."

"There's no such thing as a former agent." Manon picked up a canister from the jumble on the chest of drawers and spooned tea into a Wedgwood teapot. "Have you thought about running?"

"Of course not."

"Suzanne."

"I can't—oh, all right, yes." Manon was perhaps the only person she could admit it to. She couldn't even discuss it with Raoul. Suzanne dropped down on the settee. Her body ached as though she'd been pummeled black-and-blue. "I did. For about five seconds."

Manon got up from the dressing table bench, picked up a bottle of cognac from atop a stack of boxes, filled a glass, and put it in Suzanne's hand. "This calls for something stronger than tea. Don't tell me you realized you couldn't bear life without him. At this point in your life, after the Peninsula and Waterloo, you should know just how much you can bear."

Suzanne closed her hand round the glass. Her fingers were shaking. She willed them to be still. "No, not that. I can't take the children away from him. I can't take him away from them."

Manon frowned, the bottle in one hand. "I'll own I've never had that problem. Roxane's father would have had an apoplexy or called me a liar if I'd named him as her parent. And Clarisse's was too busy advancing his own career to notice. Actors. Possibly the only worse choice for a lover than a fellow agent."

Suzanne pressed the glass against her temple. "There was a time I was mad enough to think I could take Colin and leave. That Malcolm would even be glad to be free of us after he'd done the honorable thing by offering us his name. That delusion fled when I saw him holding Colin in his arms. Or as soon as I could think coherently thereafter."

"And your baby girl ties you to him." Manon poured a glass for herself. "I don't suppose that pregnancy was accidental."

Suzanne tightened her fingers round the glass. "You mean did I do it to tie Malcolm to me?"

"Or to tie yourself to him?"

"Perhaps." Suzanne stared into the depths of the glass. "At least in part. The end result is the same."

Manon took a thoughtful drink of cognac. "I told you I was afraid the girls were getting too fond of Crispin. It will make it difficult when it ends."

"Who says it's going to end?" Suzanne asked, despite or perhaps because of her conversation with Malcolm the evening before.

"Love affairs always do. Your husband knowing the truth about you makes it more likely Crispin and I will part."

"Malcolm doesn't know any more about you than he did before. He won't learn more from me."

"Of course not." Manon dropped down on the settee beside Suzanne. "In any case, that's my lookout, as Crispin would say. We were talking about you. I understand not wanting to deny your children their father. But they also need their mother."

"Malcolm won't throw me out." Suzanne choked down another sip of brandy. "I thought he might, but now I see—"

"His feelings for you are too strong?"

"His feelings for me are blasted to bits. But he isn't going to deny the children one of their parents, either. He's told me as much. We're even still investigating together."

"So you're safe."

Suzanne took a swallow of cognac. It burned her throat. "I have a roof over my head and more money than nine-tenths of the world and no more risk of arrest than I did yesterday. I'm more fortunate than most former Bonapartist agents."

"And you feel as though your life's been shattered."

Suzanne cast a sidelong glance at her friend. "You claim not to believe in love."

Manon kicked off her slippers and drew her feet up onto the settee. "I claim not to believe love lasts. Quite different from denying it altogether."

"Are you telling me I'll get over it?"

Manon leaned back on the settee, arms hooked round her knees. "You'll find a way to go on, because that's who you are. You may even take another lover. As to whether you'll ever care for another man as you care for Malcolm Rannoch, I don't know."

"Careful, Manon. Take that one step further and you'll be talking like a romantic."

"I'm an actress. I know how to observe." She curled her fingers round her brandy glass. "I don't know that I could do it."

"Lose the man you love?"

"Go on living with him after the love burned itself out."

Suzanne hunched her shoulders against an inward chill. "As you said, I don't have much choice."

The whistle of the teakettle punctuated the stillness. Manon got to her feet and splashed steaming water into the teapot. "Who else knows?"

"No one. That is, Blanca told Addison. Malcolm's valet. I told her to tell him," Suzanne added at a sharp look from Manon. "He's in love with her. In fact, they're going to get married, despite the revelations. He won't betray either of us."

Manon set the lid on the teapot. "Who else might find out in the course of this investigation? Because if you're exposed, Mr. Rannoch will be suspected as well."

"That's absurd." Though Suzanne's tone was sharpened because Manon had given voice to a fear that lurked at the back of her mind.

"He's known to be a brilliant agent." Manon carried the tea tray to the hamper before the settee, an unlikely vision of domesticity as she gave voice to the harsh reality of a spy's life. "To believe he went on for years without suspecting—"

"I wouldn't let that happen."

"I don't see how you could stop it." Manon dropped back down on the settee. "They'd hardly take your word as a former Bonapartist agent yourself. Nor do I think Mr. Rannoch would stand by while you were accused."

Suzanne's hand tightened round her glass. "You're saying I've put him in even more jeopardy than I realized?"

"I'm saying you have to acknowledge the risks. To both of you. It's something you'll be living with for the rest of your lives if you stay together." Manon tilted her head back against the frayed damask of the settee. "If I learned that Crispin was a British agent— Well, I'd be shocked. It's hard to imagine someone more seemingly guileless than Crispin. And of course I wasn't working as an agent when we met. But if I had been, if I learned he'd entered into our liaison for what he could learn from me—" She turned her glass in her hand, frowning at it. "I'd be angry. At him, but mostly at myself for being so gullible. To be deceived in a lover is bad enough. For a spy to be so deceived goes to the very heart of who we are."

Suzanne tightened her grip on her glass. "Yes."

Manon turned her head and sent Suzanne a shrewd look. "As to whether I'd ever be able to get past it—I don't know. I think at some point I'd recognize that Crispin had only done something I'd have been proud to pull off myself."

Suzanne met her friend's gaze. "Are you saying you think Malcolm could get past this?" She heard the incredulity, and the suppressed undertone of hope, ripple through her own voice.

"Is that so hard to imagine? He's a spy himself. If he's honest at all—and I think he is—he has to acknowledge you've achieved something he might have done himself."

"Malcolm—" Suzanne took another drink of brandy. "Malcolm is a good agent. But I don't know that he'd ever do what I did."

"Perhaps you're underrating his abilities." Manon leaned forwards and lifted the teapot to pour two cups of tea. "Or overrating his scruples."

"He's a brilliant agent. But he's also a British gentleman. Despite Shakespeare, he thinks that honor is more than a word. I didn't just betray him, I betrayed his comrades through him. And in turn he'll think he betrayed his own honor. I don't think he'll ever get past that."

"Crispin's a British gentleman as well." Manon set a cup of tea on the chest before Suzanne. "But he can be surprisingly broad-minded."

"So can Malcolm." Suzanne picked up the cup. Before she married Malcolm, tea had been a rarely drunk, exotic beverage. "But the core is still there. Beneath the liberal reformer, beneath the Radical politician, beneath the spy. We come from different worlds."

Manon poured the last of her brandy into her tea and took a sip. "Yet you believe in many of the same things. You understand him very well. I don't think it's out of the question that he could come to understand you."

Suzanne set aside her brandy—she needed her wits about her—and took a sip of tea. Hot and astringent, the sort of jolt she needed. "I never told you—that night you escaped from Paris. When I went back to your house pretending to be you to draw off Fouché's men. A man came to the door. Pushed his way into the house. Handsome, dark haired. Obviously in love with you."

"Oh, God." Manon groaned. "Renard. The Vicomte de Valmay. He made my last months in Paris rather entertaining, but he could be importunate. What did you do?"

"Managed to pretend to be you talking through the door, but he insisted on going to sleep in the passage."

"That sounds like him."

"So I climbed out the bedchamber window and in through the dressing room window and emerged in the passage in the guise of a new housemaid."

Manon smiled. "You're a wonder, Suzanne."

"I have to confess I rather enjoyed it. But this man—Valmay—he obviously cared for you. He was desperate to know if you had another man in the room with you. When I finally assured him you did not, he settled down in front of the door to wait for morning."

"He fancied himself in love with me. Or at least he was in the moment." Manon took a sip of brandy-laced tea. "I wrote to him after I reached England. Tried to say I was sorry while making it clear the whole affair had been light for me in the hopes he'd treat it similarly."

"Was it light?"

Manon shrugged. "I couldn't afford for it to be anything else. I never can, and in this case given the climate I knew I might have to leave Paris. Probably as well I left before I could grow more fond of him." She drew a breath. "I confess it was . . . difficult when I first came here. The English are . . . different."

Suzanne smiled despite herself. "Spoken with admirable restraint."

Manon smiled as well. "I've got used to it. The fact that they don't say what they're thinking and that wall of reserve one can never break through and the casual anti-French comments they don't even seem to realize they're making. And the rain—somehow rain is so much more agreeable in Paris—and the lack of a good cup of coffee, though I finally found a passable café run by an émigré." She set down her cup and drew her feet back up onto the settee. "But even as a leading lady at the Tavistock I'll always be an outsider here."

"I know the feeling."

Manon rested her chin on her updrawn knees. "The girls are losing their accents."

Suzanne pictured her own children in the nursery that morning. "Colin and Jessica seem wholly British. With Continental polish, perhaps, but their roots are here."

Manon nodded. The look in her eyes might have been called wistful, were that not so unlike Manon. "I confess I missed Renard dreadfully at first. Like a lovesick schoolgirl. It was all bound up in my feelings about home of course. For a time I wondered—"

"If you really had loved him?"

"Well, we can all have delusions." She reached for her cup. "Finding work helped a great deal. I'll forever be grateful to you for introducing me to Simon. And then meeting Crispin helped as well. In the end I realized it was probably as well I left when I did. Renard was starting to act tiresomely like a husband, and I was in danger of letting him slip under my guard." She frowned into her cup. "As I'm afraid I've allowed Crispin to do. Crispin's so cheerfully carefree one doesn't take him seriously. Until suddenly there he is, worked into the fabric of one's life."

"He's impressed me these past days."

Manon's fingers curved round the cup. "Yes, me as well. He'll make some girl a good husband."

Suzanne studied her friend, seeking clues in Manon's contained face. "Doesn't it—"

"Bother me?" Manon tossed down a sip of tea and brandy. "Why should it? It's not as though I want to be married myself."

"You may not want to be married in the general run of things, but married to—"

"To Crispin?" Manon settled the cup in its saucer. "I care enough about Crispin not to want either of us to grow bored."

"Are you so sure you would?"

Manon gave a peal of laughter. "My dear Suzanne. When have I not?"

"People change. I never thought—"

"That one man could hold your interest?"

"That I'd believe in fidelity."

Manon shook her head. "Crispin claims to be bored by his world, but in truth he's so entrenched in it he can't see its limitations. I'm not going to turn him into a social outcast."

"You wouldn't necessarily have to. Malcolm and I have a young friend from Brussels—"

"Rachel Garnier. I know her story. Very touching. A whore who was also a spy who married a vicomte and is now accepted into Brussels society. But Mademoiselle Garnier was able to create a new identity for herself. Or rather your husband was able to create one for her." Manon shot a look at Suzanne.

"It's true," Suzanne said. "Malcolm is good at creating cover stories."

"So Mademoiselle Garnier passes as the daughter of a minor aristocrat. It's different when one has reigned over the Comédie-Française. I'm never going to blend into a new identity like Rachel or—"

"Me?"

"For example."

"I'm fortunate."

Manon pushed her loosely dressed hair back from her shoulders. "I like my life. I like being an actress. I wouldn't give it up.

Another reason marriage to Crispin would be an impossibility. Even if he considered it. Which of course he wouldn't."

Suzanne considered the way Crispin looked at Manon and saw him playing with Roxane and Clarisse the day before. "I'm not so sure of that last."

Manon shook her head. "If he has a moment of madness I shall have to talk him out of it. If he's too persistent I'll take another lover."

"I think that might tear him in two."

"He'll recover like Renard. And thank me in the end. Renard married the younger daughter of the Comte de Lisle last month. He wrote to tell me himself. He even seems to consider it a love match." She reached for the teapot to refill their cups.

"And it cost you a pang."

"No. Perhaps a bit." Manon set the teapot down. "It's another piece of my past gone. Ridiculous how eager I am to hang on to it. Cécile Vérin, one of the opera dancers from the Comédie-Française, was in London last month visiting her sister. She stopped by the Tavistock, and we talked for hours and then met for coffee the next day. I always thought her rather a vapid little thing, but I couldn't get enough of the news from home."

"I know the feeling, though I never precisely had a home in the same way." It was one of the things that would always tie Suzanne to Raoul.

Manon reached for her cup. "And then a fortnight ago it was Claude Lorraine. Do you remember him? He had a wine shop and acted as a courier. He managed to stay on in Paris during the White Terror, but recently he decided to resettle in England. We didn't work together much, but to be able to discuss missions—" She took a sip of tea. "It never will be the same as coffee. I was quite surprised to realize Claude had worked with—" She broke off in the midst of setting down her cup.

"Manon?" Suzanne leaned towards her friend. "Whom did Claude know?"

"Oh, damn." Manon returned the teacup to its saucer. "I keep forgetting you aren't one of us anymore."

"Not to hear Malcolm tell it."

"You have conflicted loyalties."

"Manon, this is important. If it's to do with France and the Tavistock it could connect to the investigation and that could be important to Crispin. I won't tell Malcolm unless I have to."

"Crispin." Manon's mouth curled round his name. "You think I have conflicted loyalties as well?"

"Yes."

"Suzanne—"

"Manon, you know what's at stake. Who else may have been a French agent?"

Manon sat back on the settee. "Very well. Claude apparently worked with Jennifer Mansfield."

CHAPTER 33

Malcolm stepped beneath the Doric portico into the solid sandstone environs of Brooks's. He had joined the club because it was the haunt of Whigs (and a way to refute his Tory father's membership in White's). But aside from dining with colleagues or stopping in after the House rose for a drink to postmortem a vote or strategize a new bill, Malcolm wasn't in the habit of spending much time at the club. There was something damnably odd about an atmosphere with no women. He preferred to be home with Suzanne and the children and to invite David and Oliver Lydgate and William Lamb and other colleagues home where Suzanne could be part of the strategizing. Yet many men spent more time in their clubs than they did at home, and it was almost a cliché that gentlemen sought refuge from domestic disturbances at their clubs. Irony bit him sharp in the throat.

He relinquished his hat and gloves to the footman and climbed the stairs to the Great Subscription Room. The white moldings, pale green walls, and rose-colored curtains had a restrained, slightly worn elegance. As though it would be a bit pretentious for the furnishings to be too new. Even the fire glowing beneath the pristine mantel had a subdued crackle. Groups of men were gathered round baize- or linen-covered tables playing hazard or whist. A murmur of voices, whiffle of cards, and rattle of dice rose to bounce off the barrel ceiling.

"Malcolm." The voice came from a sofa set to one side. It was William Lamb. He set aside the copy of the *Morning Chronicle* he'd been reading and moved a little to the side to make room for Malcolm. "Meeting someone?"

"Actually, I came in search of your father-in-law." Malcolm dropped down beside his friend.

"Bessborough?" William's eyes narrowed. "He's part of your investigation, isn't he?"

"Caroline told you?"

"A bit. With Caro it can be hard to pick out truth from hyperbole. But I gather you have questions about some sort of club Bessborough and your father were in and it touches on your current investigation."

"That's it in a nutshell." Malcolm glanced round the Subscription Room. "Is he here?"

"No, but he should be shortly if he holds true to form. My father-in-law is a creature of habit." William grinned. "Of course you realize if you're seen sitting here too long, you'll ruin your reputation as the M.P. most resistant to the charms of life at the club."

Malcolm managed an answering smile. "Good to keep people on their toes."

William folded the paper. He had a keen mind and a good eye for detail, but he gave no sign of noticing anything amiss with Malcolm. "How's Suzanne?"

"Well." Malcolm settled back on the sofa, one arm draped along its back. To anchor himself. "Busy with preparations for the holidays."

"It's your anniversary soon, isn't it?"

Christ. There was no escaping reminders of his marriage. "My word. I knew you had a memory for detail, Lamb, but I didn't know it extended to social events."

"A friend's marriage is hardly a mere social event. I remember getting the news just before Christmas."

"And were as shocked as the rest of my friends that I'd taken a wife?"

"Hardly." William pressed a crease from the paper. "I wished you"—he hesitated a moment—"every happiness." The coda *that I didn't find* lingered in the newsprint-and-claret-scented air.

"It's December seventh," Malcolm said. In two days' time. Her gift was stowed in his chest of drawers. He'd imagined giving it to her when they woke on the morning of their anniversary. Now he hoped it didn't serve as a reminder of all they had lost. "I still ask myself how I had the temerity to offer for her." That hadn't changed.

"Always knew you were a man of sense, Rannoch."

"We scarcely knew each other." That was even truer than he'd thought at the time.

"Caroline and I had known each other our whole lives." William drew a breath and set the paper aside.

"How is Caroline?"

William smoothed his fingers over the newsprint. "Tolerably well, all things considered. Calmer than she's been. Though she's got a fixation in her head about this play at the Tavistock. An alternative version of *Hamlet*?"

"That appears to be genuine." Malcolm retreated into the safer waters of investigation. "It was in the keeping of Lord Harleton. And it seems to be connected to a club he was a member of. The same one Lord Bessborough and my father were involved in. Called the Elsinore League. Ever heard of it?"

William shook his head. "I wouldn't have thought Bessborough and your father had much in common."

"Nor would I. There may be connections to their time in Ireland. Cordy and Suzanne"—somehow he couldn't call her Suzette now—"spoke with Caroline about Bessborough's involvement. That probably accounts for her interest."

"Does it?" William's voice was dry as the best fino. "I thought it was because Caroline hoped she could use it to pique Byron's interest."

"I hadn't heard."

William shot him a smile. "You're a good friend, Malcolm." He glanced down at the folded newspaper. "She says it's over. I think she protests a bit much."

"Byron's in Italy."

"Oh, I think it's over as far as Byron's concerned. But not in Caro's head." William smoothed a creased corner of the paper. "Do you have any idea how much I envy you, Malcolm?"

Malcolm's throat tightened. Was it going to be like this forever? Not being able to discuss his personal relationships with his friends? Not that he'd precisely been eager to discuss such details before, even with his closest friends. But not discussing details was different from keeping the very nature of his marriage a secret. "I think it's often easy to envy from the outside."

William gave a twisted smile. "I've seen you with Suzanne. That night a fortnight ago when we went to Berkeley Square after the House rose and hammered out the details of the Habeas Corpus argument. It's as though your minds lock together." His fingers curled round the sofa arm. "I love Caro. I think she loved me when we married. Perhaps she still does. But our minds couldn't be more different. I don't understand her." He leaned forwards and scrubbed his hands over his face. "God knows I've tried."

It was nothing anyone who had observed the tortured marriage of William and Caroline Lamb didn't know, but it was the first time Malcolm had ever heard such words from his reserved friend. William didn't speak about his feelings any more easily than Malcolm did himself. He touched William's arm. "Caro's been troubled since childhood."

William stared at his hands. "Sometimes, more than anything else, I long for peace," he said in a low voice. "And yet when I think of life without her—It's like blotting out the sun."

Malcolm's fingers tightened. He couldn't think of a more apt description of life without Suzanne. The Suzanne he thought he'd known. And yet that Suzanne was gone.

"In some ways she'll always be the girl I married," William said. "Or at least I'll always see her that way. And yet—one can't go back. As much as she swears the past is done, as much as I swear to put it behind us, it's always there, at the back of one's mind. Infidelity casts a long shadow."

"It makes it difficult to trust. And intimacy and trust go hand in hand."

William shot a look at him. "Well spoken for a man who's never had to deal with the loss of either."

Malcolm looked into his friend's gaze. It would mean a lot to answer William's honesty with honesty, but he couldn't do so without risking Suzanne's safety and his children's future. "You deserve better, William."

"In many ways I'm more fortunate than most. If—Oh, here's Bessborough." William lifted a hand to signal his wife's father.

"William." Bessborough moved towards them and recognized his son-in-law's companion. "Good lord, Malcolm, what are you doing here? Don't tell me that pretty wife of yours has given you cause to seek refuge?" He gave the hearty laugh of one who didn't believe it for a moment.

"Actually, I was hoping for a word with you, sir."

"With me?" Bessborough's eyes narrowed. He cast a glance round the room, then dropped down in a chair beside Malcolm and William. "See here, Rannoch, I already told your wife everything I know about the Dunboyne business. Sorry if you don't believe me—"

"Actually, I wanted to talk to you about the events of a decade or so earlier. You spent time in Paris in the 1780s, didn't you?"

For a moment, Malcolm would have sworn Bessborough's impulse was to turn tail and run. Instead the earl settled back in his chair, arms folded in a defensive posture. "Here and there. Pretty much everyone used to pop over to Paris regularly before the Revolution."

"Did you spend time with my fath—Alistair Rannoch and Dewhurst and Sir Horace Smytheton?"

"Among others. Smytheton and Dewhurst were more or less expatriates in those days. Your father spent a lot of time in Paris as well. Used to take a house and give very agreeable parties. He and Dewhurst rather tended to compete, but they were two peas in a pod politically. Loyal not so much to the king as to what the monarchy stood for. They disliked Necker because he'd supported the American Revolution. And I remember them going on one evening about Cardinal Rohan. Got quite vicious. But then they were both supporters of Marie Antoinette, so Rohan's opposition to the Austrian alliance had never sat well with them. They were quite smug when he fell from power over the affair of the necklace."

Malcolm leaned back in his chair. "Were you involved in smuggling works of art?"

Bessborough's shoulders jerked straight. "What the devil—"

"Would you prefer it if William left?"

Bessborough's gaze shot to his son-in-law. "No, I think I prefer to have him present."

"I know about the Elsinore League smuggling art treasures, sir. It seems to be the source of the collection I inherited from my father."

"Alistair would go on about art, and he couldn't afford half the things he coveted. Always thought it was dangerous." Bessborough drew a breath and cast a sidelong glance at his daughter's husband.

"Sir—" William leaned forwards, hesitated, glanced at Malcolm. "I don't believe Malcolm will share information on those sorts of details from three decades ago. He's trying to unravel a larger mystery."

Bessborough released his breath and leaned back. "Took a few pieces." He seemed almost relieved to speak. "Harriet liked them. Brightened up the house. Until—"

"Your debts got the better of you," William said.

"Just so." Bessborough met his son-in-law's gaze squarely.

"But you were still involved?" Malcolm asked.

"Helped them out a bit after that."

"For a share of the profits?" William asked.

Bessborough shifted in his chair. "Er . . . yes."

"Did they ever smuggle jewels?" Malcolm asked.

"Jewels?" Bessborough coughed. "No, it was art they wanted."

"They never smuggled diamonds?"

Bessborough gripped the arms of his chair. "What the devil do you know?"

"Not nearly enough. So they did smuggle diamonds?"

Bessborough's gaze shifted to the side. "I think that may be what gave them the idea for the whole enterprise. It was before the

Revolution. Eighty-five or '86. Dewhurst gave me passage back to England on his yacht. Never one to stint, Dewhurst. Had the devil of a head and went looking for some claret. Opened a crate and picked up a bottle only to hear it rattle and see something sparkling inside. Dewhurst came into the cabin and nearly took my head off. Then later he said he was having a necklace made for his mistress and not to make too much of it. But if that was the case, I don't know why he acted so concerned in the first place. Later, when the art smuggling began, I decided he must have got his start with diamonds."

"When was this?" Malcolm asked.

"I told you, '85 or '86."

"Can you remember which?"

Bessborough frowned. "Must have been '85. Probably October. Harriet was pregnant, and Caro was born not long after I got back. Is that important?"

"It may be very important indeed," Malcolm said.

"Suzanne, my dear." Jennifer greeted her with a smile. "Do come in. I'm just having a cup of tea and going over Simon's notes. I've always been good with lines, but I find I have the most dreadful time keeping this version straight from the original. Let me pour you a cup of tea."

There was something to be said for the British ritual of tea, Suzanne thought as she settled herself on the faded blue-striped chintz of the sofa. It gave one something to do with one's hands. "I've just been talking to Manon," she said. "I didn't realize you and Claude Lorraine were acquainted."

Jennifer went still, the blue-and-white teapot in one hand. Then she filled a cup and set down the teapot without rattling the china. "How foolish. I should have guessed Manon would put the pieces together. I don't think I realized what good friends you are. You take milk, don't you?" She added milk to the tea and gave the cup to Suzanne with a steady hand.

Suzanne took a sip of tea. "You must have been surprised to see Claude."

"Or I'd have been more discreet? You're quite right, I didn't handle it at all well. But now what's done is done and there's no sense wasting breath denying it."

"Those old rumors didn't lie, did they?"

Jennifer studied her own blue transferware teacup. "I never thought of myself as a Revolutionary precisely. Merely a French-woman, who thought conditions in my country were intolerable." She took a sip of tea and regarded Suzanne with a level gaze over the rim of the cup. "I make no excuses for the excesses of the Revolution. I refuse to take responsibility for such madness. But the excesses didn't make me want to go back to 1788."

"I can understand that."

"Can you? I believe your own family fled France during the Terror."

Was it Suzanne's imagination or did Jennifer lay the slightest stress on "believe"? "My parents were far from monarchists," Suzanne said truthfully.

Jennifer leaned forwards and picked up the milk jug. "It was difficult in those days for France to sort out our future. And I confess I took distinct exception to Britain attempting to dictate what that future should be." She splashed milk into her tea.

"I can understand that. I confess I didn't at all care for the sight of Allied soldiers thronging the boulevards after Waterloo." Suzanne took another sip of tea. "I think many Spaniards felt the same about both Britain and France during the war in the Peninsula. And so you became an agent for your country?"

Jennifer picked up a silver spoon and stirred her tea. "Spoken with such charming restraint, Mrs. Rannoch. Yes, it was much as I told you and your husband. As an actress with throngs of young men crowding my dressing room after performances—I don't mean to boast, but I believe one could call them throngs—I was in an admirable position to gather intelligence. English aristos could still come over to France and they tended to flock to the theatre. Actresses rather have a reputation." She took a sip of tea. "Some of it deserved."

"Your masters wanted you to infiltrate the British expatriates working with the Royalists?"

"Who were already using the theatre as a meeting place. Dewhurst was my first target. He presented a challenge. Whatever he was, he wasn't a fool."

"And Sir Horace," Suzanne said.

"Quite, as Horace would say. Horace was in Paris more and my handlers thought he'd make a better source than Dewhurst. Odd now to think how these things begin." Jennifer lifted the cup and cradled it in her hand. "Horace and I settled into a routine. We were supposed to be partners working for the Royalist cause. In fact, I was gathering intelligence from him. But as time went on, I found I relished the partnership more than anything."

Suzanne's fingers tightened round her cup.

Jennifer leaned forwards to refill her cup. "Intelligence has a certain glamour when one is young and the cause is young. The compromises, the double crosses, the petty betrayals, the collateral damage. They all begin to add up. One looks at one's children and thinks of the future. Not an abstract future but a specific one." She sat back and looked at Suzanne. "You're young, but I think you've been in the game long enough to understand."

"My husband left the game," Suzanne said. "As best he could."

Jennifer's mouth curved in a smile. "Yes, one can never really leave. But I had some fellow spies who were sympathetic. They were able to start the rumors that I was suspected for my supposed Royalist activities. Then of course Horace was determined to get me safely to England." She glanced into the depths of her cup and shook her head. "More than anything I think it would bother Horace that his great act of daring in getting me out of Paris was in fact carefully orchestrated by French agents. I'd like to spare him that at least."

"He never learned the truth?" Suzanne said.

Jennifer shook her head. "Dear God, he would curse himself for a fool. We settled in England. I went to work at the Tavistock and Horace became a patron. We had a child. I did my best to forget I'd ever been a French agent. Much of the time I actually succeeded." She looked at Suzanne again, like an aunt regarding a favorite niece. "You're probably too young to understand this. But there's a point where whom one looks at across the breakfast dishes every morning matters more than one would have thought possible. At least for some of us." She set down her teacup. "I think I'm safe from prosecution. After all, I didn't betray the British. But I don't know that Horace will be able to forgive me. One could say it's only what I deserve."

Suzanne tightened her grip on her teacup. Here was someone she could confide in, but for a host of reasons she could not do so. How many families had been smashed by this investigation? "Sir Horace loves you very much."

Jennifer reached for her teacup. "Horace loves the woman he thought I was."

"Surely by now that's who you are. You said in the end what mattered was looking at him over the breakfast dishes."

"To me. But I'm not sure I'll ever be able to persuade Horace of that." Jennifer took a quick sip of tea. "But that's my lookout, as Horace would say. I'm sure you have more questions for me?"

Suzanne swallowed, at once wanting to linger in personal waters and relieved to be clear of them. "You worked with my husband's father—Alistair Rannoch?"

"No." Jennifer returned her cup to its saucer. "I didn't work with Alistair as a French agent."

"Did you know he was a French agent?"

"No." Jennifer twisted her cup in its saucer. "That's the thing, my dear. The thing I couldn't tell you when you and your husband informed me Alistair was a French spy. Well, not without blowing my own cover, and I fear my protective instincts were too strong. I had no notion Alistair was a French spy. In fact, I'm quite sure he wasn't."

Suzanne had thought she was beyond surprise, but she blinked like a novice instead of a trained investigator. "How can you be sure?" As Raoul often said, there were dozens of spymasters.

"Because before Dewhurst I was supposed to be gathering intelligence from Alistair. Who was a Royalist agent."

"You're sure it wasn't simply a case of one intelligence network not knowing what another was doing? You know how muddied the intelligence game can be."

Jennifer shook her head. "I too have little faith in the perspicacity of spymasters, but my masters knew too much about him. Besides—" Her mouth curved in a faint smile. "If I do say so myself, if Alistair had been a French agent I would have discovered it."

"That I confess has the ring of truth."

"Thank you." Jennifer splashed some more milk into her tea. "Alistair was working with the Royalists and genuinely trying to help them. But his real interest was the Elsinore League."

"You mean his real interest was indulging himself?"

"No. That is, he certainly did indulge himself. But the Elsinore League was far more than a hellfire club."

Suzanne leaned forwards. She had the odd sense they had got to the heart of the investigation. "They smuggled works of art."

"That was the least of it." Jennifer frowned. "Horace still won't discuss it. But their work was political."

"On which side?"

"Well, obviously not the French."

"Are you saying the Elsinore League were working for the British? Or the Royalists?"

"By process of elimination." Jennifer twisted a heavy citrine ring round her finger. "I woke in the middle of the night once to hear Horace arguing with Alistair and Dewhurst. Try as I might—and I tried hard—I couldn't make out the substance of the argument. But I heard Horace protesting about the risks they were running. And Alistair say, 'This isn't a game, Horace. I think you forget what we're fighting for. What we've always been fighting for from the first. And to whom we owe our allegiance.'"

Suzanne kept her gaze close on the other woman's face. "Which you took to mean—"

Jennifer studied the play of lamplight on the pale yellow stone in her ring. "I have no proof. But ever since then I've suspected the Elsinore League was a British spy ring."

CHAPTER 34

"Mr. O'Roarke!"

At Colin's cry, Laura looked up from Jessica, who was crab-crawling over the paving stones at a rapid clip. Colin had run to the Berkeley Square fence and was clutching the black metal railing, pulling Berowne with him. The cat let out a squawk at the sudden change of direction. A tall figure in a gray greatcoat was approaching along Berkeley Street. He stopped, lifted his hand to Colin, hesitated a moment, then approached the square.

"Good day, young Colin."

"Have you come to see Mummy and Daddy?" Colin scooped up Berowne. "They're Investigating. But you could come in and see us."

Laura watched a reluctant smile spread across O'Roarke's face. Colin was hard to resist. Still O'Roarke hesitated a few moments longer, then moved to the square gate. Laura had the oddest sense that in doing so he was moving far more than a few steps and that his feelings about the move were decidedly conflicted.

Jessica paused in her crawling to study the new arrival, one hand on the paving stones.

"She has her own way of crawling," Colin said.

"It seems quite effective," O'Roarke observed as Jessica resumed crawling, left leg tucked under her, right foot flat on the paving stones, left hand propelling herself forwards, right raised in the air, clutching a leaf.

O'Roarke tipped his hat to Laura. "Miss Dudley, isn't it?"

Laura got to her feet and inclined her head. "Mr. O'Roarke."

Colin tugged at O'Roarke's arm. "Can you throw a ball? Daddy plays catch with me, but he's been busy."

"I think I can manage." O'Roarke hesitated a fraction of a second. "I used to play catch with your father when he was a boy."

Colin stared at him. "That was a long time ago."

"So it was."

Colin relinquished Berowne's lead to Laura and snatched up the ball. He made a slightly erratic throw, which O'Roarke caught one-handed. Colin let out a whistle of approval. "Wizard."

O'Roarke shrugged off his greatcoat and the game continued for about ten minutes. Wind cut through the square, tingling Laura's cheeks and slicing through the merino and broadcloth of her gown and pelisse, but the children seemed impervious. As did O'Roarke. Laura studied the man and boy. O'Roarke was younger than she had realized, probably not much more than fifty and fit for a man of his age. Which made sense for a veteran of the Peninsular War. They said he had fought with the *guerrilleros* and before that in Ireland. He'd known Mr. Rannoch since he was a boy and had met Mrs. Rannoch after her marriage. Presumably. Her contact's words from yesterday ran through Laura's mind.

At length, Jessica crawled into the midst of the game. O'Roarke rolled the ball between her and Colin for a time, then left them to play and dropped down on the bench beside Laura.

"You're kind to them," she said.

"They're engaging children." He watched as Colin carefully angled the ball to his sister. "One forgets. I'm not about children much."

"You seem very adept with them."

"I spent more time with young ones in the past."

"With Mr. Rannoch."

"Yes, among others." He settled back on the bench. "I was friends with the family when he was a boy."

Rather a good friend if he'd taught Malcolm Rannoch how to play catch, though from the little Laura had seen of Alistair Rannoch, it was difficult to imagine him in that role. Laura watched Jessica crawl over the paving stones after the ball. "She crawls all over the house, but for some reason she seems to enjoy the paving stones."

"Her mother's sense of adventure."

Impossible not to wonder if those few words held more than passing knowledge of Suzanne Rannoch, though two days ago Laura probably wouldn't have noticed. "She definitely has that." Laura stroked the cat, curled up in her lap.

"They're fortunate to have you."

It sounded oddly like thanks. Laura met his gaze. "Mr. and Mrs. Rannoch are very devoted parents. They spend far more time with their children than most parents in their set. It makes a nurse or governess less important."

"Still. You're with them a great deal. You went to work for them in Paris?"

The question was asked in the lightest, most casual of tones, but all her defenses slammed into place. "Yes. Mrs. Rannoch said she knew she'd found the right governess when I didn't bat an eyelash when the kitten jumped up on the tea tray and began to lap the cream during our interview." Laura rubbed Berowne behind the ears.

"Clearly the right quality for this family. Did you expect to take up residence in England?"

"She warned me Mr. Rannoch was considering leaving the diplomatic service." Laura had felt mixed emotions at the news, though she'd had little choice. She'd been under orders.

O'Roarke leaned back on the bench in the sort of posture that invited confidences. "Happy to return to England?"

"In a way. I went to work on the Continent in search of adventure." That much was true, though she'd found far more than she could possibly admit to. "But England seems less staid and dull now. Or perhaps I've grown more cautious as I've grown older."

"Spoken by a very young woman."

"Not so very young. I've been a governess for some time." And she'd hardly been in the first blush of youth when she became a governess, but she glossed over those early years, as they were difficult to account for.

O'Roarke shifted on the bench and crossed his legs. "There is something about home. Something one perhaps doesn't appreciate until one is older."

She turned her head to look at him, aware of her bonnet brim impeding her view. "But England isn't home for you, is it?"

"No, for all the time I've spent here. In truth I've lived so many places it's difficult to call any home. But I suppose I'll always think of Ireland and Spain and France as home before England."

She turned her head to look at him. It was a personal admission, and he did not seem a man who made personal admissions easily. Letting down his guard? Or giving the appearance of doing so to make a breach in her own defenses?

"It must be agreeable to be close to your family after so many years," he said.

Her defenses slammed into place. "My family are gone," she said, in the tone she'd mastered to discuss them.

"I'm sorry. Particularly difficult at Christmas."

For a moment she could taste mulled wine and disappointment on her tongue. Berowne let out a yowl of protest as her fingers tightened on his fur. She hoped O'Roarke would put it down to painful memories. Which was the truth, though not in the way he thought. Her family would be gathering for the holidays soon. They were far from gone. The only way she'd been able to risk coming back to England was the certainty that her path would not cross with theirs. Only of course, she couldn't really be sure of it at all. She couldn't so much as leave the house without half-expecting to catch a familiar face out of the corner of her eye.

"I'm accustomed to being on my own." She gave Berowne an apologetic stroke between the ears. Mollified, he twisted his head so she could scratch under his chin. "And Christmas is really a holiday for children after all."

"So it is." O'Roarke's gaze followed Colin as he retrieved the ball from a hedge under Jessica's watchful eyes.

"Do you have children of your own?" Laura asked.

"No, I haven't been so fortunate." His tone was easy, but she was skilled enough at keeping her own defenses in place to recognize them in others. "So I enjoy the children of my friends."

"As do I. That is, of my employers." She forced her fingers not to tighten on Berowne's fur again.

Jessica crawled over to the bench with determination and pulled herself up. A smile broke across O'Roarke's face. "Well done, Miss Jessica."

"Ma," Jessica announced, and pointed straight up in the air.

"You don't say," O'Roarke said.

Laura smiled despite herself. "Mrs. Rannoch says she despairs of ever being certain Jessica means her when she says 'mama' because she uses it for so many things."

Jessica gripped the edge of the bench and bounced on her heels, face screwed up with concentration beneath her red velvet hat.

O'Roarke reached out and touched her small hand. Again, Laura had the sense he was giving way to impulse against his better judgment. "It's a big thing, I would think, to hear one's child say one's name for the first time."

Laura's throat closed as though she had swallowed hot coals. "Yes," she said. "I would think so as well."

"Malcolm." Crispin nearly collided with Malcolm in the passage outside the Subscription Room at Brooks's. "Thank God, I was looking for you. That is, I came here because I couldn't think where else to go, but you're just the person I want to see. Can we talk?"

Crispin's hair was even more disordered than usual, his face haggard, his gaze dark with confusion. "Of course." Malcolm took his friend's arm and steered him into the nearest sitting room. "What's happened?"

Crispin took a turn about the room, sat down, ran a hand through his hair, sprang to his feet, sat down again. "Manon's told me. She said you already knew." He stared at Malcolm, fear overtaking the confusion in his gaze. "I hope to God she's right or I've just been an unconscionable fool."

"I suspected." Malcolm dragged a shield-back chair over and

sat facing his friend. "And you haven't admitted anything. You're to be commended."

Crispin slumped back and stared at the plaster frieze on the ceiling. "Manon thought—I'm not sure what. That I'd throw her over or something. As if—I mean she was only spying for her country. It's no more than you've done."

Malcolm nearly choked. "A novel viewpoint."

Crispin's gaze shifted to Malcolm's face. "I'll own the revelations about Father surprised me, but he was spying on his own side. Betraying people he knew."

"So you find the thought of betraying strangers easier?"

"You're the spy. You tell me."

Malcolm swallowed. He felt as though he'd taken a mouthful of burned coffee. "It corrodes either way. But though it shouldn't be worse with people one knows, of course it is."

Crispin nodded. "Manon says I'll never understand and she wouldn't want me to. I daresay she's right. All I need to know is that it doesn't change the way I feel about her." He paused, then said as though relishing the words, "I'm going to marry her."

"My dear fellow. I'm happy for you." The words came unbidden. Oddly, as with Addison, Malcolm found he meant it.

"Shocked?" Crispin straightened his shoulders and lifted his chin. He put Malcolm in mind of a defiant schoolboy.

"Surprised."

Crispin faced him squarely. "Because she's an actress or because of the other?"

"Both. One doesn't expect—"

"Gentlemen to marry their mistresses?" Crispin's mouth twisted. "That's what Manon says. I'm still trying to talk her into it. But I will. I'd made up my mind to it before I even knew about all this. Now it's more vital than before. How else can I protect her and the girls?"

Manon Caret did not strike Malcolm as a woman who would take kindly to the idea of being protected, any more than Suzanne would. "If you want to persuade her, stress protecting the girls."

"Yes, that's what I thought." Crispin's fingers tightened on the arms of his chair. "I'm not going to be talked out of it."

"Have I tried to talk you out of it?"

"No." Crispin sat back in his chair. "I was sure you would."

"My dear fellow," Malcolm said, without planning his words. "I wish you very happy. And I have the greatest admiration for you. You're a brave man."

"I'm a man in love."

"Love is an act of bravery."

CHAPTER 35

Colin's and Jessica's voices carried on the air as Suzanne approached Berkeley Square. Normalcy. At least their lives were still untouched. Though sooner or later surely they would notice the constraint between their parents. Colin was a sensitive child and sharp-eyed. She was surprised he hadn't picked up on it already. Still, for the moment, Suzanne could indulge herself in the fantasy that all was as it had been.

She started across the street to the garden and saw what had been hidden by a tree. A man sitting on the bench beside Laura. All Suzanne could see was the back of a beaver hat and shoulders of a gray greatcoat, but something in the angle of his head was unmistakable. She quickened her steps.

"Mummy." Colin ran over to the black metal railing. "Mr. O'Roarke came to see us. Well, to see you, but he played catch with me. And Jessica, she can roll the ball. Wasn't that splendid of him?"

"Splendid." Suzanne put a hand on her son's head, anchoring herself. "Good day, Mr. O'Roarke."

"Mrs. Rannoch." Raoul lifted his hat.

"Where's Daddy?" Colin asked. "Is he Investigating somewhere else?"

"Just so, darling. He'll be along in a bit." Suzanne stepped through the square gate. Jessica crawled over the paving stones and flung her arms round Suzanne's knees. As Suzanne scooped her up, Malcolm came into view down Hill Street. Suzanne swallowed at the image they must present, she holding Jessica, Colin chattering to Raoul. But after a brief gaze that took in the scene, Malcolm merely said, "O'Roarke. I suppose you have news."

"Yes. Forgive me for calling unexpectedly—"

"No, it's as well. Let's go in the house."

"Mr. O'Roarke threw a ball with me, Daddy," Colin announced.

"Splendid, old chap. Very good of him. I know I haven't been playing with you as much as I should."

Colin's gaze shot from Malcolm to Raoul. Suzanne realized that her fairy-tale window of the children being deaf and blind to the undercurrents in the house was fast closing.

They crossed the street to the house and went into the library, just as they had the day Malcolm asked Raoul about his parentage. *Three—was it really only three?—days ago.* A different world in which Malcolm had been able to turn to her for comfort.

"I know I'm the last person you want to see just now," Raoul said.

Malcolm gave a dry smile. "I think Fouché ranks a bit higher on the list."

Raoul's answering smile was equally dry but had a bit less of an edge. "For once I can say I'm pleased to be outranked by Fouché."

Malcolm waved a hand towards the Queen Anne chairs. "Sit down, O'Roarke. We're still in the midst of an investigation."

Raoul dropped into one of the chairs. Suzanne sat on the sofa. Rather to her surprise, Malcolm sat beside her instead of taking the other chair, though not close enough to touch, even accidentally.

Raoul leaned forwards, fingers tented together. "I think it's time—probably past time—I told you both what I know about the Elsinore League."

"You mean you know as well?" Suzanne asked, startled into speech.

Raoul's gaze shot to her. "What do you know?"

Malcolm looked from her to Raoul. "You mean they *were* a French spy ring?" he asked, overlapping Raoul's question.

"Not according to Jennifer Mansfield." Suzanne picked her way through Jennifer's revelations. "She thinks they were a British spy ring."

"With two French agents as members?"

"Malcolm—" She wasn't going to be able to keep Jennifer's confidence. But Jennifer herself had seen that. "According to Jennifer, Alistair wasn't a French spy."

"How does she know?"

It still stuck in Suzanne's throat to betray someone else's secrets. "Because the French set her to gather intelligence on Alistair."

"She was a good agent," Raoul said.

"You knew?" Suzanne asked.

He nodded. "I knew most French agents. It's why I could never credit the supposed revelations about Alistair."

Malcolm glanced at Raoul, then looked back at Suzanne. "Tell me. Tell me everything she said."

Suzanne recounted her exchange with Jennifer Mansfield. "I have to say I believe her when she says that if Alistair were a French agent she'd have found evidence of it," she concluded.

Malcolm gave a short laugh. "Her talents ranking considerably higher than mine."

"But she was looking for evidence, darling. You had no reason to investigate me."

"Very true. I was too blind even to see the need to look for it. If Alistair wasn't a French spy how do you account for the letters to Harleton?"

"The references to the Raven are because somehow he knew about me and knew what his daughter-in-law being exposed would do to the family."

"Whatever his opinion of his putative son. All right, that makes sense. But when he talked about how they could ruin each other—"

"I think he was talking about the Elsinore League," Raoul said.

Malcolm's gaze shot back to Raoul. "Was Jennifer Mansfield right? Were they a British spy ring? And if so why do you know when Carfax doesn't? Although knowing Carfax, he could have simply had his reasons for not telling me."

"Very likely," Raoul said. "But as it happens they are not a British spy ring. Nor are they simply a hellfire club."

"Jennifer said she overheard Alistair saying they had to remember what they were fighting for and to whom they owed their allegiance," Suzanne said. "To whom do they owe their allegiance?"

Raoul's mouth curved. "Themselves."

"You mean they were driven by self-interest?" Malcolm said. "In the service of what?"

Raoul sat back in his chair. "I can't claim to have been privy to the group's founding. I went to university in Paris, and I wouldn't have been in their set in any case. But as I understand it, this group of young men joined forces with the aim of working to ensure their mutual benefit."

"In politics?" Malcolm asked.

"In politics. In the army. I think the goal was at first to work within Britain, but some, your fath—Alistair in particular, had ambitions with larger scope. They saw that the world was changing. Like many, they wanted to influence that change. But not in the service of a particular set of beliefs or ruler or even a particular country. The goal of the Elsinore League is to maintain a balance of power on the Continent favorable to the League's members."

Suzanne stared at him and felt Malcolm doing the same. "You're saying they tried to influence international events to benefit themselves?" Malcolm asked.

"I'm saying they did." Raoul crossed one booted foot over the other. "They're powerful men. They've pooled their resources to become even more powerful." He smoothed a crease from his sleeve. "Did you ever wonder why two astute politicians like Castlereagh and Canning let things get so far between them that they actually fought a duel and Canning ended up wounded?"

"The Elsinore League were behind that?" Suzanne asked.

Malcolm's mouth tightened. "Father never liked Canning."

"In the fallout, Alistair received a cabinet position himself," Raoul said. "And Dewhurst was able to get funding for his Royalist activities which Canning had been holding up. I'm quite sure the League are also responsible for exacerbating Wellington's difficulties after his time in India. Wellington's temper is certainly part of it, but without the League, Richard Wellesley would have been able to get his brother a command in the Peninsula much sooner."

"So in that case their interference benefited the French," Suzanne said.

"Inadvertently."

"And Hugo Cyrus was promoted to general," Malcolm said.

"Quite."

"How do they do it?" Malcolm asked. "Blackmail?"

"Frequently. Sometimes more complicated ruses worthy of an intelligence mission. There are enough of them to provide cover for each other, and the one who gets his hands dirty is rarely anywhere close to benefiting from that particular manipulation. They have friends and relatives to protect them. And they've made themselves feared."

"I wonder if they knew Lord Harleton was a French spy," Suzanne said.

"They must have done," Malcolm said. "Dewhurst suspected him."

"I suspect they'd have seen it as an advantage," Raoul said. "In aiming for a balance of power favorable to their own interests, it would help to have a foot in both camps. Or rather several camps."

"Did you know Harleton was a member when you recruited him?" Suzanne asked, before she could think twice.

"You recruited Harleton?" Malcolm asked Raoul.

"For my sins. And yes, I suspected he was an Elsinore League member at the time. It was part of why I thought he'd make a doubly interesting asset."

Malcolm folded his arms. "So Harleton and my wife shared a spymaster."

"I hadn't thought of it that way," Raoul said, "but you could say so. Save that Harleton was purely a source of information, not a field agent. And I never trusted him."

"And you trusted me?" Suzanne asked, genuinely curious. It wasn't a word they used easily.

"As much as I trusted anyone."

"How did you learn about the Elsinore League in the first place?" Malcolm asked. "Did they try to recruit you?"

Raoul laughed. "Hardly. As I said, I didn't run in their circles."

"How then?" Malcolm's gaze drilled into the other man.

Raoul hesitated. Suzanne saw his fingers tense on the chair arms. "From your mother."

Malcolm's gaze locked on Raoul's own. "She stumbled across evidence in Alistair's things?"

"There was no stumbling about it. Arabella had been investigating the Elsinore League for years."

Malcolm stared at the enemy spymaster who had fathered him. "She—O'Roarke, are you saying you recruited my mother to spy for you?"

Raoul returned his gaze. Suzanne saw something shift in her former lover's eyes, something she could not have put a name to, save that she had the oddest sense they were about to step over some sort of invisible barrier. "No," Raoul said. "I'm saying she recruited me."

CHAPTER 36

Suzanne could not suppress a gasp. Malcolm's gaze was trained on Raoul. "My mother recruited you to be a French spy?"

"No. Arabella's sympathies were surprisingly liberal, but she was loyal to her country. She was working against the Elsinore League."

Malcolm shook his head in disbelief. "How——"

"I believe she learned about them when she was on the Continent with your grandfather. Talleyrand may have told her some details, possibly Peter of Courland as well."

"They're known abroad?" Suzanne asked.

"Oh yes. I believe they have international members."

"Is Talleyrand a member?" Malcolm asked.

"I've wondered about that, though I'm now inclined to think he was more interested in investigating the League. Which may be why he piqued Arabella's interest. At first I think she was merely curious. Later——"

"After Tatiana was born," Malcolm said.

"Yes. Learning about the League became a welcome focus, a distraction. But the more she learned about them, the more convinced she became that they needed to be stopped."

"And you?"

"Agreed with her. They were opposed to everything I was working for—in Ireland, in France, in Britain. Even as I worked for other causes that one remained."

Malcolm swallowed. Suzanne could see the past swirling like bits of mosaic in his head. "Is that why she married my—Alistair?"

"She denied it was the only reason, but I think it was part of it. She already knew he was one of the founders."

"Dear God."

Suzanne touched her husband's arm, dragging him back to the present.

"Why in God's name didn't you tell us any of this sooner?" Malcolm asked.

Raoul drew in and released his breath. "Because I had given my word to your mother. She didn't want you involved. The League have proved themselves willing to kill those who stand in their way. And I think she didn't want to put further strain on your relationship with Alistair."

Malcolm gave a short laugh.

"You thought of him as your father," Raoul said. "Or at least Arabella believed you did."

Malcolm drew a breath.

"I can understand if you have trouble believing it," Raoul said.

"No." Malcolm frowned at his hands. "The odd thing is I've never been able to make sense of why my mother married Alistair. This at least has some logic to it." He looked up at Raoul. "Did she use her knowledge of the League to force Alistair to get you out of Ireland?"

Raoul's mouth tightened. "It was more than that. Simply knowing about the League wouldn't have hurt Alistair. They were too careful. Arabella had learned something about a particular mission of theirs, something she could tie Alistair to directly. Something that would destroy him."

"What?" Malcolm's voice was frayed to the breaking point.

"She wouldn't tell me. I had to piece together that it was even to do with the League."

Malcolm pushed himself to his feet and took a turn about the room. "I think I may have an idea. In October of 1785 Bessborough saw diamonds hidden in a bottle of claret on Dewhurst's yacht. We found loose diamonds hidden at Harleton's house. And Bessborough mentioned that Dewhurst and Alistair hated Cardinal de Rohan."

This time it was Raoul's turn to look at Malcolm in shock. "Good God."

"Malcolm." Suzanne stared at her husband. "Are you saying Alistair and Dewhurst and Harleton stole the queen's diamonds?"

"The irony being that they never really were the queen's diamonds." Raoul ran a hand over his hair as though in an effort to reorder his thoughts. "In fact, the necklace was designed for a royal mistress."

"Madame de Pompadour," Malcolm said. "Louis the Fifteenth commissioned the necklace for her, didn't he? But then the king died before it was paid for."

"And the jewelers tried to sell it to Marie Antoinette." Suzanne conjured up bits and pieces of the story she'd heard as a child. "But she refused."

"Perhaps because she didn't want a necklace that had been designed for her father-in-law's mistress," Raoul said. "Perhaps because she saw the folly of such extravagance in a time of privation. She wasn't nearly so heedless as her reputation would lead one to believe. Leaving the jewelers in a quandary. Until an enterprising young woman named Jeanne de la Motte enters the picture."

"Did you know her?" Suzanne asked.

"I met her once or twice. Striking. And a keen understanding. Under different circumstances she might have made a good agent. She seems to have been driven by personal ambition. She and her lover tried to entrap Cardinal de Rohan into buying the necklace by creating a false correspondence with Marie Antoinette in which the queen asked him to buy it for her. They even hired a prostitute to impersonate the queen. Supposedly their motive was greed. They planned to make off with the necklace themselves. But I've always wondered if there was more to their choice of Rohan."

"Dewhurst was in France then," Malcolm said. "He'd gone to school there. Alistair and Harleton were in and out. They could have found Jeanne, they could have financed her."

"She was tried," Suzanne said. "She didn't implicate them."

"She was probably well paid not to." Malcolm took another turn about the room. "She sought refuge in England after she got out of prison."

"And they hid the diamonds?" Suzanne asked.

"They couldn't have sold them," Raoul said. "At least not all at once. They might have taken bits and pieces through the years."

Malcolm nodded. "Aunt Frances has a diamond pendant Alistair gave her, a particularly fine stone. I wouldn't be surprised if—" He broke off.

"It's all right," Raoul said. "I already knew about Fanny and Alistair."

"I should have realized. You seem to know more family secrets than I do myself. More to the point," Malcolm continued, "the diamonds could be what Harleton was referring to in his quarrel with Alistair when he said Alistair would take 'it,' too, given the chance."

Suzanne shook her head. "To meddle on that level—"

"They wouldn't have known quite the extent of it at the time," Raoul said. "If Malcolm is right, their aim was to bring down Rohan. They're clever men, but I doubt they foresaw that the public wouldn't believe Marie Antoinette was innocent of the conspiracy. That the affair of the necklace would be seen, at least in retrospect, as playing a role in bringing down the French monarchy."

"So if the truth came out, diehard Royalists like my father and Dewhurst would be seen as having helped incite the Revolution."

"Yes, that might well have seemed like too much even to them," Raoul said. "I can see Alistair going so far as to save my hide to keep the secret. He valued his reputation."

"Though in other ways he strikes me as more of an Iago than a Rodrigo," Malcolm said.

"This explains what Alistair and Harleton and Dewhurst had to fear," Suzanne said. "But it doesn't explain why someone would have wanted to kill Alistair and Lord Harleton. It doesn't even precisely explain the importance of the manuscript unless someone thought it could lead to the diamonds."

"Alistair and Harleton had the power to destroy Dewhurst," Malcolm pointed out. "But he could equally destroy them, and it's difficult to see why it should come to a crisis now."

"Carfax was on to Harleton," Suzanne said, sorting through the mosaic of information. "Harleton could have used the diamonds to pressure Dewhurst and Alistair to protect him."

"Which would give Dewhurst a motive to kill Harleton but not Alistair." Malcolm prowled back into the center of the room. "We know Rupert saw the three of them meeting in secrecy at his sister's not long before Harleton was killed, and Rupert says the meeting appeared contentious. It's not a stretch to think that related to the diamonds in some way."

"Suppose someone had uncovered their involvement and wanted revenge," Suzanne suggested. "Someone connected to Jeanne de la Motte? Or to Cardinal de Rohan?"

Raoul's gaze shifted between them, a faint smile curving his lips. "It's edifying to listen to your expertise. I can't match either of you as an investigator, but I should add that the League don't always work in concert. Obviously all the members can't be in on every scheme."

"You think some of the other members learned about the affair of the diamonds and took revenge?"

"I think it's not unimaginable that other members would have thought Alistair, Harleton, and Dewhurst had overstepped their brief." Malcolm dropped down on the sofa beside Suzanne again.

"Dewhurst." Suzanne frowned at a loose thread in her sleeve. "He's what's out of place in all this. If the motive was vengeance or even to silence the conspirators, why is Dewhurst untouched? Has he simply avoided it? Or—"

"Is he the one behind the attacks," Malcolm finished for her.

"And I think you're right, we—you—haven't arrived at the importance of the *Hamlet* manuscript yet," Raoul said.

"Which is where this whole thing began." Malcolm scrubbed

his hands over his face. "Who would have thought we could uncover a conspiracy of this magnitude and still be looking for answers."

"Darling—" Suzanne reached out and gripped her husband's hand. She had no right to either the endearment or the gesture anymore, but somehow both came naturally.

Malcolm to her surprise did not jerk away from her touch or her words. Perhaps he was unaware of both. His gaze was fixed on the cool gray light, spilling through the windows onto the Aubusson carpet and oak and bronze velvet, touched with winter. "I always saw my mother as a victim. Of circumstances, an unfortunate marriage, the demons that drove her. Someone who reacted, who sought escape. And I suppose she was all those things at times. But she was also—" He shook his head. "I can't imagine. She actually married Alistair to obtain information—"

Suzanne thought it was her jerk of response that made him break off. He swung his gaze to her though he didn't release her hand.

"It can seem a reasonable option at the time," she said.

He didn't flinch away, from her gaze or from the implications. "I think Arabella despised Alistair even then. And you didn't—"

"Despise you? No. Far from it. I already knew you were one of the best men I'd ever encountered. Which I suppose makes what I did worse."

"Not taking your children into account."

She swallowed. Her throat ached, not with loss but with sympathy. "I don't imagine your mother was even thinking about children at the time. I didn't, until I knew I was carrying Colin. By the time she was pregnant with you, she was locked into her choices."

Malcolm's mouth twisted. "I always knew her children weren't at the forefront of the choices she made. This doesn't change that."

"And yet she gave up her greatest bargaining chip to save her son's father."

"Or to save the man she loved or the man whose cause she believed in. Or whom she needed to further her own ends. In an odd way one could argue O'Roarke made more decisions taking me into account than she did."

For a moment, she felt that saying anything would be akin to treading on broken glass. "I can't pretend to understand him, Malcolm, particularly after the past three days. But I think you matter to him more than you realize."

His brows drew together, but he didn't give an instinctive denial. He glanced down at their clasped hands. She thought he would drop hers at once when he realized he was holding it, but instead he squeezed her fingers. The barest contact but enough to send a shock to the soles of her shoes. "There's a lot to discuss but no time to wallow. Not now. We have work to do."

"Darling?" Cordelia set down her pen and looked at Harry across the library table. "Is something wrong?"

Harry smiled at his wife. She had an ink smudge on her nose and her hair was slipping free of its pins and she looked impossibly lovely. "Do I look as though something's wrong?"

"Well, you don't generally stare at the same page for a quarter hour."

Harry glanced down at the Cicero speech on the table in front of him. "Probably a mistake to even try to work until the investigation is wrapped up. But I felt the need to make the attempt." In truth, what he'd felt the lure of was time in the library with Cordelia, the familiar smells of ink and leather and paper, the sound of pens scratching, and Livia and Drusilla playing with their dolls on the carpet before the fireplace. What had once been his solitary refuge was now the heart of family life.

Harry flipped the book shut. "It's odd how one can live with a person for years and then realize one doesn't really know them at all."

Cordelia flexed her fingers. "Unless you've made some sort of unexpected discovery about me, I assume you mean—"

"Archibald. He seems to have paid rather more attention to me than I credited at the time. Strange how one can miss so much about events one lived through."

"Or one sees them later from a different angle." Cordelia

glanced at her children. "God knows I was dreadfully inclined to neglect everyone's perspective but my own as a child." She picked up the pen and twirled it between her fingers. "There's always seemed to be something a bit elusive about Archie. As though there's another story hidden beneath the surface that we may never know. Every so often I'd get little hints of it. I remember we were once sharing a drink after we'd been to the theatre and he said, seemingly apropos of nothing, that the most beautiful woman he'd ever known had never been his mistress. I've always wondered what the story was behind that."

Harry frowned, something teasing at the edge of his consciousness.

"Colin said he got to see Mr. O'Roarke," Livia announced from the hearth rug in the silence. "He came to Berkeley Square."

"Yes, I imagine he needed to talk to Malcolm and Suzanne." Cordelia turned towards the girls.

"I like Mr. O'Roarke," Livia said, fingers busy plaiting a doll's yellow hair. "He tells good stories. When are we going to see him again?"

"I expect sometime in Berkeley Square. Perhaps at Jessica's birthday party."

"I keep thinking we'll see him at Uncle Archie's. Don't, Dru, you'll tear it." Livia snatched a doll dress from Drusilla's fingers.

Cordelia cast a quick glance at Harry and went to pick up Drusilla, who had started to cry. "Why would you expect to see Mr. O'Roarke at Uncle Archie's?"

"Because I saw him there before."

"Recently?" Cordelia asked.

"No, before Waterloo. Before we lived with Daddy. Here, Dru can have this one." Livia held out a sturdy wool doll dress.

Cordelia dropped down on the hearth rug with Drusilla. Harry got up from the library table and walked towards his wife and daughters.

"Darling," Cordelia said as Drusilla snatched up the proffered doll dress. "What exactly did you see?"

"It was when we were staying with Uncle Archie when our

house was being painted. I woke up one night and went to find you, and I got confused because it was a strange house. I saw Uncle Archie downstairs in the hall talking to a man I'd never met before. It was Mr. O'Roarke." Livia looked between her parents. "They were talking quietly, as though it was something secretive. But then it always seems like grown-ups have secrets."

CHAPTER 37

"Amazing how we see a man and woman together and jump to certain conclusions. As though no other sort of relationship were possible." Harry stared at his uncle through the afternoon shadows that filled Archibald's study. "You weren't Arabella Rannoch's lover."

"No?" Davenport topped off his glass of port. "Then why on earth would I have told her son I was?"

"To explain your interactions with her in '98. Dewhurst had already jumped to that conclusion and told Malcolm."

"My dear boy." Archibald took a sip of port and paused, as though evaluating the vintage. "You saw Arabella Rannoch. You were old enough to appreciate her charms."

"You told Cordy the most beautiful woman you'd ever met was never your mistress."

"Arabella was a lovely woman, but that could refer to any number—"

"It could. But somehow I'm quite sure it referred to Arabella."

Archibald took another sip of port. "That sounds a bit imprecise for a scholar. I'm not saying I was blind to Arabella's more refined qualities, but if you imagine our relationship was about reading poetry or poring over obscure texts—"

"No, I think it was about passing secrets to the United Irishmen."

The glass tilted in Archibald's fingers. He righted it, stared at it for a moment, then set it on the table. The business of a few seconds in which Harry's image of the man who had raised him shifted irrevocably. "Between the Julio-Claudians and your intelligence work, you see plots everywhere, Harry."

"On the contrary. I can't believe I grew up in your household and didn't see this much sooner."

Archibald reached for his glass again. Now that Harry had his uncle's game, he could recognize evasive action. "See what?" Archibald asked.

"You were passing information to Lady Arabella Rannoch, who was giving it to Raoul O'Roarke to pass along to the United Irishmen. The only thing I'm not sure about is if you were helping the French as well."

Archibald turned the glass in his hand. "I could deny it. I probably should. You don't have proof, and I doubt you'll come by any. Not enough to convince others. And yet—" He regarded Harry for a moment. "It's like claiming not to have feelings for the love of one's life somehow."

Harry swallowed. Somehow, in the last few minutes, he had stumbled into a different world. "You—"

"I was a young man in search of adventure. More perhaps. Meaning. Something other than being an idle fribble." Archibald's thin mouth curved in a dry smile. "You're surprised? You thought an idle fribble was precisely what I was? But then that was a pose. Only of course as the pose goes on, it becomes harder and harder to find the reality within it."

Harry studied the man he thought he was just beginning to know. "You're telling me you read Paine and Locke and were driven by a belief in the Rights of Man?"

"Is that so hard to believe?"

"Of the man I thought you were. Obviously I didn't know you."

Archibald pulled a handkerchief from his pocket and mopped up the port that had spattered on the marble tabletop. "Even as a heedless schoolboy, I knew things were bad in Ireland. I had friends among the United Irishmen. But I think it was the Elsinore League that tipped me over the edge."

Harry kept a careful gaze on his uncle's face. He felt as though if he so much as glanced away he would miss a vital clue. "The Elsinore League were hardly revolutionaries."

"On the contrary." Archibald stared at the red stains on the embroidered linen of the handkerchief. "When I joined the League it seemed amusing. I took their talk about adjusting the balance of power in the world to favor themselves largely as bluster. But as time went on it became clear it was a great deal more. It crystalized everything that was wrong with my class. Though even then I doubt I'd have acted without her."

"Arabella Rannoch?"

Archibald nodded. "She sought me out at several entertainments. At first I was flattered. Then I realized she was trying to sound me out for information about the League." He folded the handkerchief into quarters and ran his thumb over it. "I confronted her about it. And I told her if she was interested in information about the League, I'd be delighted to help her."

Harry stared at his uncle. The shadows in the room seemed to have deepened. "You were spying on the League?"

"To begin with. They needed to be stopped. Arabella was searching for information that would do that, or at least keep them in check. But even with me working inside they were clever. Little was committed to writing. And they had powerful friends. We gathered information. We managed to scuttle one or two missions. Then one day I was complaining about Dewhurst and Bessborough's insufferable smugness on the Irish situation. Arabella said she had a friend who would very much agree with me. The next thing I knew I was picking the lock on Dewhurst's dispatch box during that now infamous dinner party and giving Arabella information to pass on to Raoul O'Roarke."

"And it went on after?"

"Yes." Archibald regarded Harry for a long moment. "You were a spy yourself."

"And I can't claim to have been driven by any such idealism, even at the start. But—"

"You were spying for your own country?"

"It seems to make a difference. I don't know that it should."

"A remarkable admission, Harry. I'm proud of you." Davenport returned to the table with the decanters and poured another glass of port. "I went on working against the League. Occasionally I gave information to O'Roarke about Ireland and France." He crossed to Harry and put the second glass in Harry's hand. "But it changed things as you grew up. I became more cautious."

Harry's fingers closed round the glass, though he was scarcely aware of what he touched. "You surprise me."

"I couldn't replace your parents. Or what your parents should have been. But I didn't want you left alone with your only remaining relative branded a traitor."

Harry stared into his uncle's face. Davenport's face looked harder than Harry remembered, but at the same time there was an unusual warmth in his eyes. Archibald Davenport had always been something of a stranger. Why should that matter more now? "Are you saying you gave up your . . . activities?"

"A spy can never really give up his—or her—activities. You should know that better than anyone. But I moderated my work as I could. I had to be more careful in any event. You were damnably curious."

Harry had a memory of coming into the library to find his uncle slipping papers inside a book. "I thought you were trying to conceal communications from your mistresses."

"Yes, I tried to convey that impression. A reputation for debauchery can be good cover for a spy." He gave a faint smile. "Not that it was entirely cover." He adjusted the globe beside his desk. "You took me by surprise when you went to the Peninsula."

"Having friends in harm's way could hardly have been novel for you."

"Friends, yes. Having the closest I had to a son in that situation was . . . rather different."

Harry watched his uncle. Davenport's face seemed even more closed, as though he was tightly guarding his emotions. "Did it change your actions?"

"The Irish rebels were always close to the French. I wasn't without sympathy for the French. But suddenly I was determined not to pass along anything that might relate to the Peninsula."

How odd that a choice of intelligence information should be the strongest declaration of affection one had ever received from one's uncle. How odd and how appropriate to their family. "That must have been a challenge."

"I managed as best I could." Archibald retrieved his own glass and took a sip. "After Livia was born I had a fresh concern. She was—"

"Essentially fatherless. I abrogated my responsibilities in those early years."

Archibald watched him a moment. "One might also make the argument you did a great deal for her given the circumstances. I'm very fond of Cordelia, but there's no denying she put you through hell."

"I never thanked you," Harry said. "For looking after my wife and daughter in my absence. Whatever else is between us, I'm grateful for that."

Davenport waved a careless hand. "I'm fond of them both. Amazing the diversion a young child creates. But given the circumstances of Livia's birth and Cordelia's somewhat precarious position in society, my exposure would have made things infinitely worse." He paused for a moment. "It will be easier for all of you now."

Harry forced a sip of port down his throat. "Easier?"

"Cordelia has vouchers for Almack's again. No one who sees you with Livia thinks about her paternity. You should be able to weather my disgrace tolerably well."

"You think I'm going to expose you?"

"It's your job. A job you're very good at. And as you've made clear through the years, you really don't owe me much."

"Do what you must, Malcolm." Harry looked at Malcolm across an anteroom at Brooks's. "I'm getting him out of the country."

Malcolm shot a look at Harry. "What makes you think that will be necessary?"

"Damn it, Rannoch, you're one of the most honor-bound men I know. I wouldn't ask you not to inform Carfax."

"No, you wouldn't ask it. But that doesn't mean I intend to inform Carfax."

It was Harry's turn to shoot a gaze at his friend.

"I like to think I have a healthy sense of the limitations of the gentleman's code," Malcolm said. "The war is over. I hardly see what would be gained by exposing your uncle."

Harry studied his friend's face. Malcolm looked oddly unconflicted, and yet at the same time the defenses were thick in his gaze. "Why—"

"Because there's been enough killing. Because he was driven by some of the same goals I share." Malcolm paused. Harry could feel the air weighted with the sort of admission they seldom made to each other. "Because he's your uncle."

"He—"

"Committed a crime? That will be on his conscience. I think all of us in intelligence, on all sides, have more than enough on our consciences."

Harry swallowed. "When we talked about loyalty to Crown and country or the lack of it, I never realized we'd be talking about my family." He studied Malcolm for a moment, wondering, not for the first time, what else might have lain behind that conversation. Malcolm's face gave nothing away.

"It's nice to find abstract principles hold up when faced with the reality," Malcolm said. "Harry"—he touched Harry's shoulder—"I know it must be hard. Especially given that your relationship had begun to improve."

Harry frowned. "My uncle isn't the man I thought he is. And yet I think I'd take the man I've seen today over the man I thought he was." He looked sideways at Malcolm. "That probably sounds mad."

"Or like you have a healthy sense of priorities." Malcolm watched him for a moment. "It means a great deal, having a father."

"Careful, Rannoch, you're speaking to the original loner. It might have meant something once. I'm too old now to need a father."

For a moment, Malcolm's gaze was thick with unknown ghosts. "I used to think that. But I don't think we ever really are." He took a step towards the door. "I won't turn your uncle in to anyone. But he owes us some answers. So does Raoul O'Roarke."

CHAPTER 38

Malcolm slammed the door of the Berkeley Square library shut. "Talk. Both of you. We should be done with secrets."

His words were addressed to Archibald Davenport and Raoul. Harry and Cordelia were also present, as was Suzanne. Harry had brought his uncle to the house. Malcolm had summoned Raoul without telling Suzanne why, though he had specifically said he wanted her at the conference he'd called.

"My dear boy," Archibald said. "Surely you can't be naïve enough to think any of us could ever be done with secrets."

Malcolm folded his arms across his chest. "The two of you and my mother were trying to bring down the Elsinore League."

"Among other things." Raoul glanced at Suzanne and Cordelia, who were both seated, and dropped into a chair. "For what it's worth, I suspect Archie, like me, was suffering from a misguided desire to protect the younger generation. Or possibly ourselves. Ask us what you will."

Malcolm's gaze shot between the men. "Was anyone else in the Elsinore League working with you?"

"No." It was Davenport who answered. "As far as I know, I was the only traitor."

"You uncovered the Dunboyne information and leaked it to the United Irishmen," Malcolm said.

"As I admitted to Harry," Davenport said. "What I didn't say is that Alistair persuaded Dewhurst when to set the attack. I'm quite sure his aim was to get rid of O'Roarke."

Raoul gave a wry grimace. "The Elsinore League were dedicated to advancing their own interests. Of all sorts."

"Did either of you know Alistair and Harleton and Dewhurst were behind the affair of the necklace?" Malcolm asked.

"What?" Davenport said.

"You're a bit behind me," Raoul said. "You'd better explain, Malcolm."

Malcolm explained about their discovery at Harleton's country house.

Davenport dropped down heavily into one of the Queen Anne chairs. "Good God. I thought the League couldn't surprise me anymore. I was wrong." He frowned. "You say something in the *Hamlet* manuscript led you to the hiding place?"

"A different version of Hamlet's letter to Ophelia," Suzanne said. She recited the poem.

Davenport's frown deepened. "Odd—The raven and the dove sounds like Dewhurst's crest. And the bit about the blood sounds like their family motto."

"I thought their crest was a bear rampant," Malcolm said.

"The one they use now, that they acquired with the earldom. They upgraded, as it were, when they were given the Dewhurst title. This crest and motto went with the original title, Baron Caruthers, before it was even a viscountcy. The odd thing is, Harleton was asking me about it just a fortnight or so before he died."

"About the Caruthers crest?" Harry asked.

"About the motto actually, and if it had had something to do with blood."

Suzanne exchanged a look with her husband, all else momentarily forgot.

"If there's a reference to the Dewhurst—Caruthers—family in

the same lines that told us where the treasure was hidden it's an old reference," Cordelia said.

"It was written by Eleanor Harleton and Francis Woolright," Malcolm said.

"Francis Woolright?" Davenport asked.

"Eleanor Harleton's lover," Malcolm said. "He was an actor in the Chamberlain's Men. With a mysterious past."

Suzanne's fingers tensed on the sarcenet of her skirt. "Was there a Caruthers son who disappeared around that time?"

"Only one way to find out." Harry scanned the shelves. "You do have a *Debrett's,* don't you, Rannoch? Deadly dull, but it does have its uses at times like these."

"Alistair would have had a full set. He had an outsider's fascination with the aristocracy." Malcolm dragged over a set of library steps and retrieved a gilt-spined volume from one of the higher shelves. He carried it over to the library table and set it down on the brown-veined marble in the light of a brace of candles. "Odd," he said, opening the book.

"What?" Suzanne moved to her husband's side.

"There's a marker in the book on the page with the Dewhurst listing." Malcolm pulled out a paper and turned it over in his hands. "It appears to be a bill from Alistair's tailor. But what's interesting is that he was looking up the family." Malcolm ran his finger down the page of names that marked the line of a noble house. "Guilaume Caruthers came over with William the Conqueror, who made him a baron. Henry the Fifth created the first baron's several-times-great-grandson Viscount Caruthers after Agincourt and then Henry the Eighth made his great-great-grandson the first Earl Dewhurst. His son—" Malcolm froze, his finger on the page. "His eldest son, Robert, is listed as presumed dead in 1592."

"Not so surprising perhaps," Raoul said. "A young aristocrat with a love of the theatre. The only way he could pursue that life would have been to disappear."

"You make it sound like an easy choice," Cordelia said.

"Easy? Not in the least. But for a chance to work with Shakespeare and pursue his dream instead of managing estates and hobnobbing at court—I can understand him making it."

"So can I," Cordelia said.

"But Woolright and Eleanor Harleton married," Suzanne said. "And had children. Including a son."

Malcolm nodded. "While Dewhurst is descended from Woolright's younger brother. Which means there's another whole line out there who are the rightful heirs to the Dewhurst earldom."

"And Alistair Rannoch had figured it out," Suzanne said. "Though he'd have had no particular reason to use it against Dewhurst."

"But Harleton would." Malcolm's mouth turned grim. "Suppose Harleton showed the manuscript to Alistair."

"Alistair was hardly a Shakespearean scholar, but he had enough wit to investigate those lines," Raoul said. "Especially if Harleton pointed them out to him as the key to the hiding place. And if Alistair shared his information with Harleton—"

"Harleton might have tried to use it to blackmail Dewhurst into protecting him from Carfax," Malcolm said. "But Dewhurst decided it was safer to get rid of both men who could threaten his possession of the title."

Suzanne's hands closed on her elbows. "Dewhurst has to know there's no controlling the manuscript now."

"No," Malcolm agreed. "That's why he stopped trying to recover it. But he'd be worried about who else Harleton might have told or who could put the pieces together—"

Suzanne met her husband's gaze. "Crispin."

CHAPTER 39

Crispin unlocked the stage door of the Tavistock with the key Manon had given him and went down the darkened passage. A faint glow shone from the stage. "Darling?" he called.

"I'm afraid she's not here yet."

Crispin frowned at the voice. *Good God, that sounded like*—He strode through the wings to the edge of the stage. One rehearsal lamp was lit, casting greasy light over bare boards and rehearsal props and the tall figure of a greatcoated man. *"Dewhurst?"*

"Good evening, Crispin." Dewhurst surveyed him without surprise.

"What are you doing here? How did you get in?"

"After my career in France, the door of a theatre is hardly of great moment to me."

"But why—"

"I wanted to talk to you."

"You sent me the note?" Alarm, unfocused but sharp, quickened Crispin's blood. "Where's Manon?"

"She'll be along presently. I wanted to talk to you first." Dewhurst's gaze moved over him. "You went to school with my son, Crispin. I can't help but view you as a father might to a certain extent."

"Thanks." Crispin took a step closer to the earl. It seemed

important to hold his ground somehow. Why had Rupert Caruthers stopped talking to his father? He must have had his reasons. "I'm a bit old to need a father."

"Spoken like a very young man. I've been concerned about this liaison of yours for some time."

Crispin folded his arms across his chest. "Surely a man in your position has more important things to worry about than a love affair."

"Actually, it's my position that gave me the cause for concern." Dewhurst surveyed him with what might have been pity. "My dear boy, there's no easy way to say this. The lovely Manon was a French agent."

Crispin swallowed the instinctive retort. He had to be careful to protect Manon. "Just because she's French and an actress—"

"My dear boy." Dewhurst crossed to Crispin's side and put a hand on his shoulder. "It's considerably more than that."

Crispin squelched the impulse to jerk away from Dewhurst's touch. "Assuming that were true—and I don't for a moment admit that it is—what makes you so sure I haven't known all along?"

"I can't but admire your loyalty to your mistress, Crispin, mistaken as it may be. But you're also a loyal Englishman. You wouldn't."

"With all due respect, sir, you don't know me at all."

Dewhurst's gaze hardened. He took a step back, pushing Crispin away. "You fool. You've succumbed to her wiles."

"Call it what you will."

"*Chéri?*" Manon's voice came from the wings. "Where are—"

"Don't come out here, Manon!" Crispin yelled. "It's a trap—"

At least that was what he meant to say. He only got the words half-out because Dewhurst's fist smashed into his jaw and sent him crashing to the stage floor. Manon's footsteps pattered against the boards. Then he heard her go still. Dewhurst had pulled a pistol from his greatcoat. "You leave me with no choice but to get rid of the pair of you," Dewhurst said.

Crispin stared up at the earl. "You're mad."

"I'm a man who knows how to do what needs to be done."

* * *

Malcolm ran down the passage from the stage door, Suzanne beside him, to see Crispin sprawled on the floorboards, Manon standing in the wings, and Dewhurst holding a pistol on them.

"Don't be a fool, Dewhurst," Malcolm said. "You can't kill all of us."

Dewhurst jerked instinctively, the pistol swinging towards Malcolm. And therefore Suzanne, damn it. But they were better able to protect themselves than were Crispin and Manon.

"You don't know what they've done, Rannoch."

"I know what you've done. And I know what you fear losing. More to the point, so do Harry and Cordelia and Archibald Davenport and Raoul O'Roarke. You can't contain this."

Dewhurst's gaze filled with rage and the recognition that he was trapped. "Then I can at least take out one harlot of a spy."

His arm swung towards Manon. Crispin screamed and tried to hurl himself at her. Suzanne, running full tilt, got there first and knocked Manon to the floor. Malcolm hurled himself at Dewhurst. They slammed into the boards. The gun went off, and Malcolm heard his wife scream.

CHAPTER 40

For a moment, every ounce of blood in Malcolm's veins turned to ice. He saw what happened in agonizingly slow fragments, as though he were moving through water. Manon collapsed on the boards, Suzanne sprawled on top of her, stiffening at the impact of the bullet, blood spurting from her shoulder. Then she screamed and somehow he could breathe again.

He was across the stage on the floor beside her, holding her in his arms. He could feel the shudder of her breath against him. He was dimly aware of Manon's anxious gaze as she knelt beside them. Suzanne's eyes fluttered open. "Darling. Malcolm. I'm fine."

"You're bleeding." The blood was soaking through the sleeve of his coat where he held her. He tugged at his cravat, still holding his wife.

"I'll hold her, Mr. Rannoch," Manon said.

A satisfied grunt came from across the stage. The conclusion of a series of thuds Malcolm had scarcely been aware of. Crispin had tackled Dewhurst and was sitting atop the earl's chest. As Malcolm glanced up, Crispin drew back his fist and slammed it into Dewhurst's jaw.

"Is he unconscious?" Malcolm asked.

"For the present." Crispin stared down at the earl. "I never until now understood the impulse to commit murder."

"Don't let him move." Malcolm was stripping off his cravat. The bleeding had slowed on Suzanne's arm.

Suzanne turned her head towards Manon. "Help me get my clothes off so Malcolm will see I'm not dying."

With Manon's help, Suzanne got her spencer off and her bodice loosened, an easier task thanks to the nursing flap. Malcolm pulled a flask from his greatcoat pocket and splashed some whisky on the wound, then bound his cravat round it. A temporary dressing, but it would do until they got home.

Dewhurst stirred. "What—"

"Shall I hit him again?" Crispin asked.

Dewhurst drew a breath of outrage. "You arrogant—"

Footsteps thudded in the wings. Rupert appeared at the edge of the stage. "Malcolm, I came when I got your message—Good God."

"Rupert," Dewhurst said.

"Don't." Crispin slammed a hand on Dewhurst's chest. "Don't even try to lie your way out of this. You have four witnesses."

"Witnesses to what?" Rupert asked.

"Your father tried to kill Manon and me," Crispin said.

The sort of silence that follows the discovery of Polonius's body fell over the stage.

Malcolm helped Suzanne to her feet, his arm round her. With his free hand, he reached in his greatcoat pocket and pulled out his pistol. "Let him get up," he said to Crispin. "But don't even think about running, Dewhurst."

Dewhurst stood and smoothed his coat, quite as though he were in a diplomatic council chamber. "I must say, I never thought this is what it would take for you to be talking to me again, Rupert."

Rupert stared at his father. "My God, sir. Whom were you working for? Besides yourself."

Dewhurst regarded his son as though Rupert had already retreated an uncrossable distance and there was no calling him back. "For you."

"Don't put this on me." Rupert fairly spat the words. "I had no say in the matter."

"For my descendants. For your Stephen. For people like us."

Dewhurst took an impatient step forwards, as though he could physically breach the gulf between them. "Damn it, Rupert, don't you see there's been a war for the past twenty years and it's not a question of countries. Our way of life is under attack. Your way of life too, Rannoch." His gaze shot to Malcolm. "From the Jacobins in France, from the machine breakers here at home, from the upstarts like O'Roarke in Ireland, from the rabble all over the Continent who employed people like her." He jerked his head at Manon.

"And that was the point of this Elsinore League of yours?" Malcolm said. "To attack the rabble?"

"Simply fighting the French did nothing to mend matters here in England. We wanted to preserve an appropriate balance of power. To keep our friends in positions to wield influence."

"And line your own pockets," Suzanne murmured.

Dewhurst ran his gaze over her. "That wasn't our goal, Mrs. Rannoch."

"No?" Malcolm said. "I can't but think it was at least Alistair's. Cardinal de Rohan had insulted your friends—"

"Rohan was a threat to France's stability and with it that of the Continent."

"So you set him up for ruin," Malcolm said. "And helped bring down the French monarchy and turn France over to what you would call the rabble."

Dewhurst twitched his cravat straight. "We were young. It was an unfortunate incident. But we learned from our mistakes."

"Mistakes which could ruin you."

Rupert was staring at his father as though he had transformed into another creature. "After what you did to Bertrand, I wouldn't think any action of yours could surprise me. But by God—Have you no limits?"

"Of course I have limits. I know precisely to whom and what I'm loyal. I know what I owe to my name and my family. Something you've always been inclined to forget, Rupert."

"Don't you dare." Rupert's voice rose to echo into the flies. "I'm loyal to the people I love. That has to come first."

"You. Both of you." Dewhurst looked from Rupert to Malcolm

and shook his head. "If we lose this war it will be due to people like you. Not understanding where your loyalties lie. Putting the personal before the needs of your family."

"Family are personal," Rupert said.

"That's just where you're wrong, my boy. Family are a trust. An obligation. One's role in life."

Rupert stared hard at his father. "I don't think you gave a damn about family. I think it's a façade. I think you're driven by one thing and that's power for yourself."

"Alistair certainly was," Malcolm said. "I imagine it was a good alliance as long as your self-interests coincided. But then they diverged. When was that? After your difficulties two years ago in Paris?"

"Those difficulties were all in your head."

"And Wellington's and Castlereagh's. You haven't been assigned to a diplomatic mission since. You're out of the corridors of power. But Harleton still tried to blackmail you into protecting him, didn't he? Did he threaten you with the truth about the necklace?"

"Harleton thought he was going to be exposed." The words seemed to be torn from Dewhurst's throat. "He threatened to expose the business about the diamonds if Alistair and I didn't protect him. He broke the one cardinal rule of the League."

"Which is?"

"Never to use our information against each other. We knew our interests might diverge, but we never turned on each other."

"And so you got rid of Harleton," Malcolm said.

"You can't seriously expect me to answer that."

"My God," Rupert said. "I didn't think you could possibly prove more of a monster—"

"That's what I thought at first," Malcolm said, "but the pieces don't add up. Harleton couldn't have made your role in the affair of the necklace public without ruining himself along with you and Alistair. He might have blustered and made threats, but the two of you would have laughed in his face. And it didn't explain why you wanted the *Hamlet* manuscript. Until we made a discovery in the manuscript itself that made it all fall into place."

The fear that shot into Dewhurst's gaze, though quickly veiled, told Malcolm he was on target. "Do pray enlighten me," Dewhurst said.

"I think my wife should do that, she's the one who put the pieces together. Darling?"

It was only the start in Suzanne's gaze that made Malcolm realize the endearment he'd employed unthinkingly. He kept his gaze steady on her own, not taking it back. "It was really Archibald Davenport," she said. "He discovered the real secret in the *Hamlet* manuscript. The identity of Francis Woolright."

"Who?" Rupert said.

"An actor in Shakespeare's company who was Eleanor Harleton's lover. And married her after her husband was executed in the wake of the Essex rebellion."

"Entertaining as this ancient history is," Dewhurst said, "what the hell does it have to do with—"

"Because Francis Woolright's real identity was a secret, one he guarded closely. He'd left his family to become an actor, and he had no desire to go back. Yet he or Eleanor Harleton cared enough about his heritage to hide it in a speech they added to the manuscript."

Rupert frowned. "Are you saying—"

"The speech mentions a raven and a dove. Which I believe is the original emblem of your family."

Rupert stared at his father. "By God—"

"Don't listen to them, Rupert, it makes no sense."

"On the contrary. It makes a great deal of sense." Rupert swung his gaze to Malcolm and Suzanne. "Did this Francis Woolright and Eleanor Harleton have a legitimate son?"

"Yes," Malcolm said.

Rupert's gaze moved back to his father. "All this talk about rights and legitimacy. And you aren't even the rightful Earl Dewhurst. I'm not Viscount Caruthers."

"That's not—"

"You tried to have Bertrand killed to get an heir to a title that isn't even rightfully yours."

"What about Alistair?" Dewhurst demanded.

"Alistair was the one who pieced together the truth about Francis Woolright after Harleton showed him the manuscript," Malcolm said. "You had to get rid of both of them."

Dewhurst folded his arms across his chest. "You can't prove any of that."

"Perhaps not," said Rupert. "But we can damn well try."

CHAPTER 41

Crispin put a glass of cognac into Manon's hand. The girls were safely asleep upstairs. She and Crispin had both stared at them for a long interval, though Manon had refused to meet his gaze afterwards. "Are you sure you aren't cold, darling?" He reached for a shawl that was draped over a chairback.

"I'm fine, Crispin." Manon jerked away from his hand. She was leaning back on the settee, calling on her acting talents to maintain her usual negligent attitude. "It was Suzanne who was almost killed, not me."

"It was you Dewhurst was trying to kill." Crispin stared down at her with that look that said he wanted to put his arms round her again. And if he did so it would undo her.

"If it comes to that he was trying to kill you, too." Manon's fingers tightened round her glass. She stared at it for a moment, the fear of those moments on the Tavistock stage shooting through her, then took a quick sip. To prove she could do so.

Crispin took a turn about the hearth rug. "Malcolm says I should point out to you that marrying me is by far the best way to protect the girls."

"Malcolm Rannoch said that?"

"Yes." Crispin frowned at the memory. "I was braced for a fight and sure he'd try to talk me out of it."

"So was I." Manon considered Suzanne's British husband. "I wouldn't have thought a man of his type would be able to see beyond the confines of his world. Though I must say he impressed me today."

"What about me?"

She smiled, wondering how many more times she'd stare into those blue eyes. "You impressed me as well, *mon cher*. It was quite masterful how you took down Lord Dewhurst."

Crispin took a step closer to the dressing table. "Don't try to change the subject. I mean what about me being able to see beyond the confines of my world? Malcolm's right: If you marry me, it will be easier for me to protect the girls."

She tilted her head back, surveying his familiar features, the curly hair that fell over his forehead, the curve of his mouth, the unexpected stubborn strength in his jaw. How had she ever been so foolish as to let him become so important to her? "Do you think I would marry only to protect the girls?"

He swallowed. The look in his gaze was fear. It occurred to her that he was terrified she wouldn't say yes. "No, of course not. But I also know you're concerned for their safety. As am I."

"My dear Crispin, if you've learned anything at all about me you must realize I've done rather well protecting them my entire life."

"And you think I'm a callow amateur, blundering about in a game I don't understand."

"Never that, *chéri*. Though it's quite true you don't understand it. Fortunately for you."

"God." He took a turn about the hearth rug. "It's a wonder you ever wasted any time on me at all."

"Crispin . . ." She hesitated, words she dare not say hovering on her lips. For to say, *It's precisely because I love you that I can't marry you,* would be to give the game away. "I couldn't possibly consider our time together wasted."

"An agreeable interlude then?" His mouth twisted. "Look, Manon, I know your past—No, that's not what I mean," he added as she gave a sharp laugh. "I know you've been with men who are more brilliant than I. I have no illusions. But the one thing I do have is an old family name and a title and fortune and all the trappings that go with it. I know that seems particularly hollow after today's events, but it gives me a certain influence. Which I know is precisely what your people were fighting against, and I daresay there's a great deal to be said for their argument, but right now, here, it's an advantage." He dropped down on one knee before her. "For God's sake, let me do what I can."

"My dear Crispin." She reached out and touched his face. "It's the most generous offer I've ever received. But you'd get tired of it, you know. Having a wife who couldn't be received in your world."

"You mean the world of my father? Who was a French spy himself? I don't give a damn about it. But I can't imagine a world without you and Roxane and Clarisse." He sat back and scanned her face. Suddenly he no longer looked like a schoolboy. "Or are you saying you'd get tired? Of me?"

"No." She touched his face again, against her better judgment. "I never thought I'd say this to a man, but oddly enough, I don't believe I would."

He seized her hand and drew it against his mouth. "Well then."

"If the truth ever came out—"

"We'd go to Italy or Switzerland or America. I've enough money. Amazing how that can cushion most blows."

She drew a breath, hovering on the edge of something she hadn't thought possible. "I wouldn't give up the theatre."

"I wouldn't want you to."

"There'll always be a risk—"

"Life's a risk." He got up on the settee beside her and took her in his arms. "It helps to take the risk with the right person."

Manon laughed, despite herself. "You're very stubborn."

"Say it."

"Yes."

"Yes, what?"

She drew a breath that trembled between fear and wonder. "Yes, Crispin. I'll marry you."

* * *

Cordelia pulled the door of the night nursery closed on her sleeping daughters. "Do you want to talk about it?" she asked Harry.

"Yes. No." Harry gave a twisted smile. "That is, I'm not at all sure I do, but I probably should."

Cordelia leaned against the closed door and touched her husband's face. She and Harry had gone to Dewhurst's house in case he was there and so had missed the confrontation at the Tavistock and had only arrived at the theatre in time to speak briefly with a subdued Malcolm and Suzanne. "What will happen to Dewhurst?"

"Rupert is determined to try to bring him to justice and to find Francis Woolright's descendants, but I don't know if either will be possible." Harry rubbed a hand across his eyes. "Odd. Rupert wants his father brought to justice. And I'm profoundly relieved that Archibald won't be."

Cordelia scanned her husband's tired face. "The scope of what they did can hardly be considered the same."

"No. In fact, it's not a great leap for me to find myself in sympathy with Archibald's views. Still. I never thought his fate would be a matter of such moment to me as it has been these past few days."

"Parents." Cordelia glanced over her shoulder at the nursery door. "The bond is there whether we realize it or not."

"And perhaps having our own children drives that home."

Cordelia leaned her head against her husband's shoulder. "Do you think Malcolm and Suzanne will be all right?"

"It was just a flesh wound to her arm." Harry stroked his fingers against Cordelia's hair. "It looked worse than it is."

"That's not what I meant." Cordelia lifted her head to look at her husband, struck by how very precious the tenderness in his gaze was. "Something's . . . shifted between them these past few days."

"I know." Harry's mouth turned grim. "That is, I know something's changed between them, though not why."

"And?" For a moment Cordelia felt like a child, desperately wanting to be reassured that fairy-tale endings were possible.

But Harry was never one for false reassurance. He touched her hair again, his gaze clouded with concern. "I'm afraid only time will tell."

Malcolm knotted off a clean dressing round Suzanne's shoulder. "It's good to be home."

She looked up at him. The light from the tapers on her dressing table shadowed his eyes and sharpened the bones of his face. "Do we have a home?"

"It's time Berkeley Square became ours and not Alistair and Arabella's."

Her fingers closed on the silk and lace of her dressing gown. "You can't seriously want me here."

He pulled the dressing gown up about her shoulders. "I don't see where else you'd be."

"Don't, Malcolm." She steeled herself against the seductive brush of his fingers. "We've settled that we're sharing a house. That doesn't mean we have a home. Or that you want me in it."

He dropped down on the dressing table bench beside her. "At the moment, the prospect of you being anywhere else is bloody terrifying."

Her fingers closed round his wrists. "I know what this is, and it won't work."

"What is it?"

"I almost died, and you've had a rush of remorse."

"If you mean contemplating a future without you adjusted my thinking, you're right."

"But it won't last." She tightened her grip on his wrists, wondering how many more times she'd be able to touch him. "We'll settle into everyday prosaic reality, and you'll remember all the reasons you have to hate me."

He slid his fingers behind her neck. A glint of familiar laughter lit his eyes and made her heart turn over. "When have we ever been able to exist in everyday prosaic reality for five minutes?"

"Don't be clever, darling, you know what I mean. You'll go over every secret I might have exposed. You'll think of every one of your friends who died in battle. You'll think that through me you betrayed comrades and Crown and country and that your own honor was compromised."

"You don't believe in honor."

"No, but you do."

He turned his hands in her grip to brush his thumbs against her fingers. "I wonder if Cordy put Davenport through this?"

"It's not the same."

"On the contrary. I'd say it's remarkably similar. He told me she did her best to argue to him that it couldn't possibly work. That he couldn't forget."

"It's one thing to forget infidelity. It's another—"

"You don't call what you did infidelity? Betrayal is betrayal, my darling."

She swallowed. "Cordy regrets the past."

"And you don't?"

"Of course I do. But I can't say I'd behave differently if I did it again."

He pulled one hand free of her grip and brushed the backs of his fingers against her cheek. "I doubt you would. I think I know you that well."

"Can you seriously tell me you think you can go on as we did before?"

"I should hope we won't. We'll be a deal more honest." The laughter faded from his eyes. "We have two children. I don't think either of us has much choice about where and how we live."

She couldn't suppress an inward flinch. Though it was no more than the truth. "You said it yourself. You don't want Colin and Jessica to grow up with two parents at each other's throats like—"

"Like I did?" His mouth curled with derision. "I don't think we could be like Alistair and Arabella if we tried." He drew a breath. She felt it rough against her skin. "I wonder sometimes if Arabella kept us in Scotland so much because the atmosphere in Berkeley Square was so poisoned. I don't think that was all of it. I think she genuinely did find being a mother wearing. And God knows packing the children off to the country isn't unusual in our set. But I think it was part of it." He looked at Suzanne for a long moment. "I can't imagine you packing your children off."

"Well, I'm not an aristocrat."

"I don't want the children to grow up afraid to trust."

"Nor do I. But it's a bit of a challenge when their parents don't trust each other."

"You don't trust me?"

"Poor word choice. I trust you with my life, Malcolm."

"Yet you thought I could take the children away from you."

"I'd never seen you pushed to this extent."

"We have to find a way to go on. Not just to live under the same roof. To keep the atmosphere from being poisoned." He watched her in silence a few moments longer. "It must drive you mad. Planning seating arrangements, ordering dinners, answering cards of invitation. That isn't what you were trained for. What O'Roarke trained you for."

"Sometimes it drives me mad. Sometimes I find myself enjoying it. And then I think I'm a hypocrite."

"Enjoying the trappings of a life you're fighting against?"

"In a nutshell."

"I feel much the same when I make use of being the Duke of Strathdon's grandson."

"You don't have any choice about being the Duke of Strathdon's grandson."

"I could repudiate my heritage."

"And upend your life and destroy your family's."

"Which is what telling the truth would have done to you." His gaze locked on her own. "Whatever else, I don't doubt you love Colin and Jessica. And our marriage began to protect Colin after all. At least on my side."

Once again she felt a well-deserved flinch. She curled her hands into fists at her sides. "Plenty of couples in the beau monde live nominally under the same roof but lead separate lives."

His gaze hardened. "So they do. Is that what you want?"

Her nails bit into her palms. "I'm trying to figure out what you want."

"To be honest, I don't know."

"You should be able to fall in love, forge your own life."

"That isn't an option anymore. I don't mean that as an accusation, it's a statement of fact. We've forged a life. Even if it's a false one, we have to make it work."

She met his gaze. "There are different ways to make it work. You don't have to be married to fall in love."

His gaze hardened to polished steel. "You're giving me permission to take a mistress?"

"In the circumstances I hardly think my permission is required."

She felt the tension that ran through him. "Are you saying you want to take a lover?"

"No! That's the last thing—I'm trying to find a way to give you the life I took away."

"It's too late for that, Suzette. It was too late the moment we married. Maybe the moment we met."

His words bit her in the throat. "If—"

"Save your energies for more important battles." His gaze flickered over her face. "Don't get any ideas about disappearing."

"I'm not. That is"—something compelled her to scrupulous honesty—"I thought about it, but I couldn't leave the children, and I couldn't take them away from you."

"Well then. It comes back to the children, and what we owe them."

He was offering her more than she would have dreamed possible a few hours before. She should be grateful. Much of her life, after all, had been making do with the cards she was dealt. The ache of loss would ease and she would stop feeling torn in two. "Every time you open your mouth you're going to wonder what I'll do with the information."

"Probably. It will make for some strained conversations for a time."

"You won't be able to leave the room without locking your dispatch box."

"Yes, well, I do finally learn my lessons."

A host of losses ran through her head. Laughing over a draft of one of his speeches in exhausted delirium. Passing pages of the *Morning Chronicle* back and forth with the toast and coffee. Marking up the draft of a dispatch, fingers smeared with ink. "We won't—"

She saw a flash of the same sense of loss in his own gaze. "No."

"Then what—"

"The children. Some of the things we believe in. The investigations that always seem to find us." He looked down at her for a moment. "When Dewhurst fired his pistol, I knew that whatever our life together may hold, I infinitely prefer it to life without you."

"We've been through a crisis. We haven't resolved anything."

He took her face between his hands. She could feel the warmth of his breath. For a moment she thought he was going to kiss her. But Malcolm had always been too honest to seek escape in passion or romance. Or perhaps he couldn't bring himself to kiss her. "Let's just take it a day at a time and see what happens."

"You don't know—"

"When we both put our minds to something we're usually rather successful."

EPILOGUE

The smell of citrus shaving soap wafted through the close air in the space behind the screen in the tea shop. Laura swallowed, tasting stewed tea and self-disgust.

"Well?" His voice, low and even, came through the shadows.

"Mr. and Mrs. Rannoch and Lord Caruthers are trying to trace the descendants of Eleanor Harleton and Francis Woolright and to build a case against Lord Dewhurst."

"And Dewhurst, I understand, has taken himself off to the country. I shall be interested to see the next move."

"You don't mean to come to his rescue?" She should stay out of it, but she couldn't resist asking. It would be even worse, somehow, to work for someone who came to Dewhurst's aid.

He snorted. "This is the second occasion on which Dewhurst has shown appallingly bad judgment. And he broke our one inviolate rule."

"Turning against fellow members of the League?"

"Quite." His shoes creaked as he shifted his weight from one foot to the other. "What about the Rannochs?"

She hesitated, partly because it stuck in her throat more and more to disclose details about her employers, partly because she wasn't sure of the answer. "They seem easier with each other."

to normal eventually, you know. Difficult as it may be to imagine it at times."

Malcolm met his friend's gaze and managed a smile. "Define 'normal.'"

Harry gave a wry laugh that smoothed over the undertones Malcolm was sure his friend was as aware of as he himself.

Across the room, Suzanne got to her feet, Jessica in her arms, and moved towards Malcolm and Harry. The pendant of blue topaz and aquamarine that he'd given her for their anniversary sparkled at her throat. He'd been afraid it would be a reminder of a past they would never recapture. But it just possibly might be a promise of the future.

Suzanne's gaze seemed to hold the faintest of questions, as it often did these days, but she gave a bright smile. "The princess seems to be getting a second wind. Shall we bring in the cake?"

"Sounds like a good plan." Malcolm held out a finger for Jessica to grasp hold of. Jessica lifted her head from Suzanne's shoulder and smiled at him. She had run about with glee at the start of the party and then had taken a nap in Suzanne's arms.

Harry lifted his glass. "Here's to Jessica."

Malcolm took a drink of champagne and lifted his glass to Suzanne so she could take a sip. The sort of simple interaction that for a time it had seemed they never would recapture. Her eyes widened for a moment, then she smiled, a quick, seemingly casual smile that, like a line from Shakespeare, held layers of meaning.

Malcolm returned the smile and put an arm round his wife and daughter. "And to another year of adventures."

HISTORICAL NOTES

The *Hamlet* manuscript referred to in this book is fictional (as are Francis Woolright and Eleanor Harleton), but there are three different versions of *Hamlet* that we know of: the First and Second Quartos and the First Folio. The First Quarto version of the play wasn't rediscovered until 1823, which is why Malcolm only mentions two versions. As Malcolm also says, there are mentions of an earlier play that was a source for *Hamlet,* perhaps by Thomas Kyd, perhaps even by Shakespeare himself.

The Dunboyne affair is fictional, but the events of the United Irish Uprising within which it is set are very real. The Elsinore League and their involvement in the affair of the queen's necklace are also fictional, but Jeanne de la Motte did seek refuge in England after she was released from prison and the necklace is thought to have been taken to Britain.

Selected Bibliography

Creevey, Thomas. *The Creevey Papers: A Selection from the Correspondence & Diaries of Thomas Creevey, M.P.* Edited by Sir Herbert Maxwell. London: Murray, 1904.

Foreman, Amanda. *Georgiana: Duchess of Devonshire.* New York: Modern Library, 2001.

Gleeson, Janet. *Privilege and Scandal: The Remarkable Life of Harriet Spencer, Sister of Georgiana.* New York: Crown, 2006.

Granville, Harriet. *Letters of Harriet Countess Granville 1810–1845,* vol. 1. London: Longmans, Green and Co., 1894.

Gronow, Rees Howell. *Reminiscences and Recollections of Captain Gronow,* vol. 1. London: John C. Nimmo.

Lever, Tresham. *The Letters of Lady Palmerston: Selected and Edited from the Originals at Broadlands and Elsewhere.* London: John Murray, 1957.

Shakespeare, William. *Hamlet.* Ashland: Blackstone Audio, 2011.

Shapiro, James. *A Year in the Life of William Shakespeare: 1599.* New York: Harper Perennial, 2006.

Tillyard, Stella. *Aristocrats: Caroline, Emily, Louisa, and Sarah Lennox, 1740–1832.* New York: Farrar, Strauss & Giroux, 1994.

THE
BERKELEY SQUARE AFFAIR

Teresa Grant

About This Guide

The suggested questions are included
to enhance your group's reading of
Teresa Grant's *The Berkeley Square Affair.*

DISCUSSION QUESTIONS

1. Compare and contrast the relationships Malcolm, Harry, Crispin, Rupert, and David have with their fathers and surrogate fathers.

2. The loss of a father figures prominently in this book as in *Hamlet*. What other issues and themes in *Hamlet* have parallels in the book?

3. How might Malcolm's reaction to the revelation of Suzanne's secrets have been different if Suzanne had told him instead of him working it out for himself?

4. Did you guess who was behind the deaths of Lord Harleton and Alistair Rannoch? Why or why not?

5. What do you think lies ahead for Crispin and Manon?

6. How do you think a grown-up Colin and Jessica might react if they learned the truth about their mother?

7. Which of Malcolm and Suzanne's friends do you think would have the hardest time accepting the truth about Suzanne? Which do you think would be the most understanding?

8. How do you think Malcolm and Suzanne's relationship will play out in the next few weeks?

9. Francis Woolright turned his back on his heritage. Which other characters in the book do that?

10. Whom do you think Laura Dudley was reporting to?

11. Suzanne and Manon say Malcolm and Crispin can never entirely escape the mind-set of being British gentlemen. Do you think that's true?

12. How are the decisions Malcolm and Suzanne make shaped by the fact that they are parents? How do you think they

would have dealt with the revelation of Suzanne's secrets if they didn't have Colin and Jessica?

13. Hamlet sees the ghost of his father. What metaphorical ghosts haunt the characters in the book?

14. Raoul O'Roarke played a huge role in both Malcolm's and Suzanne's lives, and as he himself says, many of the things he's done could be considered unforgivable. How did you feel about him by the end of the story? What do you think lies ahead for his relationship to both the Rannochs?

15. What role does solving mysteries together play in Malcolm and Suzanne's relationship?